RAVE REVIEWS FOR DAWN THOMPSON!

THE BROTHERHOOD

"*The Brotherhood* is a terrific paranormal romance that continues the fresh concepts of *Blood Moon*."

—*Midwest Book Review*

"Not only is the writing lyrical, beautiful, it was chilling, dark, sinister, a near perfect vampire story rooted in vampire mythos origins, a cunning hybrid of a regency romance and a sexy, vampire tale that leaves you breathless and wanting more."

—Deborah MacGillivray, Author of *Riding the Thunder*

BLOOD MOON

"Thompson's new trilogy kicks off with a chilling, mesmerizing vampire novel whose fast pace and adventures are guaranteed to keep your blood pounding. Thompson's tale catches your attention and will have you spellbound from beginning to end."

—*RT BOOKreviews*

"Dawn Thompson's exquisite prose brought to life the lush Moldovian surroundings. *Blood Moon* was a frightening, enthralling, and stirringly erotic novel. I thoroughly recommend it to anyone who is not looking for a typical vampire novel....I look forward to continuing the exhilarating journey."

—Mystic Castle

THE FALCON'S BRIDE

"Thompson's intriguing time travel intelligently blends 17th-century Irish legend with Regency sensibilities, passion, mystery and a wondrous love story of two engaging characters—the stuff of myth and magic."

—*RT BOOKreviews*

"Dawn Thompson is...a force to be reckoned with....This was an absolutely spellbinding effort by Ms. Thompson....[A] riveting and unforgettable read! I highly recommend this book!"

—Marilyn Rondeau, Reviewers Internati...l C...tion

"Those looking for p

W9-DFH-282

A RISING HUNGER

She hadn't taken one step when he was beside her. She hadn't even seen him move. He was, indeed, more wolf than man, but what moved him was a supernatural energy that defied description. His scent overwhelmed her—mesmerized her. She inhaled him deeply —leather, and the cold, crisp north wind, laced with his own distinct feral essence, mysterious and evocative. It set her heart racing and undermined her balance. If he hadn't reached out and seized her arm, she might have swooned.

"And just where do you think you're going?" he growled.

Paloma avoided his eyes; they were searing toward her. A strange iridescence had come over them. An odd greenish color rimmed in red had replaced the sparkling onyx of those Gypsy eyes. Her heart sank. She had never seen anything as terrifying as the look of them searing toward her in the semidarkness, for the fire was dwindling.

"Well?" he prompted. "Answer me!"

"It's best if I go," she said. "Surely you can see that."

"I see nothing of the sort."

DAWN THOMPSON

THE RAVENING

LOVE SPELL NEW YORK CITY

*For DeborahAnne MacGillivray,
PR person, Webmistress, multitalented author
in her own right, and treasured friend,
in appreciation for all you do.*

LOVE SPELL®

February 2008

Published by

Dorchester Publishing Co., Inc.
200 Madison Avenue
New York, NY 10016

ISBN 10: 0-505-52727-8
ISBN 13: 978-0-505-52727-1

The name "Love Spell" and its logo are trademarks of Dorchester Publishing Co., Inc.

Printed in the United States of America.

10 9 8 7 6 5 4 3 2

Visit us on the web at www.dorchesterpub.com.

THE RAVENING

PROLOGUE

England, the Cumberland border, November 1871

Paloma danced beneath the autumn moon. It was full and round, shining down upon the fells. She needed no music. It lived in her heart, drowning out the sorrow of her reality among the Travelers. She needed no partner, no Lord of the Dance. Hadn't she stolen out onto the fells to get away from the rest? It had been thus since her father passed and her stepmother took a new husband.

It was warm for the cusp of November; warm enough to go about with naught but her paisley shawl for a wrapper, warmer than it had been last year when the caravan came this way. Soon, they would be traveling south, to Dartmoor or Cornwall, where the winters were milder. But winter seemed so far away as Paloma danced under the autumn stars, like so many winking eyes looking down from the indigo vault overhead. Dancing was in her blood.

All at once, the vista changed. A sooty cloud

passed before the moon, casting deep shadows over the fells. Cold suddenly, Paloma shivered. Was it an omen of ill boding, or just what it appeared—an innocent passing cloud? It lasted but a moment, before it drifted on and the moon shone down again. But now it shone upon another figure crouching in the tall grass a few yards off, watching her—*a wolf*. Where had it come from? They'd heard the howling for days, but no wolves had been seen. That was as it should be, since there were no wolves in England any longer . . . unless the tales of phantom wolves— vampires that took the form of wolves—were true. But surely not. Those were naught but fables told to frighten wayward children.

For a moment the creature didn't move. How beautiful it was, a dusky shade of gray in the eerie filtered moonlight. Its iridescent eyes were mesmerizing. Paloma missed her step. The music in her head faded then. She heard nothing but her rapid heartbeat, and saw nothing but those two glowing acid-green eyes rimmed in red burning toward her. She could not unlock her gaze from them.

All at once, the creature sprang up and started to advance. Taking slow, measured steps, it began slinking toward her. She wanted to run, but her feet were rooted to the spot. She wanted to scream, but her throat closed over the sound. The wolf prowled nearer, but then it wasn't a wolf any longer, it was a naked man. In the blink of her eye, it surged into a silvery streak of displaced energy that brought it so close to her she could smell its foul, sickening-sweet stench, like rotting flesh, and feel its fetid breath puffing on her skin.

How the creature towered over her, its skin the color of gray-green mold stretched so tightly over its frame the veins showed through. It was aroused. She could feel its hard shaft forced against her belly as it encircled her waist with one thin arm, threw back its bald head and bared its long, curved fangs stained with the residue of old blood that looked black in the moonlight.

Through a blurry haze, Paloma stared transfixed as the creature slowly lowered its fangs toward her arched throat. How strong it was. Why couldn't she move? Why couldn't she tear her eyes from its hideous face? It uttered a guttural chuckle as if it read her thoughts, swooped down and sank the slippery fangs into the base of her arched throat. When its long talons plunged beneath her embroidered blouson, plucking at her nipple, her heart nearly stopped. When those talons started to lift her skirt, she screamed, and screamed again—a bloodcurdling sound that carried on the cool wind that had suddenly risen.

Raised voices from the camp rumbled in her ears. The vibration of heavy footfalls carrying toward her, shuddered beneath the soles of her boots. Snarling like the lupine animal it had been when it first appeared, the creature threw her down and, just as swiftly as it had changed before, it changed again. It wasn't a naked two-legged creature that loped off into the deep darkness beyond the thicket, abetted by another cloud shutting out the light of the moon. It was the beautiful great gray wolf that had so mesmerized her, its guttural howl living after it, reverberating in the very marrow of her bones.

Out of the corner of her eye Paloma watched the bobbing torches approaching through a mist of tears. Her body seemed as light as a feather; as if the wind would carry her off if she didn't hold tight to the tall grass her hands had fisted into. The fells were swimming around her. The torches were suddenly so close she felt their singing heat. Several thrust full in her face narrowed her eyes, and she turned her head aside, with a groan.

A woman gasped. "*Vampir!*" she shrilled. "*She has been bitten!*"

"Aye," a gruff man's voice returned, making the sign of the cross. "There! Look there!" he cried, pointing toward a shaggy gray, bushy-tailed blur disappeared among a stand of young saplings, "—a wolf in camp!"

His words were scarcely out when the creature changed again, and a huge black bat soared skyward from the place where the wolf had been. Silhouetted against the moon, the creature climbed aloft, its dark wings sawing skyward through the still night air. The others seemed not to notice. Were they blind?

The man reached to lift Paloma into his arms, but the woman stopped him with a firm hand. "No!" she said. "Leave her. See? She loses consciousness. She will rise a vampire. We cannot bring that with us. Are you mad?"

"We cannot just leave her, Kesia," the man said. Was that her stepfather's voice? *Yes* . . . She shuddered at the sound of it. He was bending over her. He smelled foul, of strong onions and sweet wine. Dazed as she was, she shrank from him—from his familiar touch.

"I see the way you look at her, Seth," the woman snapped at him. "I see the way your eyes stray to that fiery mane of hers—that fair Irish skin." She spat to the side and wiped her thin lips on the back of her hand. "You lust!" she accused him. "Leave her, I say. She is naught to me, and too much of a temptation to you. We break camp now—tonight. Hear the wolves howling? Come away before they have their way with us all!"

"What of the old woman?" he said. "She will not agree to leaving Paloma behind."

"You leave the old one to me," Kesia snapped at him. "Now, come!"

Help me, Paloma wanted to say, but the words would not come. Her numb lips seemed paralyzed. *Don't leave me*, her mind cried out, but they didn't hear—couldn't hear—even if she had been able to speak the words aloud. It was as if she no longer existed to them. They had already told the others gathered there that a vampire lurked among them, and mass hysteria had broken out as they doused the fires, packed up their gear, and broke camp, like a cloud of swarming bees.

Paloma tried to rise, but vertigo held her down. Time meant nothing then, as she drifted in and out of consciousness. She'd heard what they said. She dared not succumb to the lure of oblivion that would have her wake undead.

The wagons had started to roll; their motion visible, when the cloud cover let her see it. The charged voices grew distant. They were really leaving. . . . But surely not. It was moon madness . . . a dream . . . a terrible nightmare . . . *wasn't it* . . . ?

CHAPTER ONE

Whitebriar Abbey, Cumberland, England,
the Winter Solstice, 1871

Milosh sat his horse just inside the forest curtain at
the foot of the tor, staring through a veil of cold rain
splinters toward what remained of Whitebriar Abbey,
no more than a burned-out shell at its summit. He
hadn't come this way in thirty years. This was the last
thing he would have expected. The sight of the great
house, standing wounded against the twilight sky,
brought physical pain.

Milosh shrugged his saturated greatcoat closer
about his neck and shoulders. Rain dripping from his
wide-brim slouch hat was trickling down his neck
from the wet hair resting on his collar. He was chilled
to the bone.

"Easy, Somnus," he said, soothing the sleek black
stallion underneath him, while crooning to it, sotto
voce. The restless horse had begun to prance in place,
tossing its long, wet mane. As if in reply, the animal

bobbed its head, puffing visible breath from flared nostrils, and snorted.

Milosh paid no attention to the obvious protest. Narrowing his eyes to the rain, he spurred the rambunctious horse on and it bolted out into the thicket. The wind had picked up and the rain was fast turning to ice. He was heading into the gale, and the splinters of freezing rain stung his face and beat about him relentlessly. The horse balked as they started to climb, but the Gypsy would have none of it. Leaning low over the animal's neck, he whispered: "It is now or not at all. The tor will be as a sheet of glass in no time. Then where will you sleep out of the weather, eh?"

As if it understood, the horse complained in reply and began its high-stepping ascent, every muscle in its sleek, black coat rippling. There had to be some shelter remaining in the place. Instinct moved Milosh toward that possibility. There was a perfectly respectable inn in Carlisle, but that would not do. As inhospitable as it was in its present state, he would sleep in Whitebriar Abbey one last time before moving on.

Still complaining, the horse danced crazily up the tor, slip-sliding on the slick, icy crust forming underfoot. The closer it carried him toward the summit, the more Milosh's heart sank at the devastation. As he climbed, his mind's eye saw in rampant flashes the Abbey as it used to be, standing proud against the gales, facing the cruel north wind unscathed.

Destroyed by fire. That's what the vicar in the valley had said; a fire of mysterious origin. No word of its occupants, the Hyde-Whites. They were not harmed. They were seen soon after the ferocious blaze, but then disappeared. There had been no word of them since. Milosh heaved a ragged sigh. He was six months too late. Maybe there would be some clue inside, something his extraordinary perception would disclose. When he was here last, the Abbey was under siege by vampires. It was snowing then—a virtual blizzard. This was worse, this icy cold that stabbed a man to the very marrow of his bones.

It was the winter solstice. At home, at the foot of the Carpathian Mountains, there would be bonfires and feasting and pageantry. Many of the celebrations were remnants of the old religion practiced in secret there still or openly under new guises, like the bonfires in fall and winter, and the May pole in spring. And then there were the colorful events, tribal mysteries, whose roots were planted deep in Romany custom. Yes, Milosh was homesick, but he could not go home—not yet, it was too soon. Some still might live who would remember. Only sixty years had passed since he'd set foot on Romanian soil—a mere blink in time's eye to a vampire who had roamed through the world for nearly four centuries hunting the very thing he had become.

By the time he reached the summit, the ice had bent the grass spears low. Somnus snorted dourly, flashing eyes that glowed with an iridescent radiance, and glanced behind at Milosh in the saddle. The two shared a unique bond. Of all the horses Milosh had commanded over the years, Somnus was the closest to him. The animal was *vampir*, like the Gypsy himself, having been bitten by a vampire; Milosh had saved the wild black phantom, and made him his own. Somnus would be his last. Like himself, the stallion would not age, but rather wander through the centuries with his master.

The stables were still standing, having mostly escaped the fire, and Milosh breathed a ragged sigh of relief as he climbed down and unsaddled the horse.

Somnus had grazed before the rain began, but Milosh was never without a treat for the horse. He drew an apple from his greatcoat pocket and lured the stallion into one of the intact stalls. Searching the others, he found an old horse blanket and draped it over the animal's back. Then turning on his heels, he sprinted out into the icy rain again, and made straight for the Abbey.

He entered where the west wing used to be. The front door was still intact, but the roof above the Great Hall was gone, as was everything up to the staircase that divided the house in two. He climbed over burnt timbers, heaps of blackened slag besotted with the rain, and scattered furniture, some of which was barely recognizable. The stench of it rushed up his nostrils and for a moment that was all he could smell. It wasn't until he had cleared the second-floor landing and turned into what remained of the east wing that another scent rose above the rest—an unfamiliar scent. Such always flagged danger and Milosh froze in his tracks, his head raised as he sniffed the cold air. When he lowered his head, he did so slowly, his eyes snapping in all directions. He was not alone.

Adrenaline surged through his blood. He was always on guard, elsewise he would never have come through the ages unbitten since that one fateful time so long ago, when the nightmare began. Making no sound, he prowled to the toile suite, where he had stayed as a guest so long ago. The master suite and yellow suite across the hall had been gutted, but several suites on the north side of the hall were in fairly good condition, but for smoke damage and crumbling plaster exposed to the weather. The toile suite was one of these. Aside from a dusting of soot over everything, the rooms were reasonably intact; at least the sitting room was as he strolled through it. The unfamiliar scent was stronger there, and Milosh was on his guard as he sauntered into the vast bedchamber.

Lifting down the tinderbox from the mantle, he lit a candle. A fire was wanted if he was ever to dry his soaked clothes. His wool greatcoat had absorbed the icy rain like a sponge. He spied a few logs stacked beside the hearth and chucked them into the hearth. More were needed if he was to keep the fire going through the night, and he strode back into the sitting room and collected what was there. Arms loaded, he was striding back into the bedchamber when a small hooded figure slammed into him as he crossed the threshold, catching him off balance.

"Hold, there!" he thundered, but his words were wasted. Two small hands gave him a shove and he backpedaled into the wall beside the door, dropping the wood in his arms. The impact of his body slamming against the singed wall at his back dislodged a heavy mirror, which fell, striking him a blow to the head that drove him down on the floor.

His slouch hat spared him being cut by the mirror shards raining down around him. Dazed, he shook his head to clear his vision. The room swam around him. Through the vertigo, he saw that his assailant was a woman, slight of build though fleet-footed. Her hood had fallen back in her haste, and her long mane of bright coppery hair streamed out behind her as she fled.

"Wait!" he called after her. "Who are you . . . what are you doing here . . . ?"

A strangled outcry replied as she darted out into the corridor, the hem of her cloak dusting the woodwork.

Milosh ground out a string of blue expletives as he righted himself. Four hundred years roaming the planet doing battle with bloodthirsty vampires only to be knocked off his feet by a mere slip of a girl? He must be getting old. It was degrading. In his haste scrambling upright, he leaned upon several slivers of the broken mirror, and quickly drew back his hand. The shards cut deep into his right palm, and blood gushed from the wound. Things were much simpler when such geegaws were made of polished metal that did not put a body to the hazard.

Muttering a fresh string of profanity under his breath, the Gypsy clenched his fist over the ragged gash and staggered after the girl. She was nowhere in sight when he reached the landing. Still dizzy, he opted to employ his extraordinary power to leap great distances, and soared over the debris in his path. He touched down running through the gaping hole that had once been the west wing of the Abbey.

His eyes, narrowed in the stabbing rain, flashed in all directions. *Where could she have gone so quickly in such a downpour, more ice than rain?* He wasn't left long to wonder. His gaze had scarcely come around to the stable when he saw her leaving it at a gallop astride Somnus, her cloak billowing about her like a great black sail.

Cupping his hands around his mouth, he shouted at the top of his lungs: "Stop, thief! That is my horse you're stealing!"

The girl made no reply, and Milosh gave an earsplitting whistle meant to bring the stallion back, but Somnus galloped on, his high-pitched whine siphoned off on the wind, and disappeared down the ice-crusted tor a good deal faster than he'd climbed it.

Milosh ground out another oath and trudged toward the stable. No one else had ever been able to mount the phantom horse, much less ride him, which many a thief had discovered these past thirty years.

In any other circumstances, Milosh would have praised the girl for her fine seat astride the stallion, and excellent horsemanship in general to sit such a horse bareback. As it was, quite something else was streaming from his clenched lips.

Anger set his blood racing, and with it came the fangs that always descended whenever his temper flared, or he was in need of a weapon, or had become aroused; this reality had not ended with the feeding frenzy. He would always bear the mark of the vampire—bloodlust or no.

There was only one way to catch the girl, and he stripped off his clothes, leaped into the air, and hit the ground running on the four thickly padded feet of *canis dirus*, his wolf incarnation. Truth to be told, the Gypsy was more at home in the skin of the great white wolf than he was in his mortal flesh. It had been that way since the blood moon ritual he'd learned of in Persia had freed him from the bloodlust. Though he was still and always would be a vampire, once the feeding frenzy was eliminated, his instincts and prowess in the body of the wolf increased until they carried over into his human incarnation. He was more wolf than man, able to destroy the undead in either body.

He sniffed the rain-washed air. The strange scent he'd smelled earlier rode the wind. So this was the foreign scent he'd smelled—*her scent*. It filled his flared nostrils still. He recognized it now—herbal and clean, a blending of rosemary and lavender—all manner of herbs—a fragrance of the wild—of the wood—of the earth, mysterious and evocative. It played havoc with his senses, reminding him of his early days . . . and of home.

The great wolf snorted as it skidded down the steep incline in a gait that more closely resembled a limp owing to its gashed right front paw. It was definitely less graceful than its usual surefooted prowl, when sinew and muscle meshed in a flawless mechanism that felt more comfortable to Milosh than his two-legged stride. At the moment, he was too enraged to care.

The snorting wolf staved on in mindless pursuit. He was the hunter now, that feral instinct having taken over. Was her scent a memory or was she near? Either way, Milosh couldn't shake it. On his last visit to Whitebriar Abbey, he'd had the snow to show him his quarry's tracks. Now, he had to rely upon his extraordinary sense of smell. He wasn't too concerned. He also had the horse's scent, and since the other had made such an unsettling impression upon him, he decided to trust Somnus's musky odor instead. It led him through the brake and the thicket at the foot of the tor, past what remained of the dormant, sheared-off woad canes, then finally into the forest.

Above, the canopy of interlaced boughs kept much of the icy rain from penetrating to the forest floor. A cold green darkness prevailed under the pines. Reflected light from the shadows twinkled in the wet patches that hadn't escaped a sprinkling. The white wolf's breath puffed from its flared nostrils. The ice underfoot had slowed the blood flow in its gashed front paw, but the nagging pain remained. Now and then a high-pitched whine testified to that. His extraordinary night vision was charged now in the deep dark of the forest. He saw the path ahead as if through a bloodred veil, and though he strained and tested his power to its fullest, he detected no sign of horse or rider. Where could she have gone?

All at once, he stopped in his tracks. The scent was stronger now, but that was not what made the great wolf hesitate. It was the plaintive howling of other near and distant wolves that raised the hackles on his back. Waves of déjà vu washed over him at the sound. It brought back memories of the siege that had taken place there thirty years ago, of Sebastian, the vampire that hunted *him* as he did it, and of the Brotherhood that had driven the creature back, but could not—for all their number—destroy it. Could it be happening again? More pointedly, could he have brought it here? If it was, and he had, whoever the girl was she was in grave danger, and he sprang forward, her scent ghosting through his nostrils, and plunged deeper in among the ice-glazed trees in search of her.

CHAPTER TWO

Paloma had taken shelter in the ruins of Whitebriar Abbey when the wolves she feared so began to howl at twilight. Now, it was full dark, and she was thrust into the midst of them, and if that wasn't enough, she had become a horse thief! Making matters worse, she had no idea where she was going in the icy downpour.

If only that man hadn't come, she would have been safe and reasonably dry until morning, when the wolves always stopped howling. As it was now, she was in the midst of them and she was soaked and cold . . . so cold. Did the strange intruder belong at that burnt-out manor? From what she could see hiding in the dressing room, it had seemed familiar to him, the way he prowled through the rooms, and he seemed to know just where to find the tinderbox to light the candle. Still, the image he presented didn't seem right for a lord or a squire. He did not have the manner of a fine gentleman likely to preside over such a place, nor did he resemble a common peasant.

If truth were to be told, he looked to be Roma, a man in his late thirties; certainly no older than forty. If he was a Gypsy, he wasn't part of her Travelers' band. She had never seen him before. She would have remembered such a one as he.

She had gotten a good look at him from her vantage peeking through the dressing room door in the dark. He was tall, and seemed muscular, made to look more so in the fine caped greatcoat he sported, which broadened his shoulders substantially. The wet slouch hat he wore hid most of his features, though she did notice a handsome face all angles and planes, and dark flashing eyes gleaming in the candlelight from beneath the soggy brim of the hat. Gypsy eyes, deepset and evocative, snapped in all directions as if he sensed her presence.

For a split second, Paloma had almost been willing to make her presence known and trust those eyes. But then she remembered what had befallen her this past month. Gypsy or no, she dared not trust him. She dared not trust *anyone*, not even such a one as he, who evidently possessed the same Romany blood as she.

It was when he moved through the rooms that she fled. There was something in his demeanor—something feral. It had taken her a moment to identify it. He moved with the gait of a wolf. In a flash, she saw the wolf that had bitten her—relived its mesmerizing stare—saw it approaching in all its rhythmic glory. It was then that she bolted.

The horse was a godsend. She would have scampered down the tor on foot if she hadn't heard it complaining in the stable as she passed. Paloma had ridden horses since she was a child, but never had she ridden such a one as this beneath her now. It almost seemed human, the way it seemed to be trying to communicate with her—tossing its proud head as it pranced along, taking turns she never anticipated as it bolted through the forest. Could it be deliberately carrying her away from the mournful sounds of wolves howling? It certainly seemed so. It was a Gypsy horse, after all, strongly built, with feathered feet and forelegs, rare in black stallions; a crossbreed no doubt. Could it sense that she was Roma, too? It certainly seemed that way, but such a thing would be preposterous. Though she had always found them sensitive, horses did not possess that kind of perception.

The deeper she went the more tangled the ground cover became. Nettle and thorn, glazed over with ice, clacked and clattered as the horse's hooves displaced them. It was getting harder and harder to control the animal, and Paloma finally gave him his head. Leaning low over his strong, rippling neck, she felt the veins in it bulging— felt the blood thrumming through them. All at once, she could smell the horse's blood. She hadn't fed. In her haste to find shelter before nightfall and then the escape, there hadn't been time. Paloma began to shake. What was happening to her?

All at once the horse reared back on its hind legs and loosed a blood-chilling whine. Unprepared, Paloma fisted her hands in the animal's wet matted mane and clenched her knees against its slippery sides to keep from falling off. No mean task, as the animal began to spin in place, forefeet flying. When those churning hooves came crashing to earth, she screamed. Before her stood the very thing that struck terror in her heart—a great white wolf, with a silver streak down its back standing in her path, feet apart, shoulders hunched, its lips curled back over bared fangs dripping strings of drool. Its hackles were raised, its barrel chest heaving as though it had just run its heart out. The great ruff about its bullish neck fanned out wide about its head. Hind legs bent, front legs rigid, the wolf made several short lunges, clearly meant to intimidate. But Paloma was most frightened by its eyes, the way they stared, the red-rimmed acid-green iridescence about them, like the wolf on the fells—the wolf that shapeshifted into the vampire that had bitten her. She would carry the memory of that mesmerizing gaze to her grave. Oddly, this wolf was not subjecting her to its deadly stare. Its Other-worldly luminescence was directed at the horse. It held the animal relentlessly.

That the ethereal creature was *vampir* went without question. That it seemed more interested in the horse than it did in her was little consolation—not after what she had been through. She screamed again in spite of herself. The last thing she wanted to do was turn its attention in her direction, but that couldn't be helped; it was scream or swoon. Her throat opened and out it poured, the shrill sound bouncing off the ice-frosted tree trunks, echoing far into the distance as she spurred the animal deeply. To her horror, it wouldn't budge.

What was wrong with the horse? It had obeyed her commands until now. Paloma called to the complaining animal and slapped its neck and withers with the reins as she had before. When that failed, she dug in her heels again—more cruelly this time. The supple leather offered little resistance, but the soles and heels of the Gypsy-crafted footwear were hard wood and bit into the horse's sides savagely. Still, it would not move. The wolf prowled closer. Panicked now, Paloma glanced around quickly. Were there other wolves about? There were none that she could see, though she did hear the howls of one not too far distant. To climb down and run would be suicide. The great white wolf would make short work of her if she attempted that, and even if she did by some miracle escape it, what of the others?

The decision, however, was taken out of her hands. Before her eyes the wolf expanded, just as the wolf in the fells had done, and in a fluid surge of silvery motion surged into the shape of a naked man. *The Gypsy from the ruins!* He stood before the balking horse, white-knuckled fists on his hips, his black eyes snapping. His stiff jaw muscles twitched in an angry rhythm.

Paloma meant to scream, but all that left her constricted throat was a gasp. How finely formed he was. Reflected light from the ice-clad shadows showed her his tall broad-shouldered silhouette. She had been wrong. The greatcoat had not expanded his posture. He was magnificent, from the top of his shaggy head to the lean, muscled torso, from the narrow waist to the corded thighs that framed his thick erect manhood. He didn't seem to care that he was standing there naked and aroused before her. Could it be sheer arrogance, or did he think the darkness made him invisible? It did not. He bore the same ethereal aura as did the tree trunks surrounding them. His chest heaving with rage, he yanked the reins from her hands and gave them a vicious wrench. The horse bent its front legs and knelt on them.

Seeing her opportunity, Paloma leapt off the animal's back, but his quick hand shot out, arresting her by the collar of her cloak, and sat her back upon the kneeling animal without ceremony.

"Ohhh, no, little thief," he said, swinging himself up in front of her on the horse's back. "Hold fast to me!" he yelled, as the animal surged to its feet.

The sudden lurch as the horse extended its front legs to right itself made her grab the Gypsy despite herself. As fast as she did so, she let go as if she'd touched live coals. She'd forgotten he was naked. His cool, moist skin was stretched over rock-hard muscles, which tightened beneath her fingers. A soft moan escaped him as she grazed something else. His member couldn't possibly reach that far . . . could it?

"Hold fast, I say!" he gritted, as the horse charged back through the wood.

There was nothing for it. She had to hold on to him. The horse was fairly flying past the trees, weaving in and out among the dense ferns carpeting the forest floor. The Gypsy's scent filled Paloma's nostrils, a clean scent, of leather and the musk of exertion . . . of the woods, and the brisk north wind. She breathed him in deeply, resisting the urge to rest her head upon his strong back, inhaling the rich metallic richness of the blood in his veins—Roma blood. She longed to taste it. With the longing came bitter tears. A month ago the thought would have disgusted her. Something pinged in her sex, as though a ripe berry had burst and its hot, sweet juice had begun to trickle through her body. Her belly and thighs, pressed up against his bare buttocks, were riveted with the sensation. Her breath caught, and she bit her lip as the fangs began to crowd out her canine teeth. This, she dared not let him see.

Just then, the horse let loose a spirited whinny, turning its head toward its master. "On, Somnus!" the Gypsy said. "I will deal with you directly, you traitorous cob. And you, little thief," he went on, addressing her, ". . . do you hear those wolves howling? You should count yourself fortunate that I caught up with you when I did. You would not have lasted the night. *Oshashoy kaste sc feri yek khiv sigo athadsol*," he added in Romany.

"What have you just said to me?"

"You do not recognize the dialect?" he returned. "Curious. You *are* Roma. I said, 'the rabbit which has only one hole is soon caught' . . . and these woods are crawling with *vampir*."

"As if you are not one yourself," she snapped at him.

"Yet you do not seem to fear me," he mused, "which means that you are either simpleminded, or a vampire as well."

"You do not even try to deny it?" She was incredulous, and used the incredulity to avoid addressing the last.

He shrugged against her, sending new ripples of icy fire through her loins. "What use?" he said. "But what you do not know, little thief, is that this fine mount you stole is *vampir* also. Now sit still! Stop that squirming. You'd best prepare your case. You have much to explain when we reach the Abbey."

Milosh steeled himself against the soft pressure of the girl's supple body leaning upon him—against the occasional contact her tiny hands made grazing his sex as the horse jostled them. How soft and cool those hands were. How his traitorous manhood reached for their touch. It had been too long since he'd been with a woman. Her hot breath puffing against his cold, wet skin riddled him with gooseflesh that had naught to do with the temperature. He reached for her hands and raised them higher on his torso, away from his throbbing hardness. There was no mistaking the gesture, and the girl gasped, stiffening against him. It was too late. His loins jerked forward. The soft warmth of her belly rubbing him behind—even through the folds of her peasant skirt— and the mere memory of those tiny fingers clutching him lower, touching him innocently, was too much to bear. He moaned as the seed of his body betrayed him. It rushed from him, an unstoppable lava flow that siphoned the breath from him as well. Muttering a string of oaths under his breath, Milosh shrugged the moment off, hoping she hadn't realized what had happened, and gave another husky command to the horse, whose gait had taken on a haughty prancing air as they approached the kirkyard.

The girl was silent apace. When she spoke, Milosh stiffened as if she'd struck him. "Do you always go about unclothed in bitter winter?" she snapped at him.

"Only the undead have the power to shapeshift fully clothed," he answered over his shoulder.

"But I thought—"

"What, that I was undead? No. I am *vampir*, but not undead. I was bitten, but not drained to death. The undead are those who are killed by a vampire and later rise to serve their masters and the bloodlust that is their curse for all eternity. They are not redeemable. These I am committed to destroy, and it is often difficult because they are possessed of extraordinary powers. One of these is the ability to shapeshift clothed. Since I do not possess this power, needs must I had no choice but to leave my togs behind, considering the situation. You do not know the danger you are in."

"Those ruins are yours, then?"

"No, they are not," Milosh said—his words clipped and dour. "Whitebriar Abbey belongs to . . . close friends. Having found it thus, I took shelter from the storm . . . just as you evidently did . . . unless you are acquainted with the owners?"

"No, I'm not," she said quietly. She sounded so forlorn he almost softened toward her, but not quite.

"What, then?" he said. "Where is your caravan— your band?" A Traveler alone—and a girl to boot? It didn't ring true. She was either lost or deliberately outcast, and he would know which. She was frightened, that was a certainty, and Milosh meant to know why, and of whom—or *what,* before he delved any deeper in the distraction she was fast becoming.

"That is none of your concern!" she flung at him.

"Oh, but I beg to differ, little thief," he replied. "It is very much my concern. You stole my horse, remember?"

"You have him back," she snapped.

"Ummm, and fortunate for you that I do," he said. "Have you experience with phantom horses, then— horses that have been infected?"

"'Infected'?"

"It is a term my friends of the Abbey preferred to use in regard to the corruption that comes from the vampire's kiss." Was that a sob? Was she about to apply her womanly wiles with the deadly weapon, tears? This was the last thing he needed. He would rather face a pack of vampire wolves than a woman's tears. Annoyance ruled his posture, and he spurred the horse accordingly.

"I . . . I have never seen such an animal," she grumbled.

Ummm, just as I thought, Milosh gloated. "He'd have made short work of you before the dawn if I hadn't gotten him back in hand. Why did you run?"

"I do not know you, sir. You frightened me. I heard the wolves . . . As you say, there are vampires abroad. You yourself just admitted that you are one—"

"But not one who means you harm," he cut in.

"Then let me go! I can manage on my own."

"As you have thus far, eh?" Milosh scoffed. "If you hadn't stolen Somnus here, I might well have done. As it is now, I cannot. I will not have you on my conscience. We go back to the Abbey. Then I will decide."

Somnus balked again when they reached the foot of the tor. It was all Milosh could do to coax the creature up the grade. The girl's grip tightened around his middle, awakening his sex again. She cried out as the horse slipped, and Milosh loosed another oath.

"Stop that wriggling about!" he snapped. If only she would sit still and not provoke his manhood to rise against him, it would make matters easier. "What is your name?" he said, attempting a distraction.

"I am called Paloma," she replied.

"The dove, eh?" Milosh grunted, pulling back on the reins as the horse began to veer off course. "From the Spanish? You do not look Spanish, little thief. Hah! You do not resemble a dove, either, come to that. The name doesn't suit you."

"I will thank you not to mock me, sir," Paloma said haughtily. "The Spanish comes from my father's side. My mother was an Irish Traveler. It was she who named me thus in tribute to him."

"So that would account for your hair that flames. And where are they now, your parents, um?"

"D-dead," she said low-voiced.

"To leave you wandering the fells on the winter solstice," Milosh mused.

"You have me at a disadvantage now," she snapped at him. "Who are you, then, that you claim close friendship to the *Gadje*—the non-Gypsy in a strange land?"

"That much of the Romany language you do speak, eh?" he returned. "I am called Milosh . . ."

A strangled gasp escaped her then—not once, but twice, and then she said no more.

CHAPTER THREE

The Abbey wine cellar hadn't been looted, much to Milosh's relief. A thorough mellowing with the Hyde-White's fine Madera was in order—anything to blunt the raw edges of desire the little dove had ignited in his loins.

They were seated in the toile suite beside a roaring fire. Milosh, fully clothed now, sat sipping his wine, a close eye upon his captive, whom he'd wrapped in an afghan from the chifforobe. She was shivering so with teeth-chattering chills; the wine in her glass was about to spill over the rim as she raised it to her lips.

This was the first time he'd really gotten a good look at her. How striking she was with her long, coppery hair catching glints from the fire. It tumbled about her shoulders in a mass of waves and tendrils. Her eyes, large and on the green side of hazel, were slightly almond shaped, more in the manner of a frightened doe than her namesake, the dove. Her lips, slightly bowed and luscious, were still tinged with blue from the cold, and her skin, much to Milosh's dismay, bore no trace of her ruddy Irish ancestry; it was milk-white, so fine as to show the tracery of blue veins beneath it when the light hit it just so.

Milosh's heart sank. It was a sure sign that she had been infected. His intuition had never failed him. Even in the deep dark of the forest he'd suspected it. Those suspicions blossomed when conversation put her to the test and she seemed not to credit the condition with either fear or wide-eyed wonder. He would bide his time until dawn and see if she could bear the light of day. Meanwhile, he would put her to the test through subtle observation; he knew just how and what warning signs to look for, and he would keep his distance. She had already gotten under his skin in a way no other had managed to do in nearly four centuries. He was still marveling over that. Perhaps it was the Romany bond that linked them, or the pluck of the cheeky little gel to steal his horse—a vampire horse, at that! That was another strike against her. Only another vampire could have gotten anywhere near Somnus, much less ride him. And then there was the horse's almost comical antics on the ride back—dancing and prancing as if the creature knew something Milosh did not. Whatever she was, he wouldn't soon forget the soft fleeting touch of her tiny hands grazing his erection. Never had the touch of any living being aroused him so totally—not even, to his profound dismay, that of his poor dead wife so very long ago.

"Is something amiss?" she said, jolting him out of his thoughts.

Milosh frowned and almost laughed at the ridiculousness of the question, given the situation. "Why do you ask?" he said. Answering a question with a question was always a good way to regain lost footing.

"You stare, sir."

"Ah! Forgive me," he recovered. "I hadn't gotten a good look at you until now."

"Is that so important?"

"I believe it is," he said. "I'm seeing your Irish lineage now that I have light to see by. You lack only the ruddy complexion."

"I had it once," she said, pouting.

It was almost as if she'd spoken her thoughts aloud. He was watching her closely then. Should he address it? No. He would see if any more such thoughts lived in that pretty head before risking her silence. If there was one gift at which he excelled it was ferreting out the infected. It was what he did, who he had become—the vampire hunter. A mistake could be deadly. He had not come all this way to err in his thus-far infallible judgment.

It was that self-same gift that began his association with the Hyde-Whites, Jon and Cassandra, a little over sixty years ago on his own turf in Moldovia. Discerning their level of infection had not happened overnight. It had taken longer than he cared to recall to be certain what they were—if they could be saved, or had to be be destroyed. Then later, the gift came into use again in the matter of their son Joss. That was perhaps the most critical for him, since he had formed a lifelong attachment to Joss's parents, not to mention the friendship he'd formed with Joss himself—something unthinkable for a vampire hunter. Emotions had no place in his chosen vocation. A wrong decision made with the heart instead of the head could be fatal. A relaxed guard could end his days for good.

"Y-you couldn't be *the* Milosh?" Paloma said at last. Judging from her expression it took a great deal of courage for her to ask that question.

"Has word of me reached the Irish Tinkers, then?" he asked, amused by her innocence.

"And the Spaniards," Paloma said. "You are a living legend, sir."

"Even to the Spaniards, eh? Yes, I am he."

"And you knew these people here?" she marveled.

He nodded. "It's been thirty years since I've come this way. I was anxious for a visit." He waved his arm to encompass the entire situation. "This is what I found," he said. "I inquired in the village, and the vicar told me the fire occurred six months past. The occupants, my friends, survived, but no one knows where they've gone. I meant to wait out the storm and be on my way. There are vampires here, and I have work to do."

"I see," she said, her eyes downcast. That was one blessing. It was difficult to ignore those hazel eyes. He made a valiant effort.

"So!" he said, with flourish, adding another log to the fire for something to do with his hands; it hardly needed more wood. "Now you know my tale, it's time you told me yours, little thief."

"I do not think that is your whole tale," she snapped at him, "—nor does it entitle you to mine."

"It is enough . . . for now," Milosh said, forced to meet her eyes again. "And you *will* tell me how you came to be wandering the wilds of Cumberland alone, unheard-of for a Traveler—a girl Traveler, no less. What's more, you will tell me now. Your very life may well depend upon it—do not lie," he quickly added. "I will know if you do."

She shrugged and pulled the afghan closer about her. "There is no mystery," she said. "I got separated from the rest and lost my way."

"And they moved on without you?"

She nodded.

"Unlikely. What was your crime?"

"I've done no . . . crime, sir."

"Well, you cannot prove that to me, little thief, still smelling of my stolen horse. Try again. What was your crime?"

Paloma hesitated. "My mother died when I was five hands high," she began, "and Father married again—a shrewd woman, who raised me . . . harshly. Three summers passed, and Father died. My stepmother wasted no time finding another husband. Her eye was upon him long before my father went to his reward . . . and his eye was upon me . . ."

"He had his way with you, this stepfather?"

"No!" she cried. "I left the caravan before it came to that, but he would have done if I had not fled when I did. I was no match for his prowess."

"Go on," Milosh prompted. Her tale was believable thus far, but why wouldn't she meet his eyes? Those red-gold lashes sweeping her translucent skin were captivating, but what was she hiding?

"My stepfather was seeking me. He was drunk with wine, and I . . . I hid in a barrow; there are many on the fells . . . old burial caves. I must have fallen asleep. When I awoke, the caravan was gone. I wasn't surprised that I was left behind. My stepmother knew her husband lusted after me. That she left me behind was no surprise. He was our leader, but it was she who ruled the camp, and she despised me."

"And you made your way here? Where have your Travelers gone?"

"They go south, where the weather is warmer for the winter," she said. It made sense that they would. So far, Milosh found no fault in her tale. It was not unusual. He'd heard it told a hundred times through the ages. But still there was something . . .

"And you found your way here—just like that?" he said.

"Not . . . directly," she hedged. "I, too, needed to travel south to escape the cold to come. I am not fond of snow. I traveled west a way, but found the land too rugged, and the *Gadje* there too set against Gypsies. They pelted me with stones! Then I began to wander south, in hopes that the caravan was well on its way to Dartmoor, where we usually wintered in the past. I hoped to turn west again and find a place in Cornwall that would welcome me, or another Gypsy band to take me in. We are many in the west, but I expect you already know that. So, if you have it in mind to return me to my caravan, you can forget it. I would rather die first."

It was best not to let on that he was suspicious, and he chose his words carefully. "You cannot travel this land alone and unprotected. Hear those wolves howling? Listen well, little thief, they are *vampir*! How long do you imagine you will hold your own against such as that, eh?"

"I will travel by day."

"So do many of them, albeit with their powers reduced for the lethargy they suffer in the daytime. Still, they retain powers enough to dupe such a one as you, green as grass. You are ill equipped for fending on your own."

"I am not your responsibility."

"Ohhhh, but you are, little thief, and have been since you laid hands upon my horse. Of course, the guards, or whatever you call them hereabouts now, would probably take a different view. Horse thievery is a hanging offense, you know, or had you forgotten? What? Did you think I would just forget about that?"

"You have him back, your precious horse!" she cried, jumping to her feet.

"That does not negate the crime."

"Do not turn me in to the guards," she begged him.

"Please . . . just let me wait out the storm and be on my way."

"You aren't afraid to stay here with me? I am going to remain here also, little thief."

"If the tales of you are true . . . I have naught to fear . . . do I?"

"You have plenty to fear, my girl, but not from me."

She gasped. "Then, they are true . . . the accounts that you have found a cure!"

"No, not a cure," he corrected her, "—a remedy. There is no cure for vampirism. Once a vampire bites you, you are infected for life. The depth of the infection varies, but the effect does not."

Paloma opened her mouth to speak, but closed it again, her brows knit in an unattractive frown. Even so, she was exquisite. It was clear that she didn't understand. Why it should matter flagged caution.

"How old are you," he queried, "—how many summers?"

"I will be twenty-four summers on the ides of April," she said.

"A mere babe," he said through a guttural chuckle. "How many summers do you suppose I am?"

"The tales of that could not be true," she said. "I couldn't imagine it."

"The tales are probably accurate enough, though I dare say they have doubtless been exaggerated over time. I have lived nearly four centuries since I was bitten just a month before my fortieth summer."

Paloma gasped.

Milosh cocked his head, studying her. An audible breath released his words. "Still . . . knowing I am *vampir*, I find it shocking that you do not fear me even a little, despite who, and what I am. How is that, I wonder? The mere mention of the species strikes terror in the hearts and minds of one and all regardless."

"If you are what you say . . . what *they* say of you, why should I fear you? You have conquered the feeding frenzy."

"Oh, aye, that . . . or you could be *vampir* as well, couldn't you? That would explain your lack of fear, wouldn't it? You avoided that nicely earlier." It was a risk, but Milosh took it, hoping for a reaction. He had none. "Tell me the truth," he said, ". . . have you been infected?"

"No!" she said haughtily.

Milosh studied her a moment. There was anger in her voice. Was she clever enough—or desperate enough—to use anger to cover the guilt of a lie? Possibly. He needed to know before he closed his eyes in her company. It was time for a test. The gash in his palm from the broken mirror had begun to bleed again. He'd caught her glancing at it several times during their conversation. Now she caught him watching her.

"I-I'm sorry about that," she said, gesturing toward his hand. "It ought to be tended. It looks deep."

Milosh strode to the duffel bag he'd left there earlier and rummaged inside. It was several moments before his fingers closed around the object he sought—a silver flask filled with holy water. He snaked it out and faced her.

"I am not too adept with my left hand," he said, holding the flask toward her. "Would you mind? It is just water. If you would wash it and bind it with this—" he produced a clean handkerchief from the duffel bag "—we may avoid infection."

The test would be twofold, first to see what reaction she had to the holy water, and second to see her reaction to the blood itself.

"There used to be linen towels in the chest of drawers back in the dressing room," he told her, holding onto the flask while she went to see. While he waited, he rolled back his sleeve, and moved from the wing chair he'd occupied beside the fire to the chaise lounge at the edge of the carpet. Being out in the ice storm had evidently stopped the blood flow. Now, being close to the fire, the bleeding had begun again.

Moments later, Paloma returned with a towel, and Milosh opened the flask and handed it over, watching while she poured some onto the thick, soft cloth and began sponging the blood from his right palm. Her hands were shaking, and her jaws were clenched so tightly her sensuous lips had formed a hard, crimped line as she wiped away the blood.

"Is something wrong?" he said. She seemed to have handled the holy water without incident, but the blood had obviously upset her. What little color she had was lost of a sudden, and her breathing had become shallow and labored.

"I . . . I have never been fond of the sight of blood," she murmured.

Her whole body had begun to quake, and he took the towel from her. "Here, let me," he said, a close eye upon her as he finished the chore. She had turned away, her eyes fixed upon the smeared blood still remaining on her fingers. He poured more holy water on the towel. "Give me your hands," he said. Taking them, he began wiping his blood off her fingers, watching her expression. He did this slowly, though she tried to pull her hands out of his.

"I'm sorry!" she cried, finally wrenching her hands free. "I . . . I can't!" Spinning on her heels, she skittered into the adjoining bedchamber and closed the door behind her.

Milosh stiffened at the sound of the bolt being thrown. *Damned cut is deep,* he observed, winding the handkerchief around it. He cinched the knot in tightly with his teeth, and to his dismay encountered fangs. What had she done to him, this little mis-named dove? Was it only that, like so many women he'd encountered, she couldn't stand the sight of blood? Or was it something far more dangerous? The signs were unclear. Nothing was conclusive, and he certainly couldn't act until he was positive. Some of her reactions were suspect, while others seemed perfectly normal. This wasn't going to be as easy as he'd hoped. He wouldn't know for certain until he'd made a few more tests, and he heaved a sigh, eyeing the chaise that was too small for him. It was going to be a long night.

CHAPTER FOUR

Paloma backed away from the locked bedchamber door. Would he follow--burst in on her? It didn't seem as if he would. She laid her ear against the door and held her breath. There was no sound coming from the sitting room, and she sagged against the soot-streaked wood only to startle away from it at the sound of a deep, sensuous voice.

"Get some sleep, little thief," Milosh said from the other side. "I shan't trouble you, but I shan't be far from you . . . in case you should need me. I am a very light sleeper. . . . We'll see what needs must in the morning . . ."

Paloma didn't answer him. Backing away from the door, she stumbled to the sleigh bed and flopped on the dingy counterpane. He had lit the fire there, too. She welcomed its warmth. She was chilled to the bone.

She knew what he meant. She could hear the wolves howling in the night above the sudden tapping of hail against the windowpanes. The draperies hadn't been drawn closed, and she went to the window. Hail as big as pence coins bounced off the window ledge and assailed the pilasters outside. Paloma reached to close the draperies, and noticed her hands. They were smeared with blood. Milosh's blood. She had smelled it through his bronzed skin, clutching fast to him for dear life on the phantom horse. It had tantalized her when she made a bold attempt to cleanse and bandage the wound. Now, it struck terror in her heart, drawing her lips to the bloodstained fingers like a magnet—making her heart race—her breath come short. Her pulse was thundering in her ears as she took the traitorous fingers into her mouth and licked them clean of the Gypsy's blood.

She hadn't fed. There had been no opportunity. Now, the residue on her hands whetted her appetite for more. Long, sharp fangs distorted her mouth. That had nearly happened in the sitting room. This was Milosh—the legendary Milosh. Yes, legendary . . . and the only one who might save her. He was also a relentless vampire killer. Had her lie fooled him? It wasn't likely. At best, it gave him pause for thought. He would reserve judgment until he'd observed her longer. She would have to be on her guard.

It was said that some strange eastern ritual had made him immune to the feeding frenzy. Would he share the secret? Would it work for her? If only she hadn't gone out on the fells to dance in the moonlight. If only that other wolf hadn't caught her unaware. If only she hadn't looked in its eyes. *If only—if only—if only!* There was no use nursing regrets. She was infected, as he put it, and he could be either her savior or her murderer; that would depend upon her skills at seduction.

Her sex pinged, recalling the touch of his rock-hard member as her hands grazed it holding fast to him on the horse. There was no question that he was attracted to her. She had aroused him. She was well aware of the effect she had upon men. She had fought them off often enough . . . all save one. But that seemed to have happened to another person, in another lifetime. Now her loins were on fire just thinking about that wild ride upon the phantom horse. Milosh had brought her to the brink as well, but she preferred not to think about that. She wanted one thing, and one thing only from the enigmatic Gypsy— the secret of the blood moon ritual. How far would she go to get it? That remained to be seen. Right now, staying alive long enough to form a plan to get him to tell her his secret, and to put it into action without giving herself away, was all that mattered. How could she—a mere slip of a girl— pit her talents against a nearly four-hundred-year-old legend? If she wasn't very careful, he would find her out in a heartbeat. That was the danger. Focusing upon that, she climbed back onto the bed, clapped her hands over her ears to keep out the howling, and let sleep draw her eyelids down with the salty, metallic taste of Milosh's blood lingering at the back of her palate. Her sex was on fire. She had taken him within her in the most intimate of ways. He was part of her now. The blood in her veins thrummed in a strange erotic rhythm. Her heart fluttered in her breast differently. It echoed in her ears with the howling until she thought she would go mad. She had tasted the blood of a vampire. There was no turning back now.

It was nearly dawn when Milosh finally drifted off to sleep. It wasn't long before he awoke with a start. In the instant before his eyes focused, a familiar earthy scent ghosted past his nostrils—rosemary and lavender—*her* scent. Her warm breath was puffing against his face; a lock of her long coppery hair danced on his chest. It wasn't a dream, as he'd first thought. His eyes snapped open. Paloma was standing over him. His hand shot out, seizing her wrist, and, in one sinuous motion, he swung his feet to the floor and surged to his feet.

"What are you doing?" he said, his voice husky with sleep.

"It is almost dawn," she said. "I couldn't sleep . . . I'm hungry."

Milosh heaved a sigh. "Have you brought no provisions, then?" he replied.

She shook her head. "I have eaten all I had put by. I was hoping you had something you could share. I would have foraged for food if I hadn't encountered you, sir."

"Ummm," Milosh growled. Striding to his duffel bag, he loosened the string and reached inside, a close eye upon her as he produced a half loaf of brown bread and a slab of hard cheese. The wine still stood on the windowsill where he'd left it the night before. He pulled back the draperies, letting in the first dreary rays of light, and filled two glasses with the red wine.

"This will have to do until we go abroad again," he said. Breaking off a chunk of the bread, he handed it to her. Nodding, she took it and sank into the wing chair beside the hearth, while he cut her a piece of the cheese. After cutting a piece for himself, he returned to the chaise lounge to eat it.

"Do we stay . . . or do we go?" she said around a swallow of wine.

"That depends upon the weather."

"What do you mean to do with me?"

"I haven't decided yet," he said, blinking away the last dregs of sleep. He'd hardly slept and he was still puzzling over what she was doing poised over him when he woke.

"You cannot keep me prisoner here," she snapped at him. "Either call the guards, or let me go."

"No one is holding you here, little thief," he said. "You may leave whenever you like. On your own head be it." Milosh gestured toward the window. "Do you hear that?" he said. "Those are not wild dogs, like the town folk would have you believe. They are *vampir*. Dawn has broken and still they howl. Some can go about in the light of day. True, those that can are weaker in daytime, but any one of them could—and will—make short work of a mere slip of a girl like you if you venture among them unescorted by someone skilled in the art of defending against them."

"I'll take my chances," Paloma huffed, tossing her coppery mane.

Milosh sketched a bow, sweeping his arm wide toward the doorway. "Be my guest," he said, and finished his wine.

He was awake now. The gauze of sleep, like a film of cotton wool, had faded from his eyes. What was she playing at? Any fool could see she was terrified. And what was she about, bending over him on the chaise lounge? Hungry, she'd said. Not the way she was picking at her bread and cheese. There was only one way to find out, and he waved his arm toward the door again.

"Well? What are you waiting for—go!" he charged.

"You'll set the guards on me."

"So long as you do not make off with my horse again, I will not summon the guards."

Paloma stared at him for a long moment. That look was almost more than Milosh could bear. She had a gaze that could make a man melt.

"Go, if you're going!" he barked.

"I . . . I will!" she snapped back. Snatching the small bundle of belongings she'd left beside the door when she'd arrived, she cast one last poisonous glance over her shoulder, and marched through the open doorway, her skirts dusting the doorjamb.

Paloma hadn't lied when she woke Milosh earlier. She *was* hungry, but for blood, not food. She was just inches from feeding upon the distended vein in his neck. She couldn't help herself. She hadn't fed in nearly two days, and the feeding frenzy had nearly driven her mad. If she had succeeded, she would have spoiled any chance to extract the information she needed from the Gypsy, which was the only reason she'd hesitated.

Did he suspect her? After that, how could he not? Now, she had to modify her original plan. Ignorant of the depth of infection that would qualify her for the blood moon ritual, Paloma had intended to get him to reveal the secret to her, feigning curiosity, no matter how far she had to go to get it. He was a vampire hunter. If she told him she had been infected, he might end her days as quickly as she could bat an eye. Now, she would have to convince him that she was not a vampire before she dared try to get him to tell her about the blood moon ritual. What better way to do it than to venture forth into a pack of howling vampire shapeshifters? She must be mad. Counting upon the probability that he would keep an eye upon her— if for no other reason than to satisfy *his* curiosity—she pulled her hooded cloak about her, sorry at once that she'd left the warm hearth behind, and began her slippery descent of the tor.

The icy drizzle had stopped, and the tor seemed like an enchanted fairyland. The grass spears, bent low in their sheaths of ice, crunched like cracking glass underneath Paloma's feet as she made her way down. Much of the distance was navigated on her bottom, since keeping her footing on the grade—treacherous enough in fine weather—was nearly impossible in the hard-soled boots she wore. Still, the scenery took her breath away. She scarcely heard the wolves now, though she knew they were there. She felt their eyes upon her. It was an eerie, ghostly feeling.

Her first glimpse of the rowan tree at the foot of the hill captivated her. She stopped beneath it. Icicles dripped down like rain, gleaming in the fractured morning glare. How glorious it was to stand beneath that frosty bower. She glanced behind, but there was no sign of Milosh. Perhaps she'd been hasty. Perhaps she'd misjudged him. Four hundred years in relentless, cold-blooded pursuit of the undead would naturally harden a man. Still, she wasn't mistaken about what she felt when she'd clung to him on the phantom horse. He *was* attracted to her. She hadn't imagined his arousal—the soft moans escaping his throat when his seed left his body, the dilated gleam in his onyx eyes. There was much passion in the enigmatic Gypsy. It was contagious. If things were only different . . . if she hadn't been infected . . . But she had, and she didn't want to die—not in the dawn of her youth—not until she'd loved and lived and grown too old to dance.

Passing the kirkyard, Paloma glanced behind again. There was still no sign of Milosh. Perhaps she was mistaken. Perhaps he had just let her go, and good riddance. Now what to do? She would have to arrange to cross his path again somehow, if she hoped to ever learn about the blood moon. Right now, she had no plan, her first having failed, and she could taste danger in the very air around her.

The ice-covered gravestones in the kirkyard glistened as the light struck them. There was no sun, but it wasn't far behind by the look at the way the sky was brightening. Icicles dripping down in glassy strings tethered the stones to the ground. In any other circumstance it would have been glorious to behold. Paloma had never seen an ice storm before, and the unearthly look of the world at large took her breath away . . . until something moved. A shaggy shape stepped from behind a large Celtic cross on one of the graves—a great gray wolf, whose red-rimmed eyes cast an iridescent glow like a halo about it reflecting from the ice.

Paloma stepped gingerly, a close eye upon the beast through the spiked iron kirkyard fence. For a moment, the wolf didn't move. Her knees were shaking so, she couldn't go on. Scarcely breathing, she stopped, gripping the iron spikes for support until her hands began to stick to them. Should she run, walk briskly, or continue on as if she didn't even know it was there? And which way? The village lay to the north, the forest stretched southward between the thicket and the river, the tor was at her back. There wasn't a soul out to come to her aid on such a morning. While she tried to decide, the wolf lumbered toward her, its head down, shoulders hunched, baring long fangs trailing threads of drool as it advanced upon her. Paloma backed away from the fence. She scarcely felt the sting where the ice had burned her hands. Her thudding heartbeat was the only sound until the wolf's snarls broke the silence.

The decision was easily made. Spinning on her heels, Paloma started back toward the tor, the snarling wolf padding after her. There was no haste in its advance. It was almost as if—despite the wrought-iron fence between them—it knew it could not fail to bring down its quarry. Paloma's eyes snapped back and forth between the terrain ahead and the wolf behind, until she misstepped on the slippery ground and nearly took a tumble. Soft, involuntary sobs, dry and breathless, escaped her lips. The creature was gaining on her. All at once it stopped, backpedaled, and soared into the air and over the iron spikes with the ease of a feather. Paloma screamed as, at that instant, another wolf streaked through the air from the direction of the tor—a white wolf. It slammed head-on into the gray in midair in a snarling, thrashing, silver streak of motion that brought the two combatants to earth at her feet.

Slip-sliding on the ice, Paloma jumped out of the way, giving the creatures a wide berth, and scrambled back along the lane toward the tor. Unable to tear her eyes from the conflict, she stumbled along backward until the gray wolf's legs buckled and it fell over on its side. Then, feet rooted to the ground, she watched in horror as the white wolf severed the gray's head at the neck behind its shaggy ruff. Hands clasped over her mouth to keep the scream in her throat from escaping, she stood a captive audience of the ripping, tearing, crunching motion of the white wolf's great jaws. She watched wide-eyed as it lifted the other in the air and shook it back and forth, flinging blood in all directions until the bones and flesh and sinew gave, and the gray wolf fell to the ground in two savaged pieces.

Paloma stared down at her clothes; they were spattered with blood—the last thing she wanted. She hungered for it—thirsted for it, and she couldn't drink of it in front of Milosh. The overwhelming smell of it was driving her mad, but more important was the look of the white wolf standing—barrel chest heaving—its great feet spread apart, its eyes burning toward her not unlike the eyes of another wolf that had stared her down on the fells.

Cold chills riddled her body, as hot blood rushed through her veins. The shock of hot against cold threatened to render her senseless. All at once, the wolf lying dead in the snow began to shrivel before her eyes. Steam rose from the carcass, and it was a wolf no more. A man lay there in its place, his severed head several feet off. After a moment it disappeared as if it had never been, and Paloma screamed and bolted, running south toward the forest, leaving her bundle of belongings behind in the lane.

She hadn't gone ten yards when something slammed into her back, driving her down in the ice-crusted grass. She cried aloud as the breath was knocked out of her, and rolled over to see that it was the white wolf that had knocked her down. It was covered with blood jowl to heel, but it didn't appear to have been bitten. Straddling her body, its thick footpads firmly planted strategically on her cloak to prevent her from rising, the animal licked her face. Paloma's heart was shuddering in her breast, her breath coming in spastic explosions. The heady scent of the blood and the musk of the wolf filled her nostrils. She could not breathe for the suffocating smell forced upon her. Threaded through it was Milosh's unmistakable scent—leather, and the clean north wind. Man and wolf were separate entities, and yet somehow they were one.

The wolf's tongue warmed her cheeks. It was almost as if it was trying to tell her it meant her no harm, as it cleaned the blood spatter from her cheeks. There was no question that it meant to prevent her from escaping. Paralyzed though she felt with fear at the savagery she'd just witnessed, Paloma found the strength to shove the wolf away with both her hands, scrambled to her feet, and started to run. The direction didn't matter. Until that moment, she had no inkling of the entity she'd stumbled upon at the burnt-out ruins of Whitebriar Abbey. The legends were evidently true. The Gypsy, Milosh, was a force to be reckoned with, and all she could think of then was escaping him. The image of the decapitated creature emblazoned upon her memory would remain until her dying day. She was flirting with sudden death, and all she could think about then was putting as much distance between herself and the great white wolf as her trembling legs could manage.

All at once, her feet went out from under her. Something yanked on her cloak, and she landed hard on her bottom in the ice-glazed thicket. Her head snapped toward the cause of her unladylike predicament. Behind, the white wolf sat on its haunches, its jaws clamped upon a good chunk of her mantle. The look in its eyes was deadly. What did it mean to do with her? That was fairly obvious. The minute she struggled to her feet, the animal scarcely gave her time to retrieve her bundle before it trotted off toward the tor with her in tow, without a backward glance.

The wolf paid no heed to her appeals that it slow its pace. Could the Gypsy not hear human speech in his animal incarnation? How could that be, when she'd heard tales of how the great Milosh could communicate with his mind? All at once cold chills washed over her. Could he be doing that right now? Could he be reading her thoughts? From that moment on she vowed to make her mind a blank whenever she was in close proximity to him. Soon, she vowed, that closeness would end.

For now, she had no choice but to trip on after the creature as it jerked her along by the hem of her cloak. It gave no quarter as it pulled her up the tor, back to the ruins silhouetted black against the dreary soot-gray clouds.

CHAPTER FIVE

Milosh was still in his wolf incarnation when they reached the Abbey ruins. It wasn't until they'd returned to the toile suite that he surged back into his human form. Paloma skittered away as he changed in a silvery streak of simmering motion and stood naked before her. His eyes were like molten fire. He had left the shaggy wolf coat behind, but not the eyes. He was more wolf than man in either incarnation, in the way he walked with a feral prowling swagger, in the sound he sometimes made when his emotions ruled him—more animal than human.

Paloma gasped when he prowled closer—nostrils flared. He resembled a fire-breathing dragon, and instinct backed her up apace, but not fast or far enough. He bridged the gap easily, seized her in his arms, and shook her none too gently.

"Now do you see why you cannot go off on your own?" he seethed. "Do you finally understand what a position you have put me in, little thief?"

How he towered over her, his muscles rippling

beneath the bronzed skin. What a magnificent figure of a man he was, ruggedly handsome, the angles and planes of his face the perfect canvas for the fire's flickering shadow play. Even his shaggy mane of hair, a mass of tousled waves barely grazing his shoulders, was like the wolf's ruff. Though it was a man who stood before her, he was so much a wolf still, in all but that he stood upon two feet. He didn't seem to realize that he was naked, something that had jarred her sensibilities from the first time he'd shapeshifted in the forest.

"Why did you let me go, then?" she snapped at him.

"Would you have listened otherwise?" he retorted. Rage flexed his muscles and drew his lips into a hard bloodless line that barely let the words escape. "Look here, little thief, I like this no better than you. The last thing I need here now is a stubborn little *chovexani*—"

Paloma's gasp cut him short. "I am not a witch!" she hurled at him.

"Oh, no?" he murmured, crushing her closer. He was aroused, and she gasped again. "Then, how do you account for this?" he said, thrusting his hardness against her. "You have bewitched me, I think, little thief. Not in four hundred years have I lost control of my member to a woman."

"Let go of me!" Paloma cried, struggling against his grip.

"Oh, I have no intention of acting upon the demands of what you feel there," he said, "—only of showing you the ultimate consequences of your wiles. That much control I still possess, but do not presume to put me to the test. I am a vampire, yes, but I am still a man, and it is longer than I care to tally since that there has lived inside a woman—and never in one as beguiling as you."

Mesmerized by his closeness, by the cool, feral muskiness drifting from his damp skin—his own male essence, laced with the scent of leather and rain-washed air, Paloma bent her head back beneath his gaze. Waves of molten fire coursed through her under his spell. It had to be a spell. She had just seen him—for he was the same entity as the great white wolf—sever the head of another creature with naught but his jaws as weapon. She had seen his razor sharp fangs slice through fur and sinew and muscle as easily as a knife slices through soft butter. The right thing to do was to throw herself upon his mercy, confess her situation, and beg him to help her. But she couldn't summon the courage. The sight of the savaged wolf beside the kirkyard fence was too vivid in her mind. She spat in his face instead.

For a moment, he froze stock-still. His lips were only inches from hers, his hot breath puffing on her cheeks, sweet with the ghost of Madera wine. His jaw muscles had begun to tic a steady rhythm. That notwithstanding, he lowered his mouth and took her lips in a searing kiss that left her weak and trembling in his arms. His silken tongue chased hers to the back of her palate as he deepened the kiss, and Paloma felt as if her bones were melting.

She struggled free and raised her hand to strike him in the face, but his fingers clamped around her wrist and he pulled her closer. How deep and black his eyes were, dilated with raw passion and rage. It was hard to tell where one emotion stopped and the other began in him, only that it was feral in essence, and flagged danger.

"Take care what you start, that it is not something I must finish," he said huskily.

Paloma opened her mouth to speak, but a firm but gentle shake as he gripped her upper arms closed it again. Though she fought valiantly to keep from meeting his gaze, she could not take her eyes from the black onyx depths of his.

"Now then," he said his voice no more than a whisper, though it smoldered with unspent passion, ". . . this is what will be. We've wasted half the day. By the look of that sky out there, more rain threatens. We cannot travel by night. The risk of vampires is too great. The one I killed is of no consequence. He was a minion. It is his maker that I seek, and he would take you down in the blink of an eye to get to me. We will have to spend another night here, in these ruins, and set out at first light in the morning."

"Set out for where?" she said.

"Most travel south, but several caravans that I know of frequent the North Country in winter. I will see you safely to one of them, and then be on my way. I cannot in good conscience leave you to fend on your own. You've just proven the folly of that."

"Who made you my protector?"

"You did, little thief," he shot back, "—the minute you stole that horse. I put you to the test, and you failed. I will not leave you like your clan did. I will not have you on my conscience." He steered her toward the bedchamber and handed her over the threshold. "I want you to close this door and stay in there," he said. "That which I killed was not the only vampire afoot hereabouts. Those that roam in daylight suffer from lethargy, but as you saw, they are well equipped to take out one such as you."

"You do not know that," she cried. "You interfered before I had a chance to—"

"*Silence!*" he thundered in a tone that would brook no opposition. "If I had not 'interfered,' that creature would have ripped your throat out. Now then, stay inside. Some of the servants' quarters are still intact.

I shall go below and see if I can find us something to eat. We need to talk. I'm going to trust you not to run off, because if you do, you'd best be warned, I will not come after you again."

Milosh tugged on his clothes with rough hands. His traitorous body needed a good scourging. He almost wished she would strike out on her own again. He did not trust her, and what was worse, he did not trust himself under her spell. Yes, something was definitely not as it should be. He could feel it—he could taste it, but there just wasn't enough proof for action. If his mind wasn't so clouded with the effect this little Irish Gypsy spitfire was having upon him, he might be able to use his powers of discernment to discover what that something was. The way things were he was at a distinct disadvantage. It was not a comfortable thing. His success over the centuries had been because he let nothing interfere with his purpose. That single-mindedness had preserved his sanity, and his life. There could be no distractions if he was to continue his work, and if the girl was anything, she was certainly that.

His lonely life had damned him. It made him vulnerable. He longed for the life he could have had—should have had. Perhaps if he confided more of his situation to her, it would help him gain her trust—at least long enough to see her safely into the hands of others who might care for her. Women always seemed to need more explanations than men, but it was his lack of experience when it came to the mysteries of the female mind that worried him. He was pulling on his top boots when that thought came to him, and her voice from beyond the bedchamber door stopped him midtug.

"Milosh . . . please," she said. "Let me come with you . . . I . . . I don't want to stay here alone."

Maybe it was the way she said his name that made him melt. It sent the fingers of a chill loose upon his spine. Or perhaps it was that he simply didn't trust her. He wouldn't examine his motives too closely. Striding to the bedchamber door, he threw it open to her misty doe-eyed gaze. She was frightened, and well she should be.

"All right, come!" he said, "But stay close to me. We two might not be the only inhabitants of this accursed place."

When they reached the entrance to the servants' quarters, Milosh hesitated beside the archway leading to the corridor that led below, to the secret tunnel Joss Hyde-White had introduced him to thirty years ago. All at once, the fine hairs at the back of his neck were standing on end. Staring into the black cavern of that corridor, he sniffed the air. His instinct told him they were not alone. His extraordinary sense of smell confirmed it. This was something he needed to explore on his own and in wolf form, and he needed to do it before dark.

"Why are we stopping?" Paloma murmured. "Is someone there?"

Milosh nodded toward the archway. "At the end of that hallway is a secret chamber leading to a tunnel that gives access to the courtyard at the second-floor level," he explained. "I've used it myself. The Hyde-Whites were all shapeshifters. The tunnel was designed to allow their animal incarnations to come and go unseen by the help. I do not know how much of that sector has been compromised by the fire. It isn't safe to explore. My wolf will . . . later . . . before dark, just in case. Come, the servants' quarters are this way." He led her through a doorway on the right, whose door was lined with singed green baize. "The fire occurred six months ago," he reminded her.

"There may be some nonperishable foodstuffs below in the pantry that will suffice until we begin our journey."

"Why can we not explore the other corridor now?" Paloma said.

"The fire has undermined that sector," Milosh explained. "Our combined weight might well be too much and cause it to collapse. The wolf has a lighter step, and it is able to leap great distances should the need arise. In such a place as this, intruders are not the only danger. The whole structure could collapse—especially after such a soaking with rain."

His answer seemed to satisfy her, and they continued on to the larder and pantry below. Most had been picked clean by looters, but they did find some dried beef, white flour, some leavening, and a jar of preserved brandied pears that had been overlooked by the thieves, having fallen back behind one of the pantry shelves. Milosh pointed out that a bit of coffee had been spilled on one of the dusty shelves, and Paloma carefully scooped it up and put it in the coffeepot she found with the other pots and kettles strewn about. There wasn't much, but it should make enough for their evening meal. The pump was still operational, and Milosh filled a bucket with water, while Paloma scavenged for a skillet and unearthed a bowl and two tin plates. There wasn't a spoon, fork, or knife to be found, but there was a small ladle, and she added that to the collection. Together, they carried their finds back up to the suite, and Milosh chucked two more logs on the fire and propped the skillet over the flames. Then, rummaging through his duffel bag, he produced a bit of salt pork he had put by, and tossed it into the skillet.

"What do you do?" she asked him, as he began mixing water into the white flour and leavening.

The Gypsy smiled. "I shall make us some *bokoli*," he said, taking a knife from his boot. "Once I cut up the dried meat, and add whatever pork that does not render to fat for the cooking, the batter will make fine pancakes. You may begin the coffee."

It was early for the evening meal, but Milosh was not one to stand upon ceremony. Gypsies kept no code of protocol for meals. They ate when they were hungry, and Paloma seemed hungry to him, and weak, probably from lack of food. She'd had nothing more than a nibble of brown bread and a sliver of cheese since they joined company, yet she only picked at her food.

"I am in no wise a proper cook," he said, sitting cross-legged beside the hearthstone, "but in my situation, with four centuries of practice, I have become quite skilled at the basics of it—especially when it comes to working with limited ingredients. You must be famished, and yet you have hardly touched your *bokoli*. How is that? Mine tastes fine enough."

Kneeling on the floor beside him, Paloma hesitated. "I'm more exhausted than hungry," she said at last. Why wouldn't she meet his eyes? ". . . But I will try," she went on quickly, nibbling at her pancake as he bent his head for a closer look. No, something was definitely not right, and he continued to study her as she set her plate aside and took up her coffee.

"Try some of these," he said, exhibiting the pears. Lifting the metal spring, he pried the glass lid open, fished out a pear slice with his fingers and offered it, dripping the brandy liqueur. Paloma shook her head in refusal. "No?" He shrugged. Popping the fruit in his mouth, he rolled his eyes. "Ummm," he hummed, licking the juice from his lips and using his finger to trap one long rivulet headed for his chin. "I've tasted none better," he said, sucking the last drop from his finger. She licked her lips watching him, and he snaked out another piece of pear from the jar. "Are you sure?" he said, offering it. "They are really quite delicious, and they should be eaten now that they've been opened. It's a pity to waste them."

Paloma reached toward the pear and retracted her hand twice. Why was she afraid?

"Here, allow me," he said, raising the pear to her lips. "You've scarcely eaten a morsel. In that way, you do resemble your namesake, the dove. Take it, please, before the juice runs up to my elbow."

Paloma opened her mouth and let him feed her. His heart began to pound. The silken feel of her warm tongue against his roughened fingers sent darts of fiery sensation stabbing through his loins. The sight of that pink, pointed tongue flicking the juice from her pouty lips was more than he could bear, and he set the jar down not a moment too soon to cancel the pressure of fangs descending. "Delicious, no?" he said, sucking the rest of the liqueur from his fingers. Her essence mixed with it was more intoxicating than the brandy. "Help yourself now," he said, shoving the jar toward her. "You need to keep up your strength."

"Perhaps just one more . . ." she said, picking out another pear slice from the jar. Watching her devour it was too unnerving. She *was* a witch. He was tight against the seam. It was time to put some distance between them, and he got to his feet and squared his posture as casually as he could manage, with a full hard arousal upon him.

"Can I trust you to stay put while the wolf goes below?" he said.

"S-suppose whatever you sensed down there . . . suppose . . ."

"Trust me, it will not," he replied. "I have been about this business long enough to know how to deal with whatever entity has taken lodgings below stairs. Sometime, I will tell you all about it. You have naught to fear in that regard, little thief."

"I wish you would not persist in calling me 'little thief,'" she said, pouting.

"Well, that's what you are, aren't you?"

"No, I am not!" she insisted. "I . . . I took your horse out of necessity. I didn't know you, sir. For all I knew, you might have been a brigand, or . . . or a thatchgallows. You are Roma. You know folk think all Gypsies are thieves. How could you take the stand of a *Gadje* against your own kind?"

"Well, you are certainly no dove," Milosh said, with a raised eyebrow, and not a little amusement.

"I . . . used to be . . ." she murmured. Were those tears in her eyes? Yes, something was certainly not as it should be with this strange little Gypsy spitfire. What deep secrets had misted those eyes? She was like a flower that hadn't opened, and he longed to peel those petals back one by one until he'd solved the mystery hidden beneath. "May I ask you a personal question?" she mewed, jolting him out of those thoughts.

"You may ask whatever you like," he allowed, with a sly wink. "That is not to say I will answer."

"How did you become a . . . a—"

"—a vampire?" he interrupted her.

Paloma nodded. Scrambling to her feet, she took a seat in a wing chair at the edge of the carpet.

"My wife was about to deliver our firstborn child," Milosh said, strolling before the hearth. It was a painful memory still, but he didn't mind telling it. Each time he did, the pain eased somewhat. "In my homeland, at the foot of the Carpathian Mountains, our caravan had made camp in the foothills at the edge of an ancient wood. Our midwife had gone into the village to help a *Gadje* family also in need. When Rosa, my wife, knew her time was short to deliver, she sent me for the woman. It was several miles, and I took the cart to bring the woman back . . ." He could see the episode unfold before his eyes as it always did when he told and retold what had occurred, and he hesitated. His mouth felt dry as he steeled himself against what was to come.

"If this is too painful for you," Paloma said, ". . . you needn't continue. I was just . . . curious."

"No," he said. "It is just that I still cannot believe what happened . . . not really. That night many in the village were bitten, including the auxiliary bishop of Moldovia, Sebastian Valentin. He was not as fortunate as I. The creature killed him, and Sebastian rose again *undead*, the kind that must be destroyed, and joined their ranks. He has stalked me ever since. We did not get on well while he lived. It has become a deadly game for very personal reasons, and it is he whom I believe we are dealing with here now—"

"In the lower rooms?" she cried, vaulting to her feet. "It is this Sebastian you fear is hiding in these ruins?"

"Shhh," he said, "Sit back down. You were the one who wanted to hear this."

Paloma eased herself into the chair she'd sprung from. "W-what did this Sebastian . . . look like?" she said.

"Why?" Milosh said, with a start. "What could that possibly matter?"

"I-in case he *is* here and tries to infect me, while your wolf is skulking about below, fool!" she snapped at him.

A close eye upon her, he continued. "He is tall and slender—bald-headed. His skin is pale gray-green like that of a cadaver, stretched so tightly over his bones that they show through, as his veins do. He wears no clerical robes. Instead, he dresses in the togs of the day . . . or goes about naked; I have seen him in both guises. His preferred creature is the bat, though I have also seen him shapeshift into the form of a wolf—a large, gray wolf." She seemed to lose all color. Her whole demeanor clenched, and Milosh cocked his head, observing her. "What? Have you seen such a creature hereabouts?" he queried. "Besides the gray wolf I killed earlier?"

"N-no," she said. "It's just that he seems so . . . hideous."

"We digress, and the day is wasting," Milosh said. "A bat attacked me in the forest as I drove to fetch the midwife. I was able to fight it off, but not until it had infected me, though I didn't realize it then . . . it was only a scratch, and I had no idea what was happening . . . that we were under siege. Later, I discovered it was the same creature that had infected Sebastian, and when it tried to attack me again, I killed it. . . . That creature was my first kill. . . ."

"You continued on your way to the village after you were bitten?"

"Yes," Milosh said. "I collected the midwife and returned to the caravan to find Sebastian attacking my Rosa in our wagon. We struggled, and I was bitten again before others from the village came to our aid and frightened him off—"

"Was there no one to look after her while you went to the village?"

"Yes, there was, but as I told you, many were infected that night. We lost a great number of our band. The entity had minions. It was the full moon, and the slaughter was widespread."

"How awful for you," she murmured.

"That was not the whole of it," Milosh went on.

"For two days, Rosa worsened, while I did not. Either he had drained more of her blood than mine, or stole back in the night and took her again, I do not know. I knew she was dying. I just couldn't bring myself to do what I knew must be done to give her peace. Then, on the third day in the darkness before dawn, my Rosa awoke undead. There was no hope for it . . . nothing to be done, and it fell to me to . . . destroy her, and my unborn child with her. . . ."

"H-how?" Paoma said. He had her rapt attention.

"The undead must be killed with a stake through the heart . . . or they must be beheaded . . . or both. There are other ways, but staking and beheading are the methods of choice—the surest. I did both . . . to be certain her soul was saved . . . and the unborn soul of our child as well, and then I buried her at the crossroads . . . which is where our people bury suicides and those suspected of vampirism. That was almost four hundred years ago. It is an old superstition that being buried at a crossroads will confuse the creature if it rises. They still do this with suspected revenants as well—those that are reputed to rise from their graves after death."

"How terrible for you!"

"Shortly after, I became a vampire hunter, which is what I have been ever since."

"Vampires drain the blood from their victims," Paloma said guardedly. "If you are still a vampire, how is it that you do not . . . infect others anymore?"

"I traveled east for some time, eventually to Persia, in search of a remedy from the holy men there," Milosh said. "They shared with me a secret ritual that, if performed under the blood moon, would arrest the feeding frenzy."

"B-but you are still a vampire?"

"Yes. There is no cure, but without the bloodlust.

I retain all of my . . . powers, I prefer to call them 'gifts,' and my fangs will appear whenever I need to defend myself, or when I am angry or . . . aroused. I tell you this so you will not be frightened if they appear all of a sudden. If they do, be assured I will have no desire to feed."

"This ritual," Paloma said, ". . . what does it entail?"

"There is not time to tell it here now," Milosh said, rising. "It is of no consequence in any case, except to another vampire. What is important now is making certain we are safe here until dawn. The day is nearly done. I need to do my work before the sun sets. Go into the bedchamber and latch the door. Stay there until I return. No matter what occurs, do not open that door to anyone but me."

CHAPTER SIX

Paloma backed away from the locked bedchamber door. Her heart was pounding—echoing in her ears. Milosh's words, *there is no cure*, came back again and again to haunt her. Her only hope was the blood moon ritual, but how could she persuade him to tell her now? If she pressed the issue, he would become suspicious. She couldn't shake the fear that he already was. She hadn't missed his intense looks, as if he meant to penetrate her very soul with those mesmerizing eyes of his.

It was becoming harder and harder to hide her lethargy. He'd noticed that, too . . . And the hunger. She desperately needed to feed. She hadn't since the odyssey began. The need for blood suppressed the need for food. What would she do when darkness fell? She couldn't go another night without satisfying the bloodlust. What would happen to her in that case? She had heard the tales of those deprived of the blood they craved going mad, or having no control of the anonymity they coveted in hiding their true nature, leaving them vulnerable to being destroyed by some zealous vampire hunter. She was in the company of such a hunter now, and she was fiercely attracted to him—more so since she had heard his sad tale. She longed to give him comfort . . . and more. Haunted by his passionate embrace, she wanted to give him so much more.

Could it have been the infamous Sebastian Valentin he spoke of that had infected her? He fit the description too closely to dismiss out of hand. If it was Sebastian, how seriously was she affected? Was she undead? Would the blood moon ritual even work? What did it all mean? The thoughts tormented her while she passed the time locked alone in the bed-chamber.

Battling the hunger, Paloma went to the window. The day was nearly gone. Soon they would face another night. Her lethargy would fade and the feeding frenzy would begin. Thus far she had been able to keep it from him, but she'd been without blood for too long. That had happened to her once before, shortly after she'd been bitten, before she realized how the vampire's kiss would affect her. It was indeed like a madness that came over her—drove her to pounce upon a *Gadje* wayfarer who gave her a ride in his wagon, which was why Milosh's tale had such a heart-wrenching effect upon her. She was riddled with guilt, filled with remorse for what she had done—what she'd been compelled to do as if she had no will of her own . . . And now, she was about to do it again . . . But how?

Milosh left his clothes in the sitting room and padded down the corridor in wolf form. The shadows were already creeping into the corners of what remained of Whitebriar Abbey. It hurt his heart to see it thus. He didn't want to leave Paloma alone, but he didn't have a choice. She would be too much of a distraction. With night coming on, whatever entity had taken refuge there would be at its most powerful. He needed all his wits about him if he were to do battle with vampires. His four hundred years' experience could testify to that.

He didn't need lit candles to find his way. The corridors of Whitebriar Abbey were etched in his memory, and he had his extraordinary vision to rely upon. It was like looking through a veil of blood, and his heightened sense of smell picked out a familiar scent before he ever neared the secret chamber.

Sebastian.

Slow, measured steps carried him down the back stairs. Prowling silently, hackles raised—the wolf followed instincts older than time as he ferreted out his age-old nemesis. Sharp fangs descended, and his heart began to beat like a kettledrum, moving the thick white fur of his barrel chest. More times than Milosh could count, he had stalked this vampire and the creature had eluded him. There was only one way to defeat the monster, and that was by surprise. By the depth of the quickening shadows, it didn't seem likely that he would succeed tonight, but still he would try, just as he always tried, with all of the passion in him, and would do so again and again, until Sebastian Valentin was destroyed.

Coming abreast of the secret chamber, the white wolf stood upon its hind legs to reach the rosette carving that activated the spring, giving access to the chamber and the tunnel beyond. The instant the door swung open, a swarm of bats poured past him into the shadow-steeped corridor. Rearing on its hind legs, the wolf shook them off as they grazed him. His guttural snarls echoed along the passage as one after another, the bats attacked him, swiping at him with their talons, beating him about the face and head with their wings. Clouds of the creatures tormented the wolf until it beheaded one of them with a vicious chomp of its vise-like jaws. A bite strong enough to behead a man sheared a bat's head off with ease, extracting a bloodcurdling shriek in unison from the fluid black mass against blacker shadows. Before the wolf's eyes, the swarm swirled into a spiral of shrill, flapping frenzy. There was no mistaking the odor now. Sebastian appeared before him, his wingspan challenging the dimensions of the hallway, his gray-green bald head scraping the ceiling, the acid-green, red-rimmed eyes glowing like live coals.

"So, I am not rid of you yet," the creature seethed as his fangs descended. "You are a fool, Milosh, to tweak my nose. You cannot win the battle you wage with me."

You always did underestimate me, Sebastian, the wolf spoke with Milosh's mind, as he always communicated when he shapeshifted, to those other vampires who had the ear to hear. *Your day will come.*

"But not today!" the creature said. Pulling back one mold-colored wing, it delivered a shattering blow to the wolf's side, lifting it off the floor, and slamming it against the soot-streaked corridor wall. "I could destroy you in a heartbeat. Have you never wondered why I have not claimed you in all these years? Eternity is much more interesting with you in it to spar with me. You live because I let you live, so take care not to anger me. I would hate to end our little game too soon."

The wolf struck hard, leaking an agonized yelp as it collapsed to the floor with an echoing thud. Pain seared through the wolf's body. Dazed, it started to rise, only to be caught by the vampire's other wing. This time when it fell to the floor, it couldn't rise.

Jeering laughter bled through Milosh's bleak semi-consciousness. "No, not today," Sebastian tittered and, before the wolf's dazed eyes and in a cyclonic swirl, the vampire melted again into a swarm of bats sawing off in all directions.

A foul stench was fanned to life by the dozens of wings as the bats soared past him. Milosh summoned all the strength of the wolf to raise himself off the floor, but it was not Milosh the wolf that rose, it was Milosh the man—naked and disoriented. It was the first time he had ever been jolted out of the body of the wolf by anyone or anything but his own power to shapeshift. That alarmed him more than the bloody gash slicing through a raised lump upon his brow that was leaking blood into his right eye. But it wasn't only the blood that starred his vision. It was the vertigo that flagged danger. It undermined his judgment and threatened to render him senseless. That he could not allow. Sebastian was loose in the house, and Paloma was vulnerable lest he protect her.

The wolf could travel faster than the man, but to his horror, Milosh could not surge back into wolf form. That had not ever happened before, either. Sebastian had proved his point. The creature seemed to delight in tormenting him, like a cat toys with a mouse before it puts it out of its misery, only this cat-and-mouse game had taken four centuries, and wasn't over yet. Could it have been the blow to the head that prevented him from shapeshifting? There was no time to puzzle over it. Leaning against the wall for support, the Gypsy dragged himself along the corridor with one thought to drive him: he had to reach Paloma before Sebastian did

Paloma had begun to pace the bedchamber carpet. How long should it take to search what remained of the lower regions? Where was he? How was she going to feed if she couldn't leave the bedchamber? Suddenly she heard rustling sounds coming from the sitting room beyond. She crept to the door and leaned her ear against the paneling. Yes, there was no mistake. Someone or something was moving about. She was just about to call out when a gentle rap at the door sent her backing away from it as if she'd been launched from a catapult.

"W-who's there?" she stammered, gripping her chest. Her heart was thundering so fiercely she could hardly hear his reply.

"Open the door, Paloma, it is me," Milosh said from the other side.

Paloma's hands were shaking hopelessly as she fumbled with the latch and finally threw the door open. "Where have you been, I've been worr—" She gasped. "W-what's happened to you?"

Milosh stood before her, leaning upon the doorjamb. He was fully dressed from his slouch hat and greatcoat to his top boots. A bloody gash crowned a thick lump on his brow, and despite his bronzed coloring he seemed pale to her. She gasped again, reaching toward him as he pushed himself off from the woodwork for fear he'd fall. He swayed, but he managed to remain upright. Feet apart, he struggled to maintain his balance, staring toward her with eyes dilated black in the light of the dwindling fire in the hearth. It was almost as if he was struggling to see her. What drew her attention most, however, was the slow trickle of blood leaking in rivulets down his face from the wound on his brow. Paloma licked her lips. She could smell it. She could *taste* it. Her heart began to pound.

"Get your things and dress warmly," Milosh said, his words clipped, spoken through clenched jaws, their muscles tickling a stiff rhythm.

"Why? Where are we going?" Paloma murmured. "I thought you said it wasn't safe to be abroad at night . . ."

"It isn't," he said succinctly. "Believe me, we will be safer out there than we are if we stay. It is Sebastian we are facing, Paloma. I just encountered him in the lower regions."

"Sebastian did this to you?" She was incredulous.

Milosh nodded. "I must see you safely to those who will protect you before I return and clean out this nest here. I cannot do that with you underfoot. I am too distracted."

"Forgive me, but you do not look in fit condition to finish anything," she observed, taking his measure. "A good puff of wind will likely knock you over."

"You think so, do you? Do not bet upon it, my girl. I do need to regroup and regain strength, however, and I cannot do that worrying about you. Now hurry!"

"But if he is out there—"

"He always feeds when he awakens. If he did not come here straightaway after you, he is feeding elsewhere. He knows you are here—just as he knew I was here. He can smell us—sense us. He toys with us. I know him well, Paloma. Do not argue with me. Get your things."

Still she hesitated. "But wait . . . if he is out there somewhere, wouldn't we be safer in here? Won't we be in more danger if we travel in the open? I hear more than one wolf out there."

"Sebastian *is* more than one wolf—and bat—and many other creatures. How else do you imagine he could have done such as this to me? He cannot be defeated in open combat; to do that he must be taken by surprise. Once I have seen you to safety, I will be about the business of that, but not until. Now do as I say!"

"At least let me clean the blood from your face," Paloma said. "It's leaking into your eye."

The thick, crimson ooze was more than Paloma could bear. She reached and wiped as much as she could away with her fingers then darted into the dressing room.

"I'll fetch a towel," she said. "There are plenty in the chest of drawers."

"We haven't time for that!" Milosh called after her, loosing a string of muttered oaths.

"It will only take a moment . . ."

Once out of his line of vision, she licked and sucked her fingers clean, just as she'd done when he cut his hand. How she abhorred the hunger that compelled her. How she detested what she was doing. It wasn't nearly enough, and she almost sobbed aloud. She craved more . . . so much more.

There was nothing for it, and she snatched a towel from the chiffonier drawer, took great care to wipe all traces of blood from her lips and face with it, and rushed back into the bedchamber as he bellowed for her again.

"Here! You do it, while I fetch my things," she said, thrusting the towel toward him. "I'll be but a moment." She dared not touch him again. It had taken all her control to force back the fangs the bloodlust had inflicted upon her, especially since her body had craved it since the first time. There was no hope for it now that she had tasted him. But at the same time, though she longed for more of the salt-sweet metallic thickness of his blood still lingering at the back of her palate, she dared not let what she could not have tempt her.

Darting back into the dressing room, she pulled on her hooded cloak, snatched her bundle of possessions, and skittered back into the bedchamber. Milosh had tossed down the towel. Taking her arm, he led her through the sitting room and into the corridor.

"Stay close beside me," he told her, shaking his head as if he meant to clear his vision. He was weaving when he walked. No, he was not in any shape to travel. A twinge of guilt struck. If anything happened to him now, it would be her fault. Tears welled in her eyes. If only she hadn't been bitten. . . . If only she could confide in him that she had been, without fear that he would destroy her. If only . . . if only . . . Why did it always come back to *if only?* It had happened, and there was nothing for it but to try and learn the secret that would spare her. He meant to deliver her to some ragtag band of Travelers and leave her. That could happen tonight. But it wasn't just the secret any more. She had tasted his blood. He was part of her now. Facing that earth-shattering revelation was almost more than she could bear. But there it was.

Together, they made their cautious way over the slippery, ice-glazed ground to the stables, where Milosh saddled Somnus. The phantom stallion seemed glad to see his master and her as well, bobbing his proud head, tossing his long, silken mane. Milosh hadn't brought his duffel bag—proof positive he meant to return and face Sebastian. He tied her bundle to the pommel, and swung himself up none too steadily.

Settling himself in the saddle, he reached out his hand. "Swing yourself up behind me and hold fast," he charged her.

Paloma did as he bade her, and rested her head upon his broad back. Did he flinch? Surely she couldn't have hurt him. Every muscle in him seemed to tense beneath her body pressed so close against him. Was he remembering another ride, when she held him thus—when he was naked, and her hands innocently grazed his erect member, bringing him to climax? They hardly knew each other then, but they knew each other now. She'd tasted his lips—his blood. No, she could never leave him. Somehow she had to persuade him not to leave her.

Somnus raced down the ice-crusted tor as if his hoofs had wings. He pranced—feathered feet and forelegs held high—through the valley, over the fells, and began following the river at the edge of the wood. They traveled a different way than they had before—southward, she surmised. She didn't ask. It didn't matter. She was taking careful note of landmarks so she could find her way back to the ruins. All Gypsies had phenomenal abilities when it came to sensing direction. It was in the blood.

They had nearly reached what seemed to be an abandoned smokehouse. The rubble beside it suggested that a house had once stood there. The iron strap hinges on the door were undone, and the door gaped open. It was then that Milosh began to sway in the saddle. It was almost as if he had been searching for some shelter for them both before the vertigo had its way with him, and not a minute too soon. Though Paloma gripped him with all her strength, he groaned and fell from the saddle to the frozen ground, unconscious.

Screaming his name, Paloma slid off the horse and knelt beside him. Prancing in circles, Somnus voiced his complaints, shoving Paloma aside with his cold wet nose as she tried to revive the Gypsy. It was no use. He was out cold. She seized the horse's reins and led him shying and complaining behind the structure, where she tethered him to a clump of bracken, and returned to Milosh, still lying as she'd left him. He was as still as death in the tall ice-clad grass. She would have thought the cold of it alone would have revived him.

She tried to lift him, but it was no use. He was deadweight. He couldn't stay as he was. She had to get him inside out of the weather. Rolling him on his back, she fisted both hands into the thick woolen greatcoat, dug in her heels, and dragged him inch by inch until she'd gotten him inside.

Paloma fell back on her bottom, her breath coming short. Gulping air, she glanced about the smoke-house. It had evidently sheltered other wayfarers in the past, for a pallet of sorts was spread on the leaf and straw-strewn floor in the corner. Constructed of brick, the ceiling rose at least ten feet. As well as she could calculate, the smokehouse itself was no larger than twelve feet square. The rafters were hand hewn. No meat hung from them now, only several long forgotten bunches of what she assumed to be herbs suspended there to dry, shackled to the walls with cobwebs and dust above a hearth that nearly filled the span of the back wall. There were several half-burnt logs in the grate. She carried a tinderbox in her bundle. At least they would not freeze to death. She scrambled to her feet and lit the fire.

Having gotten her wind back, Paloma stood and gripped Milosh's greatcoat again. This time she did not stop until she'd gotten him onto the pallet and knelt beside him. With trembling hands, she smoothed the blood-matted hair back from his broad, smooth brow. How handsome he was, the strong cheekbones, the straight nose, the noble Romany bone structure all angles and planes beneath that burnished olive skin. The onyx eyes, so full of Gypsy fire, were closed now, though she knew what lurked beneath those deep-set lids. They were filled with seduction, with hard, cruel passion, with a haunting sadness that defied description and wrenched the heart. They had the power to hypnotize, to seduce, and to cut to the quick.

Paloma traced the shape of his face, of the broad, strong jaw, of the gentle cleft in his finely chiseled chin, with a trembling finger. She had always been saddened by the lack of laugh lines in that face. She ran her fingers lightly along his cheeks where they should be. She knew why the laugh lines were absent, now that she had heard his tale. Tears welled in her eyes. This time, she could not blink them back. Blood still oozed from the gash on his brow. The scent of it was tantalizing. Her memory recalled the taste of it. Her heart began to pound louder now, the rhythm of the very blood coursing through her veins in tune with the blood in his that thrummed just as wildly beneath her fingers.

Milosh stirred with a moan. His eyes remained closed, but his lips parted. It couldn't be borne. Paloma lowered her mouth over his. Encouraged by his response, she deepened the kiss, tasting him deeply. He groaned, pulling her into his arms, his trembling hands roaming over her body beneath the hooded cloak. Was he awake or asleep? Paloma couldn't tell. He was aroused, his hardness leaning heavily against her belly, his heart hammering against her own. He slipped her embroidered blouson down, baring one breast. Her sex clenched at the touch of his thick fingers tracing the hardened nipple. Her loins felt drenched in fire, and she moaned aloud as he pulled her on top of him and took the taut aching bud in his mouth.

Paloma stared down at him, her heart fluttering wildly. Her thick, swollen sex throbbed for him—ached for him. How skilled he was with that silken tongue—teasing, taunting—bringing her to the brink of ecstasy as he sucked and circled and nipped until her moans came in involuntary waves. He had raised his wounded head off the pallet to reach her breast, and she slipped her hand underneath it in support, fisting her fingers in his dark, wavy hair, holding his head against her breast while he suckled.

Her mind was racing. She was torn between the bloodlust and a genuine, all-consuming passion for him. All at once, both emotions exploded in an unstoppable lava burst that changed her vision. She saw him now through a veil of fluid crimson. His face was distorted. Her thrumming sex was pulsating to the rhythm of her blood as the fangs descended. She could wait no longer to feed, and as he reached for her lips, she swooped down, sinking her fangs into the shaft of his thick, arched throat . . . and drank.

CHAPTER SEVEN

Milosh's eyes sprang open. Staring blankly, he made a strangled sound. It was a desperate moment before he parted dream from reality and realized what Paloma was doing to him. Her image flashed before him in fluid waves of crimson red. It was *happening*—really happening. Roaring like a lion, he seized her upper arms and shoved her off him, vaulting to his feet.

Separation tore the flesh of his throat; he barely noticed. Blood ran down his neck, puddling against his collar; he scarcely felt the hot, wet trickle oozing from two ragged puncture wounds. Raking his hair back ruthlessly, he fought the vertigo for his vision. It was a dream—a horrible nightmare brought on as a result of the blow to his head. It had to be! But it wasn't. Paloma lay curled on her side in the straw beside the pallet, sobbing uncontrollably, her fangs clearly visible. She *was* a vampire, and she had fed upon him.

He seized her arm and raised her to her feet none too gently. Pushing her lips back with his thumbs, he examined her fangs; they were dripping blood—his blood. In all his years he had prided himself upon his prowess in escaping another vampire's kiss. He'd come close, but he had never been bitten since he performed the blood moon ritual. He had no idea how being bitten now would affect him—or her, for that matter. Rage, sorrow, and desire roiled in him as he loomed over her, his breast heaving. Rage spoke.

"When?" he seethed, shaking her again. "Tell me it happened after I found you in those ruins. When, damn you? *When?*"

"A . . . a month ago," she sobbed. "Our caravan was camped on the Cumberland border. We were on our way south for the winter. I went out on the fells to . . . dance. I love to dance . . . and I wanted to get away from my stepfather. He had been eycing me with lust, and I was afraid he was going to . . ."

"But he did not?" Milosh interrupted her.

Paloma shook her head. "No," she said. "It . . . it would have been better if I hadn't wandered off and he . . . had . . ."

Milosh's lips were clamped tight over his anger, his nostrils flared, His breath was audible, and controlled. "Never that," he said.

"I am not a virgin," she snapped at him, eyes flashing. "But Seth, my stepfather, was not the one. It happened when I was just a girl of seventeen summers. I foolishly thought the *Gadje* who took my virtue would take me away. Seth and my stepmother Kesia were both hateful to me. I would not submit to him, and she, she knew he was after me, she . . ."

"What is all that to me?" Milosh interrupted.

"N-nothing, evidently . . ." Paloma said emptily.

"What did the creature look like?" Milosh queried through rigid lips. He was beyond reason. He had been *bitten.* That was all he could think of then. After nearly four hundred years he had been bitten, and by a cheeky little slip of a girl who had stolen his heart. His passion had just damned him.

"He . . . he appeared first as a wolf . . . a beautiful gray wolf," she said dismally. "It was sitting in the tall grass watching me dance. I haven't danced since . . ."

"Go on," Milosh said. He hardly recognized his own voice.

"For a moment, he didn't move from the thicket . . . and then he changed into the figure of a naked man who looked like the creature you described—thin and bald, his skin like that of a cadaver. His eyes were like magnets. Once I looked into them, I . . . I couldn't look away."

"What happened then? I need to know, Paloma, if I am to help you—if I even *can* help you now."

"He came closer . . . he was a-aroused. He seized me . . . and he bit me here—" she pointed to her throat "—and he would have had his way with me if the others hadn't come running. I screamed, I think. . . . That must have been what brought them."

"But the creature did not take you down . . . he did not enter you?"

"No," she said, "there wasn't time. Seth and Kesia found me. It was the reason they left me behind. They did not want to risk a vampire in camp. At least, that is what Kesia said. I think she was afraid sooner or later Seth would force me to submit. I have been running ever since."

"Why did you not tell me?" he demanded.

Paloma gave a start, and her posture clenched. "I saw what you did to that other . . . that creature. I saw your wolf sever its head! I was afraid you would so the same to me if you knew."

Milosh let her go, and raked his hair ruthlessly.

"You are not undead," he growled. "You could not go about in daylight if you were. You little fool! If you had only told me . . ."

"I was . . . afraid . . ." she sobbed.

Aware now of the blood still leaking from his neck, Milosh swiped at it with a rough hand. "Afraid, eh?" he snarled. "Aye, and you may well be far more afraid now for this fine treachery. I was trying to help you— see you safely to the caravan of Traveler friends who might have welcomed and cared for you. I can hardly do that now, can I? I can hardly foist a vampire off upon them! What have you been feeding upon since I found you in those ruins? You have hardly left my side."

"I haven't been . . . that is why I . . . I couldn't help myself, Milosh. It's been too long. I had to feed . . . and you were bleeding. The hunger overwhelmed me!"

Milosh sank back down on the pallet. His head was spinning. He could barely make out her image now. There came a hitch in his heartbeat, almost as if it changed its rhythm of a sudden. He shook his head in a vain attempt to clear his vision and winced, having forgotten the bloodied lump upon his brow. His brain felt as if it would burst. Was it the blood loss? How much had she drunk? He had only felt like this once before . . . in the wagon in the woods on his way to fetch the midwife. He groaned as the memory crept across his mind. Was he right back where he'd started? He groaned again.

Paloma reached toward him, but he snarled like a wolf and lurched away from her advance. "Do not come near me," he said.

"B-but, you're bleeding!"

"Oh, aye!" Malosh raved. "And whose fault is that, eh? Keep your distance. You'll get no more of my blood, little thief."

"I asked you, please do not call me that!" she cried.

"Hah!" he erupted. "You are that, my girl, it fits you well. First my horse, and now my blood! You have earned the name of 'thief,' by God! As I pointed out before, you are no dove. Now be still! I need to think!"

But it was as though a haze had fogged his brain. Try as he would, he couldn't think. He had been bitten, and by the one person alive who had the power to steal his heart . . . if he let her. No. It was better as it was. Lust was one thing. Love was a commodity he could ill afford.

Holding his head in his hands, he heaved a mammoth sigh. "I cannot go back to the bloodlust," he said, as if to himself. "Nearly four centuries ago that ended, when I learned of the blood moon ritual in Persia. I would rather be dead than go back to what I was before." He popped a bitter laugh. "That will easily be arranged," he said. "The Brotherhood will seek me out and destroy me now if Sebastian or one of his minions does not find me first . . ."

"The Brotherhood?"

Milosh nodded, not without pain. "Those I have helped partake of the rite over the years," he said. "The owners of the Abbey ruins and their son are Brotherhood. The treachery that has occurred here this night will have repercussions that are far-reaching."

"What have I done?" she sobbed.

"You may have turned the living into the dead, little thief. That is what you have done, damn you!"

"They would destroy you?" she was incredulous.

"We are *vampire hunters!*"

"Shhhhh," Paloma said. "I hear something . . ." She started toward the door, but Milosh struggled to his feet and prevented her.

"No," he murmured. "Let me. You are too green, and too distraught to deal with real danger."

Milosh stood with his ear to the door for a moment, listening before he wrenched it open. Outside, the air seemed warmer. A thick, crawling mist rushed in through the opening, swirling around him like ropes. Some crept inside the smokehouse. It seemed alive, and not unlike the mist still clouding his brain.

Malosh raised his head and sniffed the air. There was no sound, but his extraordinary sense of smell picked up something besides the clean North Country air. After a moment he closed the door. He would not alarm her.

"Whatever it was, it's gone now," he said, throwing the bolt. "It could have been a deer, or a fox. This region is a hunter's paradise. We shall have to remain here until dawn. Then I will decide what's to be done."

"You have mentioned the blood moon before," Paloma said, without meeting his gaze.

"Oh, I see," Milosh said with flourish. "So that's it, is it? You have inquired of the blood moon ritual, haven't you? I am beginning to understand what is happening here. You want to learn the secret of the blood moon. That is why you tried to seduce me! Well, little thief, you needn't have gone to such drastic lengths. I would have given you the secret gladly. You should have told me, Paloma. Now, since you have drunk of my blood, I do not know if the knowledge will help you."

"I wasn't like that," Paloma cried. "Yes, I wanted the secret, but I also wanted *you*—I did, I swear it!"

Milosh stared into her red, swollen eyes for a long moment. Perhaps she did, or thought she did, but it didn't matter now. He needed to close his eyes, but how could he trust her? He ached for sleep, but how much blood had she drained from him before he woke and put her from him? It couldn't have been enough to satisfy her after such a long abstinence. He remembered the hunger—the throbbing, pulsating frenzy to feed—stronger than the urge to mate, though that was a part of it. The bloodlust was unstoppable, and not easily satisfied.

"You cannot have fed enough," he said. "If I dare close my eyes will you come at me again, little thief?"

"I will not touch you . . . again," she snapped at him. "And you needn't concern yourself with me. I will be gone at first light. I am not your responsibility."

"You aren't going anywhere, Paloma," Malosh said in his most unequivocal voice. It was edged like a blade and bore no opposition, "—not until we see what effect my blood has had upon you . . . and what effect your bloodlust has had upon me. Do not look at me like that! You have yourself to thank for this. You've brought it down upon your own head, little thief, the minute you sank those damned fangs into this throat." He gestured toward the wounds in his neck with a scathing finger. "Now lie down on that pallet and go to sleep."

"But your injury!" she protested. "You cannot sleep upon that filthy floor."

"Never mind me."

"You will not leave me?" she cried. There was terror in her voice.

"But a moment ago, it was you who announced your plans to leave *me!*" he shot back.

"That is different . . . it is mutual . . . once we know. Please do not leave me like Seth and Kesia did . . . I beg you!"

Milosh cast her a smile that did not reach his narrowed eyes. "Do not concern yourself with me," he said. "I never sleep in a comfortable place when I feel threatened, and I am a light sleeper. Go to sleep, little thief. This is only the beginning of what your treachery has wrought."

Paloma lay curled on the musty pallet. Across the way, Milosh had fallen asleep on the straw-strewn floor with her bundle beneath his head for a pillow. Indeed, he would surely wake with the slightest provocation from such a miserable bed.

He was right. She hadn't fed enough to satisfy her old bloodlust. Dare she tell him that she no longer had the desire to feed? Had drinking his blood transferred the benefits of the blood moon phenomenon to her? Paloma wished she knew more about these things.

It would be best if she just left while he was asleep. If his blood had saved her it would save others, and he would know. He would think it was because she had gotten what she wanted, but that was not the truth of it. She could not bear to stay and see what evil she had wrought. It would be better if he were to think she was a self-serving creature and have done. Besides, she could not bear his hatred, and he would surely hate her. How could he not—especially if he reverted back to what he had been so many years ago? How could he ever bear it?

Outside, the wolves were howling. They were many, their blood-chilling voices amplified by the fog pressed up against the smokehouse in the darkness. Paloma was terrified, but she dared not wait until morning. If she were going to leave it had to be now, while he was asleep, for when he woke—*if* he woke and could bear the light of day, he would not let her out of his sight. As it was now, having been bitten so soon after a serious head injury, he was at his most vulnerable. Yes, it had to be now. She would have to leave her belongings behind, since he had made a pillow of them, but that didn't matter. She owned nothing of value. This might be her only opportunity. She drew herself up to a sitting position with the sinuous motion of a snake, and rose to her feet without making a sound.

She hadn't taken one step when he was beside her. She hadn't even seen him move. He was, indeed, more wolf than man, but what moved him was a supernatural energy that defied description. His scent overwhelmed her—mesmerized her. She inhaled him deeply—leather, and the cold, crisp north wind, laced with his own distinct feral essence, mysterious and evocative. It set her heart racing and undermined her balance. If he hadn't reached out and seized her arm, she might have swooned.

"And just where do you think you are going?" he growled.

Paloma avoided his searing eyes. A strange iridescence had come over them—an odd greenish color rimmed in red had replaced the sparkling onyx of those Gypsy eyes. Her heart sank. She had never seen anything as terrifying.

"Well?" he prompted. "Answer me!"

"It is best if I go," she said. "Surely you can see that."

"I see nothing of the sort," he snapped, sweeping his arm wide. "You cannot imagine that I would turn you loose in the midst of that. No. You are going to stay right here with me until we sort this out."

"I am not your responsibility! How is it that you cannot understand that? I never was! You made it so out of some . . . cavalier instinct. I managed well enough before we met, and I will do so again."

"And what of me?" he said. "Am I not your responsibility now that you have wiped out four hundred years of living bloodlust free in the blink of an eye?"

"W-we do not know that," she snapped.

"We do not, eh?" he chided. "Look at me. *Look!* Do I appear the same to you?"

Paloma avoided the question. "Please . . . just let me go."

"After you've done your worst, eh?"

He studied her closely, those strange red-rimmed eyes boring into her. Paloma dared not meet them, remembering the effect of the eyes of the creature that had infected her. She felt the heat they generated radiating toward her in searing waves. Her heart began to pound. This was an entity against which she knew she could not stand.

"L-let me pass," she said, knowing all the while he would do no such thing.

"You did not feed enough to satisfy the bloodlust," he said. "You should be ravenous, and yet you seem content enough. Why?"

"Shhh," she whispered. "Listen! I hear something, I tell you!"

"Do not shift the subject," Malosh said, turning her toward him. "Why are you not obsessed to feed?"

Paloma hesitated. Perhaps it was simply a curious creature of the wild prowling about outside . . . or maybe it wasn't. Whatever it was, it couldn't be any worse than what she feared she faced inside that smokehouse under the enigmatic Gypsy's spell.

"Answer me!" he seethed. "The truth, Paloma."

Paloma did meet his eyes then, only briefly. They were more than she could bear. "I no longer seem to crave the blood," she said low-voiced. "The feeding frenzy . . . it's *gone*."

"We shall see," Milosh said, pulling her into a feverish embrace that took her breath away. His lips covered hers, his silken tongue seeking deeply. Unprepared, Paloma resisted at first, but soon she could not help but respond. She was under his spell—on fire for him; she had been from the first. Now, it would no longer be denied. Her arms flew around him, drawing him closer, forcing his hardness against her. A gasp escaped her throat as his rigid member responded upon contact.

His hands roaming her body felt like firebrands blazing a trail over her as he explored every curve, every aching inch of her. Shuddering with a passion the likes of which she had never known, Paloma leaned into his ravenous kisses, arched her body against the tall, lean length of him, fisted her hands in his tousled hair until he moaned against her lips and finally scooped her up in his arms and laid her on the pallet.

His eyes, glowing like live coals, sought hers and held their gaze relentlessly while he undressed her, and himself. Time seemed to stand still as she watched him disrobe, his moves as graceful as any dancer, reminding her of how she loved to dance—to leap and whirl in the open air to the music in her mind. She heard it now, that enigmatic music—violins and flutes—and the bell-like tinkle of her tambourine. It lay just yards away in her bundle, but she didn't need it to hear its music accompanying him as he stripped off the last of his clothing and stood before her naked, staring down.

Paloma had seen lust in men's eyes before. She'd seen it in the eyes of the *Gadje* rogue who played her false, in the eyes of her slovenly stepfather, Seth, undressing her with his eyes, but she had never seen a look such as this. Milosh stood above her, his hard shaft responding to naught but the naked sight of her. The look of him thus paralyzed her mind. It was as if an invisible cord existed between them—a tether that bound not only their bodies, but their minds and souls as well in the mystery of their Roma heritage.

Mesmerized, Paloma reached out her arms, and he fell upon her there, gathering her against him, encircling her body with arms that seemed to want to crush her until the two of them had fused into one being. The effect was so overwhelming Paloma scarcely dared breathe, for even her slightest movement in those dynamic arms caused him to grip her tighter still. It was almost as if he feared if he did not clasp her to him so she would evaporate before his very eyes.

How strong he was, and yet how gentle. His hooded eyes glowed like two live coals beneath their heavy lids. His warm breath, sweet with the ghost of the wine he'd drunk earlier, puffed against her moist skin. She was his for the taking, every inch of her skin alive with tantalizing pinpricks of desire. From the curve of her arched throat, to the thatch of coppery hair between her thighs, everywhere he touched, everywhere he cherished, came alive under the masterful fingers igniting her flesh. She felt liquid fire coursing over her, bringing her to the brink of ecstasy.

Paloma's breath caught as he spread her legs and eased himself between with a serpentine motion that set her heart racing. This was a skilled lover. He was practicing restraint, but why, when she was willing, when she longed to feel his life inside her—filling her—making her whole? He was struggling with something, some inner demon. It seemed almost a battle of wits. Every corded muscle in him was flexed to its limit. His rock-hard torso felt like steel against her tender flesh. The veins in his thick neck were distended. All at once, his nostrils flared, and his lips became a thin, bloodless line, as if he meant to hold back something, as if he dared not speak for fear of losing his control.

It was then, while his eyes were riveted to hers, that he spread her nether lips, and glided fully into her on

the silken wetness of her arousal. How he filled her.
How skillfully he moved inside her, just as she imagined he would. The pulsating rhythm of his sex vibrated through the tender walls of her sheath, and her breath caught as he lifted her hips and took her deeper still. Her sex was on fire, her heart jumping wildly to the beat of some primeval rhythm, hammering—thundering in her ears.

Able to bear no more, Paloma arched her throat back, her eyes fixed upon Milosh's gaze. It had changed; with each shuddering thrust, his eyes began to glow a deeper shade of red—blood red—shimmering with iridescent fire in the light of the glowing embers. Were those tears swimming in those dilated eyes?

Sweat beaded upon his bronzed skin—upon his brow, upon the thick, hard muscles of his biceps. It ran in rivulets down his chest. Something in his posture flagged danger, but Paloma could not heed it. She lay drenched in waves of ravaging fire, helpless as her loins convulsed in rapid spurts of sensation unlike anything she had ever experienced before. It lifted her out of herself, carried her off to the thrumming of her heart that beat as one with his.

All at once, a feral sound came from him unlike anything she had ever heard. Guttural and deep, it nearly stopped her heart. Inside her, his sex swelled greater still, then froze as he growled again, and swooped down over her arched throat baring long sharp fangs leaking threads of drool.

Paloma screamed. For a moment, Milosh froze stock-still, his fangs within but a hairbreadth of penetrating the throbbing vein distended at the base of her throat. She tried to scream again, but couldn't. She couldn't move, either. Her eyes were riveted to his. Yes, those were tears glistening there. Her heart nearly stopped. Her throat closed over yet another scream bubbling up inside, as he roared again, sinking the deadly fangs into the rigid flesh of his own forearm as his seed filled her, his member pumping him dry.

Leaking a pain-wracked growl that more closely resembled a roar, Milosh threw back his head and withdrew his sex. Paloma watched in horror as he paced naked, in circles like a madman, his fangs still visible, blood leaking from the puncture wound in his forearm. She watched, scarcely breathing, as he threw the smokehouse door open, and in a streak of silvery displaced motion sailed over the threshold and hit the frost-clad ground running on the four footpads of the great white wolf. In a blink, he was gone, swallowed by the eerie mist that had covered the land like a blanket.

Dissolving into tears, Paloma scrabbled to her feet and ran to the door calling his name, but Milosh was gone. All that remained was the mournful howl of the wolf he had become amplified by the fog sounding back in her ears. Then she heard the plaintive echo as other wolves, hidden in the mist, howled in the darkness, answering the white wolf's call.

CHAPTER EIGHT

The white wolf ran until its barrel chest threatened to burst. The lungs inside seemed on the verge of collapse, but still the wolf ran on. Milosh was running mad—stark staring mad. It had been a test—a test to see if the wound Paloma had inflicted had revived the bloodlust, and he'd failed it. His worst fears were realized. After nearly four centuries of existing free of the feeding frenzy, he was again a full-fledged vampire, betrayed by love and the wild-eyed Gypsy sorceress who had stolen his heart.

Blame it upon the loneliness of his existence, upon a death wish harbored in the murky depths of his subconscious mind, or upon the haunting weariness of his lot, the effect remained the same. He had relaxed his guard. He had allowed himself to feel. He had pretended to be normal for a fleeting moment in time, and now he must pay the price. It came dear.

The misty world the white wolf bounded through was carpeted with nettle and thorn. It hardly felt the barbs pierce its fur to the skin beneath. Its cries and growls and mad, feral roars were coming in involuntary spasms over which it had no control. Milosh, its host, was on the verge of madness. What else could his wolf be? Blood dripped from its right foreleg. Milosh had still possessed enough control to turn the fangs upon himself to spare Paloma what would have been the inevitable had he stayed in the smokehouse. He had never tried such a tactic before, though his friend, Jon Hyde-White, the master of what was once Whitebriar Abbey, had done so upon a number of occasions to spare his bride before the blood moon ritual saved him. The trouble was, while the pain temporarily stayed the bloodlust, it was short lived. He had not drunk his fill. He felt the hunger yet. He must feed again and quickly if Paloma were to be safe in his company.

On the wolf plunged through the misty darkness, the blood pounding in its veins—roaring in its ears. It saw the land before it in a grotesque distortion through torrents of blood. It was as though a crimson veil had fallen before its eyes. Blinded by the thick, red curtain, it didn't see the wolf that slammed into it broadside. The animal, large and gray, didn't stand a chance. Deranged, the white wolf turned and ripped its throat out then drained it dry, as well as three others that came after. Whether these were full-fledged *vampir* or Brotherhood didn't matter then. Only later, when the wolf had given way to Milosh again, would remorse over the possibility of the latter come back to haunt him. Now, the wolf—more red than white from its victims' blood—needed to feed and get back to Paloma before she came to serious harm. She was a novice—ill equipped to deal with what she had become and what she had been spared, and Milosh dared not trust himself in her company again until he had drunk his fill and posed her no threat.

How exquisite she was. How eagerly she had welcomed him. How could he ever live without her now, without her love . . . her innocent abandon? In four hundred years, no woman had loved him as well. No woman had given him such ecstasy. For all her innocence, for she was that despite her lost virtue, she was a virgin still in all that mattered. He had touched her where no other had ever done, but at the same time, she had betrayed him—lied to him—cost him his freedom from the bloodlust. A battle was raging in man and wolf—a battle for his life, for his heart, and for the very blood coursing through it.

While these thoughts roiled in him, Milosh turned his wolf back toward the smokehouse. Soon dawn would break, and he didn't even know if he could stand the light of day any longer. Raising its head, the white wolf loosed a mournful howl into the darkness. Centuries of heartache, sorrow, and pain powered that heart-wrenching sound. Tears streamed from its eyes—wolf that it was. There was no one to see. Its pricked-up ears rang with the echo of other lupine creatures answering its bestial call. No, it was not alone in that cold, misty darkness before dawn; neither was Paloma. Some of the howling was coming from the direction of the smokehouse. There was no time to lose. Running on instinct alone, upon the extraordinary gifts that had powered infected *vampir* from the dawn of time, the white wolf's great paws scarcely touched the ground as it sped back the way it had come, with only one thought to drive it: Paloma was in danger.

Paloma had barricaded herself inside the smokehouse. Would morning never come? This had to be the longest night of her life. Outside, the structure was surrounded. What did they want of her—*what?*

Some were wolves; their howls chilled her blood. Others were in human form pounding upon the smokehouse door—slow, methodical knocks, like an automaton. The pounding came in waves. She feared it would drive her mad, especially now that the fire had dwindled to embers in the hearth, and there was precious little that she could add to it to keep it going. In the back of her mind she vaguely recalled that a vampire had to be admitted to a dwelling to gain entrance. That was all well and good, but what if the fire were to go out altogether? Suppose one of the insidious creatures, while in bat form, were to swoop down the chimney . . . Could it do that? If only she knew. And where had Milosh gone? He had loved her so fully, and then gone off in the body of the great white wolf like a madman. Had he abandoned her? It was all her fault if he hated her now. She had turned him back into what he was four centuries ago, and in the bargain saved herself from the bloodlust, albeit in innocence; she certainly hadn't planned it. She had no idea such a thing would occur when she fed from the mysterious Gypsy's blood.

A dry sob left her throat. He would never believe it was in innocence. He was convinced that she had ulterior motives. He'd said so. Her heart was aching. How could she ever persuade him otherwise now? Would she even get the chance to try?

Paloma had dressed herself, while she paced, even to her hooded cloak. She was trembling from head to toe. The eerie, disembodied voices chanted on until she clapped her hands over her ears in a desperate attempt to shut out the unearthly racket, but it seeped through her fingers nonetheless.

Thump—thump—thump. "Let me innnnn," one chanted. Was it a *child?* Gripping chills had their way with her imagining such a thing.

Thump—thump—thump. "It's so cold . . . let me innnnn . . ."

It *was* a child, but that was not the only voice, just the one that rose above the rest—vampire glamour, meant to break her down. Again and again the voices begged admittance and the wolves howled and the thumping moved the door until it shuddered. Paloma screamed in spite of her resolve to keep silent. Then, just when she thought she couldn't bear it another second, a more terrible racket riddled her with goose-flesh from head to toe. A howling, snarling, shrieking pandemonium erupted, and she held her breath as one by one the voices stilled and the wolves' guttural growls receded yelping into the distance.

Paloma was just about to relax, when there came a bestial roar that reverberated in her very soul, and then a rapid pounding at the door, like cannon fire. This was not the ghostly methodical thumping that had nearly stopped her heart before. It was a pummeling powerful enough to set the old door off its hinges. The wood shuddered, raising dust motes. Her eyes were riveted to it, her heart tumbling out of rhythm in her breast.

"*Paloma!* Let me in!" Malosh said from the other side.

She rushed to the door and laid her ear against it, hesitating.

"*Paloma!*" Milosh thundered. He pounded again, and she lurched at the vibration. "Quickly, open the door or I'll tear it off. The sun is rising!"

Paloma fumbled with the bolt. Her hands felt like two stumps. Once she'd freed the latch from its bracket, she opened the door a crack and peered through. Milosh stood naked in the mist. Rage emanated from his expanded posture, from his flared nostrils, and eyes sunken so deeply beneath his dark brows Paloma could scarcely see them. The flat of his hand against the ancient wood widened the gap and sent her skittering backward as the Gypsy burst inside on the first rays of a cheerless dawn.

Paloma gasped. "The sun has risen!" she murmured. ". . . and you are able to bear it! Oh, Milosh! I am so . . . relieved!"

"Aye, relieved," he scorned. "And what would you be if I couldn't bear it, eh?" He stormed past her, snatched up his clothes and began dressing. "Do not struggle to concoct a lie. I know what you would be—relieved then, too—and more so—in that you were well rid of me, and why not? You have what you want now—what you have always wanted from me—the secret of the blood moon."

"I have nothing that I want . . ." Paloma despaired.

Milosh waved his arm wide toward the door. "*They* would beg to differ," he snapped.

"I . . I do not understand."

"No, you do not, and that is probably the only reason I have not torn you limb from limb, little thief." He shrugged on his shirt, but not before she noticed the deep, ragged puncture wound on his forearm. "Have you suffered from the bloodlust since you fed upon me?" he said.

Paloma hung her head. "N-no," she said.

Again, Milosh waved his hand toward the door. This time he had his boot in it. "They know," he said, tugging the boot on. "You heard noises outside last night. Evidently we were overheard. Someone or some*thing* was listening when you told me the bloodlust was gone after you bit me, and they have evidently passed the word. The white wolf just fought its way through a virtual army of vampires to get to you, meanwhile battling the hunger. Foolish chit! If you had opened that door they would have bled you dry. What do you think I've been struggling with down though the centuries, eh? To keep my blood in my veins, for they think it will save them. Now that I am useless to them, they have you to drink from, and you are ill equipped to manage thwarting that. We must leave here at once. This news will spread like wildfire, and I cannot rouse the Brotherhood. You are in the gravest of danger—"

"But why?" Paloma sobbed. "I do not understand any of this. . . . What have I done?"

Milosh seized her upper arms and shook her. "You fed upon blood protected by the blood moon ritual— *my blood*. A draught is drunk that circumvents the structure of the vampire's curse under the blood moon. It is an ancient Persian ritual that must be renewed from time to time, but, while it will not cure the infection, it will stop the feeding frenzy. You have drained enough of my blood to negate it in me, but it has affected you as if you partook of the draught and performed the ritual yourself! It has made you immune to the bloodlust, Paloma, but it has drained what I needed to make me immune. You have done what none other has managed to do in four hundred years! You have finished me! It is only a matter of time."

Paloma burst into tears. "I did not mean to. You are a vampire. You know how the bloodlust compels. I could not help myself! *You were bleeding!* The sight and smell of your blood . . . it overwhelmed me. I had not fed in too long a time. You make it seem as if I did the thing apurpose."

"I have destroyed those outside that needed destroying, but others who can bear the light of day are still abroad, like the wolf in the kirkyard. They will follow you to the ends of the earth to feed upon you, hoping the same will happen to them. They will drain you to the dregs. Then you will rise undead, and you will have to be destroyed—just like my wife and child. . . . God, my God! I cannot go through it again—*not again!*"

Paloma's heart leapt with hope. That he put her in the same company with his beloved wife was all that mattered to her then. He *did* have feelings for her. She longed to throw her arms around his neck and shower him with kisses, but she restrained herself. The look in his haunting onyx eyes was deadly. His chest was heaving—straining the Egyptian cotton shirt over corded muscles as hard as steel flexing against her.

"The worst of this," he raved on, "—is that I cannot help you, and I cannot leave you. If I do, you will be dead before another dawn. . . . And if I stay you do not stand a chance. I am what I was before I partook of the blood moon rite, only far worse, if that could be. I am *vampir* in every feral, bestial sense of the word. You are in more danger from me than you are from them. When night falls again, if they do not feed upon you, I will. Do you understand now? Do you finally see what it is that you have done?"

Paloma covered her face with her hands, and Milosh let her go, raking his hair back ruthlessly. "Collect your things and come," he gritted through clenched teeth. "We have much ground to cover before another sun sets, and the sun will be high before I can calm Somnus. That noble animal entered the fray out there, elsewise I might not have made it through the night. It will take at least half an hour to quiet him."

"Where will we go?" Paloma said low-voiced. She was almost afraid to ask him. He seemed on the edge of madness.

"As far as the creature will take us before he drops," Milosh said. "Now come!"

Milosh had forgotten about the lethargy that plagued him during the daytime. There was much he had forgotten, having been so long exempt from the bloodlust and everything that went with it. Paloma was safe enough in his company until the sun set. Then, he would have to find a subject and feed before he dared submit to her presence. Anger still roiled in him—anger that he had left himself vulnerable to so easily after so many years. Maybe that was the problem; too many years. He had grown weary of the battle—of the lonely struggle to survive. Now, he had tasted something he had no right to savor, this cheeky little Gypsy spitfire clutching him so fiercely about his middle as Somnus carried them farther south. The mere touch of her sweet flesh bouncing against his rigid body as they sped over the strange terrain threatened to betray him, lethargy or no.

"Can you not renew the blood moon ritual?" Paloma said, breaking the terminal silence that was brewing between them. "You did say it must be repeated at intervals."

"I do not know," Milosh replied. He was so steeped in rage he'd forgotten that possibility. All at once, he reined Somnus in, much to the phantom horse's vexation. The animal reared, pawing the misty air with feathered forefeet, and Paloma cried out, tightening her grip upon Milosh's waist.

"What do you do?" she shrilled. "Hold him! I shall fall off!"

Milosh had almost forgotten she was clinging behind him. What had she done to him? Or had he really lost his mind?

"Down, Somnus!" he thundered, and the black Gypsy stallion made one more churning assault upon the mist then brought his deadly hooves to earth. Milosh glanced behind. Paloma still clung to him, her tiny fingers pinching through his shirt beneath the greatcoat. She had flushed crimson. How exquisite she was veiled in the mist, her almond-shaped hazel green eyes flashing like a cat's. Her hood had fallen back, and her long coppery mane rode a sudden wind that had risen . . . or was that a result of the horse's whirling? Whatever the cause, the effect was breathtaking.

"Are you mad?" she cried.

"I may well be," Milosh said through a deranged laugh, "—and if I am it is you who have driven me so, little thief."

"Why have we stopped?" Paloma demanded.

"You reminded me," Milosh said. "We must go back."

"To the smokehouse?"

"No, to the ruins."

"But why?"

"I left my duffel bag there, if you recall," Milosh reminded her. "I had planned to settle you safely and return to deal with Sebastian. I carry my tools in that bag—the tools I use to destroy vampires. I also carry holy water, and the precise combined measurements of the herbs necessary to perform the blood moon ritual. Many are needed. It is best, of course, to use fresh herbs; that is how it was taught to me. But through the ages, I soon discovered that I could not always obtain them fresh when needs must, so I dried the herbs and discovered that they hold the same properties when steeped in holy water as the fresh herbs do, as long as they are properly stored."

"And you left them behind?" Paloma said, incredulous.

Milosh shrugged as he turned the horse back toward the north again. "I told you, I meant to return," he said, "and they were safe enough. Sebastian will have no truck with holy water. He was a bishop, remember? All things holy repulse him now."

"You mean that . . . all the while . . ."

Milosh erupted in a spate of mad laughter. "Ironic, isn't it?" he chortled. "Your precious secret was right under your nose all the while, little thief. You didn't need to savage me to get it. If I had known you were in need of it, I'd have given it gladly. That is who I am—that is what I do—save those infected by the vampire's kiss, and destroy those who are beyond my skills. Will the ritual work on me now . . . after this? I have no idea, but you'd best pray that it does, because you have no idea what you're facing if it doesn't—no inkling of the danger that awaits you. And you're going to need me yet awhile. Without guidance now you do not stand a chance, and there is no one here save me to give it. Little fool! I hope you're satisfied. In your blind obsession to save yourself, you may well have killed your savior!"

Chapter Nine

It was noon before the mist finally burned off, and the sun had already passed the zenith and begun to slide low when they approached the tor. There was no reasoning with the man. Paloma wouldn't even try. Milosh had made his mind up that the secret of the blood moon ritual was all she wanted, and nothing was going to convince him otherwise.

In the beginning, she had to admit, that might have been true, but not once he'd captured her heart. Still, what she'd done to him was unforgivable. That she could not help herself excused nothing in her eyes. That she had acted in ignorance and innocence counted for naught. She had wiped out four centuries of immunity to the bloodlust in the blink of an eye—catapulted him back to the dawn of his infection—betrayed his trust. That was the worst of it. He would never trust her again.

Muted sunlight filtering through the clouds had made the landscape all around seem like a world enchanted. Ice-clad grass spears gleamed with rainbow prisms. The ancient rowan tree at the foot of the tor glistened with them. Its branches, like bony arms with skeletal fingers, clacked together as the wind passed through them, making an almost musical sound as they rode by. In kinder circumstances, Paloma would have danced to the ice music. She scarcely thought of that now, except to mourn the loss of dancing in her life. She could still go through the motions, she supposed, but it wouldn't be the same; her heart wouldn't be in it the way it was before the vampire caught her out and unaware, and changed her life forever.

Glazed over like an ice sculpture, the ruins of Whitebriar Abbey shone in the fractured sunlight. Layer upon layer of ice had spackled what remained of the facade, giving it an Otherworldly look. Rainbows bounced and gleamed off the surface, and off the shrubs and hedgerows hemming what remained of the courtyard. But Paloma's eyes were turned toward the low-sliding sun thinly veiled behind the gray cloud cover. More weather was approaching. Dared she remind Milosh that they must away quickly? As luck would have it, she didn't need to; once they reached the summit, he drove the stallion straight for the stables and rode inside.

Milosh climbed down and reached to help Paloma down as well. "Can I trust you to stay put until I collect my bag," he said, hesitating, ". . . or will you play the thief again and leave me here at the mercy of my enemies?"

"You could always take me with you, since you're so concerned about it," Paloma snapped. She felt foolish with her arms outstretched toward him in anticipation of being lifted down, and folded them across her middle.

"I took you out of here to protect you," Milosh

reminded her. "You have no idea of the danger you are facing here now. Sebastian has made this place his home. Granted, the sun has not yet set, but he has minions that protect him while he sleeps during the day. They will be abroad, and I am not at my most powerful now, since I have reverted back to what I was. My powers are limited in daylight. I must restrict myself to my physical strength, not my extraordinary strengths. Simply put, I am at a gross disadvantage defending us against the supernatural with only natural powers at my command. You see? I am honest with you, little thief, which is more than you have been with me. If you had told me the truth from the start, none of this would be happening."

"You could let me go," Paloma murmured.

"*Then*, yes, but no longer," Milosh snapped at her. "Have you so soon forgotten what occurred at the smokehouse just now? If the white wolf hadn't come on when it did you would likely be undead by now. You are not my prisoner, Paloma. I am trying to help you—teach you all that you must know in order to survive before we part, and even that is dangerous, for the sun soon sets, and then I am your enemy, too."

"Have it your way!" Paloma cried, pouting. What was the use; he would anyway.

"Hah! If I could have it my way, neither of us would be vampires. I would be courting you in proper Gypsy fashion, and we would be looking forward to a gala Gypsy wedding, with feasting and drinking, and yes, the dancing you love so. But I cannot have my way, thanks to you, and none of that can be."

"W-was that a proposal, Milosh?" Paloma said hopefully.

"No," he shot back, "—only what might have been . . . a pleasant fiction. You will soon see what really is once that sun goes down if you keep me here arguing over it. Now make up your mind—and quickly! No power upon earth can hold back the night, and it is soon upon us."

But Paloma was spared that decision. Somnus decided for her. The animal bucked and reared, tossing its long black mane, and Paloma slid off its rump and landed without ceremony on her bottom on the straw-strewn floor of the stable.

Milosh laughed, extending his hand to her. "Somnus doesn't trust you, either," he observed, lifting Paloma to her feet. As if in reply, the horse shook until every muscle rippled, and pranced in place, bobbing his head, a sly sideways glance emanating from his eye. It would have been a comical sight if the situation wasn't so grave. "So be it!" Milosh said. "The animal is smarter than the pair of us. Come, and stay close beside me."

Paloma needed no coaxing. She clung to the sleeve of Milosh's greatcoat with fingers hooked like talons as he led her through the ruins—slippery with ice— to the rubble that marked the access to what remained of the second floor. There, Milosh pried her fingers loose from his arm.

"What do you do?" she murmured. "You would leave me here?"

"No," Milosh said. "You have powers . . . gifts, if you prefer. It is time you learned to use them. Watch me, and then do as I do. This is your first lesson, little thief."

Paloma despised that he called her "little thief," but she would not call him out over it; that only seemed to make him do it more often. She chose instead to ignore it, though each time he spoke those words anger roiled inside—anger that colored her cheeks with the hot blood she felt rising there. It was the curse of her fairer-skinned complexion. It was always thus when her temper flared. She needed no mirror to tell her her countenance had betrayed her. The anger was supplanted by astonishment, however, as before her eyes Milosh leapt into the air and came down on the second-floor landing feet apart, his fists upon his hips.

Paloma gasped. "How did you do that?" she cried.

"The same way you shall do it," he replied. "*Jump,* Paloma! Bend your knees and spring forward. Do it now!"

Filling her lungs, Paloma did as he bade her and came down so close to Milosh she was suddenly in his arms, teetering on the edge of the ice-crusted landing.

"Next time," he murmured, looking deep into her eyes, "when you land . . . try to occupy your own space."

Paloma couldn't speak, nor could she meet his hooded gaze for long. His arms were strong and warm around her, his heart hammering against her breast. His hot breath puffed against her face and her body trembled against his in anticipation of the kiss she felt imminent. For one long agonizing moment, while his sensuous mouth descended, she thought those skilled lips would rest upon hers again. But Milosh froze in place as if he'd awoken from a dream, and put her from him.

"Come," he said, his voice like a whip. "The shadows thicken. There is no time to lose."

Paloma looked behind toward where she'd sprung from in disbelief that she had just leapt to such a height. Cold chills riddled her that had naught to do with the bitter cold that showed her her breath as it puffed from her nostrils. What else would he teach her? She didn't have long to wait to discover what that might be.

"I will show you what you need to know to survive," Milosh said. "More 'gifts' will make themselves known in time . . . once you are open to them. What you have just done may one day save your life."

Paloma staggered to a halt. "You read my thoughts!" she breathed, "—you *did!*"

Milosh nodded. "One day you will be able to read mine . . . but not yet. You are too full of the newness of your . . . situation for that yet. One day, however, you shall, and that gift, too, may well save your life."

"I do not know as I like it that you can read my thoughts," Paloma said, pouting.

Milosh laughed. "You should," he said. "It is that and that alone which has so far spared you."

"Spared me what?"

"You forget what I am—still am despite your treachery. A vampire hunter."

Paloma said no more as she pattered along beside him, her brows crimped in a contemplative frown. It would not be easy hiding her thoughts from him. She was thinking on that, when Milosh laughed again.

"It is only fair to tell you that it cannot be done from great distances," he said, ". . . unless, that is, you wish it so and are brave enough to try. That, too, may one day spare you being put to the hazard, but I do not think you are quite ready for such as that just yet."

"Is there anything else you have to say to shake my confidence, sir?" Paloma snapped at him. "Do feel free."

Milosh studied her for a moment. "Do you know how beautiful you are when your temper rises like that, little spitfire?" he murmured.

"Hrumph!" Paloma snorted. "You choose an odd moment for such an observation, and you haven't answered my question."

"There is one more thing you might be ready for," he said, scanning the area. "Watch closely . . ."

Part of the outer wall was still standing on the north side of the corridor alongside the suite, and he walked up it like a fly, teetering on the ice underfoot at the top.

"Well? Do you want to try?" he said.

"I shall wait for a less slippery wall," Paloma said. "Besides, I have never been overly fond of heights."

"One day, you will be glad of them, little thief," Milosh said, returning to the landing, ". . . but enough for now. Soon the sun sets and I want to be well away by then." Taking her arm, he led her to the toile suite and swept her inside. "I'll be but a moment," he said, striding through the bedchamber to the dressing room beyond. A spate of expletives soon followed, accompanied by a racket that suggested displaced furniture. Paloma stood her ground. Whatever was happening in the dressing room would brook no interference, and she was wise enough to keep well out of it. She was standing with her hand clamped over her lips when he stormed through the adjoining door like a madman.

"*It's gone!*" he seethed. "And my hope with it. I was counting upon those herbs to put it to rights. We have to find that bag. I will never be able to replace those herbs at this time of year—not until the spring, and then not even all of the species; some are late bloomers and do not appear until summer's last."

"S-Sebastian?" Paloma got out.

"One of his minions, I'll wager," Milosh said. Removing his slouch hat, he raked his hair back ruthlessly and fixed the hat in place again. "Sebastian would not have touched the holy water. More than likely, he wanted to confiscate my tools. He knew I would be returning for them. Damn and blast! That bag would have been safe enough where I stashed it in the chifforobe while I settled you, if only . . ."

"What will we do?" Paloma said, anxious to avoid rehashing her fault in the dilemma. His scathing look put paid to that, and she lowered her eyes to avoid the heat of it.

"Without that bag, I am unarmed against the undead," he said, his voice clipped and strained. "Oh, I can replace the tools, but the holy water is another matter entirely. It is not so easily gotten. I am not so fortunate as my pupil, the owner of this rubble, a man of the cloth whose vocation allowed him to concoct an endless supply. That which I possess is precious and treated accordingly."

Why did you leave it then? Paloma wanted to say, but thought better of it. His flared nostrils and crimped lips warned her against any comment then. How utterly handsome he was enraged, with his onyx eyes glittering in fractured sunlight, and color in his bronzed cheeks. One thing, however, stole the smile from her lips as she observed him then. The dark blue veins beneath the surface of that smooth, olive skin showed through clearly, reminding her that he was once again full-fledged *vampir*, and very, very dangerous.

"I left it, because it would have slowed us down, riding two to a horse, with your bag as well," he said, reminding her all too well that he was able to read her thoughts.

Paloma gasped. "Stop doing that!" she demanded, stamping her foot.

Milosh gave a start. "That's right," he said. "By all means bring them with your foot stamping. Let's have done once and for all, eh?"

"I . . . I'm sorry," Paloma said, avoiding his dark glare. "I keep forgetting there is no privacy with you.

But have no fear. If they do come, that look alone will make them wither before our very eyes. It is fierce enough to clabber cream. You will scarce have need of holy water."

Milosh cleared his throat. His scowl deepened. "We shall see," he said, "because until I find that bag we will remain right here."

Of course Milosh shouldn't have left his duffel bag behind, but he wasn't about to admit it to this cheeky little slip of a girl; neither would he admit that his brain had been addled since he met her. Wishful thinking convinced him he would be swiftly well rid of her. Leaving the bag behind was his guarantee. Now the bag was gone, Paloma was still glued to his side, and the sun was soon setting.

There wasn't much left of the ruined abbey to search. At the same time, Milosh was trying to put himself in the mind of the vampire Sebastian. Where would he hide that his minions could attend him in such an open place? What recess would a bat find welcoming to protect it from the light of day? The secret chamber? Too obvious. What remained of the servants' wing was his second choice, but that proved fruitless also. All that remained below stairs was the larder and part of the kitchen proper, and they were strewn with rubble. The upper floors had caved in upon that sector during the fire.

The darkened chambers across the hall from the suite caught his eye. These were what remained of the lush master suite, and the yellow suite he knew so well from his visit thirty years ago. It tugged at his heart to view them thus, sullied by the char and slag of fire. Only half the rooms remained, as if a giant sword had cleft them in two, the backbone of the chimney structure being all that held what was left.

The yellow suite was no more than a gaping hole; nowhere for the tiniest bat to hover. The master apartments seemed more probable. Cautioning Paloma toward silence with a rigid finger across his lips, Milosh entered the master sitting room without making a sound. Keeping Paloma well away from the ragged edge of what remained of the floor, he led her over the threshold of the bedchamber. There was no bed; it had fallen when the wall it rested against collapsed. The exquisite four-poster was now reduced to rubble with the rest below. The hearth remained, and the large oak wardrobe he remembered. *Of course! How could he have forgotten?* Sebastian had once used the very same as a hiding place and nearly killed Joss Hyde-White after exiting it. The wardrobe doors were closed now—latched tight. *The perfect resting place for Sebastian!*

"But someone would have to let him out!" Paloma whispered, answering his thoughts aloud.

Milosh's head snapped toward her. "Astute of you!" he murmured, in genuine shock that she had read his thoughts. But why wouldn't she? She was a vampire just as he was, with the same gifts, the same powers.

Paloma pointed through the gaping hole that once was the western wall. *Look,* she said with her mind, *the sun . . . it has slipped below the tree line.*

Milosh did not need to seek out the sun for proof. The lethargy was gone. Twilight had broken over him like a towering ocean wave, and with it came the bloodlust, stronger now than the last time, and more deadly. His extraordinary vision sought and found the tracery of delicate veins beneath the surface of Paloma's alabaster skin. His extraordinary sense of smell—the wolf's heightened sense—picked out the scent of her blood, salt-sweet and metallic. He licked his lips in anticipation, but it wasn't the salt of her blood that he tasted on them, it was the salt of his tears, and he spun away, but not in time; she had already seen.

Madness threatened. He was losing his focus. The flutter of wings inside the wardrobe told all too well that they had found Sebastian's hiding place too late. Paloma was right. One of the creature's minions would soon come to let him out. They could not be there then. He needed to protect Paloma from the ancient creature and from himself, whom he saw as the greater danger. Was she ready to defend herself on her own? She had to be. There was no more time for tutelage. Not only would she have to defend herself against the undead, she would also have to repel those creatures that, like the vampires that surrounded the smokehouse, sought her out to do to her what she had done to him—steal the antidote by feeding upon her blood.

Go quickly to the suite, he commanded her in thought; he dared not speak aloud for fear of being overheard. *Lock yourself in, light the fire to keep the bats at bay, and do not open the door to anyone until I come for you at dawn, not even to me do you hear—especially not to me.*

Milosh didn't give her time to reply. Seizing her in strong arms, he took her lips in a volatile kiss that aroused him completely. Then, striding to the chimney, he sprang and leapt into the bitter cold blackness below.

Chapter Ten

Paloma hadn't obeyed Milosh's directives thus far and she wasn't about to begin now. His description of Sebastian had been weighing upon her mind. She had to know if it was indeed the notorious vampire that had infected her. What she would do with the knowledge didn't enter into it. She was caught between two deadly entities—the illusive and crafty Sebastian, who had eluded his hunters for four centuries, and the legendary Milosh, determined to end the creature's days upon the earth if he had to do it with his last breath. Three determined souls, for she had joined the mix, only her stakes were higher. She hadn't the experience to do what needs must, but she had the will. Milosh could say what he would. His life had lived inside her. It was as if an ancient dam had burst and carried him away with the rushing water. This, he could not hide behind the mask he wore; there was no way to disguise the meeting of mind, body, and soul that had joined them with a bond that could never be broken. It went beyond sheer lust. Milosh knew it, though he wouldn't admit it. Paloma didn't need extraordinary powers to come to that conclusion. It was in his glittering onyx gaze—in his kiss—in what he didn't say with voice or mind . . . in the salt-laced, bittersweet taste of his tears that still lingered upon her tongue, left there by their fiery parting kiss.

A shuffling sound in the corridor outside called Paloma's attention back to the situation at hand. Slinking into the shadows cloaking the tattered remains of a tapestry on the wall beside the door, she scarcely drew breath as a hunched figure entered the room and shuffled toward the wardrobe. It was a man past middle age, whose sparse gray hair fanned out about his bare head like a misshapen halo. For a moment, Paloma thought he had seen her. His head flashed in her direction, his rheumy eyes snapping from one shadow to another. Could he hear the thunder of her heartbeat as she heard it echoing in her ears? She prayed not, but feared so. Suppose he could read her thoughts as Milosh had done? Her heart skipped a beat, as she struggled with all her might to call her mind music, the mental strains she'd danced to until the nightmare began, in hopes it would drown out the thoughts that would betray her presence there.

After a moment, the man moved on and unlatched the wardrobe. He stood aside as a swarm of angry bats sawed through the air in a racket of flapping frenzy. The shadows were in motion with their number, the air black with them. Paloma resisted the instinct to gasp, and another to cry out, watching the swarm become a vortex that funneled into one hideous entity. *Sebastian!* She recognized him at once and her heart sank; how could she not? He was the one. There was no doubt. She would never forget that emaciated body, the putrid odor of his cadaverous flesh; they were etched upon her memory.

Rooted to the spot, Paloma watched the creature seize the old man by the throat, lifting him off the floor with one bony hand, its talons denting wrinkled flesh. The creature's naked mold-gray flesh gleamed in the shaft of fractured moonlight spilling in from the gaping hole that once had been the bedchamber wall. While it illuminated the scene, the shaft the moon threw down pointed like an arrow to her feet. Terror ran her through like a javelin. But for the shadows cast by the tapestry, she was in plain sight. If Sebastian wasn't so preoccupied with his minion, he would see her clearly. She held her breath, her eyes fixed upon the moonbeam, and the dust motes dancing there as if they were live creatures treading the silvery shaft with a purpose. She was lit as though she stood within a spotlight. Sebastian's back was to her. . . . If he ever turned . . .

"You are behindhand!" the creature said to the old man dangling from his fingers in the moonlight. "You shan't be tardy again, or I will drain you dry . . ." The old man made an incoherent reply that passed as no more than a gurgle, and Sebastian shook him again. "I smell Gypsies," he seethed. "If I have been compromised, you will be the first to go, Ezra."

Paloma began inching her way toward the open bedchamber door. Her knees trembled so, she feared the creature would hear them knocking together. Meanwhile, Sebastian ended his rant by flinging the old man against the wall, causing a little avalanche of ice-crusted charred wood and plaster to rain down. The racket that made abetted Paloma's escape. It also brought other creatures out of the shadows, creatures Paloma hadn't noticed before. It was a large room, after all—even now, reduced by half—and she hadn't been concentrating upon the periphery. These were women, trailing grave clothes. The sight of those lengthening shadows in motion giving birth to heretofore invisible creatures of the night all but stopped Paloma's heart. Still tormenting the old man, Sebastian didn't seem to notice them, but they noticed her, and began converging upon her.

Paloma's heightened sense of smell picked out their scent—the moldering decay of the grave. Unlike the old man, these were not newly made creatures. These were ancient undead. If Sebastian hadn't brought them with him, he had loosed them from their graves. Backing away from them, she had nearly reached the door, when a bestial roar pierced the silence, followed by a rumble that shook what remained of the chamber until it collapsed in upon itself, raining down upon the rubble below; all but the chimney—the backbone of the abbey. From that shuddering column of brick and mortar, Paloma watched the white wolf spring—fangs extended, leaking drool—but she didn't see where it landed, or what happened to the others. Running upon feet that scarcely touched the floor she fled to the suite and threw the bolt as what was left of the opposite side of the corridor began to collapse.

In a thundering rush of earsplitting noise, the chambers fell, one after another; Paloma could hear them crumbling. The explosion as they joined the slag at the bottom filled her with terror made worse because she couldn't actually see what was happening. The vibration shook the very floor of the suite where she stood. She wondered if it would hold, or cave in as well, its integrity having been compromised with the fall of the master bedchamber across the way. Shrieks and screams and howling wolves accompanied the racket. Paloma clapped her hands over her ears and screwed her eyes shut tight. Had the secret chamber and the tunnel and what remained of the servants' quarters collapsed, too? Judging from the direction of the sound, it seemed likely.

It was some time before the dust settled and the rumbling echo of the collapse died to a surly growl. One thing was certain. What remained of Whitebriar Abbey was no longer safe, and if Milosh's duffel bag was in the midst of the rubble, the cave-in had certainly put paid to it. She leaned her ear against the bedchamber door. There wasn't a sound. What had happened to Milosh? She couldn't leave without him. The last glimpse she had of him was the white wolf sailing out of the chimney column toward Sebastian and his minions, like a nest of snakes around him, as what remained of the master suite plunged to the rubble below. She had to know.

Her hand shook helplessly as she slid the bolt. She took a step to cross the threshold only to pull up short teetering on the edge of an abyss. The corridor outside was gone. It had fallen away between the suite and the green-baize-lined door that marked the entrance to the servants' quarters at the east end of the corridor. The door was thrown open, the baize hanging in singed tatters, but that was all that remained of the quarters below stairs. The servants' door opened upon empty air. That meant the rest had fallen. Only the suite and one other chamber alongside the second floor platform were still standing. The corridor that used to exist to the landing was gone. She was trapped, the groaning timbers of what hadn't crumbled to dust shuddering beneath her feet. It could join the rest at any moment.

Paloma looked down. It seemed an awfully long way to the heap of rubble below. No signs of life were visible or audible. She swallowed dry. Milosh would know what to do. *Milosh!* Was he still in wolf form, or had he transformed back? If he had survived, wouldn't he be trying to find her—help her? It did not bode well. Suppose he were lying below buried in the slag. Suppose he needed help. If only he could read her thoughts now. She gasped. Maybe he could!

It had to be a mental communication, lest it attract the wrong ears. There was no guarantee that a mental message wouldn't do the very same; Sebastian was no doubt just as adept at mind speech as Milosh was, but Paloma had to try something.

She took a deep breath. *Milosh* . . . she spoke with her mind . . . *if you can hear me, I beg you . . . help me! Tell me what to do . . .*

Straining her ears, she held her breath again and listened, but there came no reply. Was he out of range, or was he dead? No! She couldn't bear the thought that she had driven him to his death, for that is what it amounted to, and a horrible death at that, from which he would no doubt rise undead—beyond redemption.

Again and again, she reached out to him in thought, but still no answer came. The floor beneath her began to sway. Was it vertigo, or was the parquetry actually moving? It was! There was no question. The last of the second floor was about to join the rest of the rubble, and her with it!

As she gripped the doorjamb for support, Paloma's eyes oscillated between the landing to the west, and the gaping servants'-wing door to the east. Which way? She would have to use her gift and jump, but could she jump such a distance? It had never been tested. She was, however, a dancer, and she had leapt to great and graceful heights before she was infected. *"What you have just done may one day save your life . . ."* Milosh's voice ghosted across her memory. It wasn't mind speech, but rather his cryptic augur after teaching her how to do that which she must do now.

Paloma assessed both options again. Plaster was

falling—raining down around her. It had to be now. Below was sure and sudden death. She would be dashed against the rubble. The distance to the second-floor landing was a shorter span to jump, but she could not see what lay beneath. The longer span, to the green baize door, showed the land below the gaping hole beyond it clearly; something blacker than the shadows moved there, picked out in obscure silhouette by the light of the moon. But it was the flapping frenzy of bat wings from the opposite direction that made up her mind—that and the sudden jolt as the floor beneath her feet gave way. She bent her knees, spread her arms for balance, and sprang toward the gaping green baize door and the unknown.

In the lee of a hedgerow some yards from the wounded abbey, Milosh looked up from the remains of the vampire he'd just dragged there and savaged, its blood running down his fangs to his naked chest beneath. The rest had fled. His head snapped toward the last of the second floor collapsing, and a guttural howl—more like the roar of a lion—poured from his throat. This had been happening more and more frequently when, like now, he was in human form. Changing back had saved him. His two-legged incarnation had better control to ride the falling debris to the ground than the wolf would have possessed. He had become the wolf in both his incarnations, at least his intelligence had. It was only a matter of choosing which was best suited to the task at hand.

Now, it was time to shapeshift again—to put as much distance between himself and Paloma as was humanly possible until dawn cancelled the bloodlust. But could the white wolf outrun Somnus, whom he had set free to aid in her escape, since he could not chance it himself?

Keeping silent when Paloma needed him so desperately was the hardest thing Milosh had had to do in centuries. To hear her mind speech so clearly begging his help, and do nothing, was almost more than he could bear. It had clearly rent a tear in his sanity. Nonetheless, though he had bitten through his lower lip to keep from answering, it was what had to be. His motives were twofold: he needed to keep his distance or risk taking her—draining every last drop of her blood, rendering her perfect body to that which his wife had succumbed—and been faced with destroying her, too. And he had to teach her to fend for herself—the most valuable lesson of all, for he felt the cold breath of death puffing at the back of his neck. The specter dogged him, taunted him. He had felt it before, but never as strongly as he did now. It was gaining on him at last.

"Is there anything else you have to say to shake my confidence, sir?" Her words came back to haunt him. He had to give that confidence back to her. He had to know, if his time had come at last, that she could stand on her own against those like her, for her fight had just begun.

Milosh raised his eyes toward the star-studded vault above. He could scarcely see the constellations through his tears. Somnus's whistle rode the wind in the distance. Milosh howled again, answering the phantom horse's call. If it had gone as he'd planned, Paloma was astride the animal, thinking she had stolen the beast again. He almost laughed at the irony, but he was far too deranged for that. He could no longer deny what he felt for Paloma, but mixed into that was the bloodlust he could no longer control, and the hopelessness of it all. His duffel bag containing the herbs that might have saved him was gone—buried under tons of debris.

No, there was no hope for it. Circumstance had

parted them, and when he didn't surface, she would
surely think him dead—buried in the rubble. That
was as it should be. The kindest thing he could do
was what he had just done. . . . He had set her free.
He would not try to outrun Somnus after all. The
phantom horse was hers now. The animal had fallen
under her spell from the first, elsewise she could
never have stolen it, and why not . . . hadn't he fallen
under her spell himself?

Gazing down at the female creature he had just
drained to the dregs, Milosh heaved a ragged sigh.
Soon the vampire would rise again undead. That he
could not conscience. Despite it all, he was the vampire hunter still. In a sudden streak of silvery motion,
he once again became the great white wolf, straddled
the stirring vampire, and severed its head with super-
human jaws just as he had done to other *vampir*
through the ages. Then, with the help of his extraordinary hearing, he set out following the phantom
horse's cries.

He'd heard the sawing rustle of bats wings soaring
overhead since the rest of the Abbey collapsed. The
racket had grown distant now. No doubt Sebastian
had gone off in search of a new resting place; that
would take precedence now. It would have to be se-
cured before dawn. His immortal enemy would have
to wait a little longer for their final conflict . . . until
Milosh was certain Paloma was safe and away. This
he would do from a distance. He would not see her
again. It was best. With that decided, the white wolf
ran on in a southwesterly direction, keeping a reasonable distance from the horse carrying her away.

Paloma gave the horse his head. It was Somnus she
had glimpsed milling about below the servants' wing
landing before she jumped, though she hadn't seen

him clearly enough to identify him from above. It wasn't until she'd leapt to the ground through the gaping green baize door that she recognized the horse's dark silhouette prancing toward her, and not a minute too soon. Her feet had scarcely touched the ground when the rest of the second floor came crashing to earth around her.

Bats streaming from the rubble in all directions soared off into the night, their squeaking voices echoing after them. She hardly needed it, but the horse extended one feathered foreleg and half-knelt for her to mount. There was no doubting the invitation, but Paloma would not ride on until she had satisfied herself that nothing lived in the dusky heap of slag littering the tor. Now, convinced that nothing could have survived, she let the stallion carry her away. Through her tears she looked back more often than she looked ahead, hoping for the white wolf to materialize before her—praying it would appear, become Milosh in all his naked glory, and accuse her of stealing his vampire horse again. What she wouldn't give to hear him call her "little thief" just once more. But the white wolf made no such appearance, nor did he answer her desperate mind speech. It was over. Even the horse seemed to know it. There was naught to be done but follow the animal's leading. She couldn't have directed him then in any case. Her eyes were brimming with tears.

What time could it be? Not yet midnight. No matter the hour, dawn was far off. It was going to be a long night. The howling of wolves rose above the roar of the wind in her ears. Paloma resisted the urge to reach out with her mind, hoping. . . . But that was impossible, and she dared not try and risk attracting another with the same gift, or Sebastian himself. More wolves joined the mix. Was she riding toward them or away from them? Paloma had no idea, only that the magnificent horse was carrying her away from the only place that had offered her a feeling of safety since she'd been abandoned. She felt hollow inside with it taken from her, and why wouldn't she? She had left her heart behind in those ruins.

She couldn't let go of the realization that Milosh must have died a horrible death buried under the rubble that once was Whitebriar Abbey. She had robbed him of his immunity to the bloodlust and technically caused his death. Would he really rise undead from such a death? Dwelling upon that, she cried aloud, and the horse responded. The animal's high-pitched complaint seemed almost like a reprimand—a chastisement. She took it to heart. Somnus was more than a horse, he was a phenomenon, and she would heed his warning.

The stallion did not take her past the smokehouse as she thought he might. Instead, once they'd passed the kirkyard, he followed the river westward, avoiding the village proper. More than once the animal plunged into the water as if to throw any in pursuit off the scent. It was beautiful there at the river's edge, where the trees were sparse, their clacking branches letting in bold shafts of silvery moonlight. The water gurgled musically. It wasn't deep, and but for an occasional sprinkling of droplets that shone like diamonds in the eerie beams of dappled moonlight filtering through the trees, Paloma remained relatively dry.

All at once, Somnus broke his stride. Nostrils flared and ears pricked, he slowed his pace. Paloma stroked his neck and withers—rock-hard beneath her fingers—but he only bobbed his head, tossing his long, damp mane, and snorted, his cold flesh rippling. Something was not as it should be. Then she heard it. *Gunfire!* Was someone shooting at the wolves? Fools! Didn't they know that wouldn't kill them—that they must be destroyed by staking, and then burning and beheading if one wanted to be absolutely certain?

Paloma kneed Somnus gently, but the horse had come to a standstill and refused to go farther. She slid from his back and tethered him to a young sapling beside the riverbank. The grove thinned there, and she was able to look beyond the trees to a clearing on the other side of the river. The horse resisted. What was wrong with the beast? Her enhanced vision showed her a campfire, and wagons—*tinkers' wagons*, silhouetted black against the undergrowth at the far side of the brake. Had she found the safe haven Milosh had hoped for her?

Paloma crept closer, despite Somnus's complaints behind. The wolves still howled, and the gunfire seemed louder now. She had nearly reached the clearing, when two eyes like live coals rose up in between the trees ahead; they belonged to a large gray wolf. Her heart nearly stopped. *Do not look it in the eyes*, she reminded herself, backing toward the sapling where she'd tethered Somnus. He was at a gross disadvantage tied to the tree. Vampire horse or no, she could not leave him there to be savaged by other *vampir*; where there was one, there would be more. Her eyes flashing between the wolf advancing and the horse pounding the forest floor behind, she retraced her steps, fully prepared for the wolf to leap through the air and attack. But it was not the fangs of the wolf that sank hot and sharp into her shoulder. Shots rang out. The last thing she saw before she fell to the ground was the fiery burst from the barrel of a pistol.

CHAPTER ELEVEN

Milosh's white wolf crouched low approaching the thinning trees in the moonlight. He was at a disadvantage now, with his ghostly whiteness standing out in bold relief against the deep dark of the wood. The moon betrayed him as well. Oh, for a ground-creeping mist to cloak him, but there was none, and he couldn't even shapeshift back with no clothes to put on. He would be too conspicuous here, and too perfect a target.

He'd heard the gunfire. He'd also heard what sounded like a woman's scream. The heart in his wolf's barrel chest was hammering against its ribs. And then he saw the horse. Half-crazed, the stallion was bolting among the trees, trailing the reins he had gnawed through to free himself from the tether. But where was Paloma? He wasn't left long to wonder. The sweet scent of her blood flared his nostrils.

Nose to the ground, the white wolf padded over the forest floor, sniffing and tasting the blood Paloma had left behind; tantalized and at the same time paralyzed with fear that she was dead—or worse—savaged by one of the wolves he'd heard howling since he left the ruins. Zigzagging from tree to tree, he came close enough to growl a warning at the horse. As he moved on toward the clearing, the wagons came into view. Crouching on his belly, he crawled closer on all fours, using the undergrowth as a blind, wishing for the second time in mere minutes that his wolf was anything but white.

How badly was she hurt? If only he could shapeshift now and stride up to those wagons. The campfire was still burning, and there was a lantern lit in the one closest to the thicket he crouched in. All he needed to know was that she was safe. She should be, among other Roma. Had she found the help he meant for her to know? There was only one way to tell and he wasn't close enough to do it. He would have to wait, and patience was not one of his virtues of late.

Calling upon his extraordinary hearing, he strained his ears. There were three people speaking in hushed whispers inside the wagon; a man and two women. If only his heart would stop thundering in his ears, and let him hear. That Paloma had been shot was obvious. Her blood still clung to his jowls, where he'd licked it from the forest floor. The taste of it lingering on his tongue was driving him mad. All he needed to know was that she was not seriously harmed. If he were sure of that, he could leave her in the Gypsies' hands with a clear conscience. This was what he'd wanted for her after all, to see her safe among her own kind, who would welcome her—care for and protect her. It would be easier now that her bloodlust had been checked. How long it would remain so was anyone's guess; how it even happened was a mystery. He had done all he could do. They may never need know . . . at least not for a little while, long enough for her to take her life in hand. He had almost convinced himself. But he *was* convinced of one thing—she was far safer with Travelers than she would be with him as he was now. The unstoppable instinct to drink her blood—make her his own for all eternity—was a force in him stronger than life. A fierce battle was raging inside him then. Part of him was determined to let her go, while another part—the *vampir* part—was driven to drain her dry of the salt-sweet blood that even now tantalized his palate trickling down his throat.

" 'Tis naught but a flesh wound," a woman's voice said, an older voice, scratchy and hoarse sounding. "She's lost much blood, but she'll mend right enough, no thanks to Sasha and his wolf pelts. These creatures are *vampir*, not ordinary wolves like we find in other lands. Those do not exist here. What could their pelts be but tainted—dangerous even to handle? You mark my words: No good will come from robbing these creatures of their fine fur coats."

"Sasha is a fool, old woman," the man in the wagon said, "but he has sense enough to destroy the carcasses of the wolves he kills, and their pelts bring a pretty price among the *Gadje* in the villages."

"Aye, a pretty price for cursed fur," the old woman said. "Who knows what evil those infected pelts spread—how long before that evil comes home to roost, eh?"

"We will be long gone from here by then," the man said. "Let Sasha have his wolves."

"This is no wolf!" the woman said. "He could have killed her."

"It would be better if he had," a third voice said. This voice was that of a younger woman than the first. It had an edge that raised the white wolf's hackles, and it bared its fangs and leaked a low, guttural growl. "You have just said there are vampires abroad in these woods," the woman went on. "They will smell her blood and we will be set upon—*I* can smell it, and I am no vampire; the wagon stinks of it. I warned you! What? Would you wait until all our throats are torn out in our beds?"

"So, we break camp and leave these woods, woman," the man said.

"Shhhh, you two," the old woman warned them. "You will bring the others with your squabbling."

"If the others knew what *I* know—what *we* know, they would leave her, pull up stakes and go now—tonight! She can bring us naught but misery, my husband. Do you hear that—the howling? It grows closer—too close! She brings us nothing but heartache, you will see."

"Shhhh!" the old woman hissed at them again. "She grows restless. Take your carping outside lest you wake her. I have naught but herbs to ease her pain."

The white wolf's fangs were bared in a silent snarl as two figures emerged from the brightly painted wagon. The woman, striking and dark, appeared to be in her mid-thirties, her husband, a bit older, was tall and well-muscled, with deep-set eyes and angular features. It was as if his arms were connected to his mouth the way he flung them about when he spoke.

"We cannot just leave her," he argued. "I told you that before and now look! Your sins have come back to haunt you, woman. So be it! She stays. Even the old one in there says—"

The woman braced her hands on her hips and laughed into the night. "*The old one?*" she tittered.

"Be still! She will hear you!"

"So? And what if she does, eh?" the woman chortled. "The old one has no powers, fool. She puts on an act for the *Gadje*."

"She may not have mystical powers, but she has the wisdom of sages, and the gift of healing with those herbs of hers."

"Good!" the woman snapped. "Then let her tend the chit. I wash my hands of it. I will tell her myself that from this moment on *she* tends the girl. That ought to keep you out of that wagon."

They nattered on beside the campfire, the white wolf watching all the while. It wasn't the best solution, but it would have to do. At least they would keep her. The conversation he'd just overheard smacked of jealousy, but then, what Romany camp did not have its fair share of that?

He wasn't happy about Sasha's avocation. Skinning *vampir* wolves was a dirty business—and dangerous. Yes, their pelts were tainted, just as a rabid wolf's pelt is tainted. Would Paloma know this? Milosh doubted it. Not only the scent of her blood would bring more vampires to dog them, those pelts would act like magnets. They would draw them from great distances. His was not the only brotherhood. Sebastian and his minions—all those undead too far gone to be turned from their evil into hunters—had a "brotherhood" of their own. They would come with a vengeance to wreak havoc upon the caravan over their fallen brothers. He had seen such before. The pictures flashing across his mind that those memories evoked raised his hackles and made the silver streak along his spine stand on end.

It was a great relief that her wound was superficial. The old healer woman would care for her, and when she was recovered, she could stay or go as she pleased. Meanwhile, while Paloma was vulnerable, the woman would protect her from the crackle of lust he'd detected in the man's voice. The mere thought of another life living inside that exquisite body—tasting those sweet lips, feeling the warm, moist flood of her release—was driving Milosh to distraction. He was, indeed, on the brink of madness from all quarters. His passion for her, added to the blood hunger—the heart-stopping, mind-wrenching bloodlust that commanded him again after all these years, four centuries of years—had driven him like a man possessed, to the verge of the very kind of insanity from which no man returned, and no beast survived.

No, it wasn't the best of all solutions, but it was all he had, and still crouching down, his shoulders raised above his head in the undergrowth, Milosh's wolf turned and began to slink away as silently as he had approached, their heated voices echoing after him.

"I know why you want to keep her," the woman groused. "You think you can fool me—*me*, my husband? You have a short memory. You cannot see the threat she is—to us all? You would risk everything to crawl between those pale white thighs of hers. Aye— even knowing what she has become puts us all at risk. Do not dare try and deny it! That lecherous gleam in those eyes of yours damns you, Seth."

"You know nothing—*nothing*. Crawl between those thighs, indeed! The little spitfire would maim me! And if not her, the old one would. She has always favored Paloma, since she brought her into this evil world. She has told the tale often enough. She has done naught but pine and pule and wring her hands since we left Paloma behind."

"She is old, and soon will leave us," the woman said, the words dripping venom.

"At your hand, eh?" Seth returned. "I wouldn't put it past you. I never did believe your explanation of that girl's father's death." The woman sputtered and raised her fist toward him, but he seized her wrist and pitched his voice above her bluster. "You are aging,

Kesia," he said. "Like an old coin, you have begun to lose your luster. Your voice no longer has the sweet lure of the nightingale; it mimics the carrion crow now. Take care, harpy. I have married you in the Gypsy way and I can just as easily put you from me. Then, I will be free to crawl between whatever thighs I please!"

The white wolf stopped in its tracks, then slowly turned. *Seth . . . Kesia*? Had Paloma stumbled back upon those that cast her out? This, then, was the stepmother who despised her, and the stepfather whose advances she'd fought. He resisted the urge to throw his head back and howl at the moon. How could he leave her with these?

Atop the torment of separation and the hunger, now there was confusion, and the blind passion of rage. Milosh the man no longer lurked just beneath the surface of the white wolf he had become. The feral host was now pure beast enraged. Its vision was through a veil of red, like blood sliding down a wall. Its lips were curled back, its fangs extended, leaking foam and drool in strings that dripped upon the thick white ruff about its bullish neck. Deep guttural snarls bubbled up in its throat as it poised itself to spring, when from behind Somnus's cries pierced the forest stillness.

The white wolf and the phantom horse shared a common bond. They had their own means of communication. This time, however, the wolf was so deranged it scarcely heard the stallion's call. Set to leap into the center of the Gypsy camp, the horse's cry came a second time before the wolf responded, but too late. It turned, but did not see the heavy mesh net until it had come down hard upon it.

Quick hands gathered the net and raised the white wolf trapped inside it high. "I have him!" the man who threw it cried, exhibiting his catch. "This one will bring a pretty price!"

Inside, the snarling, wriggling white wolf fought to right itself, for it had been flipped upon its back when captured. Frantically, its feet churned and clawed inside the net, while its fangs stabbed at the mesh, trying to saw through the thick rope. These were the jaws that severed vampire's heads. It should be easy enough, but this rope was not made entirely of hemp. These were Tinkers after all. The rope was reinforced with metal, and the white wolf's position upside down wouldn't even let it get a grip. Besides, another strategy was wanted now. He couldn't leave Paloma with these.

"Why did you not shoot, Sasha?" Seth growled. "It could have savaged us!"

"What? And spoil that pretty pelt?" the other said. "There will be no holes in this fine hide—no bludgeoning, either. That head will make a fine trophy. We poison this one. The old one will know how, she has done so before. I will chain it to her wagon."

"Never mind the pelt. . . . Shoot it, I say!" Kesia shrilled. "It is *vampir*! I can smell it. Look at its eyes, they glow like fire. If that creature ever gets loose it will kill us all!"

"You are getting old, Kesia," Sasha said through a chuckle, his voice raised over the wolf's savage snarls. "When did you ever see an animal I hunted to ground break free, eh?"

"There is always a first time, you great lout!" Kesia snapped back. "Go with him, Seth. I will bring the old one. She need not hover over Paloma any longer. The foolish chit will sleep some now. We do this quickly, eh? Well? What are you waiting for? *Go!*"

CHAPTER TWELVE

Milosh's sanity was slowly returning. He could easily shapeshift back into human form, but that would not be wise, trapped as he was in the close confines of the net. He would be a sitting target. The two hulking Gypsies had cinched the mesh in so tightly he couldn't move his legs. They then chained him—net and all—to a wagon at the back of the caravan that rested against a thicket on the opposite side of the clearing, and lumbered off to the provisions wagon, where the wine and ale were kept, to celebrate their find.

How had it come to this? For four centuries, Milosh had prowled through the world escaping capture, only to be defeated by this little flame-haired thief that had bested him—*him*—the Milosh of legend. It was not to be believed, much less borne. He was infinitely glad the Hyde-Whites weren't there to see it.

Vampires turned vampire hunters ought have no truck with love. He'd said that once to someone on his journey, but he'd forgotten who now. There was no consolation in the accuracy of that wisdom, either.

Blinded by love, he had lowered his guard and been bitten. Driven by love, he had allowed himself to become vulnerable to the arch-nemesis he had hunted down through the ages. Because of love, he had let himself be captured by his own kind—Roma—who would poison him for his pelt! This was not how he envisioned his death. And the nightmare wasn't over yet.

Soon, the old one would come. There could be hope for him there. Something he'd heard the Gypsies say earlier had penetrated his addled brain. . . . She was skilled with herbs, the one thing that might save him. Clinging to that, he waited what seemed an eternity before two women came toward him. The one called Kesia, and an older, gray-haired woman, cloaked in a woolen shawl, who moved with the ragged gait of age, rheumatic joints, and fatigue.

"I want you to get shot of it at once," Kesia said, gesturing toward him. "It is to be poisoned. Sasha wants the pelt unblemished, and he means to sever the head for a trophy. They'll be in their cups till morning, but do it quickly; I do not want it howling and growling the whole night long, it will attract others. . . . And when you've done fetch Paloma here, to your wagon. She won't share mine and Seth's again—you keep her."

"Gladly," the old woman said. "You never should have turned her out to begin with."

"You know why I did, Michaela," Kesia snapped.

The other nodded. "I do," she said. "You were afraid of Seth taking her down."

"No! Well, that, too, but 'twas because of her being bitten. You know that, old woman. Do not mince words with me. And do not try my patience. You are getting too old to be of use here now. You are good for naught but poisoning wolves and duping *Gadje* with your bogus augur. Now, be about it. I want the chit out of my wagon."

The white wolf snarled, and Kesia backed away and strode toward the supply wagon to join the others. The minute she floated off, the old woman drew nearer the net tethered to her wagon wheel, and bent low for a closer look.

"You are a fine-looking fellow," she said. "There's a legend about a great white wolf the Roma tell—a vampire that hunts his own kind. You wouldn't be him, though, all trussed up in a snare; he is far too clever for that. You're a pretty one, though. She wants you dead, the bitch. A pity, but I dasen't cut you loose; she'll skin me . . ."

Taking a chance, Milosh transformed before her eyes. It was painful to do so in such cramped quarters. He hadn't felt such pain transforming since the early days. Time had numbed the agony of displaced organs, bone, and tissue . . . until now.

The old woman stifled a gasp, made an ancient sign against evil, and backed up apace.

"You have naught to fear from me, old one," Milosh said. "Caring for the girl in that wagon back there has brought me to this embarrassing pass. I will cause you no harm. Will you help me?"

"A . . . a *vampire?*" she breathed.

"You knew that before," he reminded her. "Your augur is not so bogus as that woman says. Cut me loose before they return . . . and bring Paloma. We must away while there is still time."

"They expect to return and find a dead wolf."

"If you do as I say, you shan't have to explain anything. There is much to tell, but no time to tell it. Paloma is not safe here, and neither are you. From what I overheard earlier, Kesia means to poison you as well. Then what will become of Paloma? Cut me loose and fetch her. We must leave now. She cannot remain here. Believe me when I say that I will leave no man or woman standing in your little band if I am opposed in this. I have strayed so far from my chosen path I do not know if I can ever find it again, so I have naught to lose, but you have much to lose, Michaela— Paloma, and your life. Now, turn me loose while they are all too drunk to notice our departure!"

"How can I, with no horse to pull the wagon? I dare not fetch one. Someone will see."

Milosh shut his eyes and drew a deep breath. *Somnus, come!* he commanded the horse with his mind. The animal had evidently eluded capture in the excitement when Sasha netted him. The stallion wouldn't have gone far. He wouldn't leave his master, or his mistress, for he had clearly become enamored of Paloma as well. After a moment, Milosh repeated the command, and the stallion pranced through the thicket and trotted to a stop beside the old woman's wagon, his eyes glowing like two fiery coals.

Michaela gasped. "It is . . . *possessed!*" she breathed, making the ancient Gypsy sign against evil again.

Milosh laughed. The sound echoed back in his ears. How strange it seemed. "No, not possessed, old one," he said. "This is *Somnus*, he has been with me these past thirty years. He is *vampir*, yes, but not possessed, and fiercely loyal to myself and your young charge. He has pulled many a wagon. Now will you set me free? I will not harm you. I have already fed this night."

Michaela loosened the chain that gathered the sack, and Milosh fell on his back as it spread open, then sprang to his feet. The old woman raked him from head to toe with wide-flung eyes, and covered her wrinkled lips with both hands.

"You cannot go about bare, naked as the jaybirds," she said. "Quickly, into the wagon! My husband, rest his soul, was about your size. I still have some of his clothes."

Milosh scrambled into the wagon, where the old woman produced a pair of soft leather boots, buckskin breeches, and a collarless linen shirt with full sleeves gathered at the wrist and trimmed with lace, much too fine for the situation at hand. There was a cloak as well, and a slouch hat, similar to the one he'd left behind at the Abbey.

"His dress things," Michaela explained. "They suit you, sir."

"I thank you for them," Milosh said. "My own are lost in the ruins of Whitebriar Abbey. I shall fetch Paloma. Can you hitch Somnus to the wagon? He will not harm you. We must away while these are too drunk to miss us. Her wound . . . you told the truth, it is not serious?"

"A flesh wound, nothing more, though it bled much," she told him. "My herbs will heal it. I gave her a sleeping draught. She will not make much sense till morning."

Milosh nodded, climbing down from the wagon. The old woman followed. "Wait!" she said, her voice no more than a whisper, though it commanded obedience. "You are Roma, sure enough, but not one of ours. What is your name, young son?"

Milosh laughed at that in spite of himself. "*Young son*," he said, the words riding a chuckle, "I am older than you are, mother. I am called Milosh, of Moldovia, my home in the Carpathian Mountains. I was born there over four hundred years ago."

He didn't wait for a reply. Bounding off with the gait of the wolf he'd so recently left behind, he left the old woman standing mouth agape, and ran to the lead wagon, where he found Paloma heaped with quilts on a bunk separated from the rest by a blanket at the back. How pale she was, how still. His heart was hammering against his ribs as he gathered her into his arms— quilts and all, for, though the weather had changed for the better, it was still bitter cold, the ice-crusted grass underfoot now white with slippery hoarfrost. It was what the old ones called *false autumn*, Nature's last stand before the snow.

He didn't carry her through the brake, where others might see, but rather on the far side of the wagons, through a stand of young saplings that hemmed it. How light she was in his arms; as light as feather down. How beautiful her face, with the dappled moonlight casting soft shadows on her alabaster skin. How could he ever have thought he could leave her? . . . Yet how could he not? The choice that wasn't a choice was like a festering sore that would not heal.

Deep in thought over that, Milosh didn't hear his pursuer until the man's hand clamped down hard upon his shoulder, and he spun to face Seth, his face flushed with an alcohol blush, his dark hair disheveled.

"Who in hell are you?" the Gypsy said, his words slurred and clipped. Raw alcohol sweated from his pores, and stank on his breath. "Where do you think you are going with her?"

"Shhhh," Milosh said, clearly confusing the staggering man. "One moment . . ." Setting Paloma down gently in the bracken, he straightened up and faced the drunken Gypsy, almost sorry to take advantage of the man in his present condition . . . Almost . . . but not quite.

He hadn't lied to Michaela. It was true that he had fed, but a little insurance wouldn't hurt, considering that the tantalizing scent of Paloma's blood leaking through the dressing Michaela had fixed upon her shoulder was driving him mad again. It was still hours before dawn, and he couldn't take chances, since he had no idea how much control he could count upon in his present condition. Besides, he needed no provocation. This was Paloma's stepfather—the very one she had sacrificed her virtue over in hopes of escaping—the one who stalked her still. He could not fault her, but he could fault the hulking brute before him. Just thinking about it brought his fangs out.

Their gazes locked just long enough for Milosh to captivate him—to use the vampire's power to paralyze the mind. The other blinked, and Milosh was on him, his fangs sunken deep into Seth's thick, sweaty neck. He drained the unsuspecting Gypsy's alcohol-tainted blood, but it was the wolf in him that ripped Seth's throat out, though he did not shapeshift to do it. The white wolf had risen that close to the surface again.

He did not sever Seth's head to prevent him from rising as a vampire. He could not do so in his human incarnation without the tools he'd lost in the ruins; only the wolf had power enough in its jaws to sever the head of its victim, and there wasn't time for that. If Seth had found him out, Sasha would not be far behind, unless the dolt had passed out from what he'd drunk, which was what he was counting upon. Later, when what had occurred was discovered, they would assume the white wolf had gotten loose and killed Seth. They would then assume that Michaela, afraid of reprisal for letting the wolf escape, had fled herself, with Paloma, whom Kesia didn't want anyway. She would have enough of a task at hand dealing with Seth when he rose a vampire. It seemed a fitting justice, and he thought no more about it.

Whatever the old woman had given Paloma had kept her oblivious of what had just occurred. Gathering her limp body into his arms again, a captive of her evocative scent, Milosh wished he'd had a dose of the stuff himself. It was a longer trek to Michaela's wagon using the saplings as a blind. To his relief, Somnus was hitched to the wagon, and Michaela was in the seat, ribbons in hand, when he reached it. Once he'd settled Paloma inside, he joined the old Gypsy and relieved her of the reins.

"'Twas me what named her," Michaela said, with pride. "So white she was when she come, like the breast of a dove. She cooed like one, too, no crying for that one."

Malosh's eyebrow lifted a notch. "I'll forgive you for it, mother," he said, ". . . since you've done right by her in every other way. A dove, she is not, she is more like the hawk."

"How have you come here?" the old woman queried, "—a person like yourself, come from afar? All Romany has heard of the great Milosh and his Brotherhood. I cannot imagine you coming to such a pass. Why, Roma mothers bring their bairns up upon tales of how you were bitten, and found a cure for the vampire curse."

"Not a cure," he hastened to say. "There is no cure. What I found was an antidote for the bloodlust."

"And it has come back upon you?"

Michaela was easy to talk to, and while the rode westward through the forest before he knew what had happened, he'd told her all that had occurred since he arrived at Whitebriar Abbey and met Paloma.

". . . And so, when I heard you were skilled with herbs, I was hoping you might be able to help me replace those I lost in the Abbey ruins," he concluded.

Michaela hesitated. "I near died when they left her behind after she was bitten," she said at last. Was she deliberately avoiding his query? "You were honest with her. She was wrong not to tell you from the start."

"Aye, but I know why she didn't. That was my fault."

Michaela clicked her tongue and shook her head. "You truly must love her if you can forgive her for that."

Milosh smiled. "I love her, Michaela, but I cannot have her—not like this . . . like I am. She is in more danger from me than the rest, as you are as well. When the bloodlust returned it was far greater than anything I had ever known before—and still is. As a matter of fact, it worsens each time the sun sets. It has become an unstoppable urge made worse by what I feel for her. It is a terrible desire that comes over me. How long before I am no longer able to control myself? She saw me—the white wolf, actually—sever the head of a vampire. *That* is why she held her peace. She knew what I was—a vampire hunter. She was infected. She feared I would do to her what I did to that poor unfortunate creature."

"Still . . ." the old woman said, shaking her head again.

"I cannot even fault her for taking my blood," Milosh went on. "It had been too long since she'd fed. She was as I fear I am fast becoming now . . . unable to control my . . . lusts."

"What is in her heart toward you? Does she love you as well?"

"That doesn't matter," Milosh snapped. "I am trying to do right by her, Michaela. What we want in this life is not always what we should have. You are wise enough that I should not have to tell you that. I was prepared to leave her if she had found a haven among her own kind who would accept her. It would have been best . . . for both of us. My head is not clear. Love fogs the brain, old woman. If it wasn't for love, I would not be in this fine predicament. But when I realized she had fallen back into the hands of those that had abandoned her, I could not leave her . . ."

"My son, my heart goes out to you."

"Can you help me?"

Michaela hesitated. Her eyes had fallen into deep shadow beneath the bandanna she wore on her head, and he couldn't read her expression. When she finally spoke it was with caution.

"What of your brethren," she said, "—your Brotherhood? Are there none among them who could spare you what you need?"

"None within range of my mental powers," he returned. "Believe me I have tried. The Brotherhood go wherever there are vampires to hunt and destroy. I need help now, and there are none close enough to give it. I do not even know if the blood moon ritual will help me any longer. For that matter, I do not know how long what she drained from me will help *her* . . . how long it will be before she, too, reverts back to what she was. These are areas of darkness. There are no guarantees. I only know that I must try. I cannot live like this, not after centuries of immunity from the bloodlust. I abhor what I have become unknowing, while I basked in the freedom of the blood moon. I cannot expect you to understand, but I am tired, Michaela. I would rather be dead than revert back to what I was."

"Can you still bear the light of day?"

Milosh nodded that he could.

"Well, that is something, at least. You are not yet undead. My husband, the man whose clothes you wear, could not . . ."

"Your husband was a vampire?" He was incredulous. He had wondered why the fact that she was suddenly in the company of vampires did not seem to faze her overmuch.

"He was bitten on the continent," she told him, ". . . twenty years ago, and destroyed by vampire hunters. Believe me, my son, while all the world denies their existence, Roma know well the truth of *vampir*. The lifestyle of the Gypsy Traveler makes him vulnerable."

"Then you will help me?"

"I will try," she said, ". . . but do not be so noble— so quick to leave Paloma. In the end, she may be the only one to save you, Milosh of Moldovia."

CHAPTER THIRTEEN

Somnus trotted along at a slow but steady pace. Though Milosh was anxious to put as much distance between Michaela's wagon and the Gypsy camp as possible, he was not afraid of being followed. Neither Paloma nor the old woman were wanted by the Travelers, and once Seth's body was found so brutally savaged Milosh was confident that not even Sasha would be too anxious to run the white wolf to ground. Unless he missed his guess, they'd seen the last of Kesia and her band. That, however, did not negate the danger. His ears were pricked to the near and distant sound of wolves howling, none of which were Brotherhood, and he hadn't forgotten word having spread among the local *vampir* that Paloma's blood contained an antidote for the hunger.

"Where will we go?" Michaela said. "Do you have a place?"

Milosh shot a look at the old woman as if she had suddenly sprouted two heads. "Here I sit in a confiscated wagon, wearing another man's clothes in an unfamiliar land—not a halfpence to my name. How could I have a place? I don't even know where we are going now. For that, you will have to inquire of Somnus."

"You are an enterprising young man, Milosh of Moldovia. I find it hard to believe that you have left yourself bereft. You are smarter than that."

"I *was* smarter than that until that little dove of yours crossed my path," he corrected her. "I have not come this way in thirty years, and then my visit was confined for the most part to the Abbey. That was my 'place' until what was left of it after the fire collapsed altogether. We stayed at an abandoned smokehouse east of the tor, but it wasn't safe after we were overheard and word spread that Paloma was immune to the hunger after drinking my blood. Vampires came in droves then. They had the place surrounded until I drove them off with the help of Somnus here."

"What do you want to do?" she queried.

"I want to leave her before she comes to harm at my hands," he said flatly. "That is what I have been trying to do—find her a place where she would be welcome . . . and safe. Tonight, I thought I had found such a place . . . but no."

"So go!" Michaela said. "She is safe enough with me. I have loved her since I brought her into this world. I make a promise to her poor dead mother to care for her. Paloma is like my very own."

Milosh hesitated. Before, he only had one who needed his protection, now there were two, and he was at his wits end in his search for a solution. "Forgive me, mother," he said, "I do not doubt your loyalty or your love, only your ability to protect her. It is all that I can do to manage it as things are, and . . . I do not mean to offend, but you are on in years, and in no wise fit to do battle with the entity I have brought to bear. My longtime enemy Sebastian Valentin stalks us. You are no match for him. In four hundred years, I have not been able to destroy him. He is as relentless as I am to end the fight however it must. I cannot be about the business of that without putting you both to the hazard."

"So! What do we do?"

Was she baiting him, this clever old Gypsy? "I cannot think as I am now," he said, ". . . the hunger prevents it. I need my immunity back . . . but at the same time I believe I would have a better chance at destroying Sebastian as I am now. Perhaps the fates have intervened to a purpose. But . . . if I stay as I am, I must leave you, and I cannot do that while she is in danger."

"She was in danger before you met her, young son," the old woman said. "If I am hearing you correctly, she was already encamped at the ruins that your Sebastian had claimed when you arrived there. How does that make you responsible for her safety, umm?"

"Old woman, do not try to confuse me," Milosh snapped. "I may be addled, but my conscience is not. If I leave her she is in danger, and now you, as well. If I do not, you are both in danger—from me. The hunger grows steadily. How long before I cannot control my . . . urges? If I go—leave her in your charge—how long before the effects of my blood upon her wear off? Are you prepared to deal with that? What Travelers' band will take in a vampire? I am a vampire hunter, Michaela; it was the only way that I could justify what I have become. I have seen—and done—horrors in that guise over the ages." He loosened the neck of the fine linen shirt she had given him, exposing an ugly rope burn at the base of his throat. "Will you be able to spare her being dragged through the streets by the neck toward her funeral pyre?" he said. "Will you be able to prevent them burning her alive on that pyre—or staking her through the heart, beheading her—not to mention what they might do to you, suspecting you are like her?"

"Will *you* . . . as you are?" she shot back.

"I will have a better chance than you, old woman . . . if I can keep control."

"She has stolen your heart," Michaela said.

"That does not matter. I have no right to affairs of the heart."

"You have had knowledge of her?"

Again Milosh hesitated, unable to meet her eyes. Was the woman psychic, or just guessing? Either way, Kesia had sold her short. Michaela was gifted. He had met many Roma like her, simple Gypsy folk who seemed to have a direct link to mystic planes of existence. Some could see into the future, others the past. Michaela's gift seemed so natural as not to be a gift at all, but rather a facet of her persona no more mysterious than drawing breath. There was no question that he trusted her affection for Paloma. What he didn't trust was the fallibility that age had conferred upon the woman.

"It was a test," he grumbled.

"And . . . did you pass the test?"

Milosh threw back his cloak and rolled up his right shirtsleeve, exposing the ragged puncture marks on his forearm. "What say you?" he said.

The old woman studied his wounds.

"If I had not done this, she would be undead now," he said, snapping the sleeve back over the fang marks none too gently. "I would have drained her dry."

"She received your love . . . willingly?"

Milosh gave a start. "I do not force my women!" he said, "—not even as I am now."

"Ummm," Michaela hummed. "It is mutual, then."

Milosh had never let himself dwell upon that possibility. He had almost convinced himself that all Paloma was after was the blood moon antidote. He looked away from the old Gypsy's sharp eyes, like two jet beads twinkling in the reflected light of the moon. They saw more than any eyes had a right to see.

"You will have to take that up with her," he hedged. "Far be it from me to presume to understand the wiles of women. I have been too long a solitary man."

"Some things never change when it comes to the wiles of women," Michaela said.

"Believe me, I am on guard against them, I've had to be . . . at least I was. I must get back to that and quickly if I am to survive here now." He hesitated. "Will you help me with the herbs I need, Michaela?" he said at last.

She pointed skyward. "The eclipse will come when that moon up there waxes full," she said. "There is not much time."

"You know these things also, do you?" he marveled.

"There are those among us who follow the mysteries of the universe," she said.

"Then you know how important it is that I not fail. I have my sources also, and there will not be another eclipse visible in these parts for more than two years, old woman. I will never last."

"If I do help you . . . will you stay, then?"

"That isn't fair," Milosh said. "By rights, I should go now—at once. Paloma thinks I died when the rest of the ruins collapsed. It is better that she continue to think so."

"Better for whom?"

"For all of us."

"How so?"

"If she is . . . attracted to me, it would be kinder not to raise her hopes, when naught can come of it but heartbreak. I am feeling my mortality, old woman. Death stalks me. Before I let it overtake me at last, I must destroy Sebastian; there is no place for her in the way of that. Besides . . . I believe all she wanted of me was the blood moon secret. If you are right and I am wrong . . . if she does have feeling for me, I would never be able to leave her, and that would doom us both. While my heart is battling Cupid's arrow, my head is unclear. No. It would be best for us both if I go."

"So go, if you're going!"

There was no doubt that she was peeved at him. He was peeved at himself. He was right—he knew it. Now was the time to go; there would never be a better moment. Why stir it all up again with no hope of a future? He could not function as he was. It was all much simpler when heart and loins were disjoined. His mind was pulling one way and his heart another, when a feeble groan from the back of the wagon snapped his head around toward the sound. He reined Somnus in so sharply the animal broke its stride and let loose a shrill complaint.

Milosh thrust the ribbons at Michaela. The wagon listed as he jumped to his feet. "Go to her!" he gritted through clenched teeth. "She mustn't see me. The wound on my brow is still fresh. She will smell my blood. *Go!*"

Michaela slipped inside the wagon, and Milosh yanked off his boots, then his cloak, shirt, and breeches, and leapt into wolf form, displacing the weight in the wagon again. Hitting the ground running on all fours, the white wolf bounded deeper into the woods, where he could see but not be seen. The wagon wasn't moving. Was Paloma all right? He squatted on his haunches, waiting for the wagon to move on, his barrel chest heaving, his extraordinary vision honed in upon the wagon, upon Somnus impatiently pawing the frosted ground. Why was it taking so long?

It struck him then that this was the most sensible solution—at least for the present—until he was sure Paloma was safe . . . as safe as she could be, a vampire among *vampir* at all levels of infection, with naught but the aging, rheumatic nurse of her childhood to watch over her. The white wolf could follow the wagon unseen, and be at the ready if needs must until Milosh was satisfied that Paloma was safe. For all practical purposes, he would be gone, but *not*, and while Paloma slept, he could seek Michaela out for news of the girl's progress, and whatever aid she could give him with her herbs. How was it that he hadn't thought of it before? Just one more testimony as to why a vampire ought have no truck with love. He wasn't thinking clearly. It was as if there was a fog in his brain that would not lift. The little misnamed dove—this irresistible *chovexani* had bewitched him!

Engrossed in those thoughts, he did not notice at first that the forest all around him was in motion. One by one, wolves prowled closer in a wide semicircular arc among the trees. There were large ones and small ones, silver and gray ones, male and female; they converged upon him there in utter silence. It was their leader, a handsome silver-gray wolf, that stepped forward and spoke to the white wolf's mind.

Master, have we come too late? the lead wolf said.

Brotherhood! The white wolf howled into the night. They had heard him after all. Tears blurred their images. How many were there? Ten, no *twelve*, one just a cub. By rights, they could—and should—destroy him.

Come no nearer, my brothers, Milosh spoke out in mind-speak. *I am vampir; I have been bitten. She who took my blood is as you are, but I am as I was before the blood moon . . .*

We know, the leader said. *We have no herbs to give you. We have been a company of wolves since our blood moon; we have no means to carry them as we are. For the most part we are as you see us. We can cover more ground this way. We gather our herbs when needs must. But have no fear. You are our master. We shall draw lots, and you shall drink the blood of the loser, just as your lady drank of yours, and restore yourself. . . .*

Stunned, the white wolf fell back on its haunches and howled again. Milosh could scarcely believe his ears. He had saved each one of these with the blood moon ritual and made them Brotherhood. Now they stood ready to save him—to make the ultimate sacrifice. This, he could not allow.

No, he said. *I will not take back what I have given you. You must keep your antidote, but you can be of assistance to me.*

Anything, the leader said. *You are the master. You have but to name it.*

Milosh hesitated. His heart was bursting. Though he must have over the years, he couldn't recall ever having shed tears in wolf form before. Their iridescent eyes swayed before him. Somehow, he stood.

My brothers, he said, *I will tell you what I need of you, but first I must know the whereabouts of Sebastian. I last saw him at the Abbey ruins. I have a task to perform, which you may help me with, but then I make an end to Sebastian Valentin. It is time.*

The leader snorted. *He is at the Abbey still . . . waiting for you.*

The white wolf bristled. *There is nothing left of the Abbey,* Milosh said.

The leader snorted again. *The main chimney shaft leads below to the subcellar. He sleeps there, in the deep dark by day. He is everywhere by night. He knows your every move.*

I thought as much, Milosh said. *The chimney shaft is far too small for a wolf to enter through. It must be closed off, forcing him to seek a new resting place, but that will have to wait.* His chest heaved, puffing visible breath from moist, flared nostrils. *The Gypsy girl and the old woman who tends her must come to no harm. I must be certain they are safe before I deal with Sebastian. If you would help me, stay close. Follow that wagon behind me. . . . We travel west. The hunger grows steadily stronger in me since I was bitten. If I should put them to the hazard, you must . . . destroy me—swear it on the Brotherhood!*

There was silence, the kind that is tasted, like death. Not even the woodland creatures voices spoke. The leader pawed the ground, its whole body rippling. *As you wish,* he said.

Milosh wasn't convinced the other meant it, and he met the animal's glazed eyes with his own, unequivocal gaze. *If you would help me, this you must do,* he said, *and you must do it without hesitation.*

We will do what needs must, the leader said, observing the others. There wasn't a sound.

The white wolf bobbed its head and said no more. The wagon was rolling again. As he turned to follow it, the wolf cub crept close wide-eyed with admiration, its bushy tail wagging, and rubbed its head against the white wolf's heaving barrel chest. The instant it happened, a she-wolf pranced forward and nudged the cub away.

Show respect, she scolded her offspring. *You must ask permission to approach the Master. Stand tall before him as he passes . . . !*

Milosh could bear no more. He remembered the circumstances of this mother and child saved by the blood moon. They reminded him of another mother and child now, just as they had then, and he bounded off after the wagon, disappearing beneath a blanket of mist that would mercifully soon bring the dawn.

CHAPTER FOURTEEN

Milosh had never considered himself master of anyone or anything. That the Brotherhood saw him as
such rocked him to the core. In his eyes, he was simply one who had the means to spare others like him
the horror of the bloodlust, and enlist them in a virtual army of vampire hunters that prowled through
the world committed to wipe out the undead among
them. He saw himself simply as one of the pack. But
this time . . . just this one time, he was glad of their
awe. He meant what he'd said. The hunger was esca-
lating. If Paloma was in danger at his hands and he
must be stopped, he needed to know that the Brotherhood would comply with his wishes and destroy what
he had become.

For the most part, Milosh stayed within the confines of the forest as he trotted along following
Michaela's wagon. The mist grew thicker in the wee
hours before dawn, rolling inland off the silver satin
breast of the lakes in the district. If it weren't for his
extraordinary vision, Milosh would not have been

able to penetrate it. The wagon, bright teal, cherry, and gold painted, as outstanding as it was, all too often became lost beneath the ghostly blanket.

They were no longer heading west. Michaela had turned Somnus southward. Unfamiliar with the area, Milosh needed to know why. He also needed her to know that he hadn't deserted them altogether . . . yet. Judging from the position of the stars, he presumed dawn to be a scant hour off. It had to be now, while he was still under cover of darkness and Paloma was still asleep. There was no sign of the Brotherhood, though he knew they were there. A close eye upon the deceptive mist for any enemy creatures afoot, the white wolf bolted from the forest into the open, loping after the wagon until he ran alongside it, catching Michaela's eye.

"So," the old woman said. "You have not deserted us after all, eh?" She tossed down his shirt and breeches from the floor beneath the seat where he'd left them, slowing the wagon just enough for him to tug them on and hop back into the wagon beside her.

Milosh's eyes flashed behind through the opening at their back. "Is she . . . ?"

"She sleeps," Michaela said. "The bleeding has nearly stopped. She will mend. My only concern now is that other vampires will pick up her scent and come for the blood they think might save them."

"Is that why you changed course?"

"I do not think traveling south will prevent pursuit," she said. "These creatures would go to the ends of the earth for a prize such as she is. We go south to Kestwick; it is a market town, where other Travelers congregate. You were right. I cannot hope to tend her long all on my own, young son. I am too old."

Milosh almost laughed. It amused him to be called

"young son" after roaming the planet for four hundred years. "Is it far?" he said, resisting the urge.

"No, not. If we keep up the pace, we will reach Kestwick before the sun sets again. You must tell me what herbs you need. Those I do not have at hand, I may be able to purchase there."

"You knew I would return."

"I hoped you would return," she corrected him. "You are either too noble or too afraid of her."

"I fear nothing, old woman," Milosh snapped, "—least of all your little bogus dove. I ease my conscience—nothing more."

"Ummmm," the old woman hummed. "The herbs, young son. . . . What will you need?"

"Borage, milk thistle, broom, rue, skullcap, and barsa weed," he said. "Can you read, mother?"

Michaela shook her head that she could not.

"No matter. I will show you when the time comes. The amounts must be exact . . . and they must be steeped in holy water."

The old woman nodded. "The skullcap and barsa weed will be difficult to find, but not impossible. At this time of year they are sold dried, and come dear. I will have to ply my trade to pay for them."

"Your trade?"

"I read the tarot, young son. The *Gadje* expect it. All will be well."

"Let me take the reins," Milosh said. "You had best lie down and rest. It is still an hour before first light. Will Paloma sleep past dawn?"

"I do not know. You will hear her if she wakes in plenty of time to make your retreat . . . if you still want to, that is?"

Milosh looked her hard in the eyes. "I do not want to, old woman, but I must," he said. "You need not fear for her safety any longer, if the hunger gets the better of me. The Brotherhood is with us after all, and if needs must, they will destroy me before they let her—or you—come to harm. Read your cards well tomorrow, old woman. Much depends upon the outcome of your augur."

They reached the market town of Kestwick before the sun was high. Milosh was well away before Paloma woke, but not in wolf form. It would not do for a wolf to be abroad in daylight in the market, especially since everyone knew the only wolves abroad in England had to be *vampir*. It would mean panic and sudden death. Instead, he roamed the market in the clothes Michaela had given him, the hooded cloak obscuring his face, and blended with the crowd, while Michaela read the tarot cards for patrons of the market.

He had no coin to make a purchase, but there were games of skill, archery, wrestling, and the like. He picked his competitions with care that they weren't too conspicuous, and by the time the sun began to slip below the zenith, he had won himself a respectable purse. Added to that which Michaela had gleaned from the *Gadje*, they had the price of the herbs, with enough left over to purchase foodstuff supplies as well.

They camped at the market until dusk. Then Michaela moved the wagon to the outskirts of the village inside a stand of ancient red oaks, divested of their leaves, that thinned sloping down to the lake. Just before the sun set, Milosh visited a kirk nestled in the valley to beg holy water. It wasn't until then that he realized how serious the epidemic of vampire infections had become. He didn't even have to enter the kirk to get it. A silver font was situated outside, clearly marked. Vampirism was fast reaching epidemic proportions, though no one would even admit there was such a thing. That was fairly obvious if the clergy wasn't willing to open their doors after dark to dispense holy water. He filled the two flasks Michaela had given him from the hooded font on a post beside the kirk doors, and started back toward the wagon with no one the wiser, just as darkness crept over the land.

There was no time to lose. It was time to take the form of the wolf. The hunger was already coaxing his fangs to descend. How could he bear another night at the mercy of the bloodlust? How could he bear to be so close to Paloma when the hunger turned him into an animal? He would deliver the holy water, then shapeshift and run mad until the dawn—well away from the temptation of Paloma if he could only manage to get away before the feeding frenzy made a mockery of his good intentions.

He had nearly reached the wagon when he heard Michaela scream. Cold chills gripped his heart like an icy fist. He froze in place, but only for a moment, before bounding over the thicket and crashing through the undergrowth at the edge of the wood.

"What is it, woman?" he seethed, coming abreast of her, his breathless voice no more than a hoarse whisper.

"Paloma!" she cried. ". . . She is gone!"

"*Gone?* How could she be gone?"

"She is, I tell you. See for yourself!"

Milosh leaped up onto the wagon and scrambled inside. Throwing back the curtain, he saw that the bunk she had occupied was indeed empty.

"How did she get out of here?" he demanded of Michaela, who had come up behind him. "How could she have gotten past you reading the tarot in front of the wagon? You would have seen her."

"She must have climbed out of the window," Michaela despaired, wringing her hands.

Milosh, unaware that there even was such a thing at the back of the wagon until that moment, pulled the gathered curtain away from what indeed was a small window above the bunk. It was gaping open. "But why would she do such a thing? She no longer needs to feed. When could it have happened? When did you last check on her?" Michaela was clearly beside herself, and he shook her gently. "*When*, woman?"

"I looked in on her last just before dark, before we left the market. She was asleep. It could have happened then . . . or here . . ."

"Out of the way, old woman," Milosh charged. Rummaging through the quilts, he fished out her peasant skirt and blouson. The blood on the latter rushed up his nostrils. There was no way to hold back the fangs. Loosing a howl so misshapen and feral he scarcely credited it as coming from his own throat, he thrust the flasks of holy water toward Michaela, stripped off his clothes, and the white wolf hit the ground running, its nose to the ground.

It happened so quickly, Paloma scarcely had time to react. Michaela's herbal draughts had dulled the pain. It was then, while she was on the edge of sleep, that the feeling began. It was as if her body was trying to expand and contract at the same time.

She could scarcely breathe. Her lungs seemed about to collapse. Tearing back the little curtain over her bunk, she pushed the window open, gasping for a breath of the cool, crisp North Country air. It didn't seem to help. All at once her clothes were too tight for her body—they were strangling her—she couldn't bear them another moment. She tore at her blouson, at her skirt, until she was free of them, but the feeling only worsened. It was as if she were too big for her skin. It began to stretch and strain around her. Her breath was coming short and rapid. There was pain then, as bones and flesh shifted, reshaping her body. She tried to cry out, but all that came from her dry throat was a strangled growl.

Panic nearly stopped her heart as the change occurred. One moment she was kneeling naked, gasping to fill her lungs beside the open window, the next, she was standing on long, slender legs—*wolf's legs*. What she could see of her body was covered with thick silver-gray fur. Her vision had narrowed until she saw through a distortion of iridescence that glittered and flickered and made everything appear elongated. At the same time her peripheral vision was expanded until she could almost see behind her. Terrified, the she-wolf she had become leapt through the window of the moving wagon and bounded into the undergrowth at the edge of the village.

Another gift? What more could she expect? There was no time to dwell upon that then. Eyes watched her from the copse, though nothing moved among the trees. Were these Milosh's Brotherhood, or something far more sinister? Whatever they were, they were watching her with not a little interest. Then, in a blink they were gone, and strange guttural sounds rode the wind. The snarls turned her blood cold, and she ran off in the opposite direction, while the creatures were occupied with whatever entity they had captured in the deep dark of the wood.

If only Milosh were here. She had tried not to think of him, of his strong arms around her, of his life moving inside her, igniting the fire of pleasures she had no idea existed. Beyond the passion of pure animal lust, she had felt the love in him. Why did he deny it? Tears welled in her silver wolf's eyes. How strange it was to feel their cold wetness, whipped by the wind of her motion. She never knew wolves could cry . . . or maybe they couldn't. Maybe that was a phenomenon peculiar to shapeshifter wolves. Somehow it didn't matter; all that did was that she could hardly see through her tears as she ran blindly through the ancient oak trees she had come upon.

Warmer air had thickened the ground-creeping mist that hid the forest floor. Paloma wished it would cover her as she parted it, weaving in and out among the trees. The sensation of running as free as the wind so close to the ground excited her. In any other circumstance, she would have enjoyed it. There was something palpably sexual about feeling the mulch of fallen leaves crunching beneath her naked wolf's paws as she ran on. She had become one with nature on a plane she had never visited before. . . . But what if she couldn't shift back? How had she changed in the first place? She had done nothing to cause the change; it had simply happened. Would she return to her body in the same shocking manner?

It was strange, but she didn't feel the cold. Was this a side effect as well? It must be. She hadn't felt it when she was subjected to the bloodlust, either. Milosh never seemed to be sensitive to the cold, come to that. She remembered him on more than one occasion stark naked in the icy rain and cold North Country wind without seeming to notice the stabbing, stinging pellets assaulting his bronzed skin. Why did everything remind her of Milosh?

She hadn't lost sight of the wagon, though it had melted into the mist. It had rolled to a halt in a little glade at the edge of the wood to the south. Michaela would be frantic when she found her missing. They hadn't had much of a chance to talk. She still wasn't sure how the old Gypsy had found her, or what had happened to the rest of the caravan. It didn't matter. The cold-blooded sound of snarling wolves had grown distant, all but one disturbance close by. Paloma needed to concentrate upon shifting back into human form. Milosh must have known she would be able to shapeshift; he did it often enough. If only he'd shown her how. These thoughts were hammering around in her brain when she came too close to a pair of wolves locked in mortal combat half-hidden in the swirling mist.

Slinking along on graceful legs, Paloma's silver wolf hugged the ancient oaks, fascinated by the whirling, streak of snarling bodies but a few yards from her, their fur so streaked with blood she couldn't identify their color. The larger of the two soon killed the other. There was no contest. It had always had the edge. Paloma should run; if she were in her human incarnation she would have, but her silver wolf stood rooted to the spot, mesmerized, as the victor ripped out the loser's throat and drank its blood until it had drained the creature dry. Sated at last, it lifted the limp carcass off the snarl of bracken and frosted gorse that grizzled that sector and severed its head with a series of bone-wrenching chomps in deadly jaws, while whipping the animal back and forth until it had severed the wolf's head.

Déjà vu raised the silver wolf's hackles as blood spattered her face; she blinked it back from her eyes. The thick ruff of fur around her neck expanded as her hackles raised until her peripheral vision showed it to her; it was silver, tipped with white, luxuriant and fine. She blinked again and the wolf before her had turned. Their eyes locked in an iridescent stream of recognition. For an instant they froze as two statues. Then, in a static rush of silvery motion, they left their wolves behind and surged into each other's arms.

CHAPTER FIFTEEN

Paloma opened her mouth to scream, but Milosh's firm, strong hand clamped over her lips stifled the sound. His other arm clasped her close against him. Her heart leapt. For one horrible instant, she thought she was seeing a ghost. Then his lips parted to speak and she saw the fangs, still smeared with the dead wolf's blood, and screamed despite the hindrance.

Milosh shook her gently. "Be still, little fool!" he seethed through clenched teeth, "—unless you fancy being set upon. These woods are crawling with creatures of the night."

"I thought you were *dead*!" she sobbed, pounding his broad chest with her fists. "How could you do this? How could you not ease my mind?"

He clutched her closer still, his hand buried in her long tousled mane of coppery hair, holding her face to his chest—avoiding her eyes. Were those tears in his, swimming in the eerie iridescence gleaming there? Tears? She would show him no pity. All this time while her heart was breaking . . . All the while she mourned his passing . . . All the while she prayed for the freedom of his immortal soul, he was alive and he did not come to her. He lived, and he did not ease her pain. He truly did believe all she wanted was the blood moon secret. He really was convinced that he meant nothing more to her than that—after they had loved so well—after their souls had touched—embraced—conjoined.

She beat him harder.

Capturing both her wrists in one white-knuckled fist, he swooped down and took her lips in his hungry mouth. It happened so quickly she swallowed her gasp. His hot, hard arousal leaned heavily against her belly. His groan filled her mouth as his silken tongue searched her deeply. Paloma's heart rose in her throat, fluttering, palpitating, echoing the pinging in her sex, making waves of drenching fire that rendered her powerless against his prowess. She wanted him—hungered for him—reached for him, for the promise and the power and the passion in that dynamic body that had possessed her mind, body, and soul.

Every muscle in him rippled against her. Every inch of his hot, moist skin defied the cold that should have turned his sweat to ice. No, he did not seem to feel the brisk November air, just as she did not. It must be a side effect of the infection. It was all so new to her, she couldn't be sure, but she could be sure of one thing . . . at the bottom of it all was her uncontrollable desire for the enigmatic Gypsy, who had opened her like the petals of a flower to pleasures no mortal had a right to know.

As if in a trance, she reached for his sex. When it leapt in her hand, he cried out as his hips jerked forward. The hand fisted in her hair pulled her head back until their hooded gazes met. His hot breath puffed against her face as his lips parted, baring the fearsome fangs. Long and curved, they hovered over her mouth. His eyes, dilated with desire, had become two glaring pools of acid green rimmed in red, like blood; she saw death in them, and still she crowded closer in his strong arms.

Milosh thrust his head back and, in one swift motion, lowered the deadly fangs to her arched back throat. Paloma didn't even flinch as they touched her flesh. Limp as a rag poppet in his arms, she scarcely drew breath as he froze in place over her, his warm tongue circling the spot he meant to pierce—searching for the pulse—the very center of her life force. It wasn't until those fangs actually began to dent her tender flesh that a glimmer of self-preservation sparked and she resisted. It was a long, terrifying moment before he raised the needle-sharp fangs and looked her in the eyes, his lips—fangs and all—a hairbreadth from her mouth.

"*Now* do you see why you are better off if I am dead to you?" he gritted. "I could rip your throat out in the blink of an eye—and will do if you tempt me more. I will not be able to help myself."

"Go ahead!" she cried. "Take my blood and restore yourself! It is my fault you are . . . what you have become. Take it, I beg you, or I shall die . . . if not from longing, from conscience. If I must die, let me do so knowing I have restored you to what you were. I cannot bear . . . *this*! I . . . *cannot* . . ."

His hand tightened at the nape of her neck and he turned her head toward the forest. "Look!" he growled, his eyes like liquid fire burning toward her. "Look there—" he pointed her head in a westerly direction "—and there, and there"—he turned her east then south none too gently. "*Look*, I say! What do you see?"

Paloma gasped. All around iridescent eyes not unlike his blinked toward her from the mist-clad trees.
They were surrounded. She gasped again.

He laughed, his head thrown back, his fangs reflecting glints of fractured light from thickening fog
rolling in from the lake beyond. "Oh, have no fear, little thief," he said bitterly. "You are in no danger from
those creatures, they are Brotherhood. They obey me!
They wait, Paloma. They wait for me to put you to the
hazard, at which point they have their orders to destroy me before you come to harm at my hands! Tell
me now that I am not better off dead to you!"

Tears blurred his image then, and she broke away,
her sobs living after her as she ran, blindly, her arms
carving circles in the ghost-like fog toward the direction she'd last seen Michaela's wagon. She could bear
to hear no more. She could stand to see the pain in
those dark Gypsy eyes not a moment longer.

"Go!" Milosh commanded the Brotherhood. "See
her to safety."

Paloma heard, but she did not need to turn to see
the wolves converging upon her. A sinister flapping
sound over her head made her heart race until she
feared it would burst through her breast. She did not
need to see what that was, either—the snarling of the
wolves told her Milosh was not her only danger in
that fish-gray swirling world she ran through.

"That is right. *Run*, little thief!" Milosh commanded, his voice booming through the darkness
amplified by the fog as if it was coming from an echo
chamber. "—And for both our sakes, stay gone and
tempt me no more . . . !"

Milosh let loose a bestial howl that echoed eerily
from tree to tree, as Paloma disappeared in the mist.
How could he have presumed to leave her? He must

have been mad. She wouldn't live a night through in the company of *vampir* and their creatures on her own, and Michaela had just proven herself incapable of looking after her. The dangers were too great, the stakes too high, and the consequences too devastating a burden upon his conscience. Like it or not, as much of a danger as he was to her himself, he could not leave her as she was . . . at least not yet, despite his fine display just now. His one consolation then was the knowledge that in the deep dark of the wood, in the cairns and barrows, on the fells and in the towns, the Brotherhood were watching, at the ready to destroy him if needs must to keep her and the old one from harm.

And now she knew it.

He had fed, but not enough. Crashing blindly among the trees appearing the color of thick, dark blood through the red haze before his eyes, Milosh once again became the white wolf and penetrated the undergrowth. Hidden in the mist, he would stalk his quarry—a deer, perhaps, or a boar. Yes, there would be more sport in a boar. Or if he were extremely fortunate, he would come upon another vampire—some creature the Brotherhood had overlooked—to slake his blood-lust, something, *anything*, to sate him, to keep him from following her. But nothing would sate the rage in his loins that burned like hellfire for the little copper-haired sorceress who had captured his heart.

It was just before dawn when Milosh dragged himself back to the wagon, sated at last in all but his hunger for Paloma's love. He was counting upon Paloma to be asleep, and Michaela to be awake, building the campfire to brew the morning coffee. He calculated correctly. Leaving the body of the white wolf, he collected his clothes from under the wagon seat where he'd left them, tugged them on with scathing hands, for he despised the fiend that lived in his traitorous body, and joined the old woman at the edge of the little clearing where the wagon stood, just as a ghost-gray dawn broke over the fells.

"You will have to do better than this, old woman," he grumbled, accepting the cup of steaming coffee she thrust toward him. "To begin with, latch that window—*all* the windows—from the outside. That way, if she means to escape, she will have to pass by you . . . Hah! Not that that would matter." He threw a wild arm into the air. "You would never have been able to stop her."

The old woman narrowed cold eyes upon him. "You can do better—so *do!*" she snapped at him. "Her days are numbered. You cannot outsmart the Fates, Milosh of Moldovia, for all that you will try. I need no tarot cards to see the outcome here. If you leave her she is doomed, and if you stay . . . it is too awful to imagine."

"Have you forgotten the herbs, old woman? The moon will be full in two days if the clouds will let us see it eclipse and turn to blood. You had best pray that they do, because I will not last another two years like *this* waiting for another." He tossed the coffee remaining in his cup in the fire, threw down the cup that had contained it, and strode toward the wagon.

"Here! Where do you go?" Michaela called after him. "Break your fast. It is all right. She will sleep some now."

"That doesn't matter anymore," he called over his shoulder, meanwhile saddling Somnus, who seemed pleased at the prospect of a ride. "Though, it is best that she does not know where I have gone. I do not need her in the way of what I must do now. I am taking a flask of the holy water. I have left you enough for the draught."

"What must you do?" the old woman said as if she hadn't heard anything past that.

Milosh swung himself up upon the agitated phantom horse that was clearly champing at the bit in anticipation of a run on the fells. "I must find Sebastian's resting place. He will have left it before I get there if I tarry here. Do you see that sky? Rain comes. It will slow me down."

"Can you not wait until the moon is full . . . until we see if the herbs will restore you?"

Milosh shook his head. "No, old woman, I cannot," he said. "I finally see why it is that I have not in all these years been able to defeat him . . . unless I am very much mistaken, I need to be as I am now—a full-fledged vampire—in order to destroy him." He kneed the horse beneath him. "If I do not return in time for the ritual, Sebastian has finished me. That is in the hands of your 'Fates,' old woman, or your 'Furies,'" he said, and galloped off into the fading mist.

Paloma was not asleep. She heard every word. Did Milosh have feelings for her after all? Oh, how she wanted to believe it. She couldn't tell from their brief conversation, only that she was in the way, and he didn't deem Michaela capable of remedying that by keeping her confined. No, he didn't want her, but he couldn't conscience throwing her to the wolves— literally—either. Well, he was right about one thing . . . barring the wagon windows would never hold her. Michaela would never be able to stop her if she had a mind to leave . . . like now.

Paloma tossed her cloak over her shoulder, for hoarfrost glimmered on the fells, and climbed out of the wagon. The snap and crackle of the campfire drew her as sparks rose up from the cluster of fragrant apple wood Michaela had gleaned from a fallen tree in the brake. Paloma inhaled deeply as the warm, fruity aroma, like roasted apples, filled her nostrils. Blended with the ghost of the coffee Milosh had flung into the flames and the smoky promise of succulent sausages and fried bread riding the dawn breeze, her mouth had begun to water.

Michaela wrapped a fat sausage in a piece of the bread and handed it over. Paloma took a bite and rolled her eyes. She was ravenous. She hadn't been this hungry since she'd been infected. She was still free of the bloodlust. Could that be the reason? When she'd been a captive of the feeding frenzy, the smell, sight—even the thought of food nauseated her.

She was eating more like the wolf she'd vacated than the well-mannered young lady she was in her human incarnation. Grease from the sausage lingered on her lips and drizzled down her chin. She wiped it away with her fingers and licked them clean. All the while, Michaela watched her. Paloma didn't need to look directly into those beady onyx eyes to feel the heat of their scrutiny boring into her; she'd felt it too often in the past.

"You knew he was alive," Paloma accused as calmly as if she'd asked the time of day. It was the only way with Michaela. One had to catch her off guard to get the upper hand; she was too sly otherwise.

The old Gypsy's hands clenched into wrinkled fists and flew to her hips. "I did," she said, jutting her wrinkled chin. "So?"

"You knew I cared for him—grieved for him."

The woman nodded. "And what can come of your caring and grieving, eh?"

"Naught can come of it," Paloma snapped. "But that does not mean that I do not care still, Michaela. My heart was breaking. You could have eased my pain."

"It was not up to me to ease your pain. It was up to him. He did not choose to do so. He thought his way was kinder . . . and so did I . . . I still do. There is naught but heartbreak in it if you do not let him go, Paloma. He walks the path of death; it is only a matter of time, and if you follow, it will take you with him." She made the sign of the cross, and then the ancient Gypsy sign against evil behind her back. Paloma would have laughed at the ridiculous gesture if she weren't on the verge of tears.

"What else have you kept from me?" she said, her voice quavering. She had scoffed down the sausage and fried bread. Needing something to do with her hands to keep from shaking answers from the old woman, she filled a tin cup with coffee and took a sip.

"Who can keep anything from you, little dove? You heard all of it I have no doubt."

Palona laughed bitterly. "Aye, I heard," she snapped. "I knew I could not trust you to tell me. 'Little dove,' eh? He thinks you misnamed me."

Tears glistened in the old woman's eyes, and she turned her gaze toward the fire. "You were when you were born," she said, ". . . as soft as the breast of a pure white dove, and hair like the flame of the setting sun. I saw great things for you in the cards. But always the moon card . . . the card of caution, and of deception, the card of false alliances, of the supernatural, and of lunacy. It has dogged you all your life, Paloma, casting shadows upon the sun."

"Superstitious augur, old woman? The blather you feed to the *Gadje*? What? You think *I* will believe it?" She threw back her head in a burst of coarse laughter.

"Hear me!" Michaela said, her voice booming like thunder. "I see the moon upon you here . . ." she thumped her wrinkled forehead with a wizened fist. "I always see it in that smooth pale brow. It has marked you. You throw caution to the winds, my dove. And what was that affair with the *Gadje* who took your virtue, but a false alliance?" She shook her head, her dark eyes flashing, "Ahhhh, so you begin to see, eh? Now Michaela's augur is not so much blather any more, eh? But wait . . . there is more. . . . What is this that has possessed you now—this that threatens your very soul if not supernatural? My poor dove, you are indeed dancing on the brink of lunacy, as he is also. All this I saw while you still cooed in your cradle, like your namesake, the dove. La Paloma! Aye, I saw, and there was not one thing I could do to save you from that which is predestined."

Paloma threw up her arms in a wild gesture. "Then why do we bother?' she said. "If I am doomed, then I am doomed, and there is naught to be done."

"There is naught that I can do," Michaela said. "That is not to say that you—"

"So be it!" Paloma cried, swirling off her hooded cloak with flourish. She tossed it down upon the hoarfrost underfoot, and began unfastening her laced girdle.

"Here! What do you do?" Michaela cried. Moving faster than Paloma had seen her do in years, the old Gypsy snatched the cloak up from the ground as the girdle sailed toward her. "Have you gone mad?"

"I am going to challenge your moon, old woman," Paloma seethed. "I am going after him. What he faces, I will face also. We are as one. Deny it he may, but he cannot change it. It is my fault he is as he is now. It is up to me to restore him as he was. I cannot do that sitting here idle with you, while he . . . while he . . . No! I must go to him. I can hardly go on foot, can I? The wolf will speed me to the tor."

"Wait!" Michaela said, arresting Paloma's arm as she struggled with the drawstring on her blouson. "If you must go, I will take you. You cannot roam the fells alone. They are crawling with *vampir*, and men with guns hunting them! And your wound!"

"The Brotherhood watches me," Paloma told her, "—the wound is but a scratch, and it is daylight. Vampires lose their strength in daylight . . . those that can bear the sun, that is. Let go! You cannot stop me. Hah! Besides, how can you take me? Milosh has taken the horse. What? Would you pull the wagon yourself, old woman?"

"I can barter for a horse in the village. I have ointment and simples—charms and tinctures . . . and the tarot."

"That will take all day, Michaela and that Phantom horse of his flies like the wind. I know. I have ridden him. We will never reach the tor in time. Let go, I say!"

"I must take you!" the old Gypsy shrilled. "I have the herbs he needs. Tomorrow night, the moon waxes full. What if he does not return here in time? *Think*, Paloma!"

Paloma stared into the old woman's misty eyes. She glanced at the bulbous fingers clutching at her arm. She never should have stopped to talk to Michaela. She should have transformed and been on her way. She knew she could never win, pitted against her longtime protector. The maddening thing was, Michaela was probably right, and she raised her head and let loose a shriek of pure exasperation she scarcely recognized as coming from her own dry throat.

The old woman shook her and thrust her cloak and girdle toward her. "Put these on," she said. "We need to do this now, Paloma!"

Paloma looked the old Gypsy in the eyes. A plan was hatching, and she hesitated. "Very well," she said, snatching the cloak and girdle from the woman's hands. "Go and get your wares—and be quick about it. It is a good walk to the village."

Michaela shuffled off toward the wagon. She'd scarcely climbed inside when Paloma tossed the clothing down and in a beat of her heart became the wolf that would be long gone when the old Gypsy climbed back down again.

CHAPTER SIXTEEN

Milosh was ready to concede that Somnus possessed more brains than he did. When they reached the tor, the phantom horse balked and pranced and champed back on the bit in his mouth until he had drawn blood, as if he knew what dangers lay ahead for his master.

"I like this no better than you," Milosh said to the shuddering beast as they rounded the rowan tree at the foot of the rise, ". . . but it must be, so you may as well settle down and carry me up this hill. We have much to do and the day soon passes."

Somnus snorted, tossed his head about—long mane flying—and balked, stomping the ground, white clouds of breath puffing from his moist flared nostrils. Something was definitely not as it should be. It didn't matter. If Milosh's theory was correct, and he hadn't been able to destroy Sebastian because he hadn't been at his full power, lacking the hunger that would give him the edge, this was the only way. It had to be now, before he drank the draught that he prayed would restore him to the entity he had been for the past four hundred years. Still, there were no guarantees. There weren't even guarantees that the draught would work now that he had reverted back to the creature Sebastian had made of him; it had never been tested in such circumstances as these before. Whatever the situation, his path was clear. He needed to find Sebastian's resting place, and if he could, destroy him in it before the sun set. If he could not, and the creature escaped him, it would fall to him to destroy the resting place to prevent Sebastian from returning to it before dawn. That would mean avoiding the creature through the night; not a palatable prospect, and either way there would be minions abroad to protect Sebastian.

The first order of business would be to replace his tools. This would be no great feat, since he always carried a blade in his boot to whittle and hone new stakes when supplies were low whenever he hunted in human form. There were plenty of fallen timbers to choose from at the ruins that hadn't been compromised by the fire and drenching rain, and he would be able to find something to suffice for a hammer. He had used makeshift tools thousands of times before when, like now, things were less than equal. And he had the holy water; the reason he hadn't come in wolf form and made better time. Each entity had its attributes. The trick was selecting the right body for the task at hand; at this, he was a master, the best of his kind. It was the reason he had lasted so long prowling through time fraught with entities normal humans refused to even accept existed.

What bothered him marginally was the way Somnus was behaving. Other than his own instincts he trusted none but those of the horse underneath him. This was hardly the first time Somnus had climbed the tor. When mounted, Milosh and the animal moved as one entity. There was never a question of who was master . . . until now. The phantom horse was actually fighting him at every pass. Three times, Milosh had to turn Somnus around when he tried to climb back down the tor. Lethargy was taking its toll. It was the price he paid for being able to bear the light of day, and it was taking all the strength that remained in his body to control the animal—strength that he would need to call upon in what he was determined would be his final battle with Sebastian. Cold chills unrelated to the bitter wind funneling down the tor gripped him with a kind of trepidation he had never felt before he reverted to the hunger. For the first time in centuries, he doubted his ability to part the way between the good and evil in him and at least walk the middle ground, where he would be safe to concentrate upon what he must do—where Paloma would be safe in his presence. That was at the root of his agony then, and it was twofold. He longed for her safety in his presence, but he also longed to be free of the madness she ignited in him—the fire that ruled his loins whether he was in her presence or not. Like now, when all he could think of was her beautiful face, her intoxicating scent, her exquisite body moving against his own, bringing him to life as he had never been awakened before. She had rocked his soul. The hellish part was, he damned the distraction she had become, and yet he welcomed that distraction—courted it until it threatened to destroy him. It was indeed a terrifying thing, but as the moth flirts with the flame, so did he flirt with the very thing that could end his existence. Now, it was sapping his strength. Coupled with battling the horse the entire distance, it was all he could do to dismount once he reached the summit and the stables, a welcome sight against the backdrop of a cloudy sky.

Milosh slid off the animal's back. He should lock Somnus in one of the stalls, but there wasn't a moment to lose. The clouds would bring the twilight early, and he didn't even bother to unsaddle the animal. If all went well, he would be away soon enough, and he tossed the reins over the post of an open stall instead and started toward the ruins. He hadn't reached the threshold when the phantom stallion reared and lurched and snapped the reins, nearly knocking him down, galloping past him.

"Hold, you black devil stallion!" Milosh thundered. "Where the bloody deuce do you think you're going? *Come back here!*" But it was no use. The horse streaked over the courtyard and back down the tor in half the time it had taken to climb it.

Loosing a string of expletives colorful enough to turn the gray sky blue, Milosh trudged toward the ruins. Behind the clouds, the absent sun had begun to slide below the zenith by the time he'd whittled enough stakes to fill the pockets of his greatcoat. A flat piece of iron of unknown origin he'd snaked from the ruins would serve in the absence of a hammer. Armed with these, he went below to the only place he could go, the maze of chimney works that comprised the backbone of Whitebriar Abbey—all that remained that was navigable for a man or a wolf; the rest was naught but a solid heap of blackened slag, accessible to naught but rodents, or possibly . . . a bat.

Was he on a fool's errand? The thought had crossed his mind. The longer he prowled through chimney structure, the more he became convinced that was the case, for wherever he searched nothing blocked out the light of day. If it was, he would have to find a suitable hiding place where he could watch and see where Sebastian exited the ruins at twilight. Another day's delay would put him behindhand for the herbal draught. No.

It did not bode well, and always there was the image of Paloma in his mind taunting—tormenting him—arousing him despite the absence of her physical body clasped to his own.

Distracted thus, Milosh did not see the light change filtering down from above. He did not feel the brick-work start to shift, or feel the loosened bits of crumbling mortar sifting down as the chimney collapsed in upon itself until it was too late. His arms flew up to protect his head as bricks rained down upon him, driving him to his knees as they buried him. *My God . . . she has finally killed me,* he thought, as her naked image, soft and supple in his mind, faded into painful, suffocating darkness.

Paloma was well aware of the presence of other wolves in the woods she bounded through. Now and then she caught a glimpse of the iridescence of a watchful eye. These were the ones Milosh had told her rarely shapeshifted back into their human in-carnations anymore. They had grown comfortable in their wolf bodies, something she secretly feared he might be contemplating himself. Would he go that far to separate himself from her? She hoped not, but she feared so. Her intuitive sense was heightening, as was her ability to read his thoughts when he was near. He must have known because he always let his mind go blank when he was in her company. It was like sifting through a pea-soup fog attempting to penetrate it.

Yes, the Brotherhood was following her, moving silently through the misty green darkness of the for-est. She lost track of them on the open fells, but still she knew they were close by, watching—always watching—through the mist. Watching through the tangled snarl of gorse and bracken hemming the brake, and the tall parched grass spears, their backs bent beneath the weight of ice not yet melted, edging the likewise ice-crusted river. Now and then she heard a distant howl. Other creatures were abroad, but Paloma didn't fear them. Their powers would diminish in daylight, whereas hers would not. She scarcely thought of any of that then. Only one thing moved her now. She had to put the situation to rights. Milosh would not have reverted to the hunger but for her. Somehow, she had to restore him as he was . . . no matter what she had to sacrifice to do it.

A dull soreness in the wound on her shoulder from all the running had begun to nag at her. Paloma refused to let it slow her progress. She was nearly there. She had crossed the river, prancing through its thin ice crust with high-stepping feet. It wasn't long before she reached the dormant woad field. There, Paloma's gray wolf turned toward the north, bypassing the village and the kirk, and headed through a stand of young saplings straight for the tor, and the derelict rowan tree at the bottom that marked the approach to what was once Whitebriar Abbey. She wished she could have seen it before the devastation. How grand it must have been.

Heavy gray clouds had brought the twilight early. The tor had just come into view when it happened. A darker cloud appeared silhouetted against the rest. Paloma's gray wolf misstepped at the edge of the saplings, and stood watching it change shape as it moved back and forth across the rest of the cloud cover. A flock of birds seeking a tree to roost in for the night? No . . . *bats!* There was no mistaking the way their wings glided through the air with a sawing motion, unlike the flapping of bird's wings. Her heart leapt. They were heading her way. Was this Sebastian, divided as she knew he could into a virtual swarm of the hideous creatures? Had Milosh flushed him out? Her heart fell at that thought. If it was Sebastian, then Milosh had failed. She strained her sharp wolf's eyes toward the summit and the ruins for some sign of the Gypsy's familiar shape, but all was still. Nothing moved but the eerie black cloud of winged creatures zigzagging across the twilight sky. They were heading straight for her.

Paloma's silver-gray wolf backed behind the saplings. They made a poor blind, with their skinny trunks and bare branches, but there was no other choice. Had they seen her? They must have. Bats could see in pitch blackness, and it was barely dusk. They honed in upon motion. She stood very still, hoping to confuse them. But it was no use. If, as she feared, it was Sebastian, divided again into many, he would sense her presence, to say nothing of picking up her scent. If Milosh had not defeated him in four hundred years, how could she, a mere novice, hope to outwit the creature?

She wasn't given time to strategize such a notion. They were on her in seconds. Before her eyes, the swarm became a stream plummeting toward her arrow straight until they soared through the trees and covered her, beating her about the head and body, about the thick silvery ruff that framed her masked face with their wings.

Spinning on its hind legs, Paloma's wolf howled into the gathering twilight, her voice amplified by the evening mist, forefeet flailing the air in a vain attempt to protect her eyes and beat back the swarm. For one terrible moment she feared she could not stand against the onslaught. She was too new in her wolf incarnation to handle such a situation cleverly. Outnumbered, she was at a gross disadvantage, with one thing only in her mind then—to keep from being bitten.

All at once the swarm of bats whorled into one

towering entity, whose arms were gargantuan wings, whose skeletal bald head challenged the treetops, and whose footpads, bearing talons, crackled the ice-crusted mulch that carpeted the forest floor. Its cadaver-gray hide, for Paloma could not call it skin, was veined with the blue of its victims' blood, and its red-rimmed acid-green eyes were burning toward her from their blackened sockets.

Sebastian.

Paloma's silver wolf howled again, but the sound was cut short as the creature raised one crooked wing and lifted her as if she were a broom straw, sending her crashing broadside into one of the tender saplings.

"Foolish chit," the creature said. "You cannot stand against me!"

Dazed, the silver wolf tried to rise but could not. Fresh blood seeped from the wound in her shoulder; the last thing she wanted facing a vampire that had just risen from its sleep. He would be ravenous with the hunger. The heart in her barrel chest began to thud against her ribs until it rose in her throat. Where was Milosh? She was a fool to think she could face such an entity alone, albeit that she had no choice in the matter. Again she howled into the darkness. The plaintive wail echoed off in the distance, bouncing from tree to tree sounding like a pack of wolves instead of one. Mournful and sad, it drifted over the fells until even Paloma shuddered at the sound.

"He is dead," Sebastian said. "At long last the joust is done!"

He could read her thoughts! Paloma desperately tried to clear her mind, but she could not. Her fogged brain could think of nothing except that the creature had told her, *Milosh was dead!*

Sebastian laughed. "And to celebrate, I shall finish

what I started in you, fair one," he said, ". . . but not . . . yet, eh? And not while you are in wolf form. I do not relish the blood of wolf, it is hardly enough to slake my appetite. You will keep until I tend to that."

Paloma could not help but think: *I will be long gone when you return.* He had killed Milosh. Nothing mattered anymore then. Milosh was dead.

"Oh no, I cannot claim that distinction," Sebastian replied to her thoughts. "I did not kill the Gypsy fool. He did that himself and saved me the bother. I have to admit, though, after all these years of sparring, his demise at the last was quite a disappointment." He lumbered closer and raised one foot, its talons inches from Paloma's head. His foul odor rushed at her, mold and decay laced with the sickening sweet stench of rotting flesh. "But you will not be gone when I return . . ."

Pinned between two saplings, Paloma's silver wolf could not move. It was over, and it didn't matter anymore. Milosh was dead, and she could not stand alone against the hideous, centuries-old entity that had somehow killed him. Her moist wolf's eyes screwed shut, she braced herself for the blow that would render her unconscious. Sharp talons closed around her. In spite of the melancholia that had crushed her spirit then, she fought to free herself, squirming in the creature's grip. But Sebastian only laughed, until from behind another sound pierced the silence. It only took a moment for Paloma to recognize it—Somnus's high-pitched whistle echoed in her ears as the phantom horse attacked Sebastian from behind.

The creature let her go. Out of the corner of her eye as she plummeted to the ground, Paloma glimpsed the horse that appeared to have climbed up Sebastian's back as easily as he might have climbed a hill. The phantom stallion's forefeet hooked in the creature's wing, pulled it down to give him access to the vampire's exposed throat. Sebastian shrieked. The horse's eyes were glowing like two iridescent coals; his lips were curled back, exposing terrible teeth that gleamed in the light of the moon. The silver wolf howled again. The sight reminded her that in one more night the moon would be full, and might have saved Milosh. But that didn't matter any more. Milosh was dead.

Shrieking with rage, Sebastian tried to shake the horse from his back, but Somnus held fast, his complaints filling the misty night air with discordant sounds so piercing, Paloma's silver wolf answered them with earsplitting cries of its own. Reverberating through the scant wood, the racket brought a veritable army of wolves bounding over the forest floor, the thunder of their footpads ringing in her ears—rumbling through the frozen ground beneath her as they descended upon the scene, fangs bared for battle.

In the blink of an eye, Sebastian loosed a heart-stopping cry, shrank down into the form of a single bat, and sawed through the mist to disappear over the fells in a furious rage of flapping frenzy over the heads of the advancing wolves.

The Brotherhood.

Somnus hit the ground with a deafening thud that shook the earth beneath Paloma. She heaved to right herself. It took several tries. She was surrounded by wolves nudging her upright, circling her until she stood on all fours, albeit shakily. Aside from being shaken, and having opened her shoulder wound, she was unharmed. A few yards off, Somnus lay on his side, breathing heavily. Paloma's silver wolf limped to his side, her high-pitched whine grating on the silence as she nudged the stallion with her cold, moist nose.

Get up! Her mind said to the horse. *He is not gone.*

He will be back. We must away before he comes. We must leave this place. . . .

The phantom horse could not answer, but he seemed to understand. Gradually, he struggled to his feet, a triumphant whistle leaking from him with success. He pranced in place, his dusky flesh rippling in the moonlight, his long mane tossed in the air. His lips were curled back dripping lather, exposing the deadly teeth, unlike that of any other horse Paloma had ever seen. It wasn't until then that Paloma realized Somnus was saddled. When he turned toward the tor, she bolted forward and ranged herself in his path.

Did you not hear me? she said. *Not that way . . . it is . . . too late. . . .*

But the horse pranced right on past her. What's more, the wolves did also. The silver wolf hesitated, glancing behind in the direction the bat had taken. The mist was vacant of life, but there was no consolation in that. Sebastian would be back. If she believed nothing else, she believed that.

Meanwhile, Somnus and the wolf pack had reached the rowan tree and started to climb. The horse leading, the wolves swarmed up the grade as if their lives depended upon it, their howls echoed back through the mist. Maybe their lives didn't depend upon it. Maybe someone else's life did—Milosh's life. Could he still be alive? If he was, while Sebastian believed him dead, the enigmatic Gypsy had the advantage.

A surge of adrenaline rushed through the silver wolf's blood, and she bounded after them, a close eye upon the fells behind, where at any moment, Sebastian might appear. The final battle had begun.

CHAPTER SEVENTEEN

The sight that met Paloma's eyes when she reached the summit stopped her in her tracks. Somnus was running wild around the collapsed chimney, his cries trailing off on the wind, as the wolves clawed at the fallen bricks. Paloma joined them, clawing at the rubble until her claws began to bleed.

Whole bricks and bits of broken bricks flew in all directions as the wolves dug deeper. Could Milosh still be alive, buried beneath the collapsed chimney column? The deeper they dug, the stronger his scent rushed up her flared nostrils, but that would be whether he was alive or dead. Sebastian must have picked up his scent as well, and counted Milosh among the dead despite it. The creature would return at his most powerful after having fed. The Brotherhood must have come to that conclusion themselves, for they dug with mindless fury en masse, like a machine, until, just a few feet belowground, something black appeared in the hole they'd dug, picked out by a shaft of misty moonlight.

Somnus charged forward, scattering the wolves as he kicked back more of the crumbled bricks until what lay beneath became chillingly plain. Milosh had been forced to his knees inside when the chimney collapsed, his arms flung over his head to protect it. He wasn't moving. Loosing an earsplitting whine, Paloma's silver wolf jumped into the hole on top of him, but was quickly usurped by the phantom horse that, with little regard for her in the way, clamped ferocious teeth into the fabric of the Gypsy's caped greatcoat, and hauled his limp form out of the rubble.

He was so still. He didn't appear to be breathing. The wolves had retreated now that Milosh was pulled clear, and Paloma's wolf pounced upon him, her forefeet planted upon his chest. *Breathe!* she called out with her mind, meanwhile licking his face with her long wolf's tongue. Still, he did not move, and she leapt off him, spun in circles, and pounced again, harder this time, landing upon all fours in the middle of his chest. Milosh coughed, took in air, and coughed again. Paloma plunged her wolf's snout down in the middle of his face and licked it all over until Somnus shoved her aside and took hold of Milosh's greatcoat again, hauling him to a sitting position.

"Get back . . . you lop-eared cob!" Milosh panted, seizing the horse's frayed reins.

He tried to rise and failed, and Paloma scanned the tor with her narrowed wolf's eyes. It was vacant. The Brotherhood had all slipped away. She wasted no more time. Spinning in a wide, ragged circle, she leapt into the gathering mist and came to ground in a silvery streak that materialized her in human form. Sobbing, she flung herself into Milosh's arms. What words she spoke were unintelligible, at least to her, though Milosh seemed to understand them as he crushed her close and clasped her fast.

"What . . . the deuce are you . . . doing here?" he got out between gulps of air.

Paloma pulled back. "That's gratitude," she snapped. "If I had not come, you would be dead down there."

"The hearth ledge spared me being crushed . . . but there was no air." He glanced about. "Where is Michaela . . . the wagon?"

Paloma shook her head. "I came alone," she said, scrambling to her feet. "Come! You cannot stay here. Sebastian will return. . . . Let me help you to the stables."

"Wait . . ." Milosh gritted. "What do you mean . . . he will return? He didn't . . . you weren't . . . !"

His eyes roamed over her body, over the fresh blood leaking from her shoulder, over the blood on her hands left behind from her wolf's paws digging him free. They came to rest upon her side. Until then, when she followed his gaze to her waist and hip, she didn't realize she'd been badly bruised there.

Milosh reached toward the ugly blue-black patches, but he stopped midway, seemingly distracted by the blood upon her hands. His eyes gleamed with a strange iridescence, and his sensuous lips took on a sudden change in shape as fangs distorted his upper lip. When he seized her wrist and brought her hand closer, she stiffened.

"That happened while I helped the Brotherhood dig you free. I will tell you, but you must let me help you inside. You cannot stay here. As soon as he has fed, Sebastian will return. When he doesn't find me where he left me, he will come looking for me here. He thinks you are dead. You have the advantage, but not for long out here in the open."

Paloma tugged on his arm, but Somnus, bored with the delay, pranced forward, nudged her aside none too gently, and bit down on Milosh's caped collar, hauling him to his feet. Staggering, Milosh grabbed fast to the horse's mane, staring through dazed eyes toward Paloma. Only then did she remember she was naked.

Milosh shrugged off his greatcoat and wrapped it around her shoulders. Paloma slipped it on. It swept the tousled ground cover at her feet, and her arms were lost inside the sleeves, but it held his scent, and she closed her eyes and inhaled him deeply as between them she and Somnus helped him inside the stables.

They had no sooner crossed the threshold when the phantom horse, on some mission of his own, pranced out again and disappeared in the darkness. Paloma stared after him. A cold wind funneled past her where the horse had stood, and she shuddered, the heavy warm wool greatcoat notwithstanding.

"He won't go far," Milosh said, gripping her arm as she moved to follow. "He is my creature. There is naught to fear."

"But you do not know. Defending me, he attacked Sebastian. The creature nearly killed him. He will when he comes back and finds me gone and you alive. Somnus is in grave danger."

Milosh put her from him. "So are you, from me, little thief," he said, his voice quavering. "Get back! Keep your distance and let me think! The night is young and I have not fed. You have no inkling of the danger you are in. . . ."

Milosh reeled away from the temptation Paloma was then. Staggering to the haymow at the back of the stable, he walked his fingers through his hair as if to keep his brain from bursting through his skull. She shouldn't have come. The last thing he needed now was another distraction. But if she hadn't come, and brought the Brotherhood, he would have died—been buried alive—and risen undead to be butchered even as he had butchered others like him over the years. The poor child had no inkling of what she had done, or what she was facing at his hands if he wasn't very careful. The trouble was he was drunk with love for her. He was also aroused, and overcome with the hunger that could well bring about her destruction. He dared not, could not, would not give in to the temptation she was. He leaked a bitter laugh. It was a pleasant fiction. He was no longer what he was when they first met. Now, the hunger ruled him in ways it never had when he was first infected. Was this a phenomenon that time had conferred upon him? Was he to live out his last days as the hunted instead of the hunter?

He sank down in the straw and drew a ragged breath. Why wouldn't the fangs recede? He needed to feed, and soon if he were to ensure Paloma's safety and his sanity. If only Michaela were here to take her in hand, he thought. The old Gypsy knew well what he was facing. Her own husband was a slave to the hunger. But Michaela was not here, and now Somnus had deserted him. He'd meant what he'd said before about the phantom horse, but Paloma could be right. Milosh had seen Sebastian in a blind rage. He would not wish such upon the faithful stallion.

It was hours yet before midnight, let alone the dawn. The hunger would soon be unstoppable. He needed to feed now, and Paloma was the only subject close enough at hand for that—and coming closer. *Bloody hell! Damn her for a contrary little vixen! Why will she not keep her distance?*

"Stay back, I say!" he thundered, his voice reverberating from the rafters. "Come no closer!"

Still she advanced, her slender frame lost inside his
greatcoat. How gracefully she moved even though it
dragged on the straw-strewn stable floor. He knew
every inch of the naked body beneath. Her charms
were burnished into his memory. The feel of her—the
touch and smell of her—lived in him, igniting a fire
that couldn't be slaked short of ravishing her, bloodlust or no bloodlust. If only she hadn't found out he
hadn't died. It would have been so much simpler.
Now, he was in danger of destroying the very thing
he loved. How could he bear it a second time?

As ridiculous as she looked then, her bare toes
peeking out from under the hem of that coat, her coppery hair tousled and spread about her head and
shoulders in wild disarray, the sight aroused him. It
was no use. She may as well have been in league with
Sebastian himself for the effect her very presence was
inflicting upon him. He was helpless against the
wiles she did not even know were wiles in her innocence. She was pure sensuality—pure love. He could
see it in those almond-shaped doe's eyes. In the dewy
lips parted in anticipation of his kiss—of the fangs
that would descend with arousal, for though she'd
lost the hunger, the fangs would always be a part of
the condition that bound them—marked them as
vampir. That was for life.

"We need to talk," Paloma murmured. "We cannot
stay here waiting for Sebastian to find us. It is the first
place he will look. Tomorrow night the moon will be
full. We need to find our way back to Michaela. She
has the herbs that are needed."

Milosh popped a caustic laugh. Scorn was his only
defense. "Well, you should have thought of that before you left her behind," he said.

"I could not sit idly by and let you face Sebastian
alone . . . as you are."

"The only way I can face and destroy him is as I am," he retorted. "I am convinced of it! In all these years, since I embraced the blood moon ritual, I have been unable to make an end of him, I think because I was not at my most powerful, having exempted myself from the hunger. There is a kind of madness that comes with it, an aberration that breeds fearlessness, like the Viking berserkers. Once it takes over it is unbeatable. Sebastian has this—he knows how to control it to his best advantage. Not having the same advantage in my altered state because of the blood moon, I have failed. I do not know how it is that I have never seen that before."

"You will be killed. . . . I know it!" she sobbed.

How he longed to take her in his arms, to comfort her, to lay her fears to rest. Instead, he stood there dumbly, not daring to reach out to her. His strength had returned; a boon of the night that banished the lethargy. His lungs had once again filled with air; his breathing was no longer ragged and short. As if mesmerized, he rose to his feet, helpless against her approach. The salty-sweetness of her blood surrounded him. Metallic and evocative, it filled his nostrils and he was undone, his own blood pumping through him pounding wildly in his ears, drowning out her soft voice, her wise words. Nothing mattered but that he take her in his arms. Nothing but the taste of her blood would satisfy his hunger. Nothing but burying himself in the soft warmth of her body would slake the madness that gripped him then.

Groaning, he seized her in strong arms, though they trembled. Every muscle in him rippled with anticipation. How malleable she was in his arms. How well her body molded to his, as if they were two halves of a whole. As if it had a will of its own, his hand slipped beneath the greatcoat. The touch of her soft flesh sent shockwaves up his arm that raced through his whole body as if he'd been lightning-struck. She shuddered under his touch and crowded closer in the custody of the strong arms that held her.

He was aroused beyond bearing, so tight against the seam of his buckskins that he had to unbutton them. Swooping down he took her lips in a kiss that drained his senses. When the tip of her silken tongue slid over his fangs, he could bear no more. Scooping her up in his arms, he laid her down in the hay and fell upon her, gathering her against him, spreading her legs to receive his hot, hard member. It penetrated her with ease, filling her, gliding on her wetness. He thrust himself deeper, to that place only he had reached, the shuddering depths of her that belonged to him alone. She breathed a strangled gasp as her sex tightened around him, and he took her deeper still, crushing her tighter in his arms, until he could feel the blood pumping through her inside and out.

All of his fine resolve evaporated, like the ice crystals evaporated in the mist swirling over the tor. He could bear no more. Outside the moon shone down, throwing shafts of fractured light into the stable through the wide-flung doors half off their hinges. Tomorrow it would be full. The hunger was always more unstoppable under the full moon, and this was to be a full eclipsed blood moon. It was building in him now.

Lost in the power of a passion he could no longer deny, he moved inside her, just as she moved to the rhythm of his thrusts. . . . Now if he could only separate the passion from the hunger. . . . But no, a film passed before his eyes, like a shade descending; a film of blood. His heartbeat moved his chest visibly. His sex moved inside her in the same torrid rhythm. The veins in her arched back throat were distended. He could see them clearly through her opalescent skin, calling to him—inviting him, while the tantalizing scent of fresh blood leaking from her shoulder called his lips there to taste her. Excruciating ecstasy. It was all he could do not to sink his fangs into her, now that he'd tasted her. What torture!

It was no use. His mouth descended, covering her own. When the tip of her pointed tongue flicked over his fangs a second time, his lips slid lower, searching for the vein that called to him. His tongue blazed a fiery trail over her throat until he felt the blood coursing through it, thrumming to the rhythm of her release.

All reason had left him then. He was the vampire. The hunger ruled him now. This was what he feared, that he would not be able to hold back the bloodlust. Loosing a wild, feral groan he couldn't recognize as having come from his own throat, Milosh threw back his head just as his sex was about to explode inside her, on the brink of it pumping him dry to the last shuddering drop, and lowered his fangs to her throat.

Deranged though he was, there was still one slender thread of sanity left in him and he hesitated, even though his fangs dented her tender flesh, and the lubricant saliva that would deaden the pain of penetration had begun to flow. He dared not move a hairbreadth. The climax must come when the fangs broke skin, and he could not sink them into his arm this time with a shirt and jacket preventing him. It was then that a racket behind caught his dazed attention. He froze, then turned and, through the vertigo of forced separation from the vampire in him he saw, through a crimson veil, Michaela's wagon. The old Gypsy was in the driver's seat, with Somnus harnessed to it and another horse trotting along behind.

Fury raised Milsoh off Paloma. He withdrew himself, crammed his aching member into his buckskins, and whipped the greatcoat closed over her nakedness in what seemed like one motion. Then staggering to his feet, he strode to the strange horse, loosed its tether, and sprang upon its back. As he spurred it into a gallop, he let loose the most savage *"Hyahhhh"* to his credit yet, and disappeared over the tor, coattails flying.

CHAPTER EIGHTEEN

Paloma scrabbled up to a standing position, slapping the hay from Milosh's greatcoat. It was still warm from his body heat, and a soft moan escaped her throat. She could still feel him moving inside her. Her sex felt thick and swollen, still throbbing for him. Were those tears she saw misting his dark Gypsy eyes? They were . . . she knew they were, albeit tears of anger. He had feelings for her, she knew that, too, yet he would do everything in his power to separate them. How could she live without him now? It would be easier to live without her soul. Even if she had to become the creature he was she would do it in a heartbeat if only he would let her—anything as long as they were never to be parted. All that remained was to convince him.

"Well, miss," Michaela said. She had climbed down from the wagon, her gnarled fists braced upon her hips. "That was one fine trick you played on old Michaela. No need to ask what you've been up to with him. Look at yourself! Get into the wagon and put on decent clothes. Well? Go on, then."

Paloma stopped to stroke Somnus's rippling neck and withers on her way past. She was genuinely glad to see the glowing-eyed phantom horse, just as he seemed to be glad to see her, judging from the way he tossed his mane and bobbed his head, and nuzzled her with his velvety nose.

"Ummm," the old Gypsy hummed, tapping her foot. "But for that black imp of the Devil coming to fetch me, I would never have found you. I do not know these fells. We never come this way when we pass through the North Country. The horse is smarter than the pair of you!"

Paloma wasn't about to dispute that. She wouldn't soon forget the way Somnus came to her defense in the valley and nearly lost his life in the process. He trusted her—knew her heart, even if his master did not. He had accepted her, but then he'd done that from the very first, when she stole him from that very stable.

Her clothes were laid out neatly on her bunk at the back of the wagon, and she dressed hurriedly. Slapping the brick dust, hay, straw, and mulch bits from Milosh's greatcoat, she began to fold it as if it were a sacred vestment. She raised it to her nose, inhaling him deeply. His scent was trapped in the fibers, woodsy, laced with leather and the clean north wind infused with his own evocative maleness. She clasped it to her breast. For the first time since the fateful night that set her on this course, Paloma wanted to dance.

She began to sway to the music in her mind, but the lilting strains soon faded, and she set the coat aside with a heaving sigh and slipped on her hooded mantle. He was going to leave her. It was only a matter of time. He was only waiting to be sure she was in good hands. It wasn't that he didn't want her; she knew he did. It was because he feared for her safety in his keeping. She had to admit, his fears had merit. She'd felt the pressure of his fangs denting the soft flesh of her throat. She had stiffened under that pressure, and yet, if letting him feast upon her blood would unite them, she would have let him, and gladly.

Raising her hood against the cold, Paloma climbed down from the wagon and faced her old nurse and mentor. One look into Michaela's sharp eyes told her a lecture was imminent.

"Well then," Michaela began, ". . . has he done his worst?"

Paloma stared at her, not sure how to answer.

"Has he bitten you—drunk of your blood and you his?" the old Gypsy clarified.

"He has tasted my blood," Paloma informed her. "But not bitten me to do so, just as I have done of his."

"Ummmm," Michaela hummed. "His first plan was the wisest. He should have stayed dead to you. Now, if the herbs fail him when the eclipse brings the blood moon tomorrow, you are lost, La Paloma; the hunger will have its way with him and he will kill you, though he means it not. He will be unable to help himself." She made the sign of the cross, followed by the furtive Gypsy sign against evil after her fashion. This time, Paloma wasn't at all moved to laugh.

"No, Michaela," she murmured. "If the herbs fail him, he will leave me, my heart will break, and I will die. He *is* my heart. It beats only for him. I am the cause of his relapse . . . of his return to the bloodlust, and if it cannot be put to rights, I will not be able to bear it."

Milosh drove the horse beneath him like a madman. He had to feed. Please God this would be the last time. If all went well, when the sun set again upon the tor he would drink the draught beneath the blood moon that would restore him as he was before he met the little flame-haired vixen that had stolen not only his heart, but his soul as well.

It was nearly midnight. There weren't many subjects abroad in such a small town at the witching hour. But for lightskirts and drunken revelers, the village streets were vacant of pedestrians. He chose a dandy exiting a public house to slake the hunger, though it did naught to slake the other hunger—that which Paloma had ignited in his loins; only she could do that.

He dared not stay long from the tor. He'd heard the wolves howling in the distance since he left the stable. Some of them were Brotherhood, yes, but others were *vampir*, local entities, Sebastian's minions, and Sebastian himself wouldn't be far behind. If all went well, he could bide his time, keep watch, and discover where the creature rested during the day, so he could destroy his nemesis once and for all.

As mad as it was, he let himself hope that the herbs would restore him, for that was the only way he could keep Paloma without putting her to the hazard. He saw that earlier. He had nearly ravaged her— drunk her blood and made of her what she had made of him; he was certain of it. As horrible as it was, he could not fault her for causing his reversal. Instead, he faulted himself for not being more prudent. If his heart hadn't gotten in the way of his common sense, she never would have been able to drink his blood in the first place. In four hundred years, he had never let down his guard—relaxed his defenses. He still marveled at that. He'd been with many women over time. What was it this little misnamed dove possessed that had so thoroughly captivated him? What alchemy was afoot between them that drew him to her like a magnet to steel? He did not know; perhaps he never would. Only one thing remained, like an indelible stain upon his mind: If the herbs did not work, he must find the strength to leave her.

Somnus was still hitched to the wagon when Milosh reached the stables, the horse beneath him lathered to a frazzling. "What is this?" he asked Michaela, climbing down.

"We wait for you," she replied. "We cannot remain here. It is not safe. Your Sebastian could return at any moment seeking her."

"Where is Paloma? Or have you managed to lose her again."

Michaela laughed. "You have worn her out. She sleeps. Let her stay so."

"It is just as well. Why did you hitch Somnus to the wagon? He is not fond of livery."

"Hah!" Michaela blurted. "We could not keep up with him, this cob you've ridden into the ground and I! Your Somnus wanted to lead us, so I let him lead. He brought me straight to you. Now we must away. It is still hours before the sun rises."

"And where do you propose we go, old woman?"

"We passed a kirkyard coming. It is set apart from the kirk proper. There, we will be safe from your Sebastian. If he is what you say he is—what he was before he fell, a bishop of the Church—he will not tread upon consecrated ground."

"His minions will," Milosh reminded him.

"And you cannot vanquish his minions?" she clicked her tongue. "I do not believe it."

"No, I can deal with those, but you forget one thing. . . . I need to be here, at the ruins come the dawn, to discover Sebastian's resting place. Two things must be for me to destroy the creature—I must be at my full power, and I must take him by surprise. It must be done before the sun sets tomorrow night, for if the herbal draught works, old woman, I will be as I was before

I met your little dove, and I will not be able to defeat him, just as I haven't been in all these years."

"What will you do if the draught does not work, eh?"

Milosh looked her in the eyes. He did not like what he saw there. There was trepidation in her dark gaze. Those eyes were all-seeing. They saw more than any other eyes could see. She had the gift of divination— no bogus tricks to fool the *Gadje* into crossing her palm with silver. But it went beyond that. She did not need to consult the tarot to predict the future.

"What? You have already made up your mind that it will not?" he said lightly, to cover the alarm that set his heart racing. It had to work. The alternative was too terrible to contemplate.

Michaela hesitated. "You want truth?" she said.

"What use to lie, old woman?"

"I see the weather signs," she said. "There is a halo round the moon. It does not bode well for clear skies on the morrow. I fear what will be if all our efforts are for naught. And there is more . . ."

"I will not hear it!" Milosh snarled. "It will work. It *must* work. You shan't sow your seeds of doubt in me. I am not one of your *Gadje* fools to be taken in by cryptic augur." Bile rose in his throat. Hadn't he just given testimony to her powers of perception—natural or supernatural? "I will not hear it, I say!"

Michaela studied him for longer than he cared to bear, her brow wrinkled in a contemplative frown. "Then we must pray that I am wrong," she said at last. "Tomorrow night will tell the tale, but now we must away, or there will be no 'tomorrow night' for any of us."

Milosh replaced some of the bricks the Brotherhood had removed to free him—enough to make the gaping hole less conspicuous—and they set out for the kirkyard at the edge of the village. There was, indeed, enough distance between it and the kirk that they could slip inside the wrought-iron gates without attracting the notice of the residents in the vicarage. They moved to the back, where the graves diminished alongside a hedgerow of well-manicured privet that marked the beginning of a small copse. Being careful to stay within the kirkyard boundaries that afforded them the protection of consecrated ground, they settled as inconspicuously as a Traveler's wagon could.

Milosh kept watch while Paloma and Michaela slept. They were not alone in that desolate place. There were wolves in the copse behind the kirkyard, their mournful howls testimony of their presence. These were Brotherhood, close enough for Milosh to reach with his mind. He wanted one thing only, to know the whereabouts of Sebastian Valentin, but dogging the wagon these in the wood had no knowledge of the ancient creature's whereabouts. Milosh reinforced his command that no harm come to Paloma at his hand or any other. He needn't have; these brothers were fiercely loyal to the savior who had spared them from the bloodlust. They would have crawled through the fires on the floor of hell itself to honor any request from Milosh.

Confident that the Brotherhood would keep a watchful eye until dawn, Milosh unhitched Somnus from the wagon and set both horses free to graze close by. It would be safe to leave his clothes behind and transform into the white wolf. He would set out in his four-legged incarnation to prowl the area and return to the tor, where he could watch until first light and try to discover Sebastian's resting place. That was the ideal solution. He by no means believed it would be as easy as he'd envisioned it, not after four centuries of failure. One thing, however, was certain—it would end here on these North Country fells. If all went well, it would happen on the tor in the ruins of Whitebriar Abbey, the once-grand home of his friends, Jon and Cassandra Hyde-White, and their son Joss, who were the closest thing to family he had known since the nightmare began.

Cold chills riddled his spine and raised his hackles as he recalled how he had first met Jon and Cassandra, newlywed and infected, and been faced with the agonizing decision as to whether they would live to join the Brotherhood . . . or die at his hands. And then thirty years later, there was the chilling decision in the matter of their son Joss, which was far worse, because he'd known Joss in the womb, and that outcome would affect them all. Now, he had returned to find the home they'd opened to him in hospitality cruelly reduced to cinder and ash in a mysterious fire, and Sebastian lurking about waiting. What was the creature waiting for? It went deeper than mere coincidence. No. It would not be easy, but before the full moon waned, it would be over, and he would know if he dared take the love Paloma offered, or be compelled to leave her forever.

Yes, his hackles were raised. Much depended upon the next few hours, and he was distracted by the plucky little Gypsy dancer who had wrapped herself around his heart and mind and soul. He had taken her—lived within the home she was—experienced rapture long denied him. How could he ever live without her now?

In spite of his resolve to keep such thoughts at bay, he could not help but think them. He was feeling his mortality in a way he never had before. Would he ever see his friends the Hyde-Whites again? If he did, would they be compelled to destroy him as he had taught them to destroy all those whose hunger madness threatened to spread the infection? If the herbs failed, would he lose his soul and become one with the undead for good and all? Had the hunter become the hunted? Pacing along the hedgerow at the edge of the little copse behind the kirkyard, Milosh tried to beat back these distracting thoughts. He needed all his wits about him now if he were to succeed; too much depended upon it. But the firestorm of memories—four centuries of them—would not let him go, and he didn't see Paloma approaching through the ground-creeping mist that had risen until the touch of her hand upon his arm spun him toward her with a jerk.

"What were you thinking just now?" she murmured.

For a moment, he stared down into the depths of the doe-like eyes that, despite her worldliness, looked upon him still in innocence and awe. What a strange little creature she was. He could see the dove in her now as she stood impaling him upon her bewitching gaze like a wood nymph in the moonlight. He hesitated to speak and break the spell. It was magical.

He flashed a smile that triggered seldom used facial muscles. "Why?" he said. "Are you still unable to read them, then?"

"I am afraid to try," she said.

"Because you fear that you cannot, while others can read yours?"

"No . . . because I fear I could . . ."

Milosh's smile saddened. "My poor little thief," he said, running his forefinger lightly along the side of her cheek. How soft it was, and warm against his roughened skin. The feel of it aroused him. She was a sorceress! a *chovexani*—witch, that she could arouse him with a look, a touch, a word, and conquer him with those misty, waif-like eyes that pleaded their case like those of a gamin in the street.

"Is it that you hate me so for what I have done to you?" she said. "I would not blame you if it was . . . that I could understand."

"How could I fault you for something beyond your control?" he said, looking away. He had to; the look in her eyes was too painful to view.

"Then . . . why . . . ?"

"You know why, Paloma," he said, taking her in his arms.

"You are going to leave me . . ." she sobbed.

He held her away, looking deep in her eyes then, his own blazing with iridescent fire. "I have no right to you," he gritted, shaking her gently. "You must trust me to know what is best for us both." No matter how he tried to rationalize the situation, it was the only way. To pretend otherwise was madness. What could he have been thinking?

"How can you know what is best for me, when you will not let me speak what is in my heart?"

Milosh dared not tell her if she were to do that, he would be undone, and she would be at the mercy of the hunger that would ultimately destroy her.

"You shouldn't be out here," he said, in a bold attempt to change the subject. "Soon I must return to the tor—"

"*No!*" she cried. "We are safe here. If you return to those ruins . . ."

"The white wolf has the gift of stealth," he interrupted her. "You need not fear. He will be discreet. If I am to succeed, you know I must discover where Sebastian rests in the daytime in order to destroy him." He took hold of her upper arms again. "Everything hinges upon that, and you must not follow me this time. I mean this, Paloma. I cannot hope to destroy Sebastian worrying about you in the way. He has tasted you. He will not rest until he finishes you—makes you what he is, *undead*, to serve him through all eternity. If he succeeds, there will be no saving you short of destroying you to give peace to your soul. My blood has spared you the hunger. . . . I cannot bring you back from the dead."

"You will be killed, Milosh."

"Not if I can help it, but you must do as I say. Now I want you to go inside that wagon and stay there. The Brotherhood watches. They will protect you. We will talk again when I return."

His hands slipped away, but she made no move to obey him. "You haven't answered my question," she said, hedging. "What were you thinking about before? You looked so . . . so tragic . . . as if someone had . . . died."

Milosh hesitated. "I was wondering if I would ever see my homeland again," he said, noncommittally. ". . . And I was wondering about my friends, the Hyde-Whites, who owned the rubble that was once Whitebriar Abbey."

"They too were vampires, you said," Paloma prompted him.

"Yes," he replied, ". . . Jon and Cassandra his bride. They traveled to Moldovia, my home in Romania, to seek help from the clergy there after Sebastian infected them. Jon was a man of the cloth himself. There is no greater prize for a vampire than corrupting God's anointed."

"And you helped them?"

Milosh nodded. "It was not easy," he said on an audible breath. "It is never easy deciding who can and cannot be saved. That is the duty of the vampire hunter. It is a lonely, painful life. Sooner or later, one must face destroying someone one has grown to . . . love. It is inevitable."

"They had a son?"

Milosh nodded. "Joss, yes," he said. "I knew that his mother carried him in her womb before Jon did. They returned here to the Abbey then, and it was thirty years before my travels brought me to this place to face the same nightmare I had faced with his parents, only this time it was more critical, considering that destroying him would have killed his parents as well. And now I have returned to find their home in ruins, and they are nowhere to be found. I do not even know if they live, only that the fire did not destroy them, but Sebastian is at the bottom of it. That I know, as surely as I know the sun will rise tomorrow. Forgive me, time grows short. I must go, Paloma."

"I do not want you to go," she murmured, reaching toward him as he began to tug off his boots, strip off his clothes, and toss them on the wagon seat. He dared not stay any longer. He was already aroused and wanting from their lovemaking earlier, longing for the rapture he had so long denied himself. That had recharged the hunger, and she was no longer safe in his company.

He arrested her hands and put her from him gently. "No, Paloma," he said, his voice like edged steel. "It must end here and now what lies between us. Let me do what needs must to make you safe. Do not oppose me. This is how it must be. . . . If you think on it, you will see that. Stay close to Michaela. Mind her. She is a good woman, and she loves you."

"I am not a child, Milosh," she snapped at him, tossing her coppery mane. How lovely she was when her eyes snapped like that. She took his breath away.

"No, you are not," he said, ". . . but you are a novice when it comes to your . . . 'infection.' I have four hundred years' experience behind me with mine. What have you—a month . . . two? Why do you think Sebastian has not been quick to finish you, eh? I'll tell you why—because he can, and easily, any time he wants to and he knows it. I am more of a challenge. Our fight is centuries old. Meanwhile, he uses you to get to me. Can you not see how he baits me with you? You are no match for that. Hah! Distracted by you, I am no match for it, either! Follow me, and he will kill us both. Enough now! I must go!"

He seized her then, and took her lips with a ravenous mouth, hot and hard against the petal softness of her own. His hand buried in the soft silk of her hair, he tasted her honey sweetness deeply, swallowed the moan in her throat, then put her from him as savagely as he'd seized her. "Good-bye, little thief," he murmured, and sprang toward the wood without a backward glance.

CHAPTER NINETEEN

Paloma stood clutching Milosh's shirt and breeches, staring after him as the white wolf he had become disappeared in the mist among the trees. She would not follow him this time. There was nothing she could do. He was right. A distraction could cost him his life. She still clutched his clothes. She buried her face in them. They were still warm, filled with his scent. She inhaled him deeply, as if she could take him into herself, but that had already happened when she drank his blood. He was part of her in a way that would join them forever. How could he think absence could separate them?

All at once cold chills gripped her. It wasn't what he'd said, it was the way he'd said it. He didn't think he was coming back. His almost savage goodbye meant *good-bye*. Realizing that, resisting the urge to follow him, was the hardest thing she'd ever had to do. She had enough burdening her conscience over Milosh as it was. She could not bear being responsible for his death.

Somehow, she made one foot follow the other and climbed up on the wagon. The mournful howl of a wolf amplified by the mist echoed from somewhere deep in the forest. Was it the white wolf—another good-bye? Tears welled in her eyes. She would not try to read his thoughts. He was too far distant anyway. Even if he wasn't, she wouldn't have tried. If she were right, she wouldn't be able to bear it.

Paloma gathered the rest of Milosh's things from where he'd tossed them under the wagon seat, and carried them inside the wagon to spare them a drenching in the mist that clung stubbornly to the fells as the weather turned warmer. Michaela was sound asleep in her bunk, and Paloma closed the wagon door without a sound. The poor woman was exhausted. Determined not to wake her, Paloma left Milosh's boots and togs on a built-in bench, one of two on either side of the door, and tiptoed to her bunk at the back of the wagon, separated from the rest by a curtain. She would not sleep, not while her heart and soul were abroad, and in danger. Instead, she curled up on the straw-filled mattress, listening to the howling of the wolves. From somewhere far off in the distance the sound of a gunshot sat her bolt upright. Could Milosh have gotten that far so soon? Was it him that the hunter had taken down? She was going to go mad. Not knowing was agony. Madness would be a kindness.

Minutes passed before she could relax enough to lie back down again. The howling of the wolves grew louder now, and she covered her ears to shut out the sound, but there were just too many of them. Were they Brotherhood, or *vampir*? Paloma didn't know. She tried to ease her body and mind into a state that would be receptive to the mind-speak of the creatures. Squeezing the bridge of her nose with fingers turned white from the pressure, she desperately tried to open the channel and let the voices in. It was a strange sort of meditation that came in involuntary spasms. The door was opening, and as she listened, fragmented voices spoke inside her head. Though it was not a familiar voice, she thrilled at the sound of it and held her breath as it repeated its message like a mantra:

Lady, do not venture from the wagon, it said. *Do not leave the kirkyard. Great danger lurks in wait. . . . You must not leave the kirkyard. . . .*

Cold chills raced along Paloma's spine, and she began to tremble. Her eyes snapped open wide. The voice in her mind was so loud she thought its owner was actually right there inside with her, but all was still. But for Michaela, she was alone.

You are only safe inside these gates, the voice said again. *Lady, listen well . . . do not leave the kirkyard. . . .*

The cryptic augur set Paloma's teeth on edge. She assumed it was from one of the Brotherhood, and therefore should be answered, but there was no way to tell for sure. Vampires were cunning creatures, not above such a deception to gain their own ends. If the voice was *vampir,* she dared not risk letting its owner know she was gifted with mind-speak; if it was not, its owner would not expect her to answer for just that reason. She kept silent, and finally the strange voice drifted off into the night. Milosh was right, she was a novice at all this, but her quick-witted intelligence was such that she was more able than he gave her credit for; now if she could only last until the dawn. . . .

Despite her resolve, Paloma had nearly dozed off when a deafening rat-a-tat-tat at the door of the wagon brought her to her feet. Trembling from head to toe, she stood rooted to the spot. It came again. It had woken Michaela, whose slurred reply reverberated through the small confines of the wagon, sending Paloma's hands to her lips in an attempt to hold back the scream building in her throat. Still, she held her ground and her breath.

"Who is there?" Michaela snapped.

" 'Tis Oswald Smythe, the sexton," the gruff voice replied. "Open up in there. I won't be talkin' to no locked door."

Muttering a string of Gypsy curses, the old woman shuffled toward the door as Paloma threw back the curtain and reached her in two strides.

Laying a finger alongside her lips, Paloma wagged her head and whispered, "Do not let him in, and do not leave the wagon!"

There wasn't time to explain. The sexton banged again. All Paloma could think of was the vampires banging upon the smokehouse door in another wood. Could this be one of them, trying to gain admittance by trickery? They were a clever lot.

Michaela hesitated, studying Paloma closely, then nodded. "All right, all right . . . I am coming," she hollered toward the barred door. It was small and round and she only cracked it ever so slightly, while from the shadows, Paloma caught a glimpse of a middle-age balding man dressed in black, holding a lantern high in one hand, and an antiquated musket in the other.

"What do ya' think you're doin'?" the sexton said. "Ya' can't just park here without so much as a by-your-leave. This is holy ground."

Michaela gave a lurch and scowled at the man. "What harm?" she snapped at him, clearly insulted. "None here is apt to complain."

The sexton began to bristle, and Paloma stepped out of the shadows, laying a firm hand upon the old woman's arm. "Good sir," she said. "We are just two women alone. We have become separated from our caravan, and fear being lost further in the dark. What harm to let us stay here until dawn? We are not revelers. We disturb no one."

"It ain't fittin', Gypsies campin' in the kirkyard," the sexton said. "Let one in and you'll have the lot. Why, what would the town folk say? No'm, you've got ta go. This ain't no Tinkers' camp, now—git!"

"My good man," Paloma said in her sweetest voice, "Do you hear that howling?"

"I ain't deaf—"

"Those are dangerous creatures abroad in that wood—"

"How do I know you ain't just as dangerous?" the sexton interrupted her.

"I suppose you don't," Paloma said, ". . . but if I were you, I would not want two helpless women on my conscience. We just heard gunshots in that copse. Please, sir, we mean harm to no one. Let us stay until the sun rises. Then we will be gone to trouble you no more."

The sexton shook his head. "I cannot," he said, jutting his chin. "The rector give me orders ta chase ya', and you've got ta go. There ain't no place for thievin' Gypsies in the kirkyard. Ya' can camp on the fells, now—*git*, I say!"

He aimed the musket then, and Paloma hesitated. The warning voice was still fresh in her mind: *Do not leave the kirkyard.* But what choice did she have, looking down the barrel of an obsolete musket that probably hadn't been cleaned in years?

"Very well," she said. "Upon your own head be it when we are found savaged by those creatures." She gestured toward the wood behind. "Let me collect the horses." The sexton grunted, and turned to go, but Paloma called him back. "The least you could do is stand by with that musket while I fetch them," she said. "I am not liking the sound of that howling." She couldn't help but recall the voice also warning her not to leave the wagon.

The sexton heaved an exasperated sigh. "Be quick about it, then," he said.

Alert for more mind-speak, Paloma motioned Michaela to stay inside, while she fetched the horses at the edge of the kirkyard and brought them back to the wagon. All was still. Could she have imagined the voice in her head? Was it a cruel trick of her imagination? It had seemed so real. Now, but for the mournful howl of the wolves, there was no sound, and she quickly brought the horses back and began hitching Somnus to the wagon.

"Where's your menfolk?" the sexton said, holding the lantern high while she fumbled with the tack. Her hands felt like two paddles, and hurrying only made matters worse. Somnus was no help, either. Shying and complaining, he seemed ill at ease at the prospect of being hitched up the wagon again. She had thought of hitching up the other horse, but dismissed the idea out of hand. If they needed to escape whatever entities lurked in those woods, the phantom horse would be the best choice.

"I have told you," she said, ". . . we have become separated from the others."

"Why two horses?" the sexton queried. "Ya' only need one ta pull the wagon."

"Two saves us unhitching the one each time we need to go where wagons cannot travel," Michaela barked from inside. "With two, you always have a fresh horse."

Paloma gave a lurch. She'd almost forgotten the old woman's presence. "What is it to you how many horses we travel with?" she snapped at the man.

"Stand back! You are in the way, and you are frightening these animals. They are not fond of firearms. We are a peaceful people."

"Ummm," the sexton grunted, strolling back apace. "Hurry up, then. I ain't got all night."

"You needn't stay," Paloma said. "I gave my word, and I shall keep it."

"Thank ye', but I'll see ya' gone and lock the gate behind ya', don't want none o' them wild dogs in here diggin' up the graves."

Paloma spun around to face him, her hands braced on her hips. "You know those aren't dogs," she said, "—and you know why we chose sanctuary here on sacred ground. God forgive you for turning us out. You'll have no good luck for it!"

The sexton strung the lantern on the musket barrel and crossed himself. "I don't know nothin' but that you're trespassin'," he said in a huff. "You're hitched, now git!"

Paloma climbed up on the wagon seat and clicked her tongue at Somnus. "Walk on," she said to the horse, meanwhile coming closer to the sexton than the man deemed safe.

He jumped back, almost tripping over a headstone. "Here!" he barked. "There's no call ta run me down."

"Stand back then!" Paloma warned.

"Little Gypsy snippity-snip," the sexton mumbled.

"Good night, sir," Paloma said. "Sleep well . . . if you can."

"Did you just curse me?" the man shrilled, crossing himself again as the wagon rumbled past him. "You take it back!"

"I do not have to curse you," Paloma called over her shoulder. "You curse yourself, turning us out—two women alone—into danger. Good night, Mr. Smythe."

Michaela's wicked cackle from inside the wagon

sat Paloma upright. "You gave him a mouthful," she tittered. "I'd forgotten your tongue could cut like a guillotine."

Paloma snorted. "For all the good it did me," she said. "Watch out the back window. See if he chains the gate shut. If he doesn't, we might be able to sneak back into the kirkyard once he retires. He cannot stand out here on guard all the night long." Michaela might be wizened with age and crippled with rheumatism, but she still possessed a pair of eyes as sharp as any crow's.

The sway of the wagon missed its rhythm as the old woman waddled to the back of it. There was silence, then she made her way back to her bench beside the door and flopped down again with a grunt. Having been awakened so rudely from a sound sleep had clearly vexed her.

"Well?" Paloma prompted.

"He has fixed the chain," Michaela said on as sigh. "Now what do we do? We cannot stray too far from the kirkyard. Milosh will return in need of the herbs."

"I did not want to leave the kirkyard at all," Paloma said. "I heard a voice . . . in my head. Some vampires have the power of mind-speak. I have not tried it before, but I did earlier, and a voice warned against leaving the kirkyard—against even leaving the wagon. I do not know if I imagined it . . . or if the voice was real."

"The Brotherhood?"

"I do not know. I hear the wolves howling in the wood, but I do not know if they are Brotherhood, either. Milosh said they would watch over us . . . I do not know, Michaela, I just do not know."

Paloma was silent apace. There were no wolves howling on the open fells, only in the wood. Were they Brotherhood? Dared she chance it? In the open, they would be a sitting target, despite the stubborn mist that would not dissipate, but in the wood . . .

Paloma opened her mind to the Brotherhood, this time trying to speak herself. Again and again she tried, but there was no reply. Had they left the wood? Was that why the voice was so adamant that she not leave the kirkyard, where she would be safe from Sebastian whether they were on guard or not? Or was it just vampire glamour? Whatever the cause, the voice was silent now, and Somnus was no help. She tried giving him his head, and he balked. Was neither option safe? There was no way to tell, and after much deliberation, she made a choice.

"We go into the wood," she said, "—close enough to the kirkyard that Milosh will be able to find us if . . . *when* he returns." She had to believe he would come. Despite the cryptic good-bye, she had to believe he would.

"What of the wolves?" Michaela said.

"We shall have to take the chance. It would be suicide to camp—two women alone—on the open fells. We would be a sitting target. Remember . . . some of the undead know Milosh's blood has spared me the hunger. It is reasonable to assume some who know have followed us in hopes that doing the same to me will save them also."

"None have answered your mind-speak?"

"No," Paloma said. "That could be because they have gone to protect him, and that is why I heard the voice before."

"If that is so, what wolves are those howling in the wood?" Michaela murmured.

"I do not know," Paloma said, turning the horse and entering the copse, ". . . but we shall soon find out. You were not with me in the smokehouse. I cannot conscience camping in the open."

The wagon lumbered over the uneven forest floor, pitching back and forth between the trees. They hadn't gone far when rustling in the branches overhead made more of a racket than the creaking of the wagon. The undergrowth was thick and unkempt there. Though they hadn't traveled too deeply in, the kirkyard was no longer visible. Acting upon instinct, Paloma reined in, leaped down and unhitched the stallion.

"What do you do?" Michaela said, poking her head out through the wagon door.

"I am setting Somnus loose," Paloma explained. "He cannot fight vampires off hitched to the wagon. He will dash it to bits! Have no fear. He will not stray."

"What of the other horse?"

"I will tether him among the trees. We may lose him, Michaela."

"Why? What do you see? You are scaring me now!"

"It is not what I see, it is what I feel . . . and hear . . . what my senses tell me. They are heightened now. There are bats in the treetops. I hear them—I smell them."

"*Sebastian?*" Michaela shrilled.

"Shhhh!" Paloma warned. "I do not know, but I will not take any chances. Quickly lock all the windows and latch the shutters. I will bar the door once I tether the other horse."

"Hurry, Paloma!"

Securing the horse between two slender oaks, Paloma kept a close eye upon the treetops. No, she hadn't been mistaken. Bats! Dozens of them troubled the uppermost branches. She barely made the wagon when they sawed through the trees, soaring toward it. She killed one, slamming the wagon door upon it as she dove inside, extracting a shriek from Michaela.

Paloma's hands were shaking as she bolted the

door shut. The bats had covered the wagon. She could hear their hideous squeaking, and wings flapping against it. That was not all she heard. The howling! Wolves! The ground beneath the wagon shuddered with their number descending upon it. The vibration riddled the soles of her boots; the whole wagon trembled with it.

Sinking down beside Michaela on the edge of her bunk, Paloma threw her arms around the whimpering woman. "Shhhh," she cautioned. Outside, the snarling, howling wolves slammed into the wagon. Some were milling about on the rounded roof. Others seemed to be battling the bats for possession of the door. Still others tried to climb up the curved sides, to no avail. The sound their sharp claws made scraping the painted wood sent shivers walking down Paloma's spine.

The phantom stallion's high-pitched whistle pierced the silence in concert with agonized shrieks from the other horse she'd tethered among the trees. Michaela would not be consoled, nor could Paloma persuade her to be still.

"What is happening out there?" Michaela sobbed, clapping both hands over her ears. "The wolves . . . what do they do? They will tip the wagon over! Feel how it lurches! Are they fighting off the bats?"

Paloma tightened her grip on her one-time nurse and mentor. "N-no," she said, her voice quavering. "These are not Brotherhood. . . ."

CHAPTER TWENTY

The white wolf met with no resistance in the forest.
The howl of wolves grew more and more distant the
closer he came to the tor. He reached it in the wee
hours before first light, that darkest hour before the
dawn breeze breathed its breath upon the land. All
was still—too still. If the Brotherhood was traveling
with him unseen in the lush, verdant undergrowth,
they made no move to make their presence known.

Well hidden among the trees, Milosh called upon
his wolf's special gifts to survey the land. He needed
to get closer if he were to see where Sebastian rested
during the day. The trouble was, the tor offered precious little in the way of shelter where wolf or man
could watch unseen. The stables were an option if he
could get close enough, but he would have to climb
the tor in the open to reach them. Another option
would be a little stand of dwarf pines behind the pad-
dock. Both would afford a clear view of the ruins. If
he was going to scale the tor, it must be now, when
the earth was cast in deepest darkness in the absence

of the moon that had long since disappeared from the sky. Without hesitation, the white wolf bounded through the scrub at the edge of the wood and loped up the steep, slippery incline to the summit.

Dismissing the stables out of hand as a likely place to wait, he moved past to the pines, standing like little old men, whose backs were bent and broken by the cruel north wind with nothing to protect them from the gales. Their skeletal arms in many cases swept the ground, and great humps marred their tortured trunks. It was a dreary, dismal place, made drearier by the ruins alongside, but it offered the best and safest vantage, and he settled down well hidden on a patch of cool moss to wait.

The eerie stillness still prevailed. It was an Otherworldly silence possessed of a strange heartbeat, or was that his heart thumping in his barrel chest? All at once, there was another sound. He wasn't alone. His sharp wolf's eyes searched the dwarf pines first; they were vacant of bats. Then his gaze came around to the thick undergrowth and swept it wide. He saw the panther first, sleek and black and beautiful, gliding among the trees. He recognized her at once, Cassandra Hyde-White. It could be no other. From deeper in, two silver gray masked wolves joined the cat. The white wolf's heart skipped a beat. He thrilled at the sight. It was Cassandra's husband Jon, and their son Joss.

Milosh's wolf howled into the darkness; relief and trepidation fueled the sound. Relief that they had not been harmed in the fire, and fear that they had come to do as he had taught them, destroy *vampir* infected with the hunger . . . *vampir* like he had become.

The wolf that Milosh recognized as Jon Hyde-White stepped forward. *Old friend, has the time come?* it spoke with its mind.

The white wolf's glance flashed among them. The panther's eyes were misted with tears; sorrow glazed those of the other two. They had come for him to do what he had taught them to do. Yes, the hunter had become the hunted. If he must be destroyed it was only fitting that it be done by . . . a friend.

Is that why you have come, my friends? he said.

We have come to do what the Brotherhood cannot bring themselves to do if needs must, Milosh, Jon's voice spoke to him.

Where are the Brotherhood? Milosh queried.

They have left this up to us, Cassandra said.

The other gray wolf pranced in place. *Father . . . I cannot,* Joss Hyde-White said. *There must be another way. . . .*

Young whelp, Milosh spoke up, *your father is right. I am no different than the others. If my time has come, better that it be at your hands than another's.* He was thinking of Paloma then. The hunger had risen in him—a hunger only she could slake with her blood . . . with her love. A high-pitched whine escaped him then, and the fangs descended at the mere thought of her. The separation of death would be the only way to protect her from him if all else failed.

I cannot bear this! Cassandra said, her panther bolting back into the wood.

Go after your mother, Jon charged the other.

Milosh's white wolf howled again, a plaintive sound trailing off into the night. *I ask only that it not be in wolf form,* he said. *Let me go to my death like a man. . . .*

Come, said Jon. *I have clothes for you in the stables.*

They must have anticipated this. How long had they been watching him? How many nights had they followed him—seen him in thrall to the hunger, the hunger he had defeated four centuries ago only to have it come back upon him tenfold at the hands of the little Gypsy thief who had bewitched him? Had they been watching all along, from the very first night? Thinking back, Milosh recalled having felt as if he was being watched on more than one occasion, but he'd shrugged the feeling off as being the Brotherhood, which the Hyde-Whites were, of course. But why hadn't he picked them out among the masses? He should have done, they were the closest to him. Had the madness taken him that far into deep darkness? If it had, the time indeed had come to put him out of his misery.

As promised, clothes were waiting in the loft. Surging into human form, Milosh leapt up and tugged on top boots, breeches, shirt, and cloak. Leaping down again, an effortless feat for him in any form, he faced Jon Hyde-White, standing feet apart, his broad shoulders enhanced by a multi-caped greatcoat, looking not a day older than he had been when they first met over sixty years ago. The shock of dark wavy hair, the penetrating eyes, the handsome face all angles and planes, were just as time had etched them in Milosh's memory. Was he facing his murderer? In any other circumstances he would have rushed to embrace him—and Cassandra, who had entered the stables with their handsome son Milosh had also mentored, Joss Hyde-White, both likewise dressed and unchanged in their human incarnation. Now, all three kept their distance. What a shock it was to see them all together, unchanged and youthful still, though he knew it would be thus.

"Young whelp, how does your beloved Cora fare?" Milosh said, standing his ground.

"She fares well," Joss said. "The Brotherhood keeps her . . . she is one of us . . . but I wanted to spare her this. She holds you too dear."

Milosh nodded. "I take it that you are immune to the hunger as we hoped?" he said, ". . . and she . . ."

". . . is as I am, *vampir*, but spared the blood hunger," Joss Hyde-White concluded for him.

"Ahhhh, it is good, then," Milosh said. His relief was genuine. He had long wondered about how it had turned out for Joss and Cora. It was a comfort that those from his past that he loved most in the world enjoyed the life he had envisioned for them—risked his life to secure for them. Yes. It was good. His only regret . . . that he had not done more for Paloma, whom he could no longer deny that he loved—not even to himself. There wasn't time; his had run out, and she was in no wise ready to stand against such as Sebastian.

"What caused this great devastation?" Milosh said, sweeping his arm wide toward the ruins. "It broke my heart to see Whitebriar Abbey thus."

"We set the fire," Jon said. "We were under siege. It was the only way to get them out of the Abbey. It was time for us to leave, and we could not conscience giving Sebastian and his ilk our home. We hoped to incinerate Sebastian in the flames, but he escaped, though not all of his minions were as fortunate."

"Ahhh," Milosh returned. "It makes sense now. None in the village could tell me how the fire started. I should have guessed."

"Can you still stand the light of day?" Jon asked him, changing the subject abruptly. Where was the Jon of old? Why could he not meet his eyes?

Milosh nodded. "How long have you been . . . tracking me?"

"The Brotherhood alerted us that you had . . . reverted back to the hunger in such a way . . . that another life had been put to the hazard . . . and that you had requested death before she came to harm at your hands. We had no choice, Milosh, but you can rest assured that your lady will be well cared for, just as we care for all the infected who can be saved from the stake and decapitation."

"You know how I came to be in this condition?" Milosh queried.

"We do."

"And you will not fault her—punish her?"

"No," Jon said around a tremor, "we cannot fault her for that over which she had no control."

Cassandra Hyde-White broke free of her son's grip and rushed into Milosh's arms. "I cannot bear it!" she sobbed. "I *cannot!*"

"Get back from him, Cassandra!" Jon thundered, rushing forward. Grabbing her arm, he attempted to pull her away from Milosh to no avail. "He is not what he once was," he reasoned with her. "He is not the Milosh we knew. Can you not see that? Look at him—*look!* Look at his eyes; they glow like two coals. See his skin, see the veins?"

Milosh put her from him gently but firmly. Searching her tears, his own eyes misted. "No, Cassandra," he said. "Jon is right. Though I am still who I was, I am not *what* I was. I am a danger to us all now."

"I saved you once . . ." she sobbed.

"But you cannot save me now," he murmured, "—not from this."

Milosh glanced about the stable. He was resigned to his fate. It was the only sensible solution, but since he had nothing to lose he would not be cheated of his last attempt to defeat Sebastian, not to mention Michaela's herbal draught that might just reverse the situation when the blood moon rose.

"You cannot escape," Jon said, his voice quavering. "The Brotherhood surrounds these fells. Let it go, Milosh. You have lived long and earned your peace.

Look at yourself! Sooner or later you will become the instrument of her death. Is that what you want? You know this is what must be."

"I do not dispute the decision of the Brotherhood," Milosh said guardedly, "only the timing. Let me have one last shot at Sebastian, which is why I am come here now . . . to find his resting place. He cannot be taken but by surprise, and by a full-fledged vampire—a slave to the bloodlust, with powers undiminished by the blood moon rite—such as I have now again become. The very thing that has spared me has spared him, also. I am convinced of it, Jon, elsewise I would have killed him centuries ago. And let me try the herbal draught one last time to see if I can reverse this madness. If I cannot, I will submit willingly. You have my word."

"Let him try. My God, Jon, let him try!" Cassandra begged.

Jon was about to reply, when the shrill whistle of a frenzied horse pierced the predawn silence, and Somnus burst through the stable doors lathered to a frazzling. His eyes were wild and glaring with a red-rimmed iridescent gleam; his head was held high, and he was tossing his long silky mane about a neck and withers overspread with saliva and foam. It clung to his rippling flesh. Visible breath puffed from his flared nostrils. Once he cleared the stable threshold, he reared back on his hind legs, loosing another ear-piercing shriek.

Milosh seized the reins and leaped upon the crazed stallion's back. "You can come, or you can stay," he gritted. "Somnus guards my lady. There is grave press to bring him like this."

"I-is that horse a . . . a . . ." Cassandra stammered.

". . . *vampir*? Yes," Milosh said, finishing the sentence that she could not.

"Wait!" Jon Hyde-White barked, seizing the horse's bridle. "It will soon be light. The vampires will retreat at dawn whether they can bear the light of day or not; the lethargy will render them impotent. I needn't tell you that. The sun will rise before you reach her. Let the Brotherhood handle it."

Milosh stared down into the eyes of a man he thought he knew but knew no longer. Could this unfeeling creature arresting his horse be the same Jon Hyde-White he'd saved sixty years ago? Was he so anxious to end his existence that he would sacrifice Paloma as well?

His eyes flashed toward Cassandra, who seemed to be thinking the same thoughts. Judging from Joss's stricken expression, he seemed likewise incredulous; Milosh was too incensed to tell. He heard nothing but the phantom stallion's frantic complaints. When his gaze came back to that of Jon Hyde-White, his Gypsy eyes had narrowed to slits, and he saw all three through a bloodred veil, like liquid fire. It was possessed of a shuddering pulse beat, hammering a steady rhythm in his brain.

"If the Brotherhood could handle it, Somnus would not be here," he seethed, jerking the bridle out of Jon's hands. "Are you so anxious to slake your lust for my head that you would extend the sentence to include an innocent?"

"If, as you say, the Brotherhood could not handle it, she is dead already . . . or soon will be, and you will join her."

"Jon . . . *please*," Cassandra pleaded. "How far can he go? He cannot escape." The horse reared, forefeet pawing the misty air with little regard for Jon in the way, and bolted forward. Milosh cast misty eyes toward Cassandra, and caught a tremor in her stricken eyes that mirrored her mind-speak: *My God, Milosh, just go!* she pleaded.

"If you would be of use," Milosh called over his shoulder as the horse streaked over the threshold, ". . . see if you can do what I came here to do— discover Sebastian's hiding place. He dies before another sun sets, and at my hands. Then—and only then will I let you take my head, old *friend!*"

CHAPTER TWENTY-ONE

Wolves were still milling about Michaela's wagon when Milosh reached it. Whether they were Brotherhood or *vampir* didn't matter. He charged through the thicket upon the phantom horse like a knight on his destrier engaged in a pitched battle, just as the ghost-gray ribbons of misty light heralded the dawn.

Forefeet flying, Somnus trampled wolf after wolf until the frost-glazed ground ran red with their blood. Milosh did not guide him. Given his head, the relentless horse spun and heaved and bucked and reared, choosing his targets until those creatures that were not trampled to death had fled. Milosh did not waste time destroying the fallen; the sunrise would take care of that. Those that had fled he took to be Brotherhood, and gave them no notice. Calling Paloma at the top of his voice, he leaped off the stallion's back and ran toward the wagon. Only then did he realize how scarred it was—the wood pitted and streaked with blood. All but one of the windows were broken, their curtains shredded to rags, and several of the inside shutters were off their hinges.

Scarcely noticing Somnus prancing crazily around the wagon, stirring the mist with his feathered feet, or heeding the animal's ear-piercing shrieks, Milosh leaped up upon the wagon and burst through the door. With Paloma's name half-uttered, he scanned the bleak interior with his extraordinary vision. Everything was in disarray. Despite the open windows, it stank of urine. Rumpled bedding, pots and basins, broken jars leaking the precious herbs, sullied with what remained of their foodstuffs, littered the floor in a hopeless mess that rendered them useless. There was no sign of Paloma or Michaela. The wagon was empty.

Bursting back outside, Milosh called Paloma's name again. Then he heard it—soft sobs coming from underneath the wagon. Dropping to his knees, he looked beneath it. Paloma crouched there, clutching one of the flasks of holy water in her hands. The other flasks were discarded beside her. She was bent over, nearly to the ground, for the wagon was low by Travelers'-wagon standards. She must have barely had room to crawl beneath it, and hardly enough room to move once she did.

"Paloma, come to me," he said, reaching his arm toward her. There wasn't enough room for him to slip under as she had, owing to the uneven ground. She skittered away from the hand that groped for her. "Paloma! It is I . . . Milosh. Are you all right? Come out from under there!"

A troop of involuntary screams poured from her and she clawed at his hand, sloshing some of the holy water on it. She was hysterical. Whatever she had suffered had taken its toll upon her. He couldn't assess what that was until he could examine her himself.

When he spoke again, his voice was soft and mesmerizing, a gift he'd used many times in the past.

"Paloma . . . the sun has risen," he said. "You are safe now, little dove," for she did seem like a wounded bird, crouching there in the matted grass white with hoarfrost, "—even from me."

Still, only her sobs replied.

"Where is Michaela?" he said. "Paloma, we cannot stay here. We must find her and go now, before they regroup and come for us. Come out of there! If you do not, I will have to tip the wagon over, and I am not at my most powerful."

Still no answer came, only her mournful sobs. They became shrill when he retracted his hand and scrambled to his feet. Extraordinary strength was one of his gifts, as he liked to call his vampire attributes, and he braced his back against the side of the wagon and heaved as hard as he could, but it was no use. With the dawn came the lethargy that diluted his strength and the powers with it and, while he did manage to raise the heavy wheels off the ground, he couldn't upend the wagon.

Catching Somnus as he pranced past, Milosh seized the horse's reins. Taking a coil of rope from his saddlebag, he tied it to the right front wheel and threw it over the top of the wagon. Then, mounting the horse, he rode him around to the opposite side, picked up the end of the rope dangling down and tied it to the pommel of the saddle.

"Back, Somnus!" he cried, spurring him deeply.

The horse bolted backward, straining against the tether, and the wagon groaned, its old wood snapping. After several tries, the left front wheel split apart with a deafening crack, shifting the weight of the wagon. It tipped over and crashed to earth on its side.

Bereft of her shelter, Paloma scrambled to her feet

and ran blindly into the wood, her screams living after
her. Slip-sliding on the frost-covered mulch, she fell
and got to her feet again twice before Milosh reached
her, slid off the horse, and seized her in his arms.
Paloma screamed. Her fangs had descended. Her
beautiful doe-like eyes were staring into his own, but
seemed not to see. Kneeling beside her, Milosh shook
her roughly. She was as rigid as steel against him, all
but her flailing arms, and her tiny, white-knuckled fists
pummeling him about the head and shoulders. He
seized her upper arms and shook her again.

"Paloma, stop!" he gritted, dodging a blow to his
temple. "You are safe now . . . don't you know me?
Paloma!"

All at once, she seemed to stop breathing. A tremor
of recognition flashed in her eyes, and she collapsed
sobbing against his chest, her hands fisted now in the
soft wool of his mantle.

Milosh tilted her head back and smoothed her tangled coppery mane from her face, brushing away some
of the dead leaves it had collected. Her flushed skin
was streaked with dirt and tear tracks, her eyes red and
swollen. To his great relief, her fangs were receding.

Malosh heaved a ragged sigh. "You haven't been
bitten?" he said, his breath suspended until she shook
her head that she had not been. He crushed her close.
"Thank God!" he murmured. "Where is Michaela?"

"I . . . I don't . . . know," she said through spastic
tremors. "W-we were together when we left the
wagon. . . . She pushed me underneath it, but she
couldn't follow . . . the space wasn't large enough for
her to fit through. . . . She told me to stay where I was,
and she ran into the wood. . . . She never came
back. . . ."

"Why did you leave the wagon, Paloma? You would
have stood a better chance inside."

Paloma gave a lurch. "They swarmed all over it!" she cried, "—dozens of them, wolves, *bats*, swarms of bats pecking—gnawing at the wood ... at the windows.... Wolves were clawing at the shutters ... tearing at them with their fangs and claws, running over the roof.... They came in waves. They were not Brotherhood, those that came first, they were *vampir* from the smokehouse ... the ones who thought my blood could save them ... they ... they ..."

"Shhhh," Milosh soothed, clasping her against him. "Shhh, little dove, they are gone now."

"But they will return, Milosh, they will return!"

Milosh soothed her with gentle hands. Her heart was hammering against his chest, vibrating through the shirt and woolen mantle. Her whole body trembled against him, and her teeth were chattering with the chills of shock. He stripped off the cloak and wrapped it around her.

"When t-the windows broke, and they began attacking the shutters until one fell off its hinges, we dared not stay in the wagon any longer. Then the other wolves came, the B-Brotherhood I think ... it must have been, and Somnus broke free of his tether and joined the battle, it was chaos ... and then Somnus galloped off. He *left* us!"

"He came after me, Paloma. I came as quickly as I could. What happened after he left you here? I am sorry, I know the memory is painful, but I need to know."

"He no sooner ran off when one of the shutters gave altogether," she said. "They were getting in! I grabbed the vials of holy water, and M-Michaela shoved me out first, and pushed me under the wagon, but she couldn't follow ... her girth ... she couldn't ... couldn't ..."

"My poor little dove," Milosh murmured against her hair. "Hush now, we will find her."

"The wolves . . . they tried to dig their way under the wagon. I splashed them with the holy water . . . then the bats tried to reach me, and I splashed them, too. They fled, but others came . . . so many others. The holy water is gone . . . I used it all. What will we do for the draught?"

Should he tell her the truth, that there would be no draught, that the herbs were strewn over the wagon floor, sullied with wolf and bat urine and what remained of the foodstuffs they had purchased at the market—corrupted beyond salvaging? Should he tell her that the draught was the least of their trouble? That he, the hunter, had now become the hunted, and that the beloved friends he'd come to call upon had now become the ones who would destroy him, and her, if he failed her—that they stalked him even now. He owed her truth, but not the whole truth all at once, at least not yet, not while she teetered on the cutting edge of madness. Her body was quaking, her doe eyes snapping in all directions as if she expected wolves to appear at any moment.

"The herbs are lost," he said, ignoring her gasp. It was no use. He may as well prepare her. She would know it anyway the minute she looked inside the wagon. "The crocks are broken and all their contents fouled by the creatures. It will have to wait."

"But the moon will be full *tonight!*" Paloma cried. "The eclipse will turn it to blood when it rises. There will not be another eclipse for years. Milosh, you cannot wait years as you are . . . as *we* are . . . you *cannot!* We will barely make moonrise as it is. . . ."

Milosh hesitated, cupping her face in his hand. "You must listen to me now, Paloma," he said, searching deep into her eyes. "We cannot remain here. It is no longer safe—"

"But the Brotherhood!" she interrupted him. "They will protect us."

Milosh shook his head. "No, Paloma, they will not. They are no longer with us. They have marked me for death."

"How can that be," Paloma shrilled. "You saved them—spared them the bloodlust. You are not undead! How have they turned against you . . . why?"

"There isn't time to tell it now. Suffice it to say it is fact. I have just driven them off, but you are right, they will return at dusk with the rest, more than likely so will Sebastian. They hunt me, each to his own purpose, and I am faced with a decision."

"What kind of decision?"

"Before I tell you, I need to warn you . . . do not answer too quickly."

Paloma stared. It was all he could do to meet those misty eyes.

"Thus far, only I am the hunted," he said. "Once the Brotherhood sees that you are immune to the bloodlust, you will be welcomed into the fold, and they will protect you. If I leave you, you will have a chance. But I fear that you are too new to the infection to decide wisely. Let down your guard and you will become as I am now—"

Paloma tossed her coppery mane and stiffened in his arms. "I've managed thus far quite well enough, I should think," she snapped, "—fending off a pack of vampire wolves and a swarm of ravenous bats single-handed."

Milosh took her upper arms in firm hands. "I asked you not to speak quickly," he reminded her. "Let me finish. There isn't much time." She lowered her eyes, and he went on quickly. "I am not denying that you did well, and I will hold that in my heart as a comfort if you should decide . . . to leave me—"

"*Leave you?*" she cried.

"Shhhhh," he warned her. "I am not sure of much, but I am positive we are not alone in these woods. Please let me finish."

"I do not want to hear this!"

"Aye, I know, but you will—you must! Now be still and let me speak!" He had to tell it now, while he had the courage, while his lethargy negated the powers that would harm her. "If I let you go now . . . while you are still immune to the bloodlust, they will embrace you into the Brotherhood. If I keep you, more than likely they will kill you also. I am the greater danger to you now, Paloma. Once the sun sets the hunger will command me and I will take you—drain you dry of your blood. I will not be able to stop myself, and you will not be able to prevent me. You were right, I am not undead, but losing my immunity to the bloodlust after four centuries has greatly altered me; *I* do not even know to what degree, only that I have never seen the like before. The hunger grows more insatiable with each sunset. It is as if I am paying tenfold for each day I lived immune. It is only a matter of time. . . ."

Paloma laid a finger across his lips. It was cool, and he closed his eyes, for it soothed the fever in his blood. He uttered a soft moan in spite of himself.

"There is no decision," she murmured. "I will not leave you. It is my fault that you have become . . . what you are. I will never leave you . . . as you tried to leave me."

"For your own good!" he countered. "I still believe it would have been best that you think me dead. How will you fare when I am? How will you stand to watch it? Because you will, Paloma. They will finish me before your very eyes. I have taught them well. . . ."

"I will never leave you," she pronounced.

Milosh looked her long and hard in the eyes, then nodded. There was no use in arguing, and at least he might be able to keep her safe from the others until the end, and mentor her as best he could until death separated them.

"Then you must do exactly as I say—exactly, Paloma." He had told her all she needed to know at present, but he didn't reveal that it was the Hyde-Whites who had marked him for death and were stalking him. Milosh didn't know if his omission was a mistake. All he did know was that they had to survive the day and another night in the area if he were to destroy Sebastian. Then, if he could manage that, perhaps they might be able to escape the fate looming over him like a pall. "We must not linger here," he went on. "We are too isolated. We need to be among the throngs at the market—anywhere where there are many people. They will not venture into crowds." He stood and pulled her to her feet alongside him. "Come. Let us see how much damage I did to the wheel tipping the wagon over. If it is not too badly broken, we shall use it; if it is beyond repair we have the horses."

"What of Michaela?"

"We shall search for her," Milosh said, grabbing Somnus's reins where he grazed as they passed by. "You know as well as I the loyalty of that good woman. If she does not come it is because she cannot come, Paloma. You must prepare yourself for the possibility that she might not be able. The carnage back there is horrendous. How you have come through it all unscathed is due only to Michaela's . . . quick thinking." What he almost said was what he was thinking: *due to*

Michaela's sacrifice, for that is what he truly believed had happened. He held his peace. Keeping her in the close custody of his arm, he led her back toward the wagon. "Come, we must away while the daylight abets us, and it is too short-lived to waste a moment. If all goes well, before the sun sets we will be far away from these accursed North Country fells."

CHAPTER TWENTY-TWO

Milosh and Paloma rode to market. The wagon wheel was too badly damaged. It wanted a wheelwright, and even if they could find one he would have to come to the site. That would take too long, and the other damage was too severe to be repaired before sunset. Besides, they could make better time on horseback.

Though they searched until noon, there was no sign of Michaela. Milosh didn't believe there would be, but Paloma was beside herself over the woman's disappearance, and he humored her as long as he dared. They were not alone in the wood. He sensed the Brotherhood watching from a discreet distance, well hidden in the copse. Somnus sensed them, too. That was obvious in the way he sidled, pranced, and snorted, baring ferocious teeth, while puffing visible breath from flared nostrils. His eyes glowed with iridescent fire, flashing every which way as they progressed. Judging from Paloma's description of the melee, Milosh wasn't surprised that the wolves kept their distance. They may not fear him, but they evidently wanted no truck with the black devil stallion they'd seen in action.

Having transformed from wolf to man in borrowed clothing, Milosh had no coin, neither did Paloma. What little Michaela had put by from her fortune-telling was scattered over the wagon floor. They gathered what they could find, bundled away what clothing could be salvaged and Michaela's tarot cards, and reached the market just as a weak sun broke through the clouds at midday.

They were too conspicuous on horseback mixing with the crowd, and though it was risky, Milosh left the horses at the village livery. Somnus seemed to understand his role in the event. The minute they reached the market, all trace of his vampire nature vanished. There was nothing Milosh could do about the horse's extraordinary Gypsy bloodline, which made him an outstanding specimen of superior breeding from his regal head and neck to the thick, feathery fringe shuddering about his hooves. The sight of him turned heads, and Milosh didn't draw an easy breath until the hulking mass of rippling horseflesh was out of sight at the livery.

Paloma sat at a little vacant table at the edge of the market, close enough to be part of the throngs, her tarot cards fanned out around her. She began shuffling some she'd held in reserve and laid them out facedown in front of her in the shape of a cross. Looking on, Milosh smiled. She was attracting a crowd. She wasn't alone. She would be safe, and he drew a ragged breath and blended into the milling masses to replenish the herbs and stores ruined in the wagon, replace the killing tools lost in the ruins, and collect the rest of the supplies they would need for a lengthy journey.

* * *

Paloma read one patron's cards after another. A steady stream visited her little corner of the market. Adept at her craft, having learned from Michaela at a young age, she knew just how much to reveal, and how much to let her subjects reveal. She craned her neck from time to time in search of Milosh. She was also seeking Michaela, hoping she was milling about in the crowd. If they didn't find her soon, they would have to leave without her, and Paloma's heart was heavy at the prospect.

The stream of patrons eager to have their fortunes told started to thin to a trickle after a while. Soon Milosh would come for her. They must away before long if they were to travel a good distance from the area before dark. That was the plan. Though destroying Sebastian was his passion, Milosh had confided that he had no doubt the vampire would follow him to the ends of the earth if needs must to finish their joust with death. Paloma knew there was more to his anxiousness to flee than the obvious. There was something he wasn't telling her, and he had closed his mind to her queries in that regard.

Thinking she was finished for the day, Paloma began collecting the tarot cards, when something cast a shadow across her table, and she looked up to see a well-dressed woman who appeared to be in her mid-twenties, wearing a bottle-green wool twill frock that accentuated her waspish waist and ample bosom. A shock of short-cropped hair that seemed as if it had been painted by the sun peeked out from underneath the hood of her indigo cloak. She smiled, and set tuppence down on the table with a dainty, half-gloved hand.

"Have you time for one more?" the woman said.

Paloma gazed up into large brown eyes, soulful and sad, that did not mirror the smile upon her lips.

The scent of meadowsweet mingled with lilies of the valley wafted from the woman on a breeze that ruffled her golden ringlets. Where did she ever find such blooms on the cusp of December?

Paloma tucked the tuppence into the leather pocket she wore on a cord about her waist and nodded, handing her the cards. "Shuffle them, cut them thrice, put them back together and return them to me," she said.

Paloma sat patiently while the woman did as she bade her and handed the cards back, then she laid out the cards in cross formation. One in the center, one crossing it, one above it, one below, then one on either side. She then placed four more cards to the right of the cross from bottom to top and set the rest aside.

"The Celtic cross," Paloma said. "It tells your past, present, and future." She snaked the center card out from under the one that crossed it and turned it over. "Justice," she said. "This card represents you, my lady. You are in a position to mete out justice to those around you." She turned the crossed card over. "The lovers," she said. "They are your obstacle. They hinder your progress. . . ."

"Will I overcome this obstacle?" the woman said.

Paloma shrugged. "We shall see," she said, turning over the card at the top. "The seven of rods," she said, ". . . the card of the underdog. . . . Your goal is to see him succeed."

"It is a man?"

Paloma nodded. "A man, yes, of many burdens. . . . You seek to lift those burdens."

"Will I succeed?" the woman said.

"Patience, my lady," Paloma said. "We shall turn another card and see. . . ." She turned the fourth card over. "This one may tell us something," she said. "It is the card of your past . . . your distant past . . . the tower," she said, uncovering the picture of a lightning-struck brick column, ". . . the card of complete change—ultimate transformation. You have suffered a life-altering phenomenon, but all that is behind you. Whatever that was affects you still." She turned the bottom card over. "Ah! Here we have your recent past, my lady," she said. "The seven of swords. The figure flees with five swords, leaving two behind. His efforts will be partly successful. You risk much, my lady, but I see that has been much the case with you for some time."

"Partial success, you say? Can you not see the outcome?"

Paloma turned over the other side card. "Here is what influences your near future, that which will occur shortly," she said, turning the card. "The Moon. The card of caution; it speaks for itself, my lady." She turned over the other side card. "The ten of swords," she said. "This card tells your innermost feelings about your situation. You are gravely troubled—torn in your decision." She studied the woman, whose face showed no emotion. She wanted to give her a positive outcome; that seemed paramount of a sudden, but thus far there was naught but desolation. Paloma was hoping the woman would reveal something of a telling nature, but she did not, and her hand was shaking as she reached for the next card. She was almost afraid to turn it over. "This card represents the influence others will have upon the outcome of your . . . situation," she murmured. "The King of Swords," she said, her voice quavering. "A man of great power and authority stands between you and your goal, my lady; he is close to your heart, but he opposes you in some matter that could cause a rift between you . . ."

"I see," said the woman. "Those last two cards . . . will they reveal more?"

Paloma turned over the next card. "This card tells the secret of your heart in the matter . . . that which you wish for. The Chariot, you long for a balance between the positive and negative forces to grant you success." She pointed toward the card. "Do you see the horses there pulling the chariot? One is black and one is white. My lady, you have a strong will that will protect you, but your inquiry is not for yourself . . ."

"And the last card . . . ?"

Paloma's fingers walked toward the top card yet unturned. "This card foretells the final outcome of your inquiry based upon all of the other cards in the reading . . ." she flipped it over. "*Death*," she said, ". . . but not yours, my lady, and not necessarily death as we know it, but more to do with rebirth, with change . . . if things continue as they are. See how the card is inverted? The meaning changes when the cards are reversed."

The woman nodded and smiled. Again the smile curved her lips, but did not reach her eyes. She looked almost as if she were about to cry.

"I am sorry I could not give you a happier fortune," Paloma said.

The woman's eyes blinked through a tremor. "You did what you do, and you did it well," she murmured.

Paloma!, Milosh spoke in her mind. She gave a lurch at the urgency of the mind-speak. *Come to the livery. . . . Come at once.*

Paloma collected her cards and rose to her feet. "Forgive me, my lady, I must go," she said, and skittered off into the crowd without a backward glance.

Milosh was waiting with the horses when she reached him. "We must away," he said, helping her mount, ". . . while the sun is still high. I have bought us what we need. We head south . . . away from the fells."

Still disturbed by her last patron, Paloma frowned

as they rode out of the market. "The reading I just gave disturbed me," she said, reflecting upon it. "I have never done such a reading . . . so dark and I fear hopeless, though I did not tell her that. I was about to ask her her name when I heard your voice calling me. I don't even know why. There was just something about her . . ."

"That lady, my little dove, was the reason I called you . . . the reason we must away now, while we still can."

"But why? Who is she?"

"That, Paloma, was Cassandra Hyde-White," Milosh called over his shoulder as Somnus took the lead, then said no more.

Time was passing. The sun was sinking low. The last thing Milosh wanted was to go back to the wagon. They needed to leave the fells behind, or at least put a good measure of distance between them and their pursuers before nightfall, but Paloma would not be consoled over the absence of Michaela. He would not give in until she struck out on her own in that direction, and then, of course, he had to follow. She was not safe alone here now. Cassandra Hyde-White's appearance at the market was proof positive of that.

What was Cassandra's message? Was she warning that Jon and Joss were in pursuit? Or had she made an appearance because it was she who had come to destroy him? Or could it be that she simply wanted to meet Paloma? Praying the latter was the truth of it, Milosh tried to ignore seeing the long tail and glossy rump of the sleek black panther he'd glimpsed disappearing into the forest as they left the market. Cassandra was following. There was no doubt. He could sense her. He could smell her. But why? And why didn't she use the mind-speak?

There was no time to puzzle over it. Paloma slid off her horse's back beside the upturned wagon, calling Michaela's name, and looked inside. No answer came.

"We cannot linger here," Milosh said, still mounted. "She is gone, Paloma, and she would not want you to be here in any case. I wanted to be well away by sunset. We will never reach Keswick now before the sun sets."

"Where is Keswick?

"It is south of here, by the lakes. . . . Now get back on that horse and follow me. We are being followed. We are safe enough while the sun shines, but come twilight you are in the gravest of danger, and I am not the least of it. There is much you do not know. Now *come!*"

Paloma mounted her horse. "Don't you think you ought to tell me what I do not know if it affects me so much?" she snapped at him.

"I did not want to burden you, but now, after what happened at the market, yes . . . needs must that I tell you, but while we ride. We've wasted too much time already."

Milosh turned Somnus southward then, and Paloma followed him reluctantly. It was plain she still longed to set eyes upon Michaela. They kept to the edge of the wood, hemming a less traveled lane that sidled through Cumbria. All the while the black panther followed them, running alongside, though deeper in the forest, but Milosh knew she was there. Somehow, there was comfort in the panther's presence, yet it flagged grave danger. He did not probe the mystery of that too deeply. Cassandra had tried to come to his defense in the Whitebriar stables, as did Joss, with whom he'd bonded thirty years ago. But not Jon Hyde-White, though Milosh couldn't fault him. He was only doing what he'd taught him to do so long ago. Still, it wasn't finished. All Milosh wanted was to secure Paloma's safety, and to destroy Sebastian Valentin, then he would submit to his fate. It had to come sooner or later. His only regret was not having it occur in his homeland, on the verdant steppes and lush green foothills at the root of the Carpathian Mountains, where his heart was, and always would be. Now, in winter, it would be barren of the wildflowers etched in his memory. No sweet scent of the summer grasses would ride fugitive zephyrs down the slopes. The land would be a study in tertiary hues, bleak and desolate and painted with hoarfrost, but oh, to see it just once more. . . . Keswick reminded him of home when he first set eyes upon it. It would have to do.

"Are you going to tell me, or not?" Paloma said, as they forded a brook in the woods.

Jolted out of his reverie, Malosh gave a lurch. "We are being followed," he said, "—pursued. The vampires who overheard us at the smokehouse have carried the tale. While those who are immune to the hunger are always pursued by those who seek to steal their immunity, drinking of your blood, because it was mine, holds some special benefit. Or so they suppose—"

"—because you are the legendary Milosh?" Paloma interrupted him.

He nodded. "Something like that," he said. "I do not fully understand it myself because it has never happened before. They evidently think my blood holds great powers, and it may well; just look at what I have become without it. The Brotherhood who once protected me now hunts me as well. They see what I have become, without the protection of my immunity, and have marked me for destruction. And then there is Sebastian. I have no doubt he will follow also . . ."

"Yes, yes, I know all that. What have you withheld? There is more—I know it."

Again Milosh hesitated. ". . . The Hyde-Whites," he said. "The Brotherhood has called them to destroy me now. All factions are closing in upon us—upon me, and if you stay, upon you."

"Your *friends*?" she cried.

He nodded. "They are doing what I taught them to do, Paloma. I am a danger to us all as I am. They would have done it back on the tor if Somnus hadn't come for me. I have agreed, but only after you are safe. The herbs might have spared me, but they are lost."

"But you bought more . . . at the market; that is why we went there."

"Yes, and we soon pass the kirk where I filled the flasks with holy water. I will do so again, and I will try. There is a place I know of at Keswick—a holy place, eons old. The moon is full tonight. If we can reach that place, and the draught works just as it did for me so long ago, and has done all these years, then we are safe. If it does not . . . well, we will just have to wait and see."

Milosh said no more. They rode on in silence. Of all his problems then, the only one that he couldn't solve was Paloma. Unless the Brotherhood were to take her in hand, there was no hope for her, a newly infected vampire fending on her own in a land infested with *vampir* predators. She would not last a sennight among them. Cassandra Hyde-White had had him to mentor her, as did Jon and Joss. Michaela could have helped in that regard, but there was no hope of that now. If only he knew Cassandra Hyde-White's mind in the matter, and could leave Paloma in her care, but he did not. All he did know then was that she was tracking them, and had not seen fit to divulge the reason why.

They reached the kirk where Milosh had filled the holy water flasks on the cusp of twilight. Keswick was still some distance away. They would never make it by full dark, which meant that the hunger would soon command him. Already the lethargy was fading. Within the hour, the accursed beast within that stirred the bloodlust would rear its ugly head and he would be at its mercy. He would have to feed, and quickly, if he would spare Paloma. That meant leaving her alone in darkness in a forest full of creatures in pursuit from all factions, long enough to find a subject to slake the hunger. His heart had begun to pound at the prospect of that, when a shadow moving alongside the lane caused Somnus to shy and complain.

Milosh slowed the horse's pace, motioning Paloma to do likewise. As the sun sank low and twilight swallowed the last of the day, the hunched figure of a woman staggered out onto the path, causing the stallion to rear up, forefeet flying. Milosh gasped. It was like an answer to his prayer.

"*Michaela?*" he breathed, bringing Somnus's feathered feet to ground.

Paloma had already leapt off her mount, reached the old woman, who had fallen to her knees, and taken her in her arms, by the time Milosh quieted the stallion and dismounted.

He reached them in two ragged strides. "Get back from her," he said to Paloma, pulling her away. Squatting down on his haunches, he took hold of Michaela and searched her eyes deeply. "You are a far cry from the wagon, old one," he said. "How have you come here?"

"How?" the old woman shrilled, gulping air into

her lungs. "I was . . . chased here! Wolves . . . bats. . . .
Most of them attacked the wagon . . . but a few set out
after me. I . . . I ran until I feared my lungs would
burst before I saw the kirkyard. . . . I fear I have run
myself to death. . . ."

"And you stayed here all the day, when it would
have been safe to move about?" Milosh probed her.
He had to be sure.

"There is a shed behind the kirk . . . where the sexton's tools are kept . . . his spades and scythes . . . and
the like. I crawled inside. I must have fallen asleep. I
was exhausted. I didn't know if it was day or night till
I came out just now." Shuddering with cold, she
pulled her cloak close about her and tightened the
drawstring on her hood. Still, wisps of her gray hair
straggled out framing her leathery face. "Where is . . .
the wagon . . . ?"

"We had to leave it behind," Milosh said. "It was
too badly damaged. Can you stand?"

Michaela nodded, and he pulled her to her feet
alongside him, but he didn't let her go. Gripping her
upper arms, he drew her so close to his narrow-eyed
stare, Paloma backed up apace, looking on.

"Have you been bitten, old mother?" he gritted
through clenched teeth. "Tell me truth."

"N-no!" Michaela said, clearly wary of the look of
him then. It was his intent. If he were to leave Paloma
in Michaela's charge, he had to be certain she would
come to no harm. "They tore my clothing . . . see?"
She slapped at her skirt, which was torn to tatters,
". . . but not my flesh . . ."

"Leave her be!" Paloma shrilled, tugging at
Milosh's sleeve. "Can you not see she is exhausted?"

Milosh looked the copper-haired little spitfire in
the eyes as if he were seeing her for the first time. His
energy was focused upon the wizened old woman,

and upon beating back the hunger that the mere sight and smell of Paloma had set loose in his loins.

"Come, Michaela," Paloma said, working her free of Milosh's grip. She stabbed him with a scathing look. "You will ride double with me."

Milosh's hands shot out and captured the old Gypsy woman again. "No," he said. "She rides with me."

With no more said, Milosh hoisted Michaela up upon the stallion's back and climbed up himself. Trapping her between the pommel and his body with the reins, he spurred Somnus. The animal bolted forward, shying and snorting, then broke into a full gallop heading south, while Paloma scurried to catch up.

CHAPTER TWENTY-THREE

They rode like the wind; it blew at their back, and though the near and distant voices of wolves in the forest howled a constant mantra, they saw not a one. That by no means diminished the threat in their presence, however. Milosh tapped the mind-speak of those closest and determined that there were both vampires and Brotherhood afoot on the byways they must travel to reach the spot he had in mind to try to revive the immunity to the bloodlust with the herbal draught.

It was still some time before the full moon would rise in the cloudless sky. Michaela was evidently wrong about the weather. At least that was one obstacle they wouldn't have to face. They would be able to see the blood moon; that enigmatic phenomenon which appeared during an eclipse, when atmospheric particles and shadows upon the earth wove their magic to turn the silver moon bloodred. Ordinarily, once the initial ritual was performed, any full moon would do to renew it when the time came. At least that was how it had always been in the past. But this was not like any of the other times. Milosh had lost his immunity. In view of that, if he were to give himself every advantage, the ritual needed to be recreated exactly as it was performed the first time. He chose a place of great mystery to perform the rite— the Castlerigg Stone Circle, situated in a natural amphitheatre in the rolling hills just outside Keswick. It was set on a high moor in an open bowl-like collection of hills above the city. The moon had just begun to rise when they reached it.

One side of the circle was flattened. They entered through a vast gap between two of the larger stones to the north, which appeared to have been designed as an entrance. A small rectangle-shaped formation of stones stood within the circle. It was there that Milosh dismounted and set Michaela on her feet. Paloma slid off her mount as well, and they tethered the horses to graze just outside the circle.

Taking the pouch of herbs he'd purchased, one of the two small pots in his stash, and a flask of holy water from his saddlebag, he set them upon one of the smaller stones inside the circle, and began gathering scrub to make a fire. Half mad with the bloodlust, he scarcely knew what he was doing. He must away and feed, while he still commanded his powers of reason enough to obey them. There was a roaring noise in his head, and he could hear the thunder of the blood coursing through his veins. His vision was narrowing, like that of the wolf. The indigo night pressed all around him had taken on a bloodred hue, and his upper lip had become distended with the pressure of fangs ready to descend. In all his four hundred years, he could not remember so violent a transition. They were getting worse.

His hands shook helplessly as he took the tinderbox from his saddlebag and lit the fire. Cold as the night was, sweat beaded on his brow as he mixed the herbs with the holy water in the pot and propped it in the fire to boil. Some of the water spilled over onto the flames, and sparks flew up in a cloud of hissing, spitting steam, driving Paloma and Michaela back from it apace. Dazed, he stared at them, seeing yet not seeing. They appeared as a wavy distortion before him, huddled together. He could taste their fear. Michaela's he could bear, but not Paloma's, and he threw the flask of holy water down on the hoarfrost-painted ground, and streaked out of the stone circle.

"Boil that and let it cool," he called over his shoulder as he ran off into the night. "Then draw off the liquid into the other pot. Do not waste a drop. I won't be long."

Milosh had no sense of direction then. He moved to the beat of his thumping heart. His temples felt as if they were about to burst, his heart hammering against his rib cage as if it would explode from his chest at any moment. He hadn't transformed. Man that he was, he moved like the wolf—saw through the eyes of the wolf, thought with the cunning of the wolf as he stomped on over the rolling hills, with one thought alone driving him. He must feed and return to the circle before the moon was high, and the eclipse begun. A feeling of ill boding that would not be denied tugged at what remained of his rational mind. Apprehension jousted with the unstoppable power of the feeding frenzy until he truly believed that he was going mad. In the grips of the bloodlust now, it seemed as if he was standing outside himself— a helpless bystander—looking on in horror while the creature he had become slaked its hunger in a way his inner self could not accept. This was not him—not what he knew himself to be—but it was going to destroy him just the same.

An aging shepherd dozing amid his flock on the hillside became his victim then. He still commanded some shred of conscience, and he didn't drain the man to death, though it probably would have been kinder if he had, and safer for Paloma and Michaela. Though satisfied for the moment, the hunger was not slaked. Soon the beast within would demand of him again, and he would be compelled to obey. Praying that the herbal draught would help, he waded through the bleating sheep, straining the darkness with eyes still seeing the bloodred gauze of bloodlust madness, in search of a direction.

Resisting the urge to let loose the howl of the wolf that lurked just under the surface then, he spun in staggering circles, calling upon the stars blinking innocently overhead to point him in the right direction to return to the circle. Could he be lost? Had he become that deranged? Raking his damp hair back with both hands, he tried to still the pulse pounding in his scalp. Shaking his head like a dog shedding water, he tried to clear his vision, but still the vertigo made him misstep on the slippery ground in motion with milling sheep.

Slowly, the blood-colored veil before his eyes began to lift, and the roar of his heartbeat pounding in his ears faded to a shuddering whisper. If only the world would strop spinning—if only he could remember why it was so urgent that it did. Paloma was safe. She was with Michaela . . . *Michaela!* Obsessed with the hunger, he had taken her at her word. Suppose she had been bitten after all? If that were the case, she would hardly have told him the truth. The whine of a man possessed by the demons of insanity spilled from his throat as he stumbled like a drunkard through the sheep in motion all around him. He studied the stars. South . . . he had to go south to reach the stone circle. The moon had nearly approached the zenith in the vault overhead. There wasn't a moment to spare.

Scrambling down the little hill, he left the sheep behind. There was no lane in that tousled sector crosshatched with thickets, hedgerows, and rolling green. He ran along the edge of the sparse stand of young saplings he'd used as a blind while climbing the hill earlier. It was all coming back to him now that his ransomed mind, momentarily appeased since he'd drunk the shepherd's blood, let him think. Yes, it was all beginning to look familiar to him—the lay of the rolling patchwork hills, the vast stretches of moorland, even the smokestack and smelter of a derelict copper mine picked out by the moonlight beyond the young trees.

He could make better time as the wolf, but he chose not to strip and change. He dared not leave his clothes behind now with no guarantee of finding others. The distant echo of wolves howling only bothered him marginally. His extraordinary intuition told him every moment counted, and it was as if his feet took flight until a dark shape sprang in his path, and the sleek black panther stopped him in his tracks with her deep, throaty roar.

It was Cassandra.

We must talk, she said in mind-speak.

"There is no time," Milosh said aloud. There was no need for both of them to communicate through mind-speak; there was no one about to overhear. "I have been gone too long. Unless I miss my guess, Paloma is in grave danger."

"*I have observed your Paloma,* she said. *You sell her short, Milosh. She is well able to fend for herself.*

"I want your word that you will not destroy her no matter what happens to me, Cassandra."

It is not Paloma that I have come to speak about, she replied.

"Then speak your piece quickly. I've already told you what needs must. I won't be gainsaid, and I won't go back on my word if that's what you fear, but I need your word that Paloma will be safe."

I will cause no harm to your lady, she said.

"Why did you approach Paloma at the market?"

I wanted to see she who brought you to . . . this pass.

"I relaxed my guard. The fault is just as much mine as hers, Cassandra."

The panther pranced before him. *She is beautiful, Milosh,* she said. *My heart is breaking for you. I came to tell you I have done all that I can, and to beg you to forgive Jon . . . he believes it's for the best . . . what must be done.*

Milosh nodded. "I know that," he said. "I do not fault him, Cassandra. He is doing as he must . . . as I taught him to do . . . as I believe he was destined to do."

He loves you as if you are of his own blood, even as I do, she went on. *He cannot bear to see what you have become, and he knows if he hesitates, he will not be able to go through with it . . . to give you peace. He is half mad with this . . . and Joss . . . he is beside himself. He looks to you as a surrogate father . . .*

"He will get over it. Forgive me, Cassandra, if that is all you've come to say, I must go. My intuition never fails me, and it is screaming at me now."

I have come to say good-bye to an old and dear friend, she murmured, *and to tell him not to return to the ruins. Sebastian is not there. Joss keeps watch over the tor just in case, because he will not have a hand in what must be.*

"Where is Jon?"

The panther turned then and trotted back inside

the stand of saplings. *You will see him when it's time*, she said, and disappeared among the trees, the mournful echo of her parting cry living after her.

Paloma snatched a stick up from the ground. Threading it through the pot handle, she lifted the boiling draught from the flames and set it aside to cool. It wouldn't take long exposed to the cold night air. Michaela rested beside one of the inner stones, watching her. Paloma didn't press her to help. Age and circumstance had obviously taken their toll.

She should douse the fire, so as not to attract attention of the living, or any *vampir* lurking about, but she wasn't sure if it was part of the ritual. Besides, the cold and damp had penetrated the very marrow of her bones. It was a cold not entirely related to the weather, for since she was infected the elements no longer had much of an effect upon her. Too much depended upon the outcome of this night's work.

Though things seemed to be going well, there was something lurking beneath the seemingly perfect surface that didn't sit well with her then. Could it be that things were going too well? Possibly. Whatever the cause, the effect was a nagging apprehension that, while it seemed unfounded, would not leave her.

Soon, the cloud of steam rising from the pot diminished to soft tufts, and Paloma set the other pot beside it, tore a piece of linen from her petticoat to use as a strainer, and laid it over the empty pot.

"Come here and help me, Michaela," she said to the old woman watching from across the way. "I need you to hold the cloth taut while I pour. We must not waste a drop."

Michaela got to her feet, her eyes trained upon the pots. How wizened she looked of a sudden. Coming near, she walked with a stagger. This was more than her usual rheumatic shuffle. She was too old to have run so far in her condition. A pang of remorse crept over Paloma. The woman had saved her life—sacrificed herself to do it, and now look at her. How could she ever repay such a selfless act? Tears shimmered just below the surface of her eyes and voice as Michaela drew nearer. The old woman stopped before she reached the pots, but she didn't take her eyes from them.

"What is it, Michaela?" Paloma said.

"I . . . I cannot," she whined.

"But why? It's cooled enough. I only need you to hold the cloth so it doesn't slip when I pour. Or would you rather pour while I hold it?"

"*No!*" Michaela shrilled, backing away. "I cannot! I'm afraid I'll spill it. . . . We've already lost one batch." She shook her head fiercely. "No . . . I cannot!"

Paloma met the old Gypsy's eyes until the look in them drove hers away, but not before she'd glimpsed tears in them. There was something else, too. Michaela seemed strangely pale, her face crazed with a tracery of blue veins. She seemed more nervous than exhausted—nervous and confused.

Paloma shuddered with gooseflesh. Had her old nurse and protector been bitten after all? There was only one way to find out, and she pretended to collect more twigs and scrub to feed the dwindling fire. Her travels took her closer and closer to the holy-water flask lying on the ground beside one of the inner stones. She reached for it. With her back toward Michaela, she didn't see her advancing until the old Gypsy had seized her by the hair and thrown her off balance, knocking her to the ground.

Grappling with Michaela, Paloma rolled over on her back. To her horror, the old Gypsy had her pinned to the ground. She looked not into the kindly sparkling eyes she had always trusted but instead into the rheumy red eyes of a monster whose fangs, dripping saliva, were inches from her throat. How strong she was. It was all Paloma could do to fend her off, calling upon her own extraordinary strength.

Paloma groped the ground. The flask of holy water was just out of reach. She clawed at the frost-glazed heath, fisting her free hand in the front of Michaela's hooded cloak. This wasn't the Michaela of her childhood, the surrogate mother who had tended her, mentored her—protected her all these years. It was all she could do to convince herself—all she could do to part the loving caregiver from the vampire Michaela had become. Tears welled in her eyes and spilled over, making cold wet tracks on her hot cheeks. She swallowed the lump in her throat. *This is not my Michaela!* she kept repeating until her brain ached, but underlying it all was the undeniable fact that Michaela had sacrificed herself to save her, for the *vampir* mob that had attacked the wagon would have killed her, and she would have risen undead and doubtless would have been destroyed by now.

"Michaela . . . *no!*" she screamed in the woman's face in hopes of jarring her out of the trance-like state that compelled her then. But Michaela's infection went deeper than hers. An unstoppable passion consumed the old Gypsy. It was as if she didn't hear Paloma's cries—as if she didn't even recognize her. There was no hope for it. The instinct of self-preservation took hold, and Paloma mustered a mighty shove, and rolled out from underneath her assailant.

Michaela seized Paloma's ankle as she scrambled away toward the flask gleaming alongside in the moonlight, reminding her that the moon was high, that the eclipse had begun. It was almost time. That gave her new energy and, kicking with her other foot, with little regard for what she struck, Paloma slithered along until her fingers closed around the flask and tugged it open. They were struggling too close to the pot of steeping herbs, but that was the least of her worries then. Rolling over, she flung the contents of the silver flask full in Michaela's face. The old woman shrieked. Steam rose from her skin, from her eyes glazed over with the thick gray cataracts of blindness.

Paloma's dry sobs broke the silence as she watched Michaela reel off, shrieking, carving wild circles in the air. In her blindness, she blundered into the pot of cooling herbs. Paloma dove, and burned her hands steadying it. Where was Milosh?

Paloma scrambled to her feet. "Michaela . . . *wait!*" that part of her still in denial called out after her. But the shrieking Gypsy stumbled off in the deep dark beyond the outer circle of the Castlerigg Stone Circle, and disappeared.

CHAPTER TWENTY-FOUR

As he stumbled down the north hill in the natural amphitheater that housed the stone circle, Milosh heard the screams. His heart leaped as if it meant to burst from his chest. Something dark melted into deeper darkness beyond the outer circle. Still the screams pierced the silence—Paloma's screams; he scarcely heard Michaela's, they were receding into the night among the howls of near and distant wolves, their shrill sound amplified by the acoustics of that strange place. It was almost magical, like a stadium for the gods. He could almost see them gathered there—the ancient Celtic deities—pagan entities that once were worshiped in such places. He was hallucinating; anything to take his mind off what he feared was happening below, while he was still too far away to prevent it.

Why hadn't he transformed into the white wolf? Too late now. Besides, he ran with the surefooted gait of the animal that lived just below the surface of his skin. Time had rendered him more wolf than man, in instinct, thought, and execution of his tasks. Human still, he was like the animal he had almost become. His nostrils flared, picking up the scents of fear and blood; his lungs burned as he gulped in the cold, sweet air.

He could scarcely command his voice to thunder Paloma's name as he skidded down to the bowl-like arena below and burst through the opening of the circle. Did she answer? Was that her voice? The blood pounding in his ears was roaring down all outside noises, reminding him that his hunger had not been fully slaked. Making matters worse, the moon was high. It was time.

He reached Paloma in one half-human, half-extraordinary leap, seized her arms, and pulled her into a volatile embrace, his hands racing over her body to reassure himself that she was unharmed.

"Are you . . . has she . . . ?" he stammered, looking deep into her eyes. The thought was too terrible to put into words.

Paloma shook her head that she had not been bitten. "M-Michaela," she said, out of breath. "T-there . . . !" she cried, pointing beyond the stones to the west.

"Stay here," Milosh said, letting her go. He loosened Somnus's tether and swung himself up on the stallions back.

"*No!*" Paloma shrilled, seizing the horse's bridle. "I'm coming with you!"

"Stay where you are!" Milosh charged. "You will not want to see this, Paloma!"

"Please, Milosh . . . please don't . . ."

Milosh pried her fingers loose from the horse's bridle. "Stand aside!" he thundered. "We are wasting time."

"*Please*, Milosh . . ." Paloma sobbed. "Let her go! There is no time . . . the moon!"

But he had already galloped out of the ring on the prancing phantom horse. "*Find*, Somnus!" he commanded the animal, spurring him deeply. Bolting like a bullet, the stallion streaked over the western hill. Milosh gave him his head. Somnus knew what "find" meant. He had worked side by side with his master to ferret out vampires for nearly thirty years. This particular vampire was easy enough to track. It was obvious that Michaela was newly infected, and in ignorance of the powers at her beck and call. She still moved in the rheumatic body of a weary old woman, and it wasn't long before he ran her to ground. Somnus cut her off as she attempted to hide in a tangled thicket, where two lanes crossed on the far side of the westernmost hill.

Milosh seized the saddlebag that held his cleaver, mallet, and the stakes he'd whittled, took the short-handled spade from the other, and slid off the horse. Immediately, Somnus hemmed Michaela in, menacing her with his high-stepping hooves. Meanwhile, Milosh stepped in front of her, feet apart, the short-handled spade in hand.

"Old mother," he said, through a tremor, gazing down with hard eyes toward her head bent low, ". . . is it you inside that pitiful shell of a carcass I see before me?"

She hissed at him like a snake, but still kept her face hidden from him.

Milosh strolled nearer. "If you will not tell me, raise your head and let me see for myself the depth of your infection, then," he said.

When she did not comply, he seized her hood in a white-knuckled fist and tilted her head up to the moonlight. Tears swam in her eyes. Thick, gray scabs ensconced them, where the holy water had burned her, and though she'd fled through the cold night air, the scars it had left behind upon her wrinkled skin still trailed the smoke that remained behind.

"Kill me!" she wailed, ". . . I beg you do, before I do to her . . . my little dove . . ."

Groaning, he raised the spade. The coherent moment was fleeting—a mere glimpse of what Michaela once had been in the midst of what she had become, a last rallying before the curse took over completely. She hissed again, a vicious sound leaking through the fangs that had descended dripping saliva. It was no use. There was nothing to be done. She was undead. Pivoting on one foot, Milosh loosed an agonized whine, spun in a circle and struck her hard in the face with the flat of the spade, pitching her over on her side in the scrub.

Michaela was only stunned. Such a blow could not kill the undead, but it gave Milosh time to collect the stake and mallet from his saddlebag. Absorbed thus, he did not hear the thunder of hoofbeats, or feel the tremor in the earth beneath his feet until Paloma's screams pierced the moonlit silence.

"Don't, Milosh!" she cried, sliding off her horse's back. She rushed to his side, arresting his arm as he knelt over the dazed Gypsy. "Is there no other way?"

"This is who I am," he gritted, trying to pry her pinching fingers loose. "This is what I do—what I have done for four hundred years—bloodlust or no. You were told to say put. You do not need to see this, Paloma. Go back to Castlerigg and wait for me. I will return directly."

"No!" she sobbed. "Not my Michaela!"

"She is undead!"

"She is not! She hid upon holy ground . . ."

"She said she did. Look at her! Where did those scars come from, eh? I'll tell you where, from the holy water—that's where. I've seen such many times—inflicted them myself. You threw it on her, didn't you—tell me truth!"

"I . . . I did, yes, but—"

"Please, my dove . . . do not let him kill your poor Michaela . . ." the old Gypsy whined.

"You see?" Paloma shrilled. "She is not undead. Milosh, I beg you!"

Milosh let loose a string of oaths in Romany, staring down into the cunning thing's scarred face. Plunging his hand deep inside the saddlebag, he took out the last holy-water flask and pulled the stopper.

"You want proof, eh?" he snarled, flinging the water over the old woman's body in the shape of a cross.

Michaela screamed, writhing on the ground, as it ate through her tattered clothing like acid, and caused more burns upon her wrinkled skin. Milosh shrank from the stench of burnt flesh, and shoved Paloma aside as the old woman spat like a viper through fangs that had become fully extended again.

"Stand back!" Milosh commanded, his taut jaw muscles ticcing a steady rhythm. "Somnus, come!" he thundered, and the great horse pinned Michaela to the ground with his feathered feet while Milosh drove the stake into her heart.

Blood spattered Milosh from head to foot; his hands were soaked in it. It sprayed the animal's chest and withers, clear to its flanks, and Paloma jumped back as it sprayed her as well. Her screams were more than he could bear, but he was not finished. She had seen the white wolf sever the head of a vampire, but never this, and never that of a loved one. Bitterly, he could sympathize with that, but there wasn't time to coddle it. The undead would rise again if its head was not severed, and he picked up the cleaver.

"Go back to the Circle," he pronounced. "Go now, Paloma!"

"No!" she countered, jutting her chin. "I would see just *who you are . . . and what you do!*"

Her words and their delivery bit him sore, but he had no choice but to continue. As if Paloma was not there, he lowered Michaela's hood and severed her head with the cleaver. Over his shoulder, he saw Paloma turn away, her soft sobs hanging in the still night air between them.

"Now, she is at peace," he murmured.

"She begged you," Paloma sobbed.

"Vampire glamour," he shot back. "You saw it evaporate in a blink." He staggered to his feet and grabbed the spade. "You may as well stay until the last now," he said.

She loosed a giddy laugh dripping sarcasm. "What more can you do to abase her?" she said.

"I will bury her," he said. "Do you hear those wolves? Would you rather *they* abase her—devour her remains?"

"W-where will you bury her?"

"Here, at the crossroads, where suicides, vampires, and revenants are laid to rest."

"Do it then," she murmured. "The moon is high. The eclipse has begun."

Milosh glanced toward the vault above. The moon indeed was high. There wasn't a second to lose. He dug like a madman. It was barely more than a shallow grave, but it did not need to be deep to be effective. A vampire whose head was severed would not rise.

Somnus left the corpse and trotted to Paloma, who looked for all the world like a lost child—a pitiful waif standing there in mute horror, but for a quiet sob escaping those sensuous lips now and then. The stallion nudged her shoulder with his sleek black nose, and tossed his silky mane. Looking on, Milosh's steely eyes misted, watching her throw her arms about the

horse's neck. He had always thought Somnus more
human than animal, but the manner in which the stallion had embraced Paloma from the moment she stole
him at the ruins was unprecedented.

His hands were trembling as he laid Michaela's
body in the grave and began shoveling the earth back
into the hole. Cold sweat beaded on his brow despite
the chill in the air, and the pressure of fangs had begun
to force his lips apart. It was the smell of blood . . . so
much blood. *The hunger*. He hadn't fed enough, and
now he was alone with Paloma.

By the time the chore was done, Somnus's mane
was wet with Paloma's tears. Despite the agony of
bloodlust, Milosh took her in his arms, soothing her
with gentle hands. He knew all too well the pain she
was feeling, and she wasn't the one who had performed the grisly chore. It was something one never
became accustomed to, and he shuddered, remembering the awful night so long ago, when needs must
compelled him to do what he had just done to
Michaela to his pregnant wife. Four centuries had not
erased the pain of that dreadful night that had
changed his life forever. It was burnished into his
consciousness. When Paloma's arms embraced him,
he put her from him with firm hands gripping her
upper arms. If he wasn't very careful, he would be
doing the same to her before the sun rose.

"Come," he said. "We must return to the Circle."
He glanced toward the heavens, where dusky clouds
now raced before the eclipse. Perhaps Michaela
wasn't mistaken after all. "There isn't a moment to
lose," he said, leading her.

Mounting, they both rode back the way they had
come. Time after time, Milosh observed Paloma
glancing back over her shoulder toward the grave of
her beloved mentor and friend. Somnus took the lead

coming down the hill west of the Castlerigg Stone Circle. The absence of the howling caught his notice at once. The fire had gone out. It would have to be re-lit. Something was moving inside the Circle. Milosh motioned Paloma to slow her pace and rein in. En-gaging his extraordinary vision, he cast narrowed eyes through the opening that marked the entrance. Through a red veil he saw the wolves milling about inside—dozens of them, snarling and snapping at one another as they fought over something on the ground.

Milosh's scalp crept back as he realized what they were doing. These were not Brotherhood; they were *vampir.* Paloma rode up alongside then, capturing his attention. How forlorn she looked. Her beautiful eyes were red and swollen. Tears still misted them, glisten-ing in the moonlight. How he longed to take her in his arms—to comfort her, only that. But he knew if he did it would go beyond comfort. His heartbeat was pound-ing in the blood coursing through his temples—roaring in his ears—thrumming in his veins. He could not control the fangs that had descended with the arousal that challenged the seam in his breeches. He could smell Paloma's blood above the rest. He could feel the softness of her skin against his own. *Madness*.

"What is it?" Paloma said, craning her neck toward the Circle. From her vantage, she could not see inside the ring. "Why have we stopped? The moon . . . we must prepare the draught."

Malosh shook his head. "Too late," he forced around the fangs that changed the tone of his voice.

"What do you mean, too late?" she said. She gasped. "Wolves!" she cried.

Milosh nodded.

"What are they eating?" Paloma murmured.

"The draught," Milosh said emptily.

CHAPTER TWENTY-FIVE

Run, Milosh! Run for your life! Cassandra Hyde-White's soft voice ghosted across Milosh's mind. The black panther was near. Though he couldn't see it, he knew it had to be if he could hear her sweet voice so clearly. It sounded so desperate. *Go now,* that voice said again, *while there is much confusion. . . . while the Brotherhood deals with these that have stolen your draught. That will not be long. We will make short work of this lot. They have become sitting targets inside that circle, but I can only distract the Brotherhood for so long. . . . Once Jon comes . . . Go, Milosh! Find a safe place to spend the night, and when dawn breaks, take your lady and flee—anywhere out of the district.*

"I will never last until another blood moon comes," Milosh whispered. "—She will never last! The curse . . . it consumes me . . . it eats away at my brain. I do not know myself when the hunger comes over me. It is much worse than it was when it all began . . ."

"What did you say?" Paloma said, ranging herself closer.

Take her and go! Cassandra murmured across his mind again. *Cross water to kill your scent. I will do what I can, but trust no other. . . . Brotherhood are everywhere. Word travels among them, and you have given them permission—sealed your own fate! My God, Milosh, go . . . !*

"Milosh?" Paloma prompted him.

"Nothing," he said. "Follow me, and stay close by. Somnus will protect us, but his powers have limits. *Come!*"

They were not alone. Milosh sensed a presence in the very air around them as they fled over the rolling patchwork hills that marked Keswick. It wasn't the panther. This was a malevolent presence. They were hopelessly outnumbered. Hunted by all factions, it would be impossible to tell when or where an attack might come. Paloma had no inkling of the danger they were facing. She was too newly infected to sense what he sensed, and she was clearly mourning Michaela's death. Her extraordinary powers had only begun to be honed to their fullest, and each unfortunate victim possessed different gifts. She was cheeky enough to meet a challenge, she'd proven that. What really worried him was that she trusted him completely; that and that alone could end her days. He was not the man he was when they first met. It could take months for her to realize her full potential. They didn't have months. The best they had was hours, the worst, minutes. Of all the factions clamoring for their blood, *he* was her deadliest enemy. If only he could make her see that before it was too late.

"We must find shelter until dawn," Milosh called to Paloma, motioning her closer so he could lower his voice. "We must do it now, while the Brotherhood makes short work of these here. We are being hunted. We cannot stand against all who seek us now."

"Where can we go? I do not know this land," Paloma said.

"Neither do I," Milosh returned, "but that matters not. First, we must cross water. It will cover our scent. There is a stream that runs through the wood at the foot of these hills, a tributary of the river just south of the tor. It is not very deep. We must travel in it apace to throw the wolves off our scent, while we search for a safe place to spend the night. I think I know of one, an abandoned copper mine I saw earlier . . . if I can find it now. I was consumed with the hunger when I passed it by. A kind of madness comes upon me when the bloodlust overpowers me."

"We aren't going to last through this night, are we?" she said. "I feel it—I know it!"

Milosh hesitated. He did not want to frighten her, but better that than have her blundering into sudden death, for that is what existed all around them. He could feel its dark vibration. He could taste it, just as she did, a thick, metallic residue collecting at the back of his palate, left there by the very air they breathed.

"I will not lie to you," he said. "I have told you this before, but now it bears repeating, because your life could well depend upon what I say. You are not safe, not even with me—especially not with me. I have fed, but not enough. The hunger is still in me. I hunger for *you*, little dove, and naught but you will slake it. Unless you do exactly as I say while I still possess my faculties—and you will know when I have lost them, believe me—indeed you will not last through this accursed night."

"Stop it! You are scaring me!"

His head flashed toward her *"Good!"* he snapped, "see that you stay so. It could save your life."

He kneed Somnus ruthlessly then, and the stallion's prancing hooves seemed to take flight, carrying him well ahead. He did not look back to see if she was still within sight; he did not have to; Paloma was an excellent horsewoman, and she was right behind him. What was wanted was a little more distance between them. He needed to be out of the range of safe conversation then, and he gave the horse a harder nudge. They were entering the pine forest, and it would not do to be overheard here. Though he saw no eyes glowing red blinking at them from the shelter of the trees, that did not mean there were no vampires abroad. He was counting upon the siege back at Castlerigg to draw all *vampir* in the area just long enough for them to find shelter. Even at that, there was still Sebastian to be dealt with, and it was his presence that fueled the stench of death Milosh could not shake as they sped through the forest.

There was no sign of life now. Not even the usually curious woodland creatures made an appearance as Milosh and Paloma sped on, their horses' hooves gouging clumps of soggy earth and mulch from the forest floor. An albino tree snake dangling down from a low-hanging branch grazed Paloma's shoulder as she passed under it, and she cried out, causing Milosh to break his stride momentarily. Slithering quickly higher on the branch, the snake seemed more frightened than she was. The sight wrenched a guttural chuckle from Milosh, though his lips barely smiled, earning him a scathing glance from Paloma. The brief interlude was short-lived. They were approaching the stream, shining like a satin ribbon in the dappled moonlight filtering through the trees. The soft murmur of its motion was a soothing sound, which Milosh would have deemed welcome in other circumstances. Now, it meant nothing more than a strategy, the means to an end—eluding the enemy. So much in nature had been lost to him since he'd fallen victim to the hunger again.

Plunging into the middle of the stream, they followed it northwest as it sidled through the forest, dividing it in two in that sector, with mossy banks on either side, where it widened farther on. Soon the trees thinned, and they exited into a thicket that opened onto the fells, where rolling moors stretched as far as the eye could see. It was safe now to leave the stream, and Milosh motioned Paloma to follow as he urged Somnus out onto what seemed familiar ground to him, searching the horizon for the tall smokestack attached to the abandoned copper mine.

It wasn't long before it came into view, silhouetted black against the indigo sky beneath the full blood moon. Set on a hillside, it appeared at close range like an excavation. No mining had been done there in recent days. A few dilapidated outbuildings surrounded the smokestack, and the remains of troughs at intervals down the incline were the only evidence that a mining enterprise once thrived in the area.

"There!" Milosh said, pointing. "We will be safe here until morning. Come, and look sharp. We must cross the open moor to reach it, and we lose our protection once we leave this wood behind."

Milosh urged the horse forward, a close eye on the surrounding land for any sign of danger. He saw none with his eyes, but his extraordinary perception told him traveling in the stream was a wasted effort. The forest, moor, and thicket were alive with *vampir*—undead and Brotherhood—waiting. It seemed to him only a matter of which faction would add his head to their trophies. *It is time.* He had lived long and helped many unfortunate souls infected by the vampire's kiss. He had earned his rest, but what of Paloma? She was in no wise ready to face what he had faced; it was all too new for her. If he could remain, they might face it together. He loved her, there was no question, but he could not remain with her as he was . . . not like this, at the mercy of the hunger. It was all he could do to maintain some semblance of control in her presence now. Soon, he would lose that control altogether.

Whenever he thought these thoughts, he had sudden random flashes of memory, seeing himself severing the head of his pregnant wife. It was becoming harder and harder to beat them back. He could not bear to go through that again. He would let the hunters take him if it came to that, but first he needed to prepare Paloma. The other random flashes plaguing him were imaginings of what would become of her with no one to mentor and protect her.

All at once a rustling sound in the treetops at the edge of the wood caught Milosh's attention. It was coming from a lower vantage, where the pines thinned to young saplings. His sharp eyes flashed toward the sound. Bone-chilling laughter flooded his mind until he flinched.

Sebastian!

The laughter grew louder, and Milosh slowed Somnus's pace. "Go on ahead," he whispered to Paloma, ". . . to those outbuildings. I will follow behind. . . ."

"Why?" she returned, slowing her mount's pace with a tug on the reins.

"Just do as I say!" he snapped.

Paloma stared, then after a moment made straight for the copper mine.

It won't be as easy as that, Sebastian said in mindspeak. *She will come to me of her own free will before 'tis done. She is my creature. There is naught you can do to change that.*

"You think not?" Milosh said. "Show yourself if you dare! Let us end it here—now."

Our time is coming, Milosh, but not quite yet. It amuses

me to watch the agony of your final hours. The sacrifice you are planning, it is truly a noble thing. Once I, too, thought noble thoughts, until I realized how empty they are. . . . Your sacrifice will be for naught. I will have her anyway, so go! Ride like the wind. Spend your seed in that exquisite body . . . while you can. It is the least that I can do, since she will be mine for all eternity. Well? What are you waiting for? Go!

Milosh strained his eyes toward the treetops. "Come out and face me here and now!" he called. "Show yourself . . . or are you too afraid to face me?"

Afraid of you, who have not even come close to defeating me in four hundred years? You are no match for my powers, though I have so enjoyed watching you try. No, Milosh, I choose the time and place for our last conflict, but be of good cheer . . . it won't be long now. Oh, and you will never find my sleeping place to catch me "unaware." Do not look so stunned. I know that is your plan. My mind powers are far reaching. How do you think I have managed to thwart your attempts over the years? The upper boughs at the edge of the wood shuddered as the bat took flight. *Go! Enjoy her while you can. When next we meet, it is your last . . .*

Milosh stared after the creature as it sawed through the midnight sky, spreading the scent of pine as it troubled the boughs flying deep into the forest. Cold chills raced along his spine. It was as if death had laid a cold hand on his back. He was feeling his mortality. In the past, there was always the hope that one day he would defeat the monster. Now, for he first time since the nightmare began so long ago, Milosh truly doubted he could.

CHAPTER TWENTY-SIX

Paloma was waiting beneath a dilapidated shelter, an old stable of sorts, when Milosh reached it. Together, they unsaddled the horses and saw to their needs, before moving on to the small, squat buildings that looked as if they once had served as an office and barracks. They were locked. Huge, heart-shaped padlocks dangling from chains, and signs prohibiting trespassers, spoke to the fact that they were unwelcome there. That couldn't be helped. They had to spend the rest of the night somewhere, and this was the only suitable place he'd seen.

The buildings were covered with woodbine creepers. At first glance, they might have been mistaken for part of the hillside from which the excavation had been dug. They passed the larger of the two buildings and paused before the smaller one. It was well hidden beneath the climbing vines, though it offered the best view of the surrounding land. Milosh drew the cleaver from his saddlebag and hacked at the lock and chain until they fell away. The old wood groaned as he pushed the door open. His extraordinary senses told him it was safe to enter, and they stepped inside, closing the door after them.

There was only one window. It was dingy and cracked, but it hadn't broken altogether. Enough moonlight filtered in to see by without lighting a candle or a fire, which would have been risky, attracting not only *vampir* but also curious townsfolk. He glanced about the interior. It was a crudely hewn one-room structure, sparsely furnished, boasting a desk, a locked chest, a chair, and a settle. There was a small hearth, and several candles shackled to the mantle with tallow and cobwebs. Milosh set his saddlebag down and turned to Paloma.

"You will be safe here," he said. "Keep the door bolted. Let no one in, including me—"

"You are leaving me here?" she interrupted him. "Please, I beg you, do not leave me!"

"I must," he said in his sternest voice. Already the pressure of descending fangs was changing the shape of his mouth. Cold sweat had begun to bead upon his brow, and the crimson veil had begun to distort his vision, narrowing his pupils like the eyes of a snake. He bared his fangs. "It is all I can do to contain them," he said. "If I remain here with you, I will *kill* you, Paloma. I will drain you of your last drop of blood. I will not be able to help myself."

"So, you leave me for another to devour. I do not understand your logic," she fumed. "I know you want to be rid of me, but—"

"Rid of you?" he seethed. Groaning, he seized her upper arms and pulled her closer. His eyes brimmed with tears. This time he could not blink them back. "I love you, Paloma," he said. "If things were different . . . if I was as I was before . . . but I am not. I am something . . . I . . . I do not even know what I am!

When the feeding frenzy comes over me I am like a rabid animal—nothing matters except that I feed. It doesn't matter where or how, only that I slake my hunger with human blood. You know the feeling from before, when you were first infected. Imagine that drive a hundred times stronger and growing more so with each setting of the sun. That I have tasted your blood . . . that I have lived inside this exquisite body I hold here now makes it worse. It magnifies the danger a hundredfold. My passion to possess you as a man possesses a woman makes the hunger unbearable, and the urge unstoppable. I have not fed sufficiently to keep the feeding frenzy at bay until dawn. I must find another subject soon or put you to the hazard. I do not know if I will be able to resist you even then. Rid of you? My God, Paloma . . . *my God* . . . !"

Paloma threw her arms around him. "It is all my fault," she sobbed. "No matter what, it comes back round to that. If only I hadn't . . ."

"No," he soothed. "Do not reproach yourself. The fault is mine. I did not exist for four hundred years by letting down my guard at first sight of a pretty face. I should have known. I should have been on my guard." Cupping her face in his hand, he tilted her head back to meet her eyes. "You must listen to me now, and do exactly as I say," he murmured, "—exactly, Paloma. Do not let what is to come all be for naught."

"What is to come?" she said. "What are you not telling me? What are you planning?"

"Shhh, there is no time for hysterics," he said. "For four hundred years, *vampir* have lusted after my blood—blood made powerful by the blood moon. Over time it has mellowed, if you will, until I have become a living antidote for the hunger, which is why the vampires hunted you so relentlessly after you drank of it—why they hunt you still. It is a thousand-fold more potent than that of the Brotherhood, whom I mentored. They did not drink my blood, they embraced the ritual—drank of the draught just as I would have done tonight, and they protect me . . . that is, they used to. They protect you now. I have become the hunted . . ."

"But what has this to do with—"

"Shhh, let me finish, there is so little time," he said. "The blood moon ritual only helps those who have not died and risen undead, but that will not keep the undead from trying. Those who overheard us at the smokehouse have passed the word. You will be set upon. You will be hunted—run to ground and savaged if you are not wise enough to escape . . . to elude . . . to outrun and outsmart your pursuers. It is the only thing that worries me. You are too newly infected. You do not even know the range of your powers yet. You have the strength, but if I only knew you had the skill it would make this so much easier to bear."

"Make what easier?"

"I am trying to give you the knowledge to survive," he said. "If you are aware of the dangers, you might be able to avoid them. Vampire glamour is the greatest deception, and the most deadly. It seduces even the cleverest of men and women. You possess it, too, and you will learn to use it as needs must, against your enemies. It is an acquired skill; the depth of it depends upon your mastery of the art."

"You aren't coming back!" she sobbed. "You are telling me this because you mean to leave me here! *You do!* There has to be another way. You say you love me . . . how—"

He shook her. "It is because I love you that I have to

go. They are going to kill me, Paloma! They must. There is no other way. The vampires will kill me, and the Brotherhood will destroy me before I can rise undead. It is what must be. It is time. I am becoming the very thing I am committed to destroy. I can no longer help the Brotherhood as I am, nor can I accept this as my fate—to run mad with the hunger until it happens anyway—until it happens to *you* because of me. I will not rest with your blood on my hands."

Milosh tried to put her from him then, but the earthy scent of rosemary and lavender—her scent—overwhelmed him. Combined with the rich metallic essence of her blood, the effect was bewitching. He hesitated. It was costly, for she broke his grip on her arms, fisted her hands in the back of his cloak, and held him fast. How could he ever let her go?

"What of *my* hands?" she said. "What of the blood upon them? How can I live knowing that I have driven you to what you are planning? Have you no care for me at all?"

"I am not planning anything, Paloma. I am simply trying to prepare you for the inevitable. The wheels are already in motion. The fells are crawling with creatures—Brotherhood and *vampir*—hunting me. I am trying to stay alive long enough to destroy Sebastian. If I do not, he will have you, and you will be lost."

"But your friends . . . the Hyde-Whites, they will protect you."

Milosh's heart skipped its rhythm. That was the hardest to bear. He had become close with the Hyde-Whites, with Jon and Cassandra, and with Joss. He had brought them into the fold of the Brotherhood. There really was no Brotherhood before Jon and Cassandra embraced the blood moon ritual and became vampire hunters, not as the Brotherhood existed now. He had taught them well. It was only fitting that Jon be the one to end his misery, but that did not minimize the heartbreak.

He shook his head. "No longer," he said. It was the one thing he was holding back. "It was my wish that one of my own end my days. Jon Hyde-White will do it. They protect you now . . . from me as well as the others."

"And what if I do not want to be protected from you?" Paloma said.

Milosh swayed in her arms. The physical pain of beating back the hunger was beyond bearing. Vertigo had begun. Her beautiful image swam before him. Their hearts beat as one in a shuddering rhythm that took his breath away; it resounded in the very air around them. Something tugged at his loins like hot pincers. Those eyes, those incredible eyes, he could not meet their gaze then, and yet he could not look away. Lost in their depths, he pulled her closer, their lips almost touching, and murmured her name.

Paloma crowded closer, and he reached for her breast. Untying the drawstring at the neck of her blouson, he spread it wide, feasting his eyes upon the creamy expanse of skin, like silk beneath his fingers, upon the tall, rosy nipples his touch had hardened. He worked them between his thumb and forefinger, first one and then the other, until she writhed and moaned and leaned into his hardness. How soft and malleable she was in his arms. She was his for the taking, forbidden pleasure opening to him like the petals of a flower, just as she had done before. But to take her now would be her death.

The fangs notwithstanding, he lowered his mouth to her breast and took her nipple between their sharp points, teasing its puckered circumference with his tongue, circling the areola he'd trapped between the fully extended fangs. He took great care not to pierce the delicate flesh with them as he drew the nipple into his mouth and sucked until she released a guttural groan. It resonated through his body, setting his very soul afire, reverberating through every recess of his being, until every distended vein beneath his skin thrummed to life.

Paloma's fangs had descended also, just as they always would whether she was immune to the hunger or not. She threw back her head, cupped her other breast in her hand and fed him the nipple. His trembling fingers found the other bud, wet from his kiss, and fondled it relentlessly until she moaned in involuntary spasms. The primitive sound riddled him with tongues of rampant fire, heat, and gooseflesh racing along his rigid spine until he feared his very bones would snap.

She reached for his sex, and he let out a bestial howl not unlike that of the wolf inside him, and shuddered as she freed his engorged member from his breeches and closed her tiny fingers around the rigid shaft. Desire fueled by longing mingled with the palpable hunger in a volatile explosion of bloodlust and passion that would only be slaked by total abandon to both lusts.

His breath coming short, he bent her back beneath his gaze. Her doe eyes, hooded with arousal, sparkled with mist in the moonlight throwing fractured beams and opalescent puddles at their feet through the cracked window glass. Milosh scarcely saw. Pain riddled his body. Madness clouded his mind. His vision had narrowed upon the translucent slice of milk-white flesh that was her throat arched for the taking, the vine-like tracery of veins clearly outlined beneath the skin, the blood coursing through them throbbing in a visible rhythm. He licked his lips; they were hot and dry, his fangs straining his upper lip—stretching it out of all proportion.

He wrenched her closer, his sex responding to the tender hand caressing it, and threw back his head, then lowered his anxious mouth to the alabaster expanse of her throat. The vibration of her life's blood palpitated through the hairbreadth of distance left between fangs and skin. His eyes were riveted to the distended vein barely inches from the quivering notch at the base of her throat. His heart was hammering against his ribs. He was so close. Her warmth rushed at him. Sanity had all but evaporated. He was the creature now—a creature of the night, hypnotized by her surrender, captivated by her passion, bewitched by her blood. When she spoke, he groaned and let loose a bestial howl, as if she had run him through.

"Have me, Milosh," she murmured. "Take me . . . make me as you are. We are already one. Why not in this as well? Anything, but please, I beg you . . . do not leave me!"

Milosh groaned again, and put her from him, raking his hair back from a sweaty brow. The cold attacked his sex now that he'd taken it back from the warm caress of her gentle hand. He could barely hear her with the blood thundering in his ears like a raging river thunders over rocky rapids. It was deafening.

"You would have me *damn* you . . . as I am damned?" he seethed, tearing at his clothes. One by one the garments fell away. "If I were to sink these fangs into your sweet flesh—and do not think I am not tempted—it would likely *kill* you! Then you would rise undead. What? You would suffer me to destroy again that which I love?"

"We do not know what would be . . ." she pleaded.

"And we aren't going to find out!" he said unequivocally. Naked, he seized her upper arms and shook her gently. "You are cold, you're trembling. I'm sorry. It is not safe to light a fire. Throw the bolt after me.

None can enter without an invitation. Admit no one, Paloma—not even me, should I return . . . not until daylight. Do not leave this place . . . no matter what occurs. You are safe . . . only if you remain inside . . ."

His breath was coming short. He could no longer control his rapid heartbeat. He was losing his human consciousness. There wasn't a moment to spare, and he let her go and threw the door open.

Paloma ran to him. "Do not leave me!" she sobbed. "I will never see you again if you do . . . !"

"Get back!" he thundered. His hooded gaze fell upon her standing so forlorn. Every instinct in him called out to slake the passion she had ignited in him—to take her, do as she begged him. He had to leave while he still possessed a thread of sanity. He inhaled her scent until his breath caught. His soul would remember it for all eternity if what he feared was about to happen. "Good-bye, Paloma," he murmured.

"No! Do not go!" she cried.

All at once a hitch in his memory made him hesitate. The wolf was straining to be born, the pain not unlike that of a woman in childbirth he surmised, for it came and went in agonizing contractions. As it finally broke free from the mercurial streak of displaced motion that gave birth to it, he spoke his last.

"There is one you can trust, and only one now . . ."

Her look alone posed the question her lips failed to do.

"The panther," he gritted. "If she comes . . . obey the panther . . ."

The last word out, the great white wolf streaked off and disappeared in the darkness.

Chapter Twenty-seven

Milosh bounded over the frost-clad fells, a silver white blur in the darkness. He could smell *vampir* on the wind his motion stirred; otherwise there was no breath of a breeze. He had left the only place he would have been safe until dawn. He had no choice. If he had stayed another moment in the little office, he would have ravished Paloma, but not just her body, he would have corrupted her very soul; that he could not, would not, do.

He scarcely remembered who he was. Only the barest sparks of recognition visited him now in random flashes. It was as if he stood outside himself looking down at a thousand eyes . . . watching from the fringes of the forest, from the uppermost boughs of saplings, great oaks, and ancient pines. Shadows moved along the periphery of his extraordinary vision, shadows only he could see. Why were they keeping their distance? They could take him out in one beat of his hammering heart. What were they waiting for? Sebastian. It had to be. It would stand to reason his ancient enemy would have something spectacular in mind. Those thoughts were lost on the fringes of a greater press gnawing at his reason then. The hunger. He had to feed before it robbed him of his identity, before he became what he detested most, an unstoppable creature unable to think. The man beneath the surface was slipping further away each time the feeding frenzy came upon him.

He'd seen it many times, man become beast, from which there was no return. Ill advised though it was by the one scrap of humanity he clung to, he howled into the night. How insidious that the very thing he so abhorred could save him from a darker fate, that of becoming a mindless predator—a bloodlusting scavenger driven from victim to victim, a slave to the hunger that damned him. If he were to let go of that tenuous thread of humanity and slip away into the deep darkness of the vampire gaining control, he would enter a netherworld of the mind, controlled by the creature he was fast becoming.

An unsuspecting stag in his path held that terror at bay. As soon as he drained its blood, his faculties began to return, and he ran like the wind on the open moor, away from the wood, away from the abandoned copper mine, and temptation. For while he had conquered the bloodlust for the moment he had not conquered his hunger for Paloma. It was insatiable.

Still, he was watched. He could feel the eyes upon him, even if he could not see them at their distance. They were mocking him. He could not escape; they knew it even as he did. It was safe enough to let him run his heart out. He wouldn't stray far, not with Paloma left behind. Brotherhood and vampire alike bided their time. Milosh knew their mind—even deranged as he was. *Vampir* had always stalked him. The Brotherhood had always protected him. More wolves than men and women, for they rarely shapeshifted into their human incarnations any longer, the Brotherhood had always rallied to his aid . . . until now. Now, they ran with the enemy, their familiar faces—for he knew every one—hidden behind wolf masks, even to Jon Hyde-White, his closest friend in centuries, the *Brother* who would kill and destroy him at his own request.

Milosh ran on. The wind he created whipped tears in his wolf's eyes that blurred his extraordinary vision. He remembered a time when racing the wind in the body of the white wolf was what he loved most— remembered how he shared that love of his wolf incarnation with Jon Hyde-White, whom, he used to chide, would rather run on four feet with the wolves, than walk upright on two as a man. Jon, a man of the cloth before he was infected, had enjoyed that facet of his situation with not a little shame, no doubt a product of his calling, but not enough to give it up. Milosh hadn't ever given his lupine experience much thought until Jon confided in him. Now, when it was too late, when he had become the hunted and freedom was so precious to him, Milosh understood at last Jon's passion, and embraced it as he never had before. There was so little time left to enjoy it.

Absorbed in those thoughts, he had entered another copse without realizing it, and blundered upon a little glade where armed men were gathering around the remains of a campfire. *Hunters!* Skittering to a halt, he bared fangs still red with the stag's blood, a guttural growl living in his throat. It didn't matter. It was too late. They had seen him.

"There's one!" a tall, bearded man in buckskins bleated.

"A white one!" another shouted. "What are you waiting for? Shoot!"

There were five men in all, scurrying around the campfire collecting their weapons. Tramping through the edges of the fire in their haste, they sent clouds of sparks shooting skyward. Some of the mulch on the forest floor began to catch fire. The hunters didn't seem to notice, but Milosh did. It was a small glade. It wouldn't be long before it spread to the trees nearby. Waves of déjà vu washed over him as he stood rooted to the spot, recalling another blaze in another wood in his homeland sixty years ago. He was fired upon then, too. He could almost feel the musket ball that took him down back then—a searing pain like no other as he spun on his heels and streaked off through the copse and out onto the open moor with the hunters in pursuit. Was it a memory, or was it real? The smell of his own blood spoke to that. This time, the wound was in his inner thigh, taken when he turned. His discipline was such that he scarcely broke his stride; he dared not. They were after him on horseback. Where had the horses come from? Why hadn't he been paying attention?

More shots rang out. Several whizzed past him as he ran. These were like the hunters in Michaela's caravan, who hunted primarily for the pelts. Being white and rare in those parts, his would bring a handsome price. He had eluded them once. Could he do so again? Milosh hoped so, but feared not. His strength was flagging from pain and blood loss. All he could think of was Paloma, alone at the abandoned copper mine awaiting his return. If he did not come . . .

All at once, he wasn't alone. Something sleek and swarthy, as dark as the night ran at his side. His racing heart leapt as he picked up the scent.

Follow me, the panther said, taking the lead.

Cassandra!

The red veil appeared before Milosh's eyes again. This time it was not due to the feeding frenzy. He was close to losing consciousness. Straining the darkness ahead, all he could see was the open moor—flatland, gentle rolling hills, and valleys that offered nowhere to hide that he could see. The panther took a sudden turn, and all at once she disappeared into the side of a little hill as if it had swallowed her whole. His gait reduced to a limp, the white wolf plunged in after her and found himself inside an ancient prehistoric barrow hidden in the hillside. His legs failed him. They were in deep darkness. Engaging what remained of his night vision, Milosh's wolf's eyes picked out distorted cup-markings on the stone walls inside the manmade hill that had been built up over the tomb—tridents, swirling suns, and circular whorls spun before him, set in motion by the vertigo. His barrel chest was heaving, his breath coming in short, ragged pants. His extraordinary vision slowly failed, showing him only the iridescent green eyes of the panther leaning over him as he lay helpless on his side, blood still oozing from his thigh.

The white wolf leaked an anxious whine.

Shhh, Cassandra cautioned in mind-speak. *Be still. Make no sound, Milosh. Listen . . . they pass us by.*

We are trapped here, Milosh said. *If the fire spreads it will cook us alive, and if they search this place, there is no rear entrance. We cannot stay here, Cassandra . . .*

The panther growled. *Hear the wolves?* she said. *The Brotherhood draws their fire. They will not find us, and the fire will not reach us; it spreads southward. But you are right, old friend, we cannot stay here. Can you stand?*

Gulping deep breaths of stale air that stank of death and decay, the white wolf tried and failed, falling back in defeat. *We . . . will need . . . help*, Milosh panted.

The panther pranced in circles, her long tail pummeling him in the close quarters. *I cannot bring the Brotherhood,* Cassandra said. *Jon is with them. If he sees you like this, he will think it kinder to . . . to . . .*

The white wolf whined, more to get her attention than from the pain. *Go then, and fetch Paloma . . . she is at the abandoned copper mine northwest of here. Tell her to bring my saddlebag . . .*

The panther snorted. *I fear to leave you here,* Cassandra hedged. *There isn't much more time left before the sun rises.*

Why should that matter? Milosh said. *I thought you said the Brotherhood was occupied with the hunters . . .*

Again, the panther pranced in circles. *I am not worried about the Brotherhood,* Cassandra confessed.

What then? Why did she hesitate? Could she not see that every second brought him closer to suffering a death that would make his destruction necessary? *What, Cassandra?*

You were right before, she said at last. *We cannot stay here, Milosh . . .*

Why?

Again, she hesitated. *Because . . . this is Sebastian's hiding place,* she said haltingly. *I followed him to it at sunrise yesterday. I was coming to find you . . . to tell you. I couldn't come sooner, Jon joined us at Castlerigg. . . . I just couldn't slip away until now without attracting his notice. I've been half mad with worry . . .*

The silence was palpable. It tasted of death. Milosh finally broke it. *How long before first light?* he said.

Again the panther growled. *Not long enough, I fear,* she said.

Then, go! Milosh returned. *Bring her quickly, Cassandra. You must try. I cannot do this alone . . . as I am . . . and I cannot leave her like this . . . at that creature's mercy . . .*

The panther leaked a strangled sound. *You cannot mean to try to destroy Sebastian like that?* Cassandra's mind screamed at him. *You cannot even stand!*

The white wolf ground out a bestial howl that backed the panther up apace. *Just do it!* Milosh snarled, *Go now . . . and do not let her out of your sight!*

Paloma paced the rickety floorboards in the little mining office. Would the night ever end? It was dark as coal-tar pitch. The moon had moved on—the eerily beautiful full blood moon that might have saved Milosh. Her heart was breaking. Milosh was right. He would never make it until another eclipse. That would be years. He would be dead by then—dead and destroyed—lost to her forever. That could have happened already, though somehow she didn't believe it had. She would have known in her heart. She would have sensed it. It was as if there was an invisible tether that joined them heart to heart and soul to soul. No. Milosh was alive—he had to be. How could she ever bear it if that tether should be severed? But if he was alive, why was she trembling so? Why had she nearly worn a trench in the old wood floor? He wasn't coming back. Her intuitive powers were screaming: *Something is dreadfully wrong!*

There was nothing for it. She gave her word she would not leave the copper mine, but she could not stay there not knowing what was happening. He should have returned by now . . . if he was going to return. There was a doleful ring—like the peal of a death knell—to his parting speech. Chills attacked her spine as she recalled his words. It wasn't the first time she'd heard finality in his parting voice, but she took no comfort in that. It was only a matter of time.

Her heart began to pound. No. She couldn't just stay cooped up inside the little mining office waiting for the sun to rise without her beloved. She reached the door in two strides and threw it wide, only to freeze on the threshold. Outside, in the deathly still darkness before dawn, the excavation that housed the mine was *moving*—crawling with creatures of the night—man and animal doggedly approaching, closing in upon her in a wall of fur, sinew, and gray corrupted flesh that she could not hope to penetrate in either incarnation.

Leaking a dry sob in frustration, Paloma shut the door again and threw the bolt. She dared not leave, and she dared not stay, her intuition told her that. Something was terribly wrong, and she was powerless to prevent it. Defeated, she sagged against the door, only to vault away from it as the pounding began on the other side.

Thump! Thump! Thump! The fists of cadaver-gray undead beat a tattoo on the old scarred wood that reverberated through her body. Was Milosh among them? Paloma could not bear the thought that he might be. Ghostly shapes as white as the morning mist rolling in off the lakes, pressed close to the cracked windowpane, their eyes glowing red, distorted and disjoined by the fractured glass.

All at once the howling of the wolves gave way to guttural snarls, as Brotherhood attacked *vampir*, the melee turning the undead away from the window with shrieks of terror. Paloma could hardly believe her eyes, and even though she was well aware they could not enter without invitation, the very sound and look and smell of them leaking in through the cracked windowpane struck terror in her thumping heart and threatened to make her retch. Another shriek poured from her throat as she remembered she was one of them.

Paloma dropped to her knees on the dusty wood

floor, her hands clasped over her ears to shut out the terrible sounds of carnage outside. Rocking there, she prayed for the sun to rise. Time was a two-faced vehicle then. In one way it brought her closer to freedom from the copper mine. In another, if it freed her, it could well bring her closer to the knowledge that Milosh was dead—slaughtered in the fray still taking place on the other side of the door. And then from outside she thought she heard something different. So in tune to the voices of wolves, when the cry of the panther rose above the rest, Paloma scrambled to her feet, as Milosh's words ghosted across her memory:

There is one you can trust, and only one now . . . the panther. If she comes . . . obey the panther . . .

The sky had begun to lighten. Pearly blue-gray streamers of mist danced on the dawn breeze. The sound of yelping wolves and the moans of undead dragging themselves off to beat the rising of the sun, grew distant. It had not broken the horizon, but soon; the distant crowing of a cock attested to that. Was it safe to leave the copper mine at last? A voice in Paloma's mind answered that question.

Let me in, child, it said. *Unbar the door and come. There isn't a moment to lose!*

CHAPTER TWENTY-EIGHT

The white wolf drifted in and out of consciousness on the musty barrow floor. His breathing had become shallow and labored. Excruciating pain remembered from time out of mind, when he first began to shapeshift, riddled him from head to toe. Sinew, bone, muscle, and flesh pulsated, stretching the limits of Milosh's wolf body until it groaned and expanded in a rush of displaced energy, propelling him into human form without his willing it.

Milosh cried out in the throes of agony the rupturing transformation brought to bear, the wound in his thigh notwithstanding. That it had happened without his participation could mean only one thing: He was dying. Even his extraordinary night vision was fading. It was still as dark as coal-tar pitch inside the barrow. Were his visual powers intact, he would have detected the presence with him in the burial mound long before the rustling of motion alerted him to the fact that he wasn't alone.

"P-Paloma . . . ?" he gritted, straining the inky blackness through vertigo, but the voice that replied was not that of Paloma, or Cassandra Hyde-White. This voice was deep and sensuous—a man's voice. It was that of Cassandra's husband Jon; he would know it anywhere.

"So, we have come full circle," Jon said, kneeling beside him on one knee. "The hunter has become the hunted, and it is his pupil who must end his days."

"Do it quickly then," Milosh gritted through clenched teeth. "I do not want to live as I am . . ."

Jon Hyde-White did not speak directly. To Milosh's surprise, he stripped off the silk scarf about his neck, and cinched it in about Milosh's thigh. "You have lost much blood," he said. "The smell of it will bring Sebastian. Can you stand?"

Milosh made an effort, but failed and sank back against the earthen floor, cold and sticky with his blood

Jon stripped off his cloak, wrapped it around Milosh, and hauled him to his feet. "Lean on me," he said. "You cannot remain here. The sun rises. Sebastian will come soon. His minions already gather to protect him."

Milosh attempted to take a step, and groaned as his knees buckled. "It is . . . no use," he panted. "I . . . cannot, Jon. Do what you must . . . what you came to do . . ."

"I came, old friend, to help you *live*, not die," Jon said. "If that cannot be, then, yes, I will be the one to give you peace. I could not bear for Sebastian Valentin to claim your soul among his foul undead. I will take your head and free that soul before I will let the creature that has damned us all possess it for all eternity. You forget what I was . . . what I still am in my heart and soul . . . a man of the cloth. Can you possibly think I am enjoying this?"

"You are about what I taught you to do," Milosh

said. "I have taught you well. I ask only that you do it quickly . . . and one more thing . . ."

"You have not heard me, Milosh—"

"I have," Milosh interrupted him. "I have, old friend. I've always known this day would come."

"Well, it shan't come yet," said another voice from the shadows. Joss Hyde-White stepped forward. "I'm sorry, Father," he said. "I won't let you do it—not to Milosh."

Jon sighed through a dark mutter. "Who is watching the ruins?" he snapped.

"The Brotherhood," Joss said.

"I left the task to *you*," Jon returned.

"I'm not going to let you do it, Father."

Jon glared at him. "Help me with him," he said, as if Milosh wasn't there. "He's lost too much blood . . . if he dies . . . I do not know what will happen as he is now. If he should rise undead . . ."

"Wait!" Milosh said, as if he hadn't heard. His heart went out to Joss. The anguish in the son's eyes pleading with the father—his two longtime friends at loggerheads over what was to become of him—was more than he could bear. He had indeed come full circle, but there was something he needed to say before judgment was meted out in that quarter. "Paloma . . ." he said. ". . . Do what you want with me, but, promise me you will look after her. It is little to ask . . . after all is said and done, my friends . . ."

"That is another issue that needs must be addressed," said Jon, as they supported him heading toward the entrance, "but not yet. Now come, before the dawn catches us behindhand and makes this conversation a moot point."

Somnus was the swiftest mount; the other was left behind to graze. Paloma was convinced she could have made better time were she in her wolf form, but that was not an option here now. She needed to carry Milosh's saddlebag, and the she-wolf could not do that. Speed had to be sacrificed, for the contents of the bag might well spare Milosh's life . . . or help him die. She dared not think of that, driving the phantom horse at a gallop alongside the sleek black panther in a direction unknown to her, with the first rays of dawn on the horizon diluting the night.

Cassandra's sweet voice ghosting across her mind had told her some, but not all of what she was facing. It was little more information than her intuition had already told her. Milosh was injured. He had been shot. He needed her. He had sent the panther to bring her. He hadn't left her at all. Over and over she repeated that mantra, as they raced over the frost-clad ground through the morning mist—every emotion running rampant in her.

The frosty air seared her lungs and dried her throat until it burned with icy fire. Her heart hammered so fiercely its shuddering hurt inside. The mist grew thicker as their course dipped into the valley. She could only see the black blur of the panther's motion in glimpses now, through eyes narrowed against the cold dawn breeze as the horse sped on. She was exhausted. But for her extraordinary strength, her stamina would have flagged long ago. *Don't let him die before I can reach him!* her mind cried out to any deity that might hear her and would listen. *Milosh . . . wait! I'm coming . . . my God, don't leave me . . . !* She had all but run the horse's heart out when Cassandra's voice knifed through the chaos in her mind.

He cannot hear you, she said. *I have been trying since we left the mine. He is either unconscious or—*

Dead? Paloma interrupted her. *Tell me not dead! I beg you . . . no . . .*

For a long moment there was silence. No sound save the out-of-sync rhythm of the horse's great hooves hammering the ground, and the panther's thick paw pads, crunching through the hoarfrost underfoot. Leaking an agonized groan, Paloma spurred Somnus relentlessly, scarcely knowing where the spurt of strength came from that drove the horse to streak past the panther, whose growl echoed back at her.

Wait! Cassandra's voice stabbed at her brain. *We are almost there, and something is . . . not as it should be . . . not as I left it . . .*

It was almost as if Cassandra didn't want to put her fears into words. Half mad with worry, Paloma drove Somnus harder, slapping his neck and withers with the reins.

Wait I say! Cassandra commanded her. *You do not know where you are going!*

"I do!" Paloma cried aloud. "I can smell him . . . I smell his blood!"

The barrow loomed before her out of the mist. Without hesitation, Paloma leapt from the horse's back, seized the saddlebag, and bolted inside through the mossy curtain that all but hid it from view. Cautiously, she followed Milosh's scent along a twist in the tunnel. It was a moment before her extraordinary vision engaged, letting her see through a halo of red in the darkness. It was as if her heart forgot to beat. It shuddered, and hung suspended in her breast. Before her, an emaciated creature that appeared to be half man, half bat, crawled on all fours lapping at the blood on the earthen floor—*Milosh's blood!* Had it eaten him? Was this all that remained of her beloved? Was this why she couldn't reach him with mindspeak?

Paloma screamed. The sound bubbled up in her

throat and hit the curved barrow walls with the force
of a cyclone, snapping the creature's head in her direction. It hissed like a viper, its red-rimmed acid-
green eyes burning toward her with something akin
to lust.

Through the red haze of her night vision, Paloma
recognized the creature, a dwarfed version of that
which had once towered like a giant, reduced now to
the proportions of the barrow. There was no question.
Sebastian, his upper body that of a bat, whose rustling
wings flapped now in anticipation, his lower extremi-
ties that of a man, except for the feet, which bore
sharp, hooked talons. His fangs, still glistening with
Milosh's blood, gleamed in some fragment of light
spared by her extraordinary vision in a place where
no light could be, since the flap of sod had fallen back
in place when she entered. Strings of drool dripped to
the barrow floor as he approached.

Without taking her eyes from the hideous creature
advancing, Paloma groped inside Milosh's saddlebag.
Her fingers closed around the flask of holy water, but
before she could remove the stopper, Sebastian's blue
gray sinew-veined wing struck her a blow that sent
the bag flying and pitched her over against the barrow's curved, earthen wall.

Dazed, she shook her head. Sebastian lumbered
closer, leaking a lascivious chuckle, and she shrank
from it, but to no avail, trapped against the cold wall
bleeding with rising damp. The sun had long since
risen. Why wasn't he asleep? Could Milosh's blood
have revived it enough to cancel the lethargy even in
this dark resting place, where it crawled to wait for
the sunset?

Sebastian laughed again. "You come to me, eh?" he
said. "High time, too."

His wing grazed her hair, and she shrank from it,

from the sickening-sweet stench of its corrupted flesh, and the foul breath puffing from its flared nostrils. His wing attempted to lift her chin. Like lightning, she sank her descending fangs into the cadaverous leather of the appendage, and shrank back but not fast enough, as the other wing came crashing down upon her, pitching her over on the barrow floor.

An unearthly shriek poured from the creature then, as it reared back, flinging its spittle. Strings and droplets burned her flesh like acid, and she scrabbled up in a vain attempt to back away. Another blow pitched her over again, and she fell atop the saddlebag in a bold attempt to rise, but it was no use.

"Take her away!" the creature shrilled. "I am too weary to do her justice."

Paloma blinked to clear her vision. They weren't alone. Two of Sebastian's minions emerged from the shadows shrouded in hooded cloaks. She could not see their faces. Her extraordinary vision was failing her. They advanced doggedly, one on each side, as she frantically searched for an avenue of escape, but there was none. She was trapped between Sebastian and the advancing robed figures, while outside, too gargantuan to come to her rescue through the narrow entrance to the cairn, Somnus's frantic high-pitched shrieks pierced her to the marrow.

"And do not touch her," Sebastian said. "The Gypsy bitch is mine!"

Paloma screamed again. The sound had scarcely trailed off when another joined it—the deep guttural growl of the panther as it sailed through the darkness, its jaws closing on naught but air, as Sebastian shriveled into the form of an ordinary bat sawing off into the deep dark recesses of the barrow. It happened in a blink. Having built up momentum, the panther collided with the curved barrow wall, its jaws crunching earth and rock. Paloma shivered at the sound, and screamed again as the panther fell in a heap of sleek black fur, muscle, and sinew in a trench full of bones along the wall.

Sebastian's minions had seized Paloma by the arms and were leading her away, deeper into the barrow. Someone was calling Cassandra's name. The voice was high-pitched and shrill. It hurt her ears. It was a moment before she realized she was screaming it. Cassandra didn't answer. The panther lay still . . . so still. Then the remnants of the red veil that had been Paloma's extraordinary vision faded, and the darkness, like a shroud, closed in around her.

CHAPTER TWENTY-NINE

"Leave me and find her," Milosh said. They had half dragged, half carried him inside the crumbling remains of what once had been a round tower folly in a small pine grove south of the barrow. All that remained was one curved wall two stories high, sloping to a pile of rubble that they'd climbed over to gain entrance. A tall arched window that had long since lost its glass to the elements loomed like an open mouth from the high wall above. The roof was gone, and the silver clouds racing above threatened rain. It was hardly a safe shelter, barely keeping out the wind, let alone man or beast, but there was nothing for it. Milosh could go no further. Besides, the greater the distance they put between them and Cassandra and Paloma, the greater the risk. "Go, I say!" Milosh gritted through clenched teeth. "We've come too far afield of the barrow. If . . . as you say . . . that burial mound is Sebastian's hiding place, they could be in grave danger. They may never find us here without a guide."

"What is this place?" Joss said to no one in particular, craning his neck skyward.

"Some rich fool's waste of coin and calluses," Jon said. "They call such structures *follies*; now you see why. 'Tis bloody useless. Come night it will be crawling with *vampir*, and there isn't enough left of it to keep them out."

"Are you both mad?" Milosh said. "Cassandra has been gone too long. The copper mine is not that far. She should have returned long since and here you stand discussing English architecture. Go! I cannot raise her with mind-speak . . . nor can I raise Paloma. Something is wrong—I know it—I feel it in my bones."

"He is right," Jon said. "You go, Joss. I will remain here and watch beside him until you return."

Joss shook his head. "I will not leave you alone with him," he said, defiant. "I know what you will do. *You* go, and I will look after him. At least then he will be alive when you return. That bullet needs to come out. You'd best go quickly, Father. He's lost way too much blood."

"The tools to see to that are in my duffel bag," Milosh said. "I told Cassandra to have Paloma bring it."

They continued to argue, and Milosh twisted on the pallet the wind had made of dried leaves and fragrant pine needles underneath him. Their voices raised to fever pitch, but they paid him no mind. Milosh closed his eyes and summoned a gift he hadn't called upon for so long he couldn't remember when he'd last hypnotized himself. If he could just dull the pain long enough to . . . *yes*! He let his mind drift . . . away from the folly . . . away from the heated argument taking place between his two long-time friends, whom he'd saved from the nightmare he now suffered. He had to. Despite all the rest, the blood loss had triggered the feeding frenzy—daylight though it was. Did he have enough strength left to shapeshift? He had to have—now, while they were occupied.

Milosh didn't bother stripping down. He needed every ounce of his physical and mental power to make the transformation. He'd managed to block what seemed like red-hot pincers attacking the wound in his thigh. Heaving air into his lungs, he shut his eyes to his surroundings and set himself free—free of the restraints of his blood-drained body—free of the pressures weighing upon his mind, nearly paralyzed with fear that Paloma had fallen into Sebastian's hands—free of the pain that threatened to rob his consciousness. In a heartbeat, he surged in a silvery streak of displaced energy, burying the pain of transformation in the urgency of necessity. Flesh, skin, and bone shrank to hackle-raised fur and sinew, and he sailed over the crumbling folly wall, still trailing Jon's greatcoat, and bounded northward through the pines with both men's raised voices ringing in his ears.

The trick was to stay focused. He could not die a natural death from the loss of blood. He could, however, risk becoming undead if he lapsed into unconsciousness. How long the hypnotic spell would last in his present condition, he had no idea. In view of that, there wasn't a moment to lose. If the spell should pass too soon, pain and blood loss would defeat his human self, while the madness of the hunger—magnified a hundredfold by that blood loss—would give the Hyde-Whites no choice but to destroy him.

Already, his body was taking on a strength source that brought him to the brink of his *vampir* lust. It was that dark quarter of his inner being he had to tap to numb the pain—that unstoppable passion of the blood thirst greater than the drive for self-preservation. He had to surrender to it in order to do what had to be done. The danger was that he would either come out of the trancelike state he'd put himself under too soon and fail, or succumb to it totally, unable to discriminate among his victims, putting the two women he loved in the gravest danger imaginable. As he was now, however, he was where he needed to be to destroy Sebastian at last. No, he hadn't forgotten about that. Sebastian was *his*. The hour had finally come, and if he had to die in the attempt, he would destroy the beast that had dogged him through the ages, and corrupted all whom he loved. It was time.

Milosh never transformed clothed—only the undead had that distinction. Still tangled in Jon's heavy woolen coat, his balance was off, and his gait undermined. Releasing a guttural snarl, he shook the coat free, and streaked on, doubling back the way they had come. As dazed as he'd been, he'd made a special effort to landmark the way—a tree here, a milestone or boulder there. He scarcely needed to call upon his mental map, however. The closer he came to the barrow hidden in the stubborn mist that would not vacate the valley, the stronger his extraordinary sense of smell picked out Sebastian's unique stench. He would know it anywhere. Moisture collected in his flared nostrils as he sniffed the damp air. He snorted it away, Sebastian's foulness with it, for just an instant, but long enough for him to pick up Paloma and Cassandra's essence riding the wind of his motion, for there was no breeze to spread it. He growled in anticipation as Sebastian's scent assailed his nose again, overpowering the rest. This time it was stronger.

All at once, the barrow rose up before him, parting

the drifting mist. The heart in his barrel chest heaved and banged against his ribs at sight of Somnus prancing crazily before it. Lather streaked the stallion's curled back lips, his chest and withers. His crazed eyes were glowing red and flashing wildly, as he reared and whirled and punished the frosty ground with his heavy feathered hooves.

There was no use attempting to calm the aberrant beast, whose frustration was evident. Milosh didn't even try. He now stood upon ground his feet had touched before. Recognition rushed up through the frost-clad ground, through his footpads, up his legs to the very core of him, like a lightning strike. He cast a brief backward glance over his shoulder. None were in sight behind him. They wouldn't be yet. He had left them in the dust of his departure. They wouldn't discard their togs here now, and he could run like the wind in the body of the great white wolf.

His long, curved fangs extended, he reared upon his hind legs, clawing the mossy shroud away from the opening and letting in the light. The scarf tourniquet Jon had tied around his thigh had slipped off somewhere along the way and fresh blood had begun to seep from the wound. Pain should have riddled him senseless, but it didn't. Just a little longer. If only the extraordinary strength he'd won in the trance would last just a little longer . . .

Snorting, the white wolf prowled inside the barrow. *Paloma! Cassandra!* his mind called out. They were here; there was no question, though no answer came when he called again and again. His heart pounding, he prowled deeper, rounding the bend to the place where he had fallen only a short time ago on the blood-soaked barrow floor. There was no blood there now. Someone or some*thing* had swept it clean.

He sank deeper into *vampir* as the bloodred veil,

like a tattered curtain, introduced his extraordinary vision, showing him the shadows. Two minions lurked there, hesitant to make their presence known. The white wolf leaked a snort that in another circumstance might have passed for a laugh. What must he look like to them—the hulking mass of hackle-raised fur and muscle bearing down upon them with fangs to be reckoned with? Milosh didn't wait to ponder it. Sailing through the air, his white wolf pinned them both to the barrow wall and ripped out their throats one by one.

There was no time to drink their blood, nor would he have if there was. He would not drink the corrupted blood of Sebastian's infected . . . at least he hadn't sunk to that level yet . . . though he'd lost so much blood it was tempting. Instead, his huge jaws severed their heads, flinging them into the musty air. One hit the low barrow ceiling, fell to the earthen floor, and rolled into the gutter against the wall, extracting a moan from the shadowy trench.

So deep in blood madness, Milosh almost didn't hear the sound. It wasn't until it came again that he recognized the panther's call. *Cassandra . . . ?* his mind called out. There was no reply. He'd heard the voice of the cat distinctly, yet Cassandra did not answer. Cold chills raised the ruff even taller about the white wolf's neck. He was losing control, slipping into outer darkness. The thrill of the kill—the taste of the blood, warm and salty, slightly metallic trickling down his throat, had whetted his appetite for more. He fought to keep it at bay. He had already evidently lost his powers to project his mind voice. Had he also lost his power to hear the voices of others? Praying not, he padded to the gutter, drawn by another cry from the panther's hoarse throat, and looked into the trench. The panther lay on her side. The severed head of the minion had come to rest upon her shoulder. Leaking another growl, he seized the head in his viselike wolf's jaws and flung it out of the gutter.

Cassandra . . . he said in mind-speak. *How badly are you hurt?*

The panther heaved her weight in a vain attempt to rise, and fell back again panting. Waves of déjà vu crashed over Milosh's soul, recalling when he'd last seen her so, over thirty years ago, when Sebastian had felled her. She was carrying Joss on that occasion, and his wolf's eyes misted with tears, remembering.

He has taken her deeply in, her voice whispered across his mind so faintly he could barely make out the words. *Go, Milosh . . . before . . .*

Her words drifted out of his mind then. His mind-speak was fading. Had calling upon his self-hypnosis cancelled it out? Had he traded one gift for another? It wasn't likely that she could hear him, but he had to try just once more . . .

You must rise up and leave this place, he said, forcing the words out with all his might. *You are not safe here with me now. . . . neither is Paloma, God help her. In order to do what needs must . . . I have had to make a sacrifice, Cassandra. I am no longer the Milosh you knew. Rise up and go . . . while you still can. . . . Keep your husband and the young whelp away. This is my kill . . . Sebastian is mine. . . .*

Milosh squeezed the words out as best he could, but it was clear she hadn't heard. The crackling static of whatever she was saying was reduced to a rumble, then a buzz, as if a swarm of bees had invaded his head . . . then silence. His mind-speak powers were gone, and with them the last thread of his humanity. Paloma's scent called him. Sebastian's stench drew him. He turned away from the panther and stalked along the narrow confines of the barrow without a backward glance. It was all he could do to resist the smell of the panther's blood—*Cassandra's* blood. His vision was closing in. All that came clear was the bloodred image directly in front of him.

After rounding a bend, the light he had let in was snuffed out. Now he must depend upon what extraordinary vision he still possessed. He was the predator, pure *vampir*. His heart beat in a different rhythm; the blood thrummed in his veins until he feared they would burst. He padded deeper. Sudden motion along the periphery of his narrowed vision bled into his consciousness. Tender arms flew about his neck. Soft sobs echoed in his ears. *Paloma*. Her scent—the very essence of her blood—flew up his flared nostrils. The white wolf reared up and shook her free with a warning growl.

Paloma struck hard and bit back a gasp. "Milosh!" she cried, tears streaming down. "You are *alive!* I feared you were dead. Don't you know me . . . ?"

The white wolf issued another warning snarl and continued on. He dared not acknowledge her, not while her blood was calling him—haunting him. Not while he still possessed the strength to resist her, and that was only due to the lure of Sebastian—so close Milosh was salivating. . . . So very close . . .

Paloma scrambled to her feet and came at him again. How much could he bear? He whipped around and bared his fangs. Shoulders hunched, feet apart, the silver streak along the ridge of his back was a razor-sharp indication of his intent. Head down, the white wolf lunged at her, its jowls leaking strings of blood-colored drool. Its snarl was deadly as it backed her into the gutter, sharp fangs tearing into the fabric of her cloak.

Paloma drew up her knees beneath her skirt and shrank from him. Only then did the white wolf back down, though its curled lips and bloody fangs menaced still. This time she did not follow.

"You are bleeding!" she said as the wolf padded toward the cavernous tunnel. "Please, I beg you . . . let me help you." She groped for the saddlebag. "I have the tools to cut the bullet out . . . Milosh, please . . . change back and let me . . ."

The white wolf's head snapped in her direction. A deep growl drew his lips back again. Paloma's hand flew to her mouth as a whimper leaked through her fingers. Could she have seen the tears in his eyes? She must have done. He could barely see her through them. He tossed his hackle-raised head back and let loose a howl that reverberated through the close confines of the barrow, loosening the damp earth overhead until some sifted down. His thunder would bring Sebastian. Milosh was beyond caring. It had to end now, and he had to end it, because this was his last. The Brotherhood could have him now—Jon could have him; the justice of his longtime friend would be swift, and kind, for he'd mentored him well. It was time. He could not live as he was with Paloma and put her at such a risk, and he could not live without her now—not burning with passion for her—not aching to bury himself in her sweet flesh—not longing to spend his life in that exquisite body, and daring not. But first . . . there was Sebastian.

The white wolf turned back to the tunnel. Paloma made no move to follow, though her sobs echoed in his ears. It was a long barrow, infiltrating the entire hilly mound that contained it. How many centuries had it stood there? Longer than he had prowled the earth, that was a certainty. The bones of those long dead lined the gutter trenches he passed; some were pulverized to dust by time. He paid them no mind. He would have had to turn his head to do that, and it would have tampered with his focus, since he could only see a narrow swath directly in front of him now. Even this gift was fading. Moving stealthily, he trained his extraordinary vision on the blood-black darkness ahead, looming like the belly of a long-dead beast, and smelling just as foul for Sebastian's presence in the midst of it.

A rustling sound . . . The white wolf pricked up his ears and ceased to breathe, listening. Yes . . . the familiar rustling of a bat's wings. Had he awakened it—taken it by surprise? That had come to be the ideal plan, since in four hundred years Milosh had not been able to destroy the creature by conventional methods. He had come to the conclusion that the only way to defeat his age-old nemesis was to come upon him unaware in his resting place. It had become his delicious fantasy, but Sebastian being the wily creature he was, that opportunity had not presented itself . . . until now.

The rustling came again. It was mid-afternoon. Sebastian would be lethargic—too lethargic to shapeshift back from bat form into a more deadly entity before nightfall, when he would once again be at his most powerful . . . Milosh hoped. Besides, Sebastian thought his minions were protecting him. Milosh had silenced them quickly with the white wolf's deadly jaws.

He snorted through flared nostrils, bracing himself as another, louder burst of rustling knifed through the stillness. There was squeaking now, as the bat came toward him, the sawing motion of its wings fanning the fetid air that came before it. The white wolf gave a satisfied snort. In the close confines of the barrow, Sebastian would not be able to shift into one of his formidable towering shapes; there wasn't room.

The noise grew louder—much louder. Amplified by the acoustics in the narrow tunnel, it sounded more like a swarm of bats than one lone creature, but his hearing was failing. The buzzing in his head driving him closer and closer to the brink—ready to nudge him over the edge into the abyss from which he would never return—had warped his hearing . . . hadn't it?

A rush of air, like a flesh-scourging wind, came funneling along the barrow, ruffling the thick fur around Milosh's wolf's neck. He strained his eyes ahead as he picked up the the motion of not one, but dozens of bats pouring out of the inky darkness, their irate voices echoing in unison as they soared past him raising dust.

Milosh's heart sank. Many times before, he'd seen Sebastian split into a virtual cloud of bats to elude capture. Was that what he was seeing now, had the creature strength enough in his daytime lethargy to divide? Or was this simply the crafty vampire hiding among a swarm of ordinary bats that his white wolf had awakened with his howling, voicing their complaints at being roused from their slumber early?

It was still daylight, as they sped toward the opening. Those that ventured forth into the light were harmless enough; no vampire would cross that threshold, but what of those that remained inside the barrow? And which one was Sebastian? He needed to cut off the head of the monster to defeat it.

Snorting out the dusky, putrid air that had clogged his flared nostrils as the bats soared past him, the white wolf growled. Milosh could smell Sebastian among them. Bolting back the way he'd come, his heart shuddered in his heaving barrel chest. He'd nearly reached the turn, when he heard it, a scream that all but curdled his blood—Palomas's scream. It rocked him to the core. She was trapped in the gutter beneath dozens of bats that had covered her like a living blanket.

If Sebastian had not split into many, he had commanded these and held some power over them. Had it happened at last? Had he finally caught the vampire at a disadvantage? If he had, Sebastian couldn't take Milosh's wolf in his bat incarnation, which was why he'd passed him by, but he could take Paloma. Was this some macabre chess match? Had Sebastian made her his pawn? There was no time to puzzle it out, and the white wolf leaped, soared through the air, and slammed into the gutter, crashing into Paloma broadside, scattering bats in all directions. Her screams ripped into Milosh's soul, calling him back from the brink. The pain in his leg was returning. His powers were ebbing away. He needed to beat back the inevitable just a little longer—long enough to help Paloma one last time.

She screamed again. Fangs extended, the white wolf's snapping jaws knifed through the flurry of flapping wings toward Paloma underneath, scattering bats he'd killed in the process in all directions—flinging their bloodied carcasses against the barrow ceiling, floor, and walls in an orgy of unbridled carnage. He had to have hurt Paloma in the process as he trampled her underfoot. That couldn't be helped now. Dead bats littered the barrow floor. These were not the bats he sought. Fighting the pain and the desperation of having come so close only to fail, the white wolf burrowed deeper, calling upon his heightened sense of smell to ferret out the only creature he sought then . . . *Sebastian.*

Paloma's flailing arms prohibited him. *Lie still!* he commanded her, forgetting he had lost his mind-speak powers. Exasperation wrenched another howl from him. One of the bats, a huge one, was tangled in Paloma's coppery mane, hissing and spitting. Its talons were caught, and the white wolf clamped it in his jaws. Most of the others were either dead, lay injured, or had fled. Was this the right one? There was only one way to tell.

Hauling himself erect, half blind with the pain that had returned tenfold as the trance wore off, the white wolf summoned the strength to grind out words he knew she could not hear: *Paloma . . . stay!* Then carrying the flailing bat in clamped-down jaws that drew no blood, he bounded through the barrow, past the bend, and bolted out into the blinding light of day through the gaping barrow portal.

The creature shrieked the last dreadful shrieks of a death scream, writhing in the white wolf's clamped down jaws. Shuddering streaks of radiant heat rose up, narrowing Milosh's eyes. The acrid stench of brimstone siphoned the breath from the wolf's flared nostrils; they were dripping moisture that arced and spat against the smoking body of the huge bat trembling in its death throes. The white wolf clamped down hard, shook the bat until its bones crunched. Snarling, the great wolf shook it again, his powerful jaws ripping, tearing, and spat it out as the light of day shriveled it to a cinder.

The white wolf staggered, its head thrust back in a triumphant howl that matched that of the phantom horse prancing in high-stepping circles. But it was not over, and Milosh gave the ancient vampire a wide berth as it expanded to gargantuan proportions. Writhing and shrieking, it shrank again to the emaciated form of the creature that had first bitten him four hundred years ago, then shriveled to a petrified cadaver, a blackened heap of cinder, dust, and putrid smoking ash.

Hell's fire streamed from the creature's smoldering

eye sockets. Its unhinged jaw worked as if it meant to speak, but no sound came from it. *Just so!* Milosh's mind cried out to no one in particular, for then he was only marginally aware that he had an audience. *It is finished . . . at last!* Ignoring the shadow shapes—some of them familiar—that crept close in the fading light of day, he threw back his head, loosed another howl that gave the birds flight from the trees. Then he lunged down and severed the creature's head.

Having done, the white wolf staggered back from the shriveled corpse at his feet, and spat out its head. Blinding pain seared though Milosh's thigh, riveting him with drenching fire. Blood loss called the vertigo that buckled his knees. It was over. Let them destroy him if needs must. He had done the thing anticipation of which had kept him alive for four hundred years. Now at last he could die.

The white wolf swayed. Panting hard, it stumbled. Its long, sinewy legs failed, and it fell in a heap of muscle, fur, and sinew at the prancing stallion's feet, as the last of the sun's rays dissolved in the twilight.

CHAPTER THIRTY

"Stay back—all of you!" Paloma cried. When they paid her no heed, she hissed at them like a viper through her fangs. The fangs had descended in the gutter, when she needed weapons against the literal quilt of bats that had covered her. That they remained, distorting the shape of her upper lip, was proof she still had need of weapons against those who surrounded her now. "I have the skill to help him," she went on. "My nurse taught me. She was healer among our caravan. Come no closer!"

Kneeling beside Milosh on the barrow floor, she dragged his saddlebag close. Jon Hyde-White had wrapped Milosh in his greatcoat, and carried him back inside the burial mound after he'd shifted back into human form. Milosh had been unconscious when that happened. Even Paloma knew spontaneous transformations were almost always a sign that death was close at hand, though she refused to believe it. Milosh looked like death. He'd lost more blood than an ordinary man could have lost and lived, but Milosh was no ordinary man. That was what she kept telling herself, and one by one, she drew a heavy candle, assorted knives, and holy water from the sack. Had she known when he bought the blades at the market what use they would be put to, she would have moved heaven and earth to prevent the nightmare that had unfolded since.

Joss Hyde-White lit the candle, and with it started a small bonfire outside the barrow to keep the vampires at bay, then returned it, wedging it in a chink in the rocky barrow wall over Milosh's still form. Outside, the Brotherhood waited, all but Jon and Joss and the panther crowding around Paloma as she exposed the wound on the inside of Milosh's thigh, and propped a small knife in the candle flame.

"Be reasonable," Jon said. "Why put him through this—why torture him? Let him go, Paloma. You only prolong the inevitable. He is too far gone. Even if you save him—"

"Stay back!" she warned, menacing him with the knife in her hand. "What? He rids you of your age-old nemesis, and this is how you reward him—with *death?* Not while I draw breath. *Stand back,* I say!"

"She is right, Father," Joss spoke up. "Let her see what she can do."

"*Silence!*" Jon thundered. The sound shook the barrow, and the roar of the panther joined the noise. Jon's head snapped toward the sleek black cat. "No! Not this time," he said in reply to Cassandra's mind-speak. Was she pleading, too? Paloma could hardly make out her words. "Look at him—*look!*" Jon argued aloud. "It is too late. He cannot come back from this, Cassandra. He will die . . . and rise undead and it will be a bloodbath to destroy him. Would you make him suffer that . . . make *me* suffer that? Let me take him now . . . as he lies unconscious . . . painlessly. Let me give him peace . . ."

A lump formed in Paloma's throat. Were those tears glistening in Jon Hyde-White's eyes? This was something deeper than she'd dreamed between Milosh and these now arguing for his life. Still, there was only one real answer.

"We are wasting time," she snapped at them, for all were milling about then, and Milosh was groaning awake beside her. "Get out and let me help him . . ."

"Paloma . . ." Jon said, exasperation crackling in his voice.

"No!" she spat at him with no less force than a snake spits venom. "If you mean to stop me, you will have to kill me! Get out—*all of you!*"

Jon, my husband . . . Cassandra said in mind-speak. This time her words were clear as a bell . . . *you must let her try. Come away with me. We need to talk. You forget what Milosh once told you—what he forced you to do . . . what saved us. She has the power to save him now . . . if he can be saved . . .*

Jon threw wild arms in the air. "And if she cannot?" he said.

If she cannot then I will do what you dread so. It is why I am the panther still . . . why I have not shapeshifted back . . . why I have not demanded you find me clothes to do so.

Paloma's jaw dropped. For a moment there was silence—utter still, until a feeble groan leaked from Milosh's parted lips, through fangs still extended. The sound called Paloma's attention back to the chore at hand.

"Sleep, my love," she crooned, running her hand along the inside of Milosh's thigh, feeling for the hard lead ball lodged beneath the skin. All at once light blazed in her face from the candle in Joss Hyde-

White's hand. For a moment, their eyes met. Joss nodded, and Paloma almost smiled. Was he going to help her? Yes!

"You don't have to," she murmured, looking away. She couldn't meet his eyes then, for the tears in them.

"You shall need me," Joss said, ". . . just for a little."

Paloma was about to protest, when Milosh's dazed eyes snapped open, drawing both their gazes. The flashing dark eyes Paloma knew were red-rimmed now, glowing toward her with an iridescent fire—the same glazed iridescence she'd seen in Sebastian's eyes the night he infected her. Cold chills crawled up her spine. Was it too late?

Milosh's hand tangled in her hair, recalling to mind how the bat, Sebastian's talons had done the same just minutes ago. No, she did not fear him, she loved him.

"Don't you know me?" she murmured to him. "Do you not recognize your little thief, Milosh . . . ?"

For one endless moment he stared at her, long enough for Joss to set the candle down, shove Paoma aside, straddle Milosh, and deliver a shattering blow to his jaw that wrenched a full-fledged groan from the Gypsy before his head fell back on the damp barrow floor.

"I told you, you needed me," Joss said, soothing his bruised knuckles. "Work your magic quickly. He won't stay out long. He has lost too much blood, and the hunger has taken him. He needs to feed. You are not safe with him now."

Paloma flashed him a venomous glance. "Leave us!" she hissed.

Joss looked at her long and hard. It was he who finally broke eye contact. "Very well," he said, "but I will be close enough at hand to come if needs must." He hesitated. ". . . I am on your side, Paloma," he said at last, "—we all are, yours . . . and *his*, no matter how it seems . . . or what you believe."

Joss moved away then, melting into the shadows, and Paloma spread Milosh's coat wider and took up the knife. This had to be done quickly. Again, she ran her hand through the fine thatch of dark silky hair along the inside of Milosh's thigh, searching for the bullet, marking the point of entry, and feeling for the direction it took. It wasn't deep, but it was in an awkward place due to the angle. In the process, her hand grazed his sex. He was aroused. Something leaped at the epicenter of her being—at her very core. Unconscious though he was, his member responded to her touch. Hot and thick, it reached for her, and a dry sob escaped her throat.

He was burning with fever. His skin was on fire beneath her fingers. Calling back all Michaela had taught her, for the old woman had been the closest thing to a surgeon the band could boast, Paloma raised the knife from the candle flame, cooled it, and began to probe Milosh's wound. It had to be done quickly, while he was still unconscious—almost comatose by the look of him, though the stubborn fangs still remained.

Her long coppery mane kept falling over her shoulder onto Milosh's leg, and she quickly formed it into a thick plait and cast it behind her back, where it would be out of the way as she worked. Praying the bullet hadn't fragmented, she dug deeper until the knifepoint met with resistance. He flinched, but did not wake, and she worked with quick, skilled fingers to lift the lead ball out of the wound in one bloodied piece.

She had no spirits to cleanse the wound, and the only water at hand was the holy water in the duffel bag. Could he still bear its touch? That would surely tell her how far gone he was, for he was always able to before. She reached for the flask, hesitated, and drew her hand back again. No. She didn't want to know—couldn't bear to know. Instead, she propped the knife in the tall candle flame again, meanwhile tearing a length of linen from the hem of her petticoat. It would have to do. Once the knife glowed blood-red, she hovered over the wound, then swallowed dry and laid the flat of the blade against Milosh's angry flesh for the full slow count of five, despite his writhing as it seared his skin.

The acrid stench of burnt flesh and hair invaded Paloma's nose, and she grimaced, more out of despair over the pain she was inflicting than the smell. When it was done, she tossed the knife aside as if it had burned her as well, loosely bound Milosh's thigh with the linen strip, and dropped her head down on his naked heaving chest as the tears came.

The heart beneath her face was beating a steady rhythm, albeit a ragged one. His skin was scorching hot; his body heat narrowed her eyes. What had she done? Had she spared his life only to see Jon Hyde-White take it as savagely as she had seen Milosh take the life of a vampire?

Fearing her body heat was raising his fever, Paloma drew herself up wearily, and closed the greatcoat over Milosh's naked body beneath it. She attempted to rise, but a firm hand seized her braided hair and pulled her down again.

"You should have let me die," Milosh gritted through clenched teeth. "But no, you are the thief again, only this time you have stolen my peace . . ."

"I thought you'd left me," Paloma murmured. "You were going to—I know you were. How could you, when you know how much I love you? How could you abandon me . . . like the others abandoned me?"

"For your own good," Milosh snapped. "I can bring you naught but harm now."

"But you are . . . yourself again . . . not like you were when you destroyed Sebastian."

"So that wasn't a dream," Milosh said, emptying his lungs. "I thought . . . well, never mind what I thought. I am not myself again—far from it—and you are not safe with me. It has been too long since I have fed. It is your blood I crave, Paloma. It is taking all the willpower I possess not to take you here now. What? You think this piddling wound in my leg would stop me? You have signed your own death warrant saving me. Once I have gained my strength, I will destroy you. I will not be able to . . . help myself . . ."

"Stop! You are frightening me now!" Paloma cried.

"*Good!*" Milosh spat at her. "Be afraid! I want you so afraid you will run for your life, Paloma! It is too late for us . . ."

"But not for me," a deep, throaty voice said from the shadows behind. "We need to talk, Milosh."

Paloma spun around to face Jon Hyde-White, staring down, his fists braced upon his hips.

"I will not leave you alone with him," Paloma insisted. "You mean to destroy him! Well, you will have to destroy me, too, in that case, so why should I go?"

The roar of the panther at her elbow sent adrenaline surging through Paloma. She hadn't heard it approach, and she lurched so violently at the sound she lost her balance where she knelt beside Milosh and nearly slid into him.

Come away and let them speak, Cassandra's soothing voice said, drifting across Paloma's mind.

"No!" Paloma cried. "He will destroy him!"

I give you my word that he will not, Cassandra said. *Come, child . . . there is something we must discuss . . .*

Paloma hesitated. What were they up to? She didn't

trust Jon Hyde-White. She knew he wasn't a cold-blooded vampire hunter bent upon taking another trophy. She'd seen the anguish in his eyes at the prospect; she hadn't been mistaken. She feared that his love for his longtime friend and mentor would compel him to put Milosh out of his misery.

"Do as she says," Jon said. "I give you my word . . . I will not harm him."

Paloma staggered to her feet. Something in his tone and the gentle lilt of Casandra's soothing mind-speak fostered trust. She cast one last glance toward Milosh. He seemed all but delirious with fever. His iridescent red-rimmed eyes burned toward her. She couldn't read their message, but she could read his pain. It was more than she could bear.

Paloma snatched Milosh's saddlebag. If it was a trick, and Jon Hyde-White meant to destroy Milosh after all, he would have to manage with his bare hands. She would not leave him the means to do it—the stake, the mallet and the cleaver. Hugging the bag to her weary body, she followed the panther around the bend toward the entrance of the barrow, out of earshot.

"I do not see what there is to discuss," Paloma said, dropping the saddlebag.

Sit you down, Cassandra said. *I think I know a way to save you both.*

Paloma stared. "You've seen him," she said. "He is with fever. He is weak and wasted . . . and he is *vampir* . . ."

But not undead, Cassandra's reply flashed across her mind, *at least . . . not yet. That is what I am hoping to prevent, because once the transformation is complete, there will be no returning for him. He cannot come back from the undead; no one can.*

"But I thought—"

You thought he had already crossed over, Cassandra's voice interrupted her. *No, child. He is fighting a valiant fight because of his love for you. He is no ordinary man. Milosh is an entity to be reckoned with. I do not believe he knows his own limits . . . or did know them before the hunger took him. His prowess has seen him through four centuries. He will fight what he abhors until he is destroyed himself . . . unless we can defeat the hunger . . .*

". . . which I have caused," Paloma said in dismay.

Do not reproach yourself. He was just as much to blame. There is no time here now for lamenting what could have been. I think I may have the answer to what could be for the both of you. It is not gained without risk, however. Are you game?

"I will try anything to give him back what I have taken from him," Paloma said.

Even if it means your own destruction?

"Even then."

Let us hope it does not come to that, child, but it is what I needed to hear. You need to seduce him, Paloma. You need to make him drink your blood.

Paloma stared into the silver green eyes of the panther. Had she heard correctly?

Yes, Cassandra said, *The trick will be not to let it go too far, or you could die.*

"He will never do it," Paloma said. "You see how he resists me. Why, even at the copper mine, he—"

Paloma, unless I miss my guess, the antidote is in the blood—your blood—the blood you stole from him. If I am right, when he feeds from you, he will regain his immunity to the bloodlust, just as he would have done with the herbs. You are soulmates. If I am correct, the blood in your veins, which once was his, will grant you both immunity, and keep you free of the hunger as long as you live. The blood moon ritual which freed him so long ago is a mystical thing, Paloma. I doubt that even he fully understands the workings of it, but

*it does work, and has done for over four hundred years that
Milosh has walked this earth; the Brotherhood is proof of that.
Why else are they hunted by* vampir, *why was he—why are
you now more than they, because you have taken his blood?*

Paloma tried to process what Cassandra was saying. If she was right . . .

There are no guarantees, Cassandra said. *But it is
worth a try. Are you willing? Think carefully, for if you
are you risk your life, Paloma . . .*

"I would have to trick him in some way."

The panther snorted. If ever a cat could laugh, this
one did now. *Did Milosh never tell you how he saved us
with the blood moon ritual?* Cassandra said.

"No," Paloma said, ". . . only that it was a difficult
task."

*Indeed it was. Sebastian infected us both, but did not
finish "making" us. That drove him to finish what he'd begun . . . to kill Jon, who would then rise undead and be lost
for all eternity—his greatest triumph because Jon was a
man of the cloth, a vampire's greatest prize—and to make
me his concubine. Since Sebastian had infected me, I was
his creature. Milosh knew if I were to participate in the
blood moon ritual with Jon, even though I gained immunity to the bloodlust and was Jon's wife, I would still be Sebastian's creature, who he could claim whenever he
desired . . . unless I became Jon's creature first . . .*

Paloma's breath caught, and the panther replied
with a purring sound as if her gasp was part of the
conversation. *Jon is a stubborn man,* Cassandra went
on, *and he would not take my blood. He was afraid of going too far—of doing to me what Sebastian had done. The
thought of it was reprehensible to him. Vampire though he
was—though we both were—and are—he still thought
with his clerical mind, which could not conscience such a
thing. We had to trick him . . . to make him do the thing he
so abhorred . . . the thing that saved us.*

"You and Milosh tricked him . . . ?"

Together, we planned a situation that forced the issue, Cassandra said. *I nearly lost my life that night, which is why I warned you of the danger. I won't go into detail, because it has no bearing upon the situation here now. Suffice it to say the seduction was successful. Jon took my blood, and we entered into the blood moon ritual as one for all time.*

"So now you mean to turn Milosh's advice back upon him," Paloma murmured, answering her own question.

I have to, child—you have to, or you are both lost. Unless he gets his immunity back he will have to be destroyed. I saw him kill Sebastian—we all did. I thought he was beyond redemption then. In all my vampir years, I have never seen the like. He will never make it until there is another blood moon to try the herbs again.

"But . . . you do not even know that such a seduction will work!" Paloma said.

Have you a better plan? I told you there were no guarantees. If this fails, we will have done everything that can be done. Are you still willing?

Paloma nodded.

Good! Cassandra said, *then this is what you must do . . .*

CHAPTER THIRTY-ONE

"Full circle, indeed," Jon Hyde-White said, folding his arms across his chest.

Milosh stared through the candlelit darkness toward the man who held his very existence in his hands, and blinked back the eerie red mist before his eyes. How proud he was of the man he'd mentored so long ago, never thinking that Jon Hyde-White would become the instrument of his death. It was as it should be. He was resigned . . . if only there wasn't Paloma.

"I ask only that you do it quickly," he murmured, ". . . where she cannot see."

Jon strolled closer. "Do you remember when you told me I had to make Cassandra my own before I could embrace the blood moon ritual?"

Milosh nodded. "Why?" he said warily. The pain was coming in waves, but the hunger was beyond bearing, and twofold. Besides the feeding frenzy, he'd lost a dangerous amount of blood that needed to be replaced at once. If he were to lapse into a coma, he could arise undead. Surely Jon knew that. The blood-lust had never been this strong. The urge was almost more than Milosh could restrain. If his strength wasn't so depleted, Jon himself would be in danger. Surely he could see that. What was he up to?

"You and Cassandra . . . conspired to trick me into taking her blood—"

". . . so that she would become your creature before the blood moon ritual, yes," Milosh interrupted him. "It had to be, Jon."

"I know that," Jon replied, ". . . and now, you need a taste of your own medicine."

"There is no comparison between what was then and what is now," Milosh defended. "It was necessary to save Cassandra from Sebastian. Sebastian is dead—destroyed. He cannot lay claim to Paloma any more."

"The situation is different, yes, but the necessity is the same, Milosh," Jon returned. "You need to take her before another does. She is ripe for the taking, and someone certainly will. She is unskilled in the *vampir* prowess."

"Just as you and Cassandra were, as I recall," Milosh pointed out, "—green as grass, yet you managed, so will she."

". . . because we had each other!" Jon sallied. "Someone will take her down before the sennight is out without you to mentor her."

"Can you not see I am a danger to her as I am? There are many others more qualified to mentor her than I—yourself, Joss, take your pick amongst the Brotherhood."

Jon had begun to pace, and the candle flickered in the draft he stirred. "True, but she loves you, Milosh . . . and you love her."

"Which is why I have to let her go," Milosh argued.

"Look at me, Jon—*look*! Am I not a fearsome creature to behold? I thirst so for human blood, if I were not felled here with this damnable leg and drained of my own, I would have set upon *you* long since to satisfy this damnable feeding frenzy."

Jon stared at him, and he could not meet that riveting gaze; anger, hurt and pain swam there. When he spoke, Milosh could not read the calm that delivered the words.

Jon heaved a sigh. "You are right," he said, drawing a small flask from his greatcoat pocket. He squatted on his haunches and lifted Milosh's head. "You need to feed, but first . . . drink," he said.

"What is it?"

"Laudanum in spring water, with one of Cassandra's herbal tisanes," Jon said, laying the flask against Milosh's fever-parched lips. "It will ease the pain, while I fetch you a subject to slake your appetite for blood. You can hardly hunt on your own as you are, old friend."

The pewter flask was cold, and soothing against Milosh's hot mouth. Though he was wary, the prospect of relief in any form overwhelmed him. His lips parted and he drank, then fell back with a groan and shut his glaring eyes, but he could not shut out the eerie red veil before them, like blood dripping down behind the closed lids.

He drew a ragged breath. The opiate was already beginning to blunt the edges of his pain, but it wasn't strong enough to beat back the fangs that seemed permanently affixed in place, it was so long since they'd receded. Why didn't these whom he held dear just let him go, and end his misery? What was the point of prolonging the inevitable? His mind reeled back to the moment he destroyed Sebastian. It wasn't a dream, like all the other fantasies had been over the years. *He* was the animal that had defeated the centuries-old vampire. The creature he had become had severed the head of Sebastian Valentin. He'd been so long immune to the bloodlust, he'd forgotten what the hunger spawned. If he were allowed to live, that creature in him would grow until it was far more terrible than Sebastian had ever been. He was helpless to prevent it, and it was cruel to prolong the agony of trying.

Milosh forced his eyes open. Was this it? Had they drugged him to give him a painless death? Adrenaline surged, and cold chills riddled his spine. He was still human enough to want to cling to the oldest instinct known to man—self-preservation. At least a part of him did.

Slowly, his field of vision narrowed on Jon melting into the shadows. Jon would wait now, until the laudanum laced with Cassandra's herbal magic had its way with him. Then he would return to finish him. Death would be a kindness . . . anything to spare Paloma. His mind's eye saw the cleaver poised above him. The swish it made slicing the stale air rang in his ears like a death knell. The pain was gone now. It felt almost as it had when he induced the trance and left the keep in the wood, but he had nothing to do with this trance except to try to fight it. But why not let go if it meant sparing Paloma? On the other hand, if there was one shred of hope . . . The answer to both questions banging around in his brain was *Paloma*.

The shadows were closing in. His whole body throbbed like a pulse beat. He was aroused. Just the thought of her hardened his sex. His skin was on fire, his breath coming short. The hunger was eating him from the inside out, like a ravenous animal, rending— tearing—sucking the very marrow from his bones. Heightened by the hunger, his whole being was immersed in fire. It spread from the tips of his toes, along his legs, and muscled thighs. It slid over his torso, along his arched throat, then turned cool when it reached his face.

A specter of the drug-induced dream was stroking his brow with gentle fingers. How skilled they were sliding over his temple, his cheek, over his hot, parched lips. His sex leapt as they entered his mouth, like the curious fingers of a child, touching his fangs, stroking them to their tapering, curved points. His sex was on fire at their touch. No other had ever caressed the very thing that could destroy them. No other had ever reverenced the very instrument of their death at his hands. She had opened the floodgates of tactile pleasure, where he was virgin still. It was more than he could bear. Never had he known such an arousal. Never had his member come to life with such total abandon as it did under this specter's skilled fingers.

He moaned. The hand lifted sharply. Where had it gone? Something moist and silken began to stroke the fangs now . . . something petal soft, licking, lingering. His eyes had drooped shut. He tried with all his might to force them open, but they would not budge.

While her tongue continued to lave his fangs, the cool fingers slipped lower, spreading the coat wide. Splayed out across his heaving chest, they followed the contours of his body, blazing a trail of icy fire wherever they touched, tracing the arrow-straight line of dark hair that striped his belly to his engorged sex, following the contours of his narrow waist and rigid thighs, tormenting him with the promise of all-consuming ecstasy. They flitted over the bandage with no more pressure than a butterfly's wing, but it was when they seized his rigid member that the hunger and the urgent need to satisfy the demands of the flesh collided in an unstoppable frenzy that raised him off the barrow floor and into the specter's arms. But it was no specter.

Paloma clasped him to her. What a glorious vision. She was naked as the day she was born, her long coppery hair flowing over her shoulders. Her breasts were half-hidden in it. Her skin, like silk beneath his fingers, was cool to the touch, soothing the fever in his flesh while igniting his blood with a flame so searing hot it threatened to set his very soul afire. He moaned when she eased him down and straddled him—cried out when she took him inside her, and roared like the beast that had killed Sebastian as she took all of him.

No, the specter in his arms wasn't just any wraith of the mind; he'd recognized her the moment she materialized before him. Cassandra's remedy had conjured Paloma. Whether flesh or spirit it was she, and he embraced the phantom eagerly. No other had ever loved him like she did, with a passion that matched his own. Her hair grazed his chest as she undulated against him, and he was beguiled. It was fragrant with the scent of rosemary and lavender, herbal and clean, of the earth, of the wood, as mysterious and evocative as ever. He breathed her in deeply. Was she flesh or spirit? She moved like a spirit, with ethereal grace, but she felt like flesh, sheathing his shaft with her moist sex.

On the brink of bursting inside her, he arched his spine. Unable to bear the silken feel of her breasts, of the thudding beat of her heart, a heart that beat only for him, he groaned, rolled her on her back, threw back his head, and sank his fangs into the soft curve of her neck, piercing her flesh, tasting her blood, letting its warm saltiness trickle down his throat. *Paloma's blood*. It was. He knew the taste—a taste like no other. It was in him—part of him for so long, how could he not know it? It was too late to stop. He was too weary of heart, mind, and soul to resist her. He had gone beyond the point of no return, feasting like one dying of thirst in the desert.

Murmuring his name, she took him deeper still. His feeding slowed at the sound of her voice. It sounded too real for the voice of a specter. That thought had scarcely passed through his fogged brain, when she arched her spine, drawing him closer still.

Raising his fangs, Milosh howled like a wolf as she dug her own fangs deeply into his throat, and drank as he shuddered to a climax that drained him dry. His last conscious sensation was the mixing of their blood as it raced through their veins with the thrum of a snare drum. The last sight he saw through his shuttered eyes was the candlelight gleaming in Paloma's tears. Then the light was snuffed out, the gentle pressure of her body was lifted sharply, and he fell back unconscious as cold air rushed into the space where her warmth had been.

Paloma crawled to where she'd discarded her clothes and struggled into them. It was done. Their coupling had left her weak and trembling. Vertigo starred her vision. She had done what Jon and Cassandra Hyde-White had told her to do. She had tricked Milosh into nearly draining her body of blood. Another moment and she would have been lost forever. That might still happen. For all she'd just risked, she had no idea if it had worked. Milosh wasn't conscious. Would he wake alive, free of the hunger as Cassandra hoped, or would he open his eyes to utter darkness in the body of the animal that had destroyed Sebastian? If that were the case, he would devour her as well, for now he had drunk his fill of her blood, and now she was his creature.

She had drunk his blood as well, not because she lusted after it, she did not. She drank because Cassandra said she must. She didn't question. If it meant saving Milosh, she would have tread upon live coals in her bare feet.

He hadn't hurt her. She'd known that the drool from a vampire's fangs when aroused produced a substance that numbed the flesh. This was one of the reasons why a vampire's victims seldom struggled. The nectar of the vampire's kiss clouded the mind, and dulled the senses of all save the hunger. No, he hadn't hurt her. He had broken her heart. He had forced her to take what she'd begged and he'd denied her. Even if it had worked, he would never forgive her now—not for this treachery. There was no forgiveness for such a betrayal, but if it had restored him, the sacrifice was well worth it. There was no way to tell if it had or it hadn't. He lay as though dead, his fangs still visible beneath his parted lips.

Crawling to his side, Paloma closed the greatcoat over his nakedness. He didn't stir. Laying her ear to his breast, she held her breath and listened. Yes, he was breathing. Paloma heaved a ragged sigh of relief, and reached higher, for his brow. It was on fire, dry to the touch. A fever was raging in him. What did it mean? Was it the wound in his leg that had brought it on, or what had just transpired between them? Hoping that the Hyde-Whites could tell her, she scrabbled to her feet, and crept softly away to where they waited beside the entrance to the barrow.

The panther reached her first. The others were keeping watch outside around the fire. Near and distant howling was the reason for that. The plaintive sound chilled Paloma to the marrow. It was still hours before first light.

Is he . . . ? Cassandra's voice ghosted across her mind.

"I do not know," Paloma sobbed. "He is not conscious . . ."

You did as I bade you to do?

Paloma nodded. "How long before he wakes from that draught?"

Not long, Cassandra said. *He will wake before dawn. Then we will know. He has lost much blood. The little he has taken from you will not be enough to suffice him through the day. He will wake wanting more, once the effects of the draught wear off. If that occurs, we will know we have failed, child.*

"And if we have . . . ?" Paloma murmured, almost afraid of the answer, for she knew in her heart there was no answer.

If we have failed, Cassandra said, *then he must be . . . destroyed for the good of all—for his good above all else. We will have done all that can be done, child.*

"You will be the one to do it?"

Yes, Cassandra said.

"Promise me that you will do it quickly," Paloma sobbed.

The panther nudged her with its satiny nose. *It will be swift, and painless, child . . . I promise . . .*

"And then, you must take me," Paloma said with resolve. "I cannot live without him after this. I am his creature. We are one. What we have done just now has married us by Romany law. That we have drunk each other's blood constitutes a Gypsy wedding—vampire or no. Not so drastic a method, of course, only a drop or two will do, but it is a very old and binding rite among Roma, the tasting of each other's blood. You did not know that?"

The panther purred. *Yes*, Cassandra said in her mind, *I did* . . .

"Promise me that if what we have done this night fails, you will do to me what you do to him. You can destroy our bodies, but you cannot destroy our souls. Let us be united if not in life . . . in death . . . I beg of you . . ."

Paloma's voice was hoarse and breathless. Her legs would no longer support her, and she squatted down and reached out to the cat. The panther roared and flicked its long, sweeping tail, stirring the musty odor of rich moist earth, dust and decay. It prowled closer and Paloma flung her arms around it.

"My neck is small," she murmured. "Your jaws are fearsome things that could snap it in one chomp. I beg you, do . . . I forgive my executioner . . ."

Cassandra made no reply. The utter still between them soaked into the very marrow of Paloma's bones. She shuddered. It was plain Cassandra believed the test had failed, and could not bring herself to grant the request. Paloma was about to voice fresh argument, when the sound of her name being called all but stopped her heart. At first, she thought she'd imagined it. Then it came again. This time, there was no mistake.

"*Paloma* . . . !" Milosh's deep baritone resonance delivered. It struck her like cannon fire coming a second time, and she scrambled to her feet and ran in a gait that more closely resembled a stagger back along the twisted barrow tunnel to where she'd left Milosh.

Wait! Cassandra said. *Let me go first. I am not liking the sound of that!*

Paloma had already left the panther behind. Her name upon Milosh's lips, however spoken, was enough to set her in motion.

"I must do this alone," she said, rounding the bend in the tunnel. "If I need you . . . you will know."

The candle was almost burned to a nub when she reached Milosh. At the sight of him, she froze in her tracks. He was on his feet, albeit shakily, one hand braced against the curved barrow wall for support. The front of the greatcoat gaped open, giving glimpses of his nakedness beneath. He was aroused, his hooded eyes gazing toward her with a look that could only be described as intense. Fangs still distorted his upper lip, and when he spoke, she lurched as though she'd been struck.

"It wasn't a dream . . . was it?" he said, his voice like cold steel slicing through the quiet.

Speechless, Paloma shook her head. It was a slow motion. She could neither read his tone nor his demeanor.

He swayed where he stood, and she took a step toward him instinctively, her arms poised to embrace him in support if he were to fall. But he did not fall. To her surprise, he pushed off from the curved barrow wall and staggered toward her.

"Has dawn broken?" he asked her, coming nearer.

Paloma held her ground. "Not yet," she said.

"H-have I hurt you?" he stammered. The effects of the draught were still working in him. He was slurring his words, but what caught her attention was the acid-green iridescence that shone from his dark Gypsy eyes.

"No," she murmured. He was almost upon her. He was favoring the injured leg. It was plain the effort was costing him dearly. He was in pain. His taut mouth and rigid posture attested to that. Paloma longed to reach out and take him in her arms. She was about to do just that, when he spoke again, his deep voice riveting her to the spot.

"Why didn't you stop me?" he said.

There was nothing readable in his face. Was this nothing more than vampire glamour? Was he luring her closer to finish what he'd begun, as Cassandra had warned? Was he angry that she had tricked him? He didn't give her a chance to speculate. Seizing her in his strong arms, he drew her against him, cupping her face in his hand.

"Little fool," he gritted through teeth clenched against the pain she saw in his eyes. "Don't you know I might have killed you? Why did you take such a risk?"

"Because I love you," Paloma sobbed, ". . . because I cannot live without you. I had to try . . ."

Fever still warmed his lips as they took hers in a kiss that rocked her soul. The pressure of his fangs leaning against her own made her lurch. She reached and traced one of the long, curved teeth with the tip of her finger, her eyes searching his.

Milosh smiled, and did the same to her. Paloma lurched again. "What does it mean?" she said. "Are you . . . are we . . . ?"

"I should take you over my knee for putting yourself at such a risk," he said, "—and I will if you ever do anything like that again."

"But . . . the fangs . . ."

Milosh took her hand in his and crimped her fingers around his sex. "As long as you are angry, excited, or aroused, the fangs will descend just as they have always done. Nothing has changed."

"The hunger?" Paloma cried, searching his shuttered eyes.

"Gone, little thief," he said. "You have stolen it away."

Paloma slid her arms around him beneath the greatcoat, her face buried in the soft silk of his chest hair, dark as raven's feathers beneath her cheek. His arousal leaned heavily against her. It leapt as their bodies collided, and he folded her closer in his strong arms.

"Technically, we are wed," Paloma said, not quite sure how he would react to the news.

"You mean to hold me to it, do you?" he murmured against her hair.

Paloma leaned back and met his gaze. "I spoke in jest," she said.

"There is no jest," Milosh said. "You told Cassandra rightly. Our marriage is legal and binding by Romany law. We are both of like mind, and blood has been exchanged. That is all it takes to solemnize the bond."

Paloma bit back a gasp. "You *heard* us?" she cried. "You have your powers back?"

He nodded. "Some of them," he told her. "The others will return in time."

Paloma strained against his embrace. "We must go and tell the others!" she cried.

But Milosh held her fast. "The others can wait," he said seductively. "We have our whole lives to socialize with the others." A slow throbbing started in her loins at the sound of that deep, throaty rumble. It resonated in her very bones.

"But your leg," she protested.

"The devil take my leg!" Milosh ground out. "It will mend"—he folded her fingers around his sex again—"but this will not wait." He wasted no time undressing her. Lifting her in the strong arms she so longed to hold her, he lifted her skirt and eased her down upon his arousal. "Forever begins now, lady wife," he murmured in her ear as his life lived inside her.

Paloma shut her eyes and let him love her—and how he loved her, with a reverence that all but stopped her heart. His deep, shuddering thrusts joined them in a way they had never been joined before. They were one, two souls joined for eternity. Paloma could not contain her joy, and once they had loved, and loved again, she waited somewhat less than patiently for Milosh to tug on fresh clothes from his saddlebag. Then rushing out to join the others, with her husband in tow, she did something she hadn't done since the nightmare began—something Milosh had never seen her do.

Paloma danced . . .

EPILOGUE

Six months later . . .

The coach rolled up the narrow path that wound its way toward Castle Valentin, Sebastian's stronghold in the Carpathian Mountains, through an eerie twilight mist. All was still. No breath of a breeze disturbed the trees that hemmed the path. The air was sweet with the taste of spring, not heavy with the stench of char and death the way Milosh remembered it of his last visit. They'd nearly reached the summit, and what remained of the castle loomed before them out of the mist, turrets pointing arrowstraight toward a full blood moon.

He pulled Paloma close. "It needs repair, my inheritance," he murmured in Paloma's ear. "Much of it was destroyed by fire long ago, but we will see to that."

"Sebastian's castle," Paloma said, staring toward it through the isinglass coach window in the eerie pink moonlight. "Can you just . . . claim it?"

Milosh ground out a throaty chuckle. "Who has a

better right?" he said. "The spoils of war, my love. I vowed one day I'd have that castle as my own. That day has come. Who else is there to claim it? The superstitious town folk will have no truck with it. That any part of it still stands is testimony to that, elsewise they would have torn it down stone by stone and pitched it into the abyss long since. Sebastian is no more, but who here will believe it? I am unknown here now. Time has granted me anonymity. Those that drove me out are long since turned under the sod. But *vampir* still infest these mountains, so it has been since time out of mind, and so it will always be. We are needed here, Paloma."

The coach came to a screeching halt, swaying on the rutted path. "I go no farther," barked the driver, tossing down their bags. There were only two. The rest, their trunks and portmanteaux, were being sent. Milosh wondered at the wisdom of that now, doubting they would ever see those trunks again. Who would venture near enough to deliver them? "Out! Are ye deaf?" the coachman shouted. "You're lucky I've brung ye this far. None below will set foot near here in the daytime, much less after dark. There be vampires here!"

Milosh climbed out of the coach and set the steps for Paloma. Handing her down, he glanced toward the castle, and glanced again. There came a hitch in his stride of a sudden, but the moment passed. He longed to say, *indeed there are vampires here.* The irony appealed to him, but he smiled instead and stood aside as the man turned the coach with practiced skill on the narrow, crumbling path. Shouting a desperate *"Hayaaah,"* he snapped his whip, his red scarf flying, and the coach tore off in a cloud of dust dredged up by the groaning wheels and the shying horses' punishing hooves.

Loose stones bouncing down the sheer-faced mountainside made a mournful sound that trailed off with no evidence that they had reached the bottom of the gorge. Milosh had come home, to the place where it all began four hundred years ago . . . *home.*

He picked up the two small cases and led Paloma back down the trail apace to a little cave-like niche carved in the mountain wall that he remembered from so long ago. Aside from a mound of dead leaves, pine needles, and dirt windswept from the road over time, it was as he'd last seen it, deep enough to keep their luggage dry.

He turned to Paloma and took her in his arms. "Our things will be safe here, while we see what lies in store," he said.

"We aren't taking them with us?" Paloma asked.

Milosh hesitated. "Not . . . just . . . yet," he said, nodding to the castle behind. "I saw a light in one of the windows when we stepped out of the coach. I think the driver saw it, too. That is probably why he was in such a hurry to get shot of us. Believe me, our bags will be quite safe here until morning, if he's any example."

". . . And in the meanwhile?" Paloma queried. "If we leave our bags, we have no weapons."

"We won't need them," Milosh said, stripping off her traveling mantle, then his own. "Our other selves shall have a look at our new abode. Since when has the white wolf had need of a cleaver to sever a vampire's head? This is why we've come, Paloma, to recruit those we can for the Brotherhood, and destroy those that cannot be saved to prevent them from infecting others as we have been infected. This is our 'forever,' little thief. Are you ready?"

Paloma pulled a face. "I wish you wouldn't call me that," she said, her tiny fists braced on her hips. "What have I stolen lately, um?"

Having stripped down to his buckskins, he helped her out of her blouson and skirt, feasting upon her nakedness in the shimmering pink moonlight. "My heart," he murmured, pulling her into his arms.

She tasted honey-sweet, unfolding like the petals of a rose in his embrace, just as she always did, yielding to a single kiss. He was aroused, but that would have to wait. A familiar snort from the stand of dwarf pines that edged the cave called their attention to a pair of red glowing eyes watching them.

Milosh ground out a guttural chuckle. "And you were worried that Somnus would not follow when we disembarked," he said, drinking in Paloma's grin at sight of the *vampir* horse. "He knows we will have need of him here. Besides, I do believe you have bewitched our Somnus. You cast your spell over both of us from the very start, my little *chovexani*. Now, come . . . we have much to do."

Stripping off his breeches, he gave a nod, and in a split second emerged through a streak of silvery displaced energy as the great white wolf. Paloma's silver she-wolf followed, and they circled one another, stirring the mist with prancing feet.

The white wolf thrust its head toward the heavens and loosed a heart-stopping howl that echoed through the cavernous mountain pass from peak to lofty peak. Yes, Milosh had come home, and together with the faithful phantom stallion, the two wolves loped up the narrow ribbon of a track that led to the vampire's castle, waiting beneath the full blood moon.

Sandra Schwab

Sweet passion...

After a magical mishap that turned her uncle's house blue, Miss Amelia Bourne was stripped of her powers and sent to London in order to be introduced into polite society—and to find a suitable husband. Handsome, rakish Sebastian "Fox" Stapleton was all that and more. He was her true love. Wasn't he?

or the bitter taste of deceit?

At Rawdon Park, the country estate of the Stapletons, Amy began to wonder. It seemed that one sip of punch had changed her life forever—that this love, this lust, was nothing but an illusion. She and Fox were pawns in some mysterious game, and black magic had followed them out of Town. Without her powers, would she be strong enough to battle those dark forces and win? And would she be able to claim her heart's true desire?

Bewitched

ISBN 13: 978-0-505-52723-3